Virtual Unicorn

e

Pho

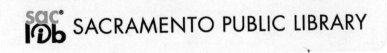

FRIENDS OF THE SACRAMENTO PUBLIC LIBRARY

THIS BOOK WAS DONATED BY
**FRIENDS OF THE
RANCHO CORDOVA LIBRARY**

The Sacramento Public Library gratefully acknowledges this
contribution to support and improve Library services in the community.

SACRAMENTO PUBLIC LIBRARY

Complete Your Phoebe and Her Unicorn Collection

Phoebe and Her Unicorn
Dana Simpson

Unicorn on a Roll
Another Phoebe and Her Unicorn Adventure
Dana Simpson

Unicorn vs. Goblins
Another Phoebe and Her Unicorn Adventure
Dana Simpson

Razzle Dazzle Unicorn
Another Phoebe and Her Unicorn Adventure
Dana Simpson

Unicorn Crossing
Another Phoebe and Her Unicorn Adventure
Dana Simpson

Phoebe and Her Unicorn in
The Magic Storm
Dana Simpson

Unicorn of Many Hats
Another Phoebe and Her Unicorn Adventure
Dana Simpson

Phoebe and Her Unicorn in
Unicorn Theater
Dana Simpson

Unicorn Bowling
Another Phoebe and Her Unicorn Adventure
Dana Simpson

The Unicorn Whisperer
Another Phoebe and Her Unicorn Adventure
Dana Simpson

Camping with Unicorns
Another Phoebe and Her Unicorn Adventure
Dana Simpson

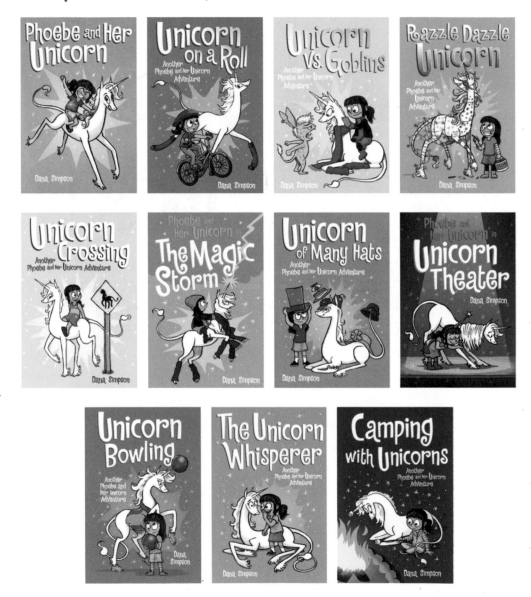

Virtual Unicorn Experience

Another
Phoebe and Her Unicorn Adventure

Dana Simpson

Andrews McMeel
PUBLISHING®

Hey, kids!

Check out the glossary starting on page 173
if you come across words you don't know.

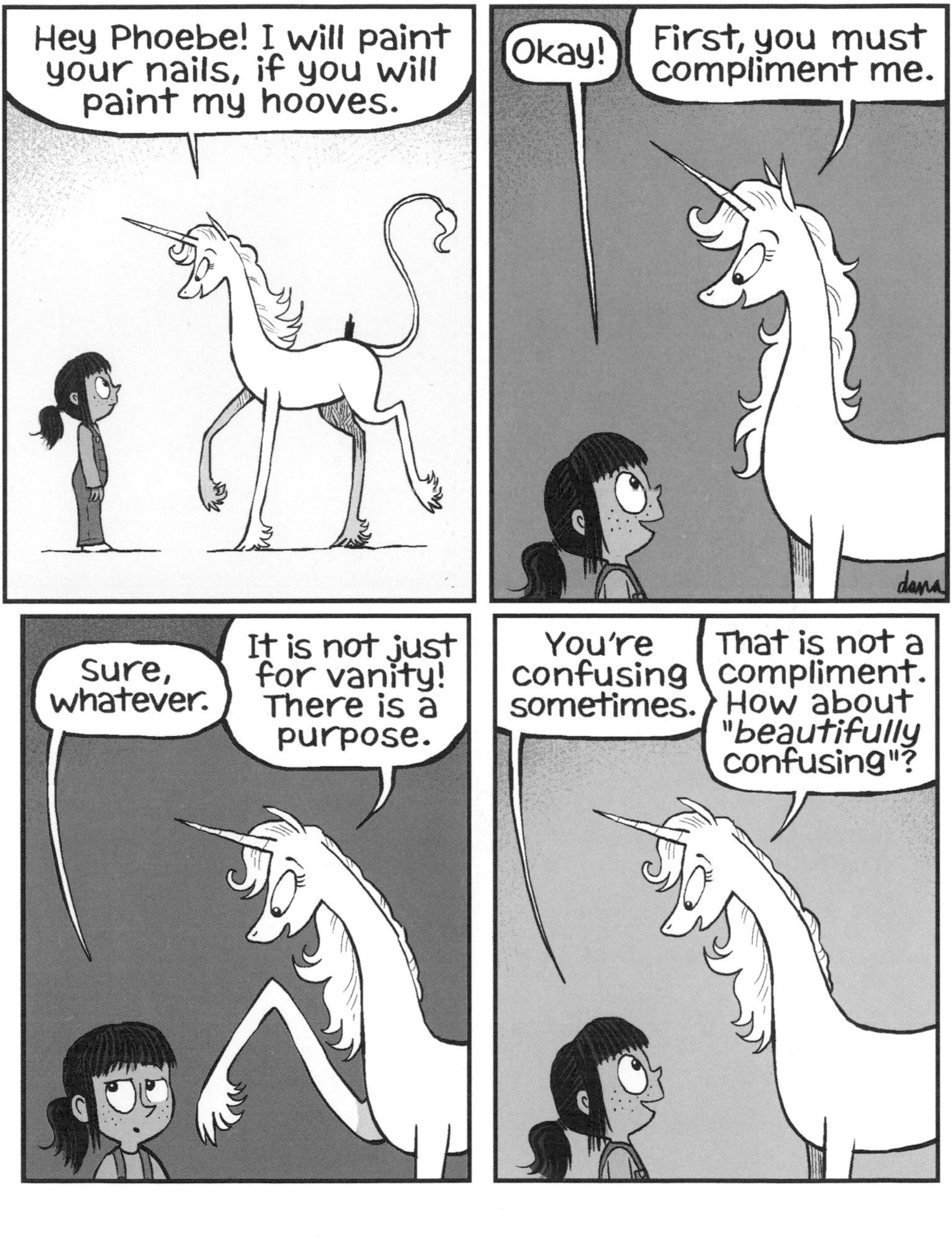
Hey Phoebe! I will paint your nails, if you will paint my hooves.
Okay!
First, you must compliment me.
dana
Sure, whatever.
It is not just for vanity! There is a purpose.
You're confusing sometimes.
That is not a compliment. How about "*beautifully* confusing"?

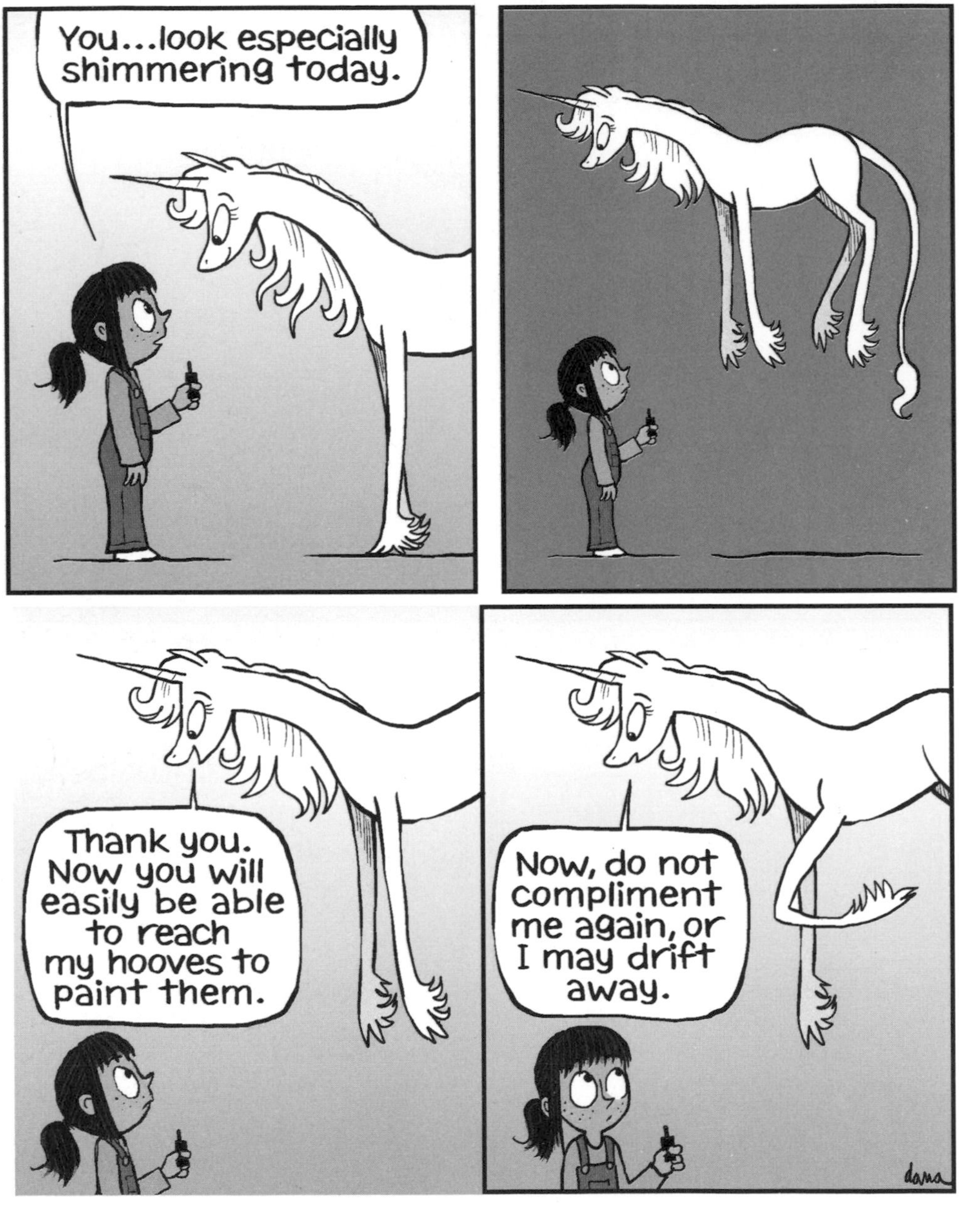
You...look especially shimmering today.
Thank you. Now you will easily be able to reach my hooves to paint them.
Now, do not compliment me again, or I may drift away.
dana

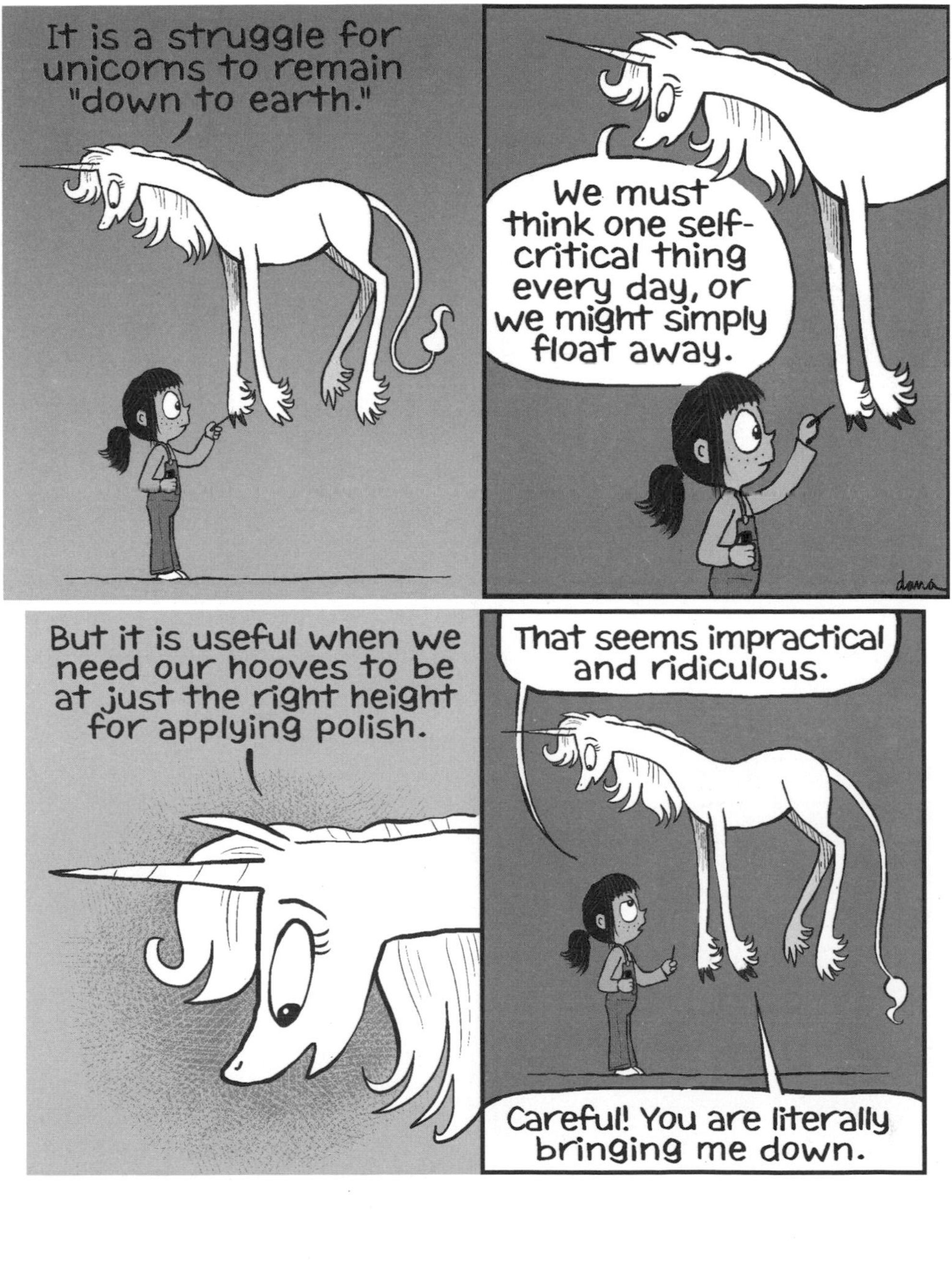
It is a struggle for unicorns to remain "down to earth."
We must think one self-critical thing every day, or we might simply float away.
dana
But it is useful when we need our hooves to be at just the right height for applying polish.
That seems impractical and ridiculous.
Careful! You are literally bringing me down.

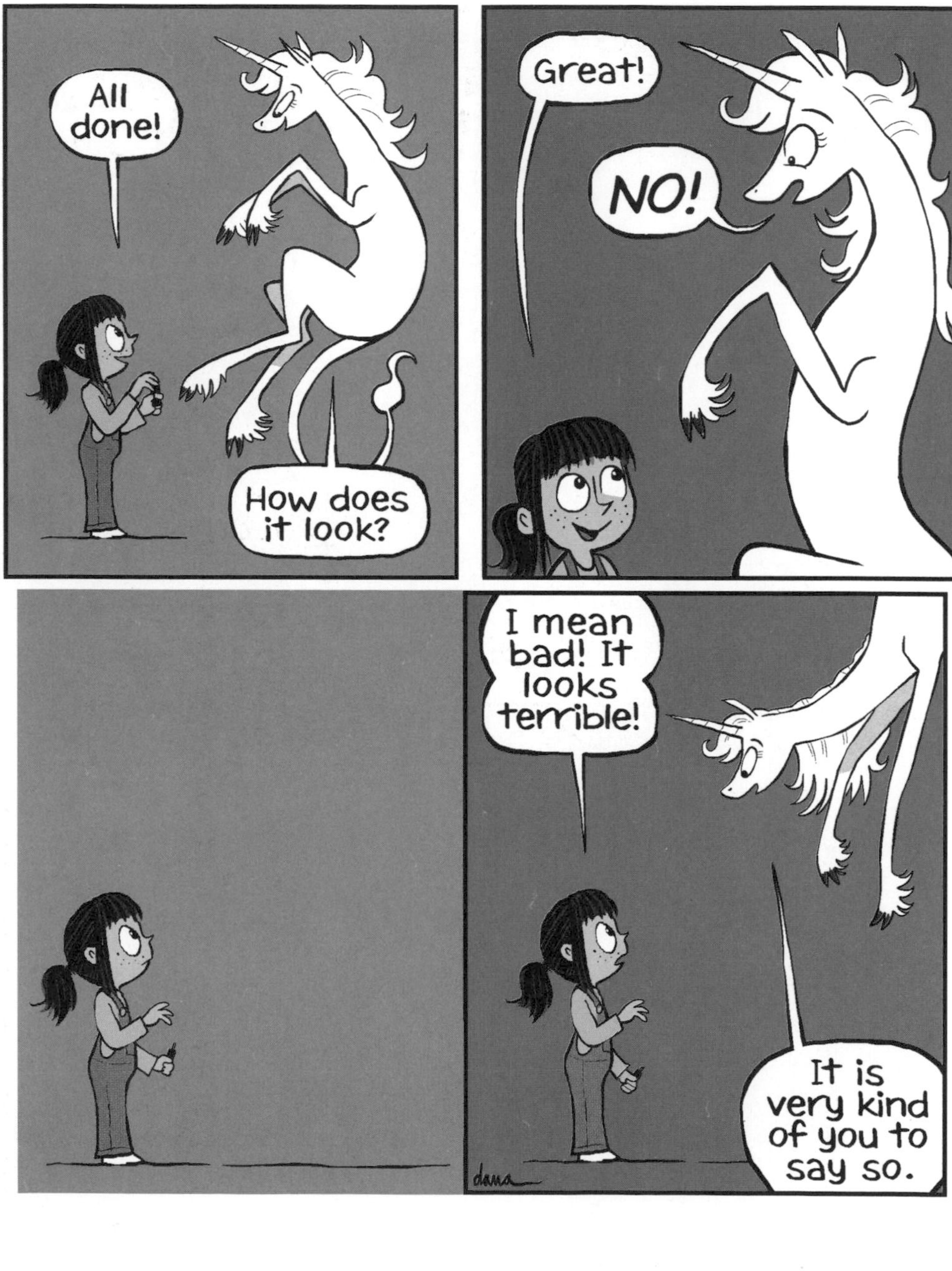
All done!
How does it look?
Great!
NO!
I mean bad! It looks terrible!
It is very kind of you to say so.
dana

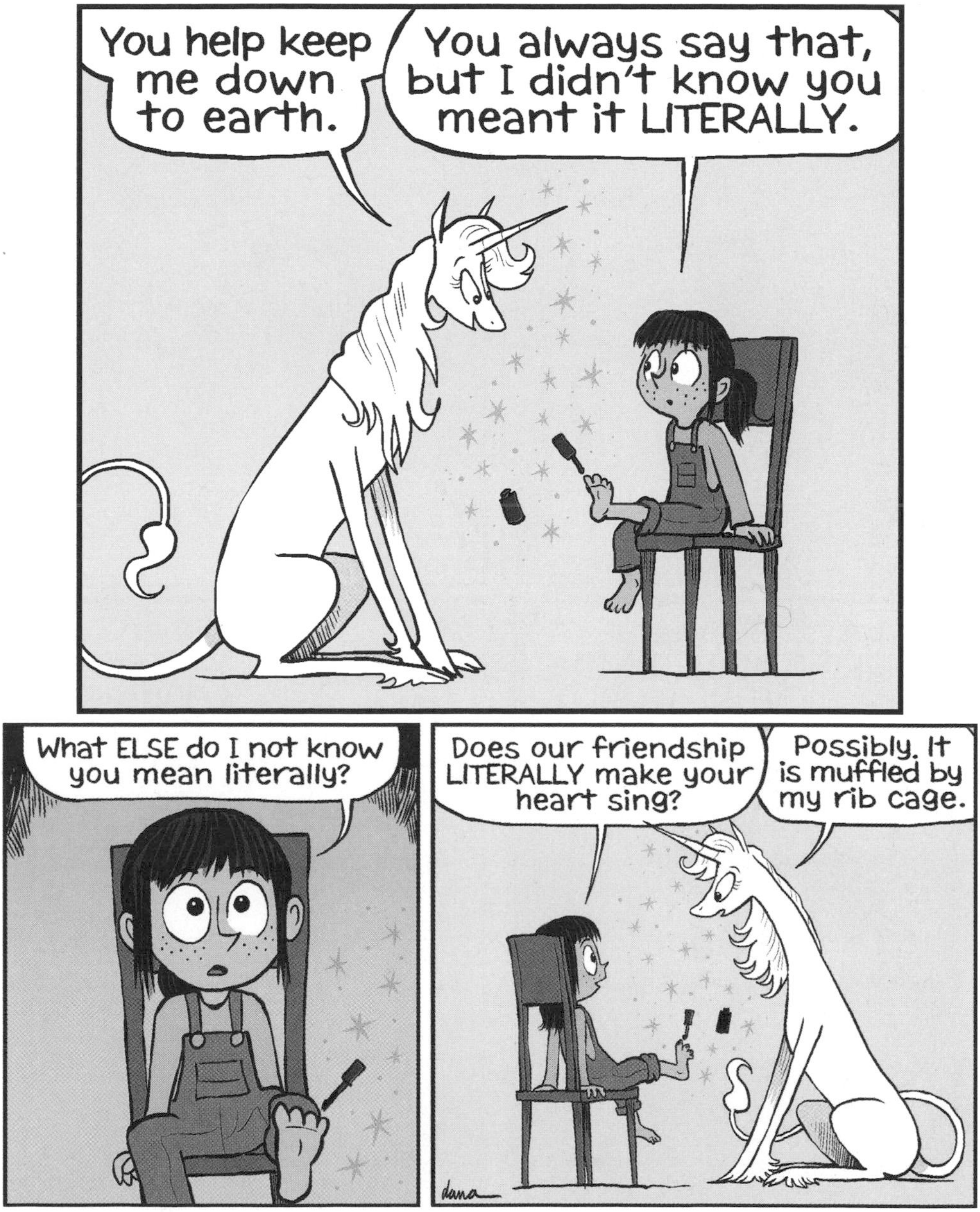
You help keep me down to earth.
You always say that, but I didn't know you meant it LITERALLY.
What ELSE do I not know you mean literally?
Does our friendship LITERALLY make your heart sing?
Possibly. It is muffled by my rib cage.
dana

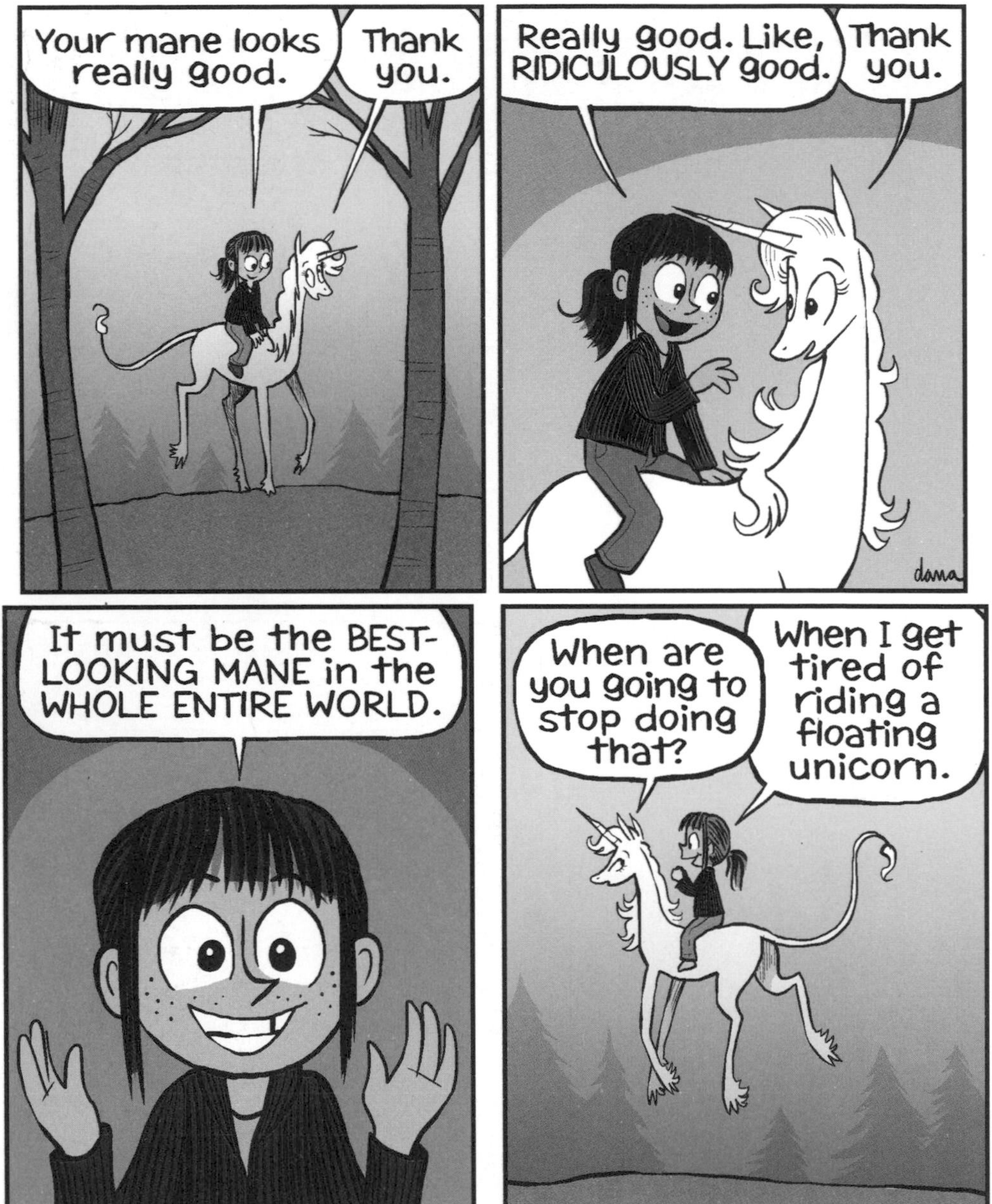
Your mane looks really good.
Thank you.
Really good. Like, RIDICULOUSLY good.
Thank you.
dana
It must be the BEST-LOOKING MANE in the WHOLE ENTIRE WORLD.
When are you going to stop doing that?
When I get tired of riding a floating unicorn.

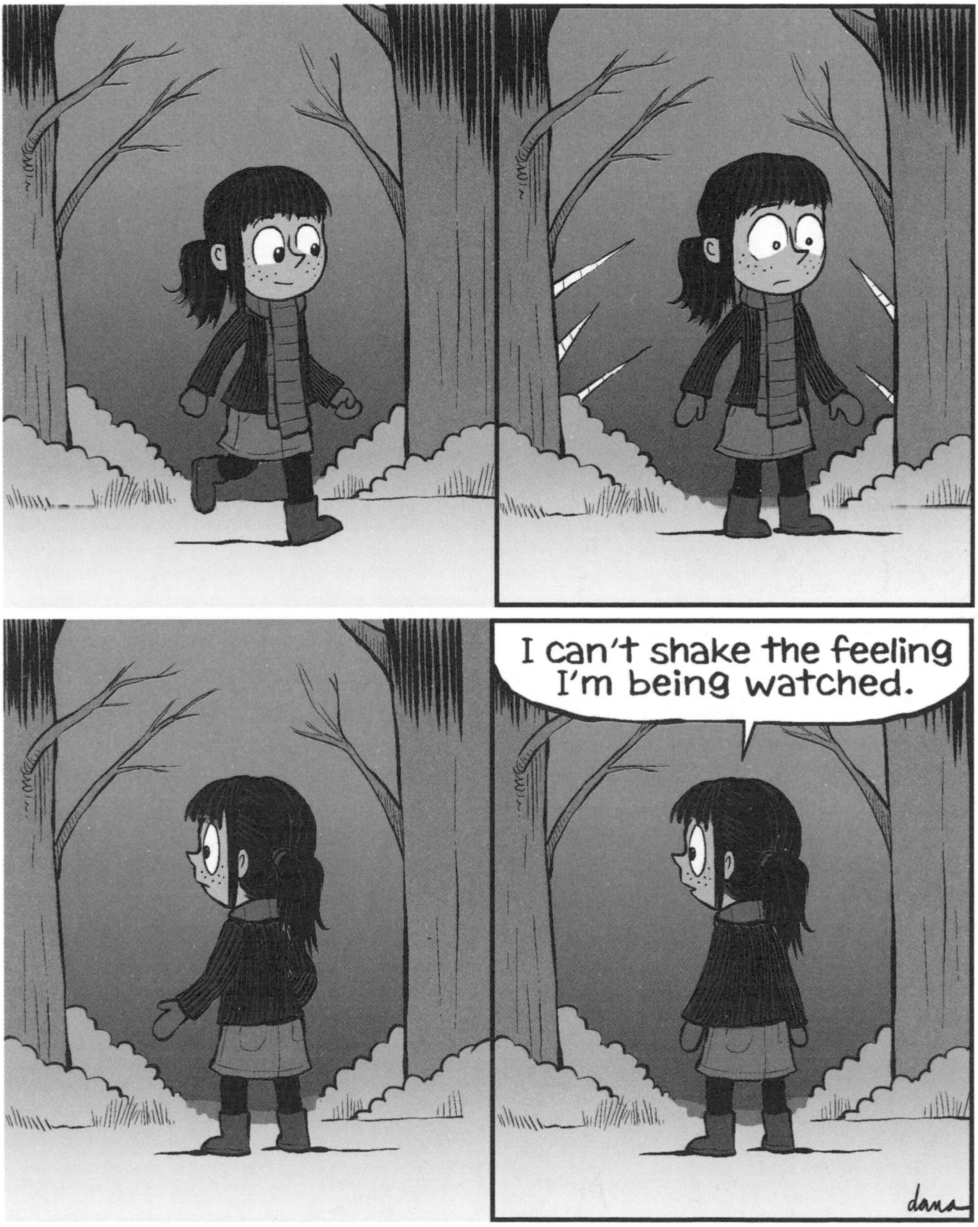
I can't shake the feeling I'm being watched.
dana

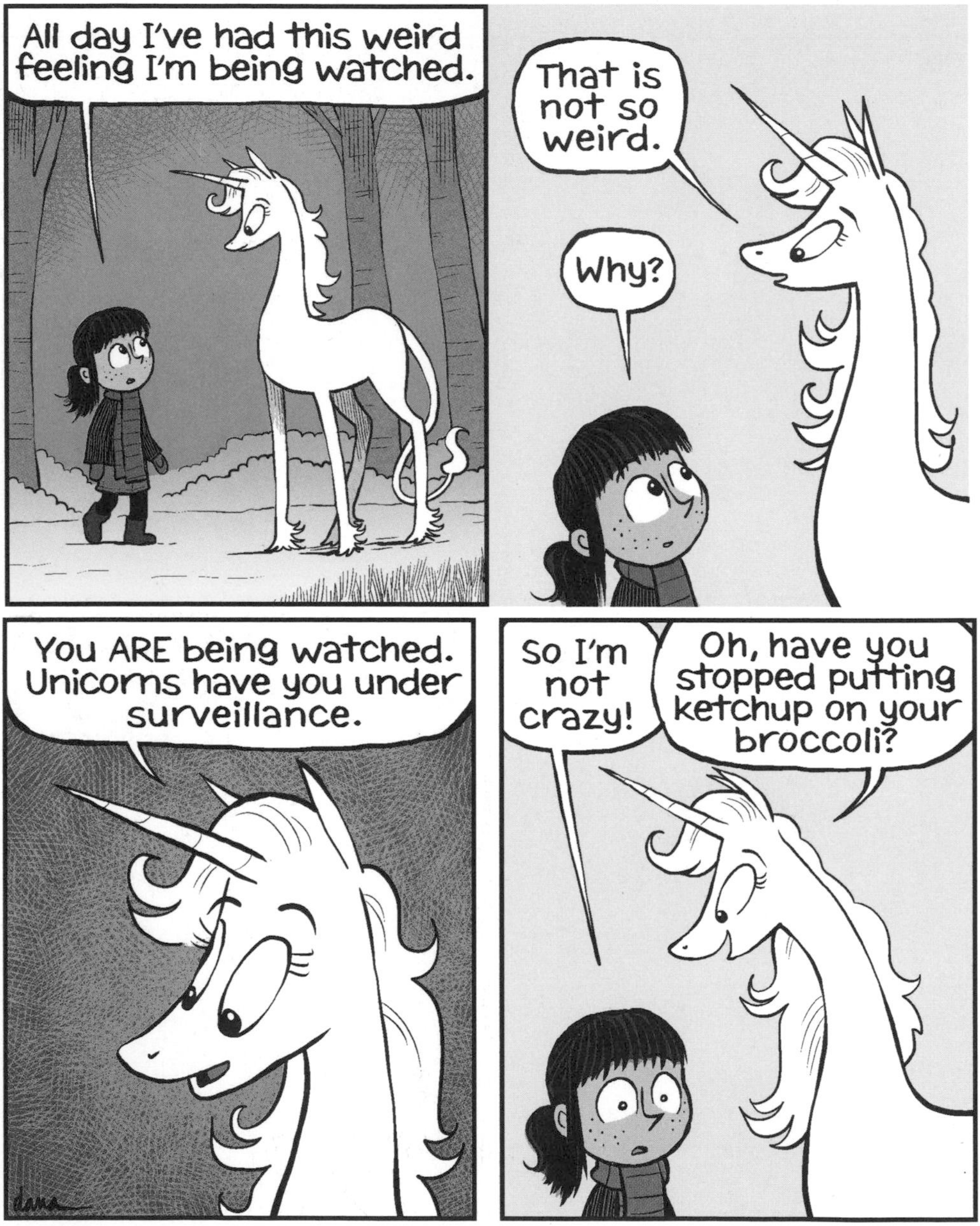
All day I've had this weird feeling I'm being watched.
That is not so weird.
Why?
You ARE being watched. Unicorns have you under surveillance.
So I'm not crazy!
Oh, have you stopped putting ketchup on your broccoli?
dana

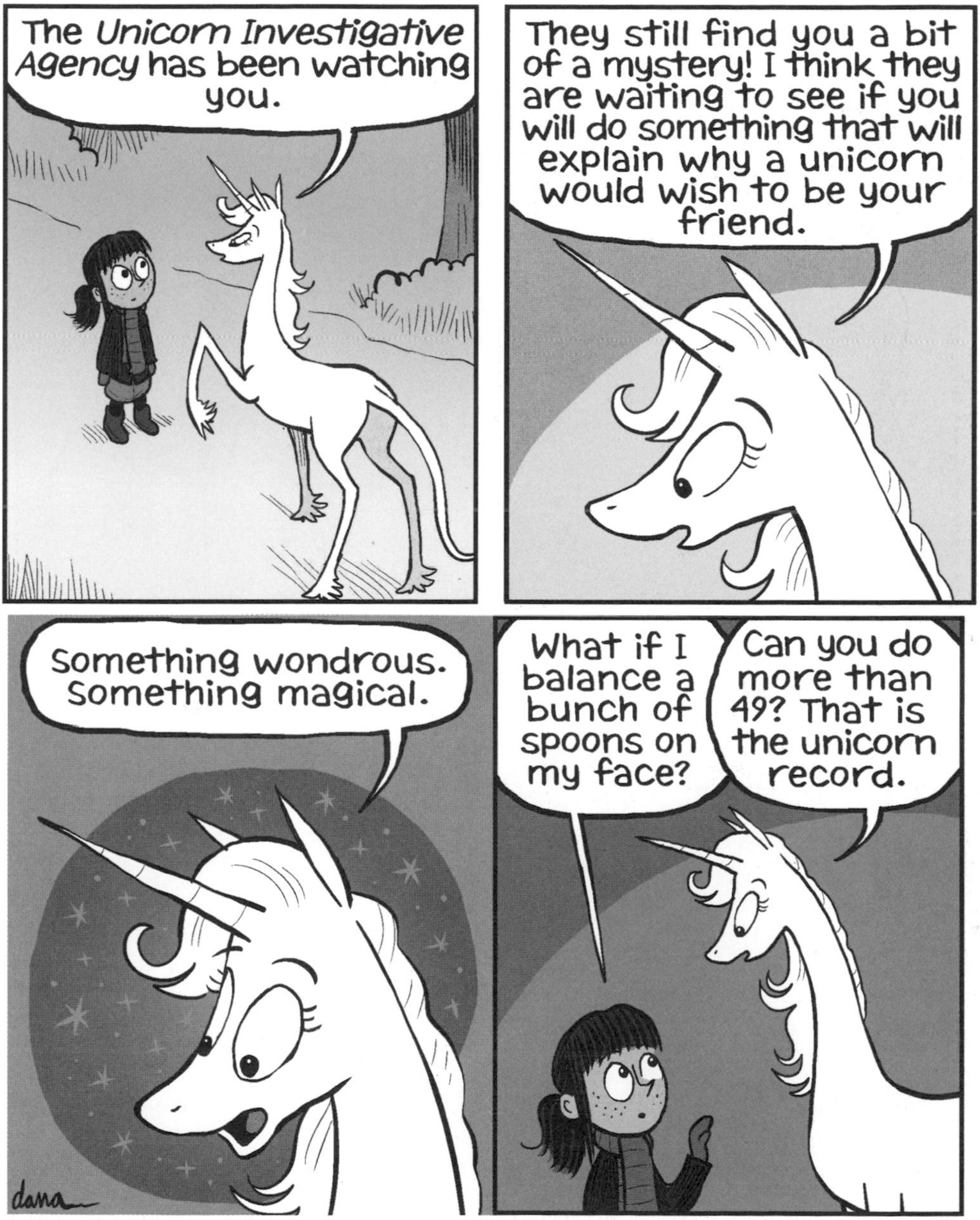
The *Unicorn Investigative Agency* has been watching you.
They still find you a bit of a mystery! I think they are waiting to see if you will do something that will explain why a unicorn would wish to be your friend.
Something wondrous. Something magical.
What if I balance a bunch of spoons on my face?
Can you do more than 49? That is the unicorn record.
dana

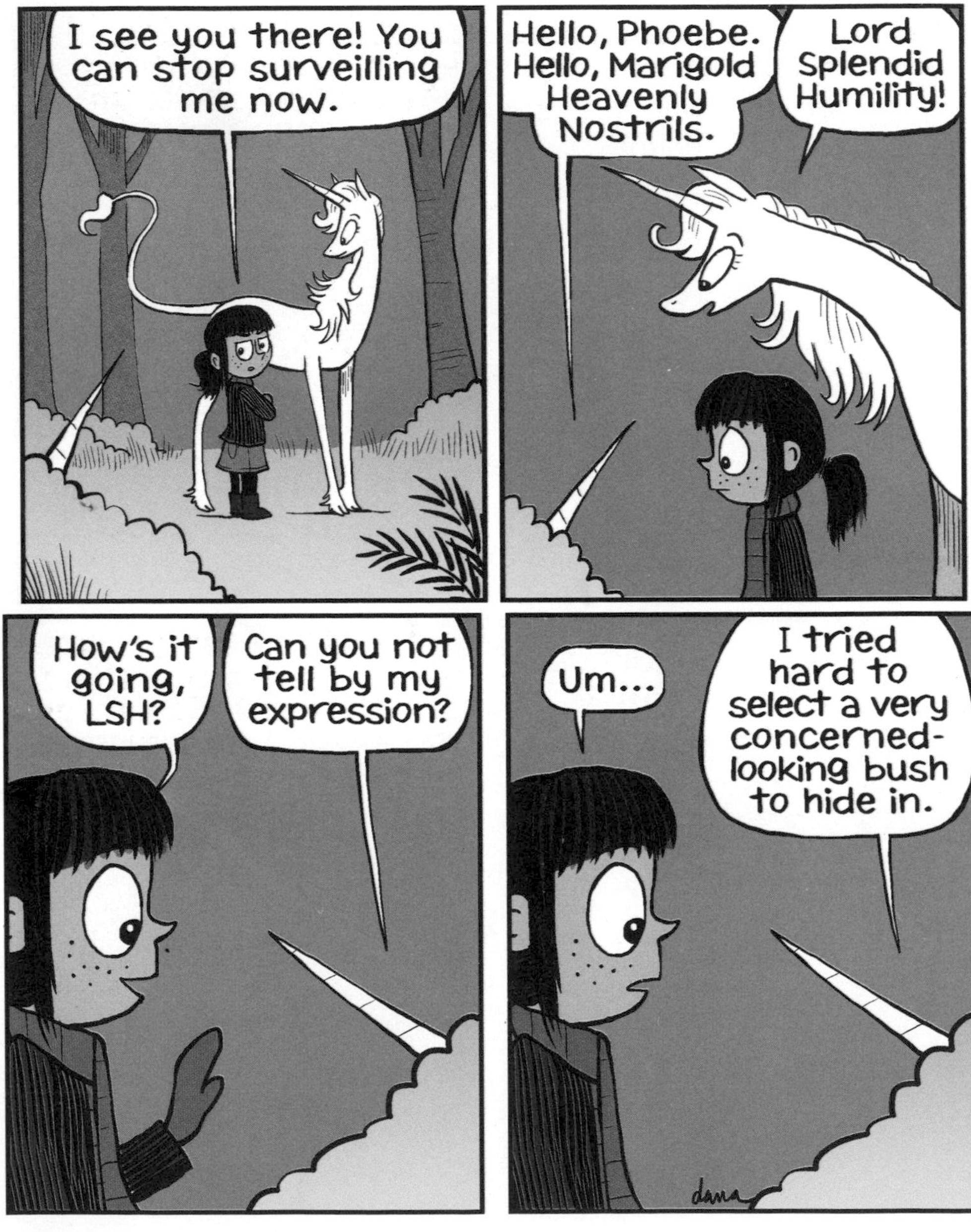
I see you there! You can stop surveilling me now.
Hello, Phoebe. Hello, Marigold Heavenly Nostrils.
Lord Splendid Humility!
How's it going, LSH?
Can you not tell by my expression?
Um...
I tried hard to select a very concerned-looking bush to hide in.
dana

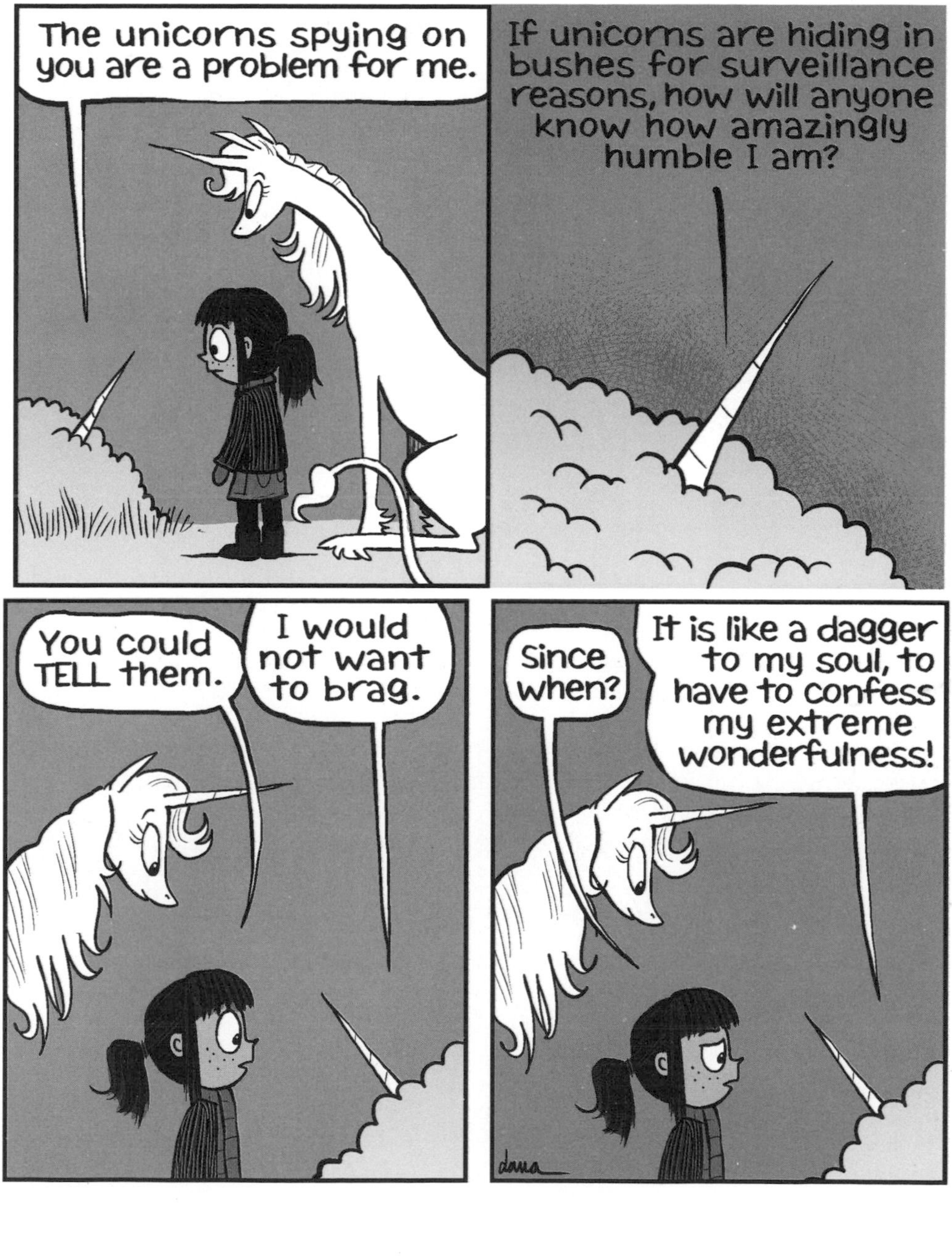
The unicorns spying on you are a problem for me.
If unicorns are hiding in bushes for surveillance reasons, how will anyone know how amazingly humble I am?
You could TELL them.
I would not want to brag.
Since when?
It is like a dagger to my soul, to have to confess my extreme wonderfulness!
dana

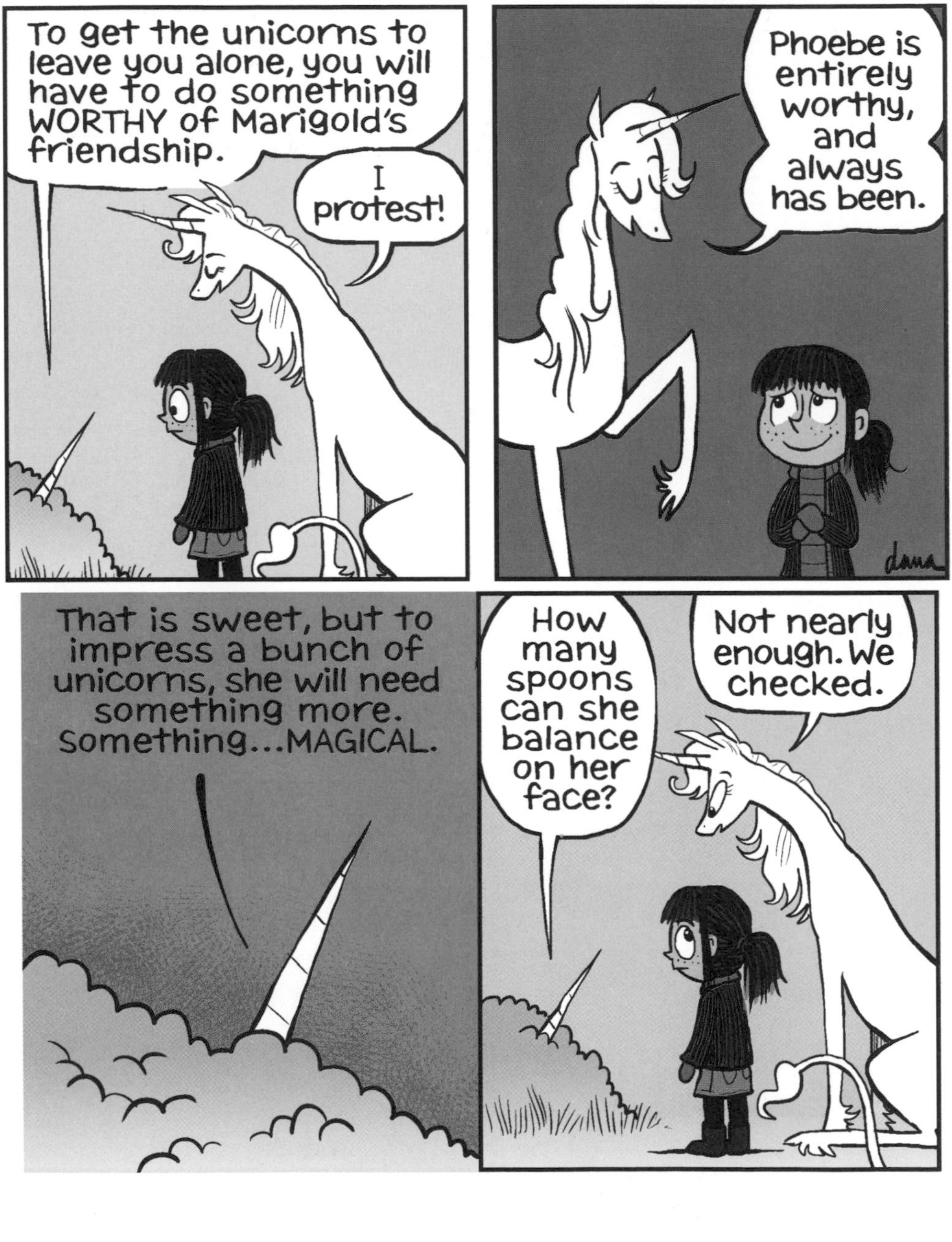
To get the unicorns to leave you alone, you will have to do something WORTHY of Marigold's friendship.
I protest!
Phoebe is entirely worthy, and always has been.
dana
That is sweet, but to impress a bunch of unicorns, she will need something more. Something...MAGICAL.
How many spoons can she balance on her face?
Not nearly enough. We checked.

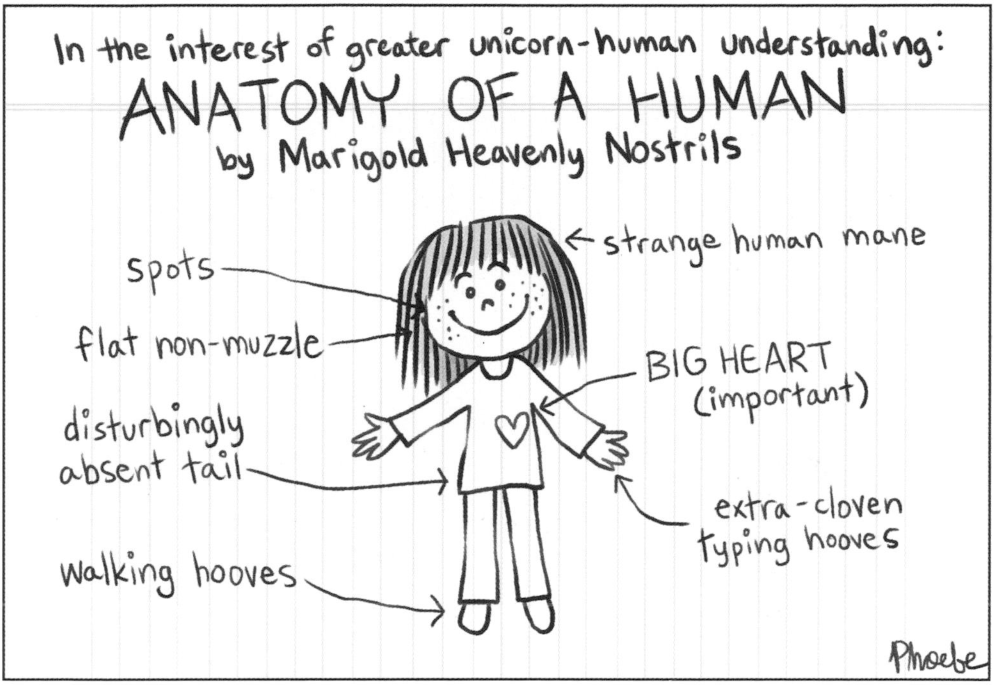
In the interest of greater unicorn-human understanding:
ANATOMY OF A HUMAN
by Marigold Heavenly Nostrils
strange human mane
spots
flat non-muzzle
BIG HEART (important)
disturbingly absent tail
extra-cloven typing hooves
walking hooves
Phoebe

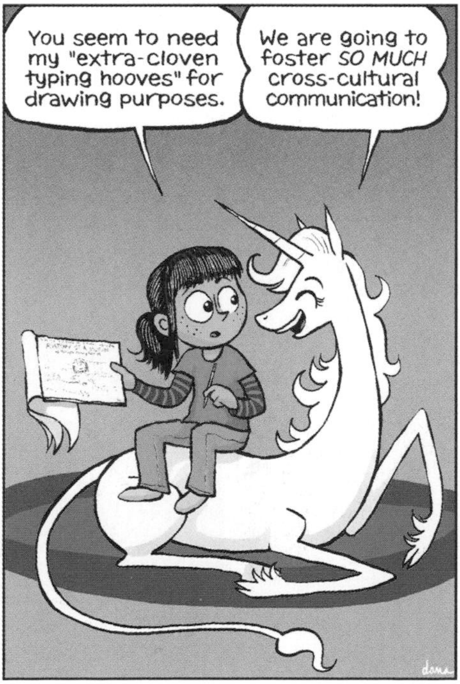
You seem to need my "extra-cloven typing hooves" for drawing purposes.
We are going to foster *SO MUCH* cross-cultural communication!

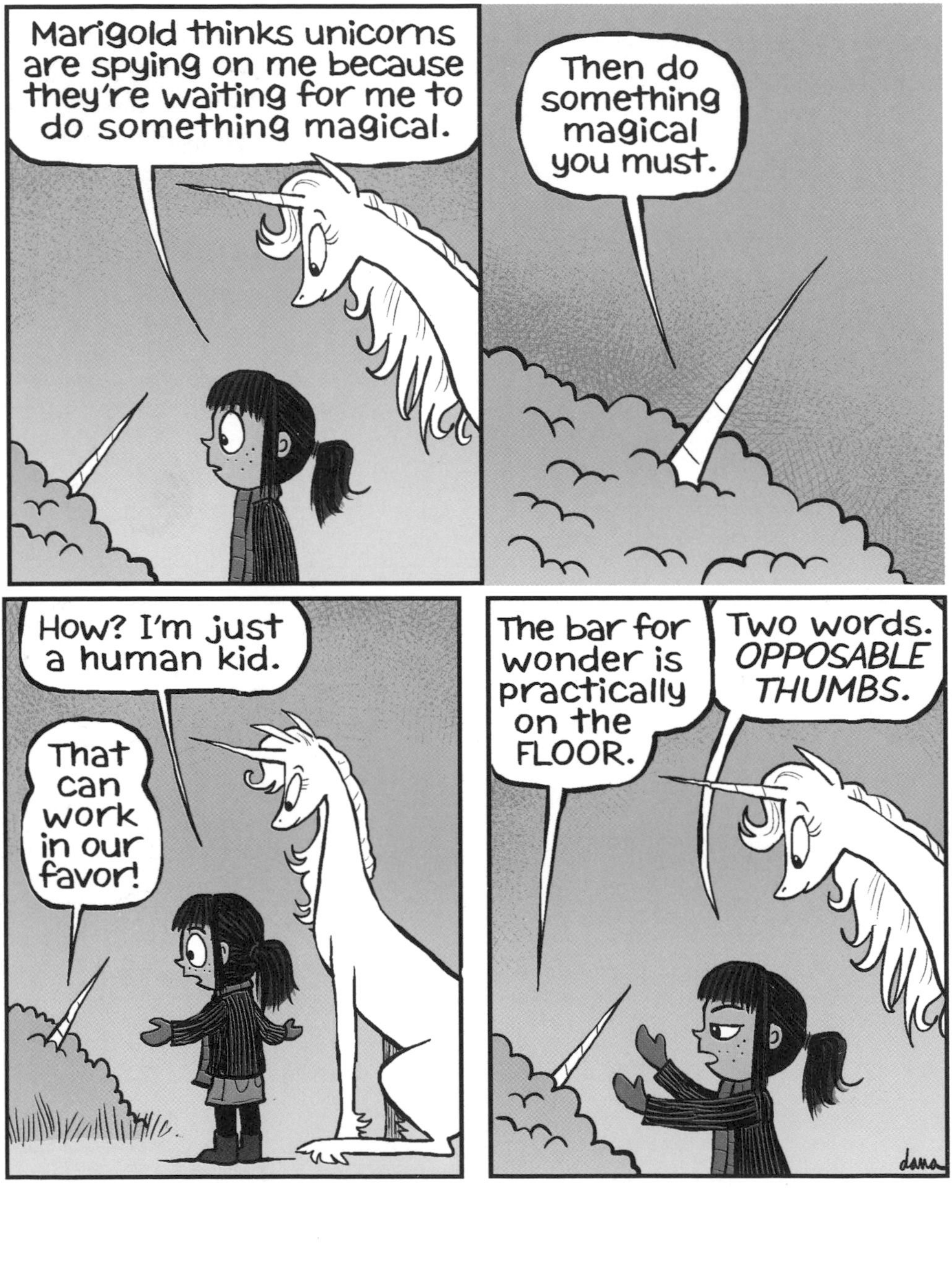
Marigold thinks unicorns are spying on me because they're waiting for me to do something magical.
Then do something magical you must.
How? I'm just a human kid.
That can work in our favor!
The bar for wonder is practically on the FLOOR.
Two words. *OPPOSABLE THUMBS.*
dana

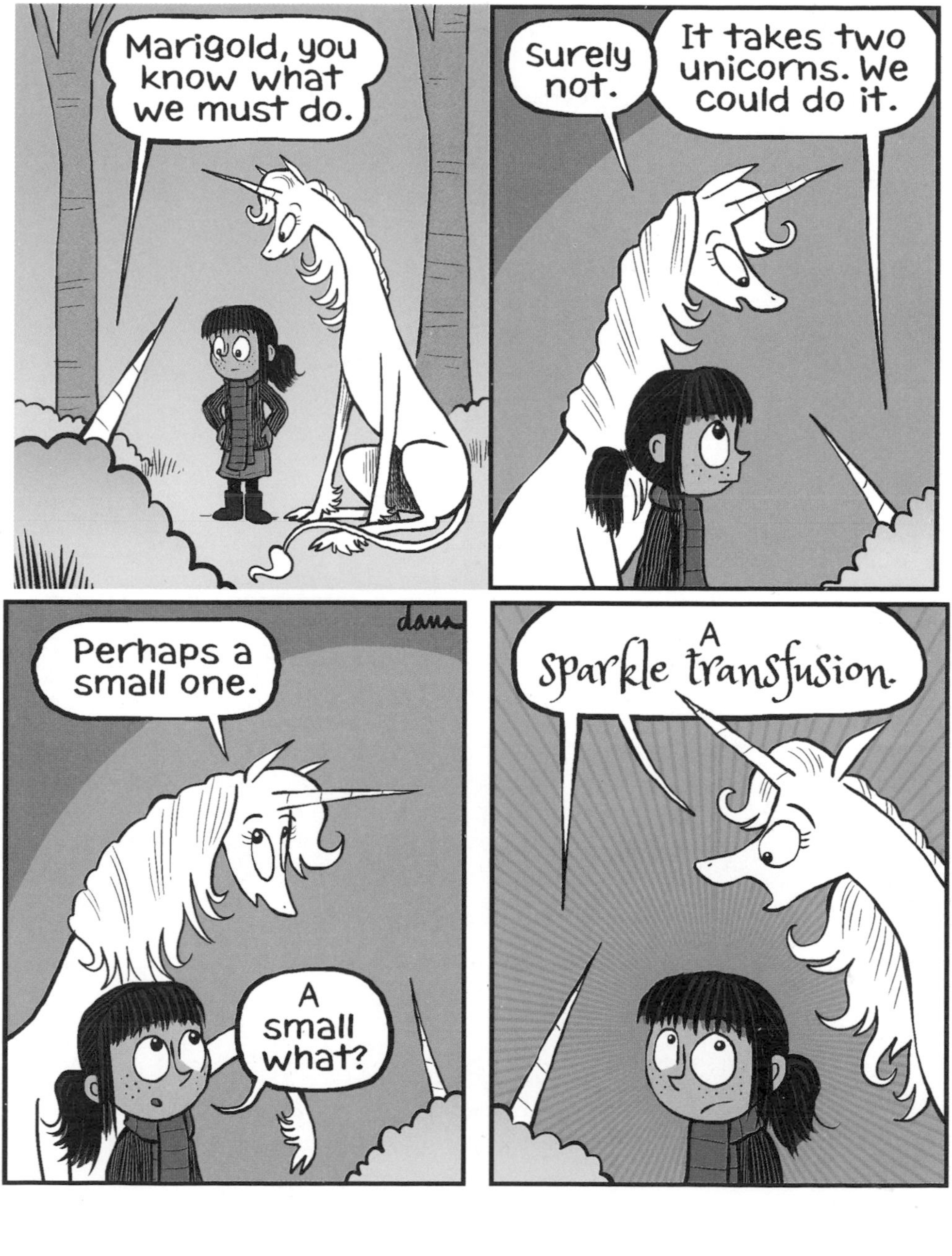
Marigold, you know what we must do.
Surely not.
It takes two unicorns. We could do it.
dana
Perhaps a small one.
A small what?
A sparkle transfusion.

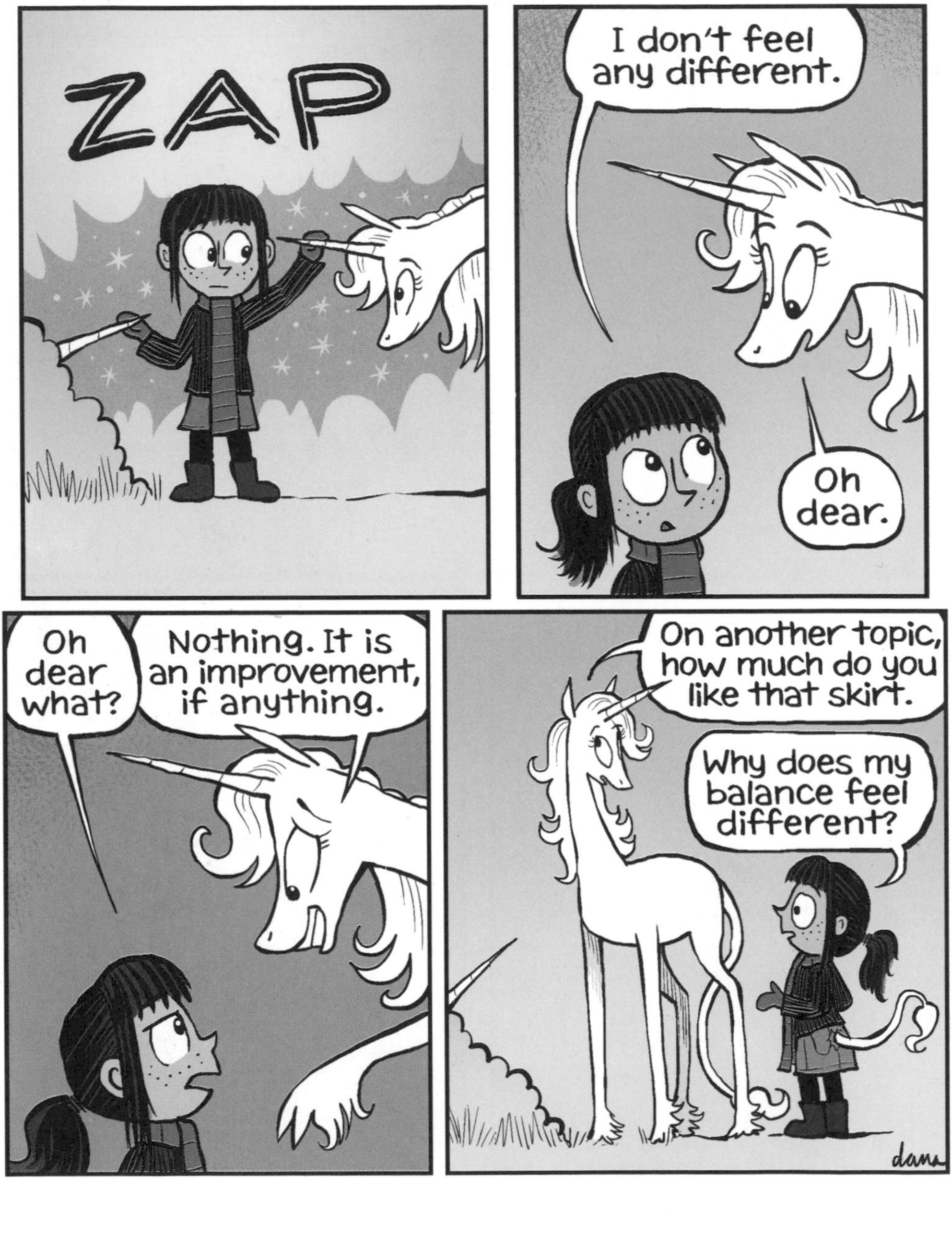
ZAP
I don't feel any different.
Oh dear.
Oh dear what?
Nothing. It is an improvement, if anything.
On another topic, how much do you like that skirt.
Why does my balance feel different?
dana

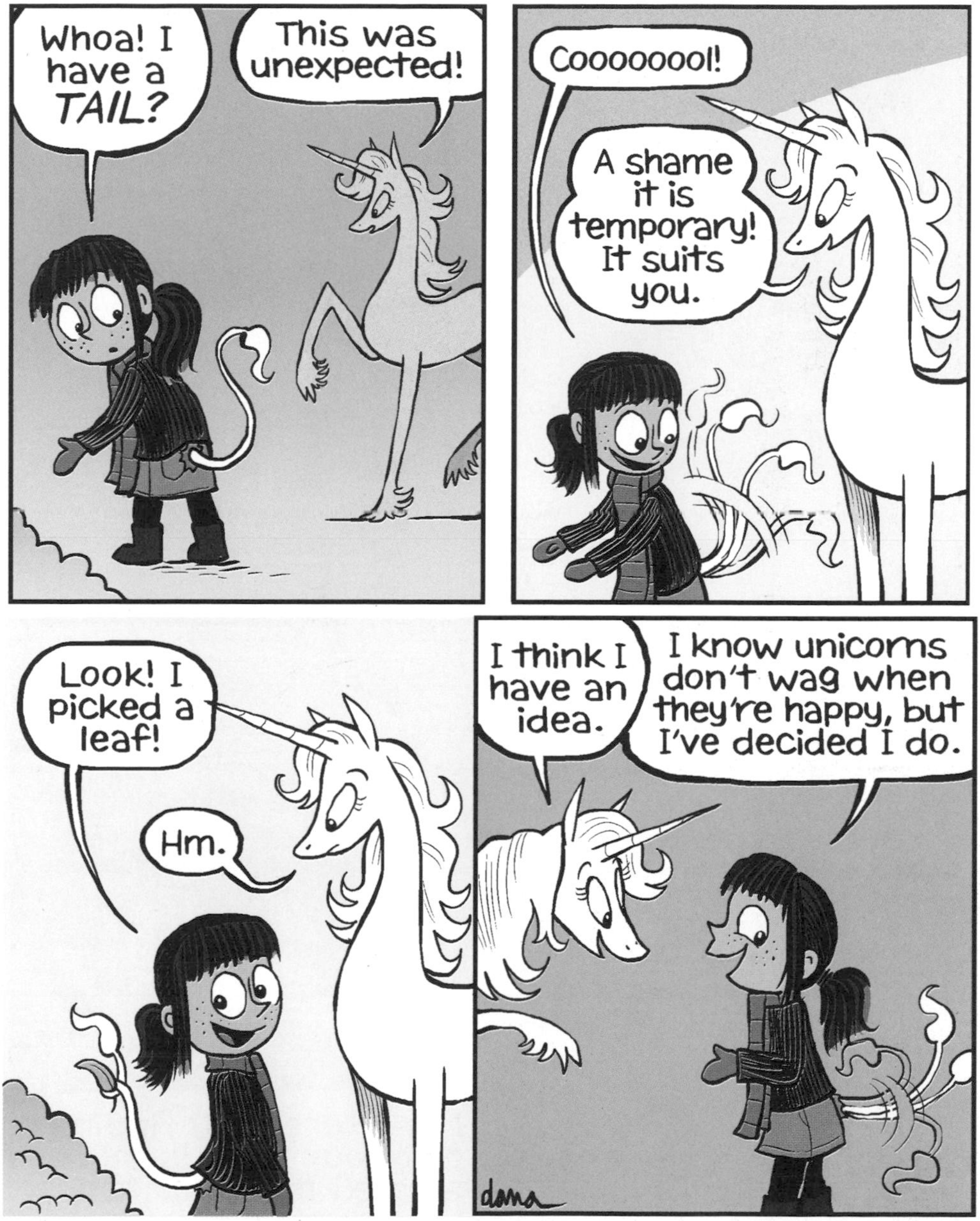
Whoa! I have a TAIL?
This was unexpected!
Cooooooool!
A shame it is temporary! It suits you.
Look! I picked a leaf!
Hm.
I think I have an idea.
I know unicorns don't wag when they're happy, but I've decided I do.
dana

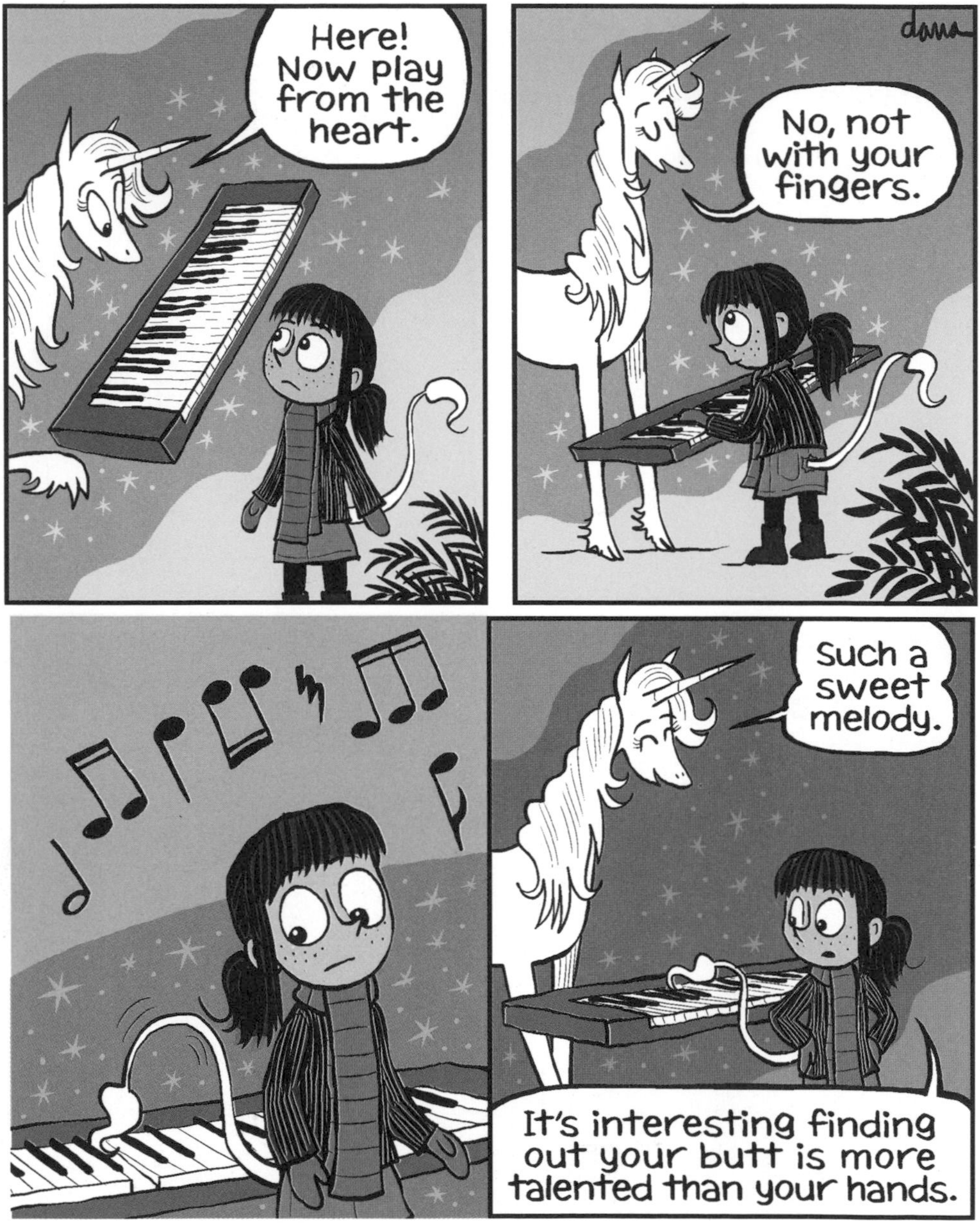
Here! Now play from the heart.
dana
No, not with your fingers.
Such a sweet melody.
It's interesting finding out your butt is more talented than your hands.

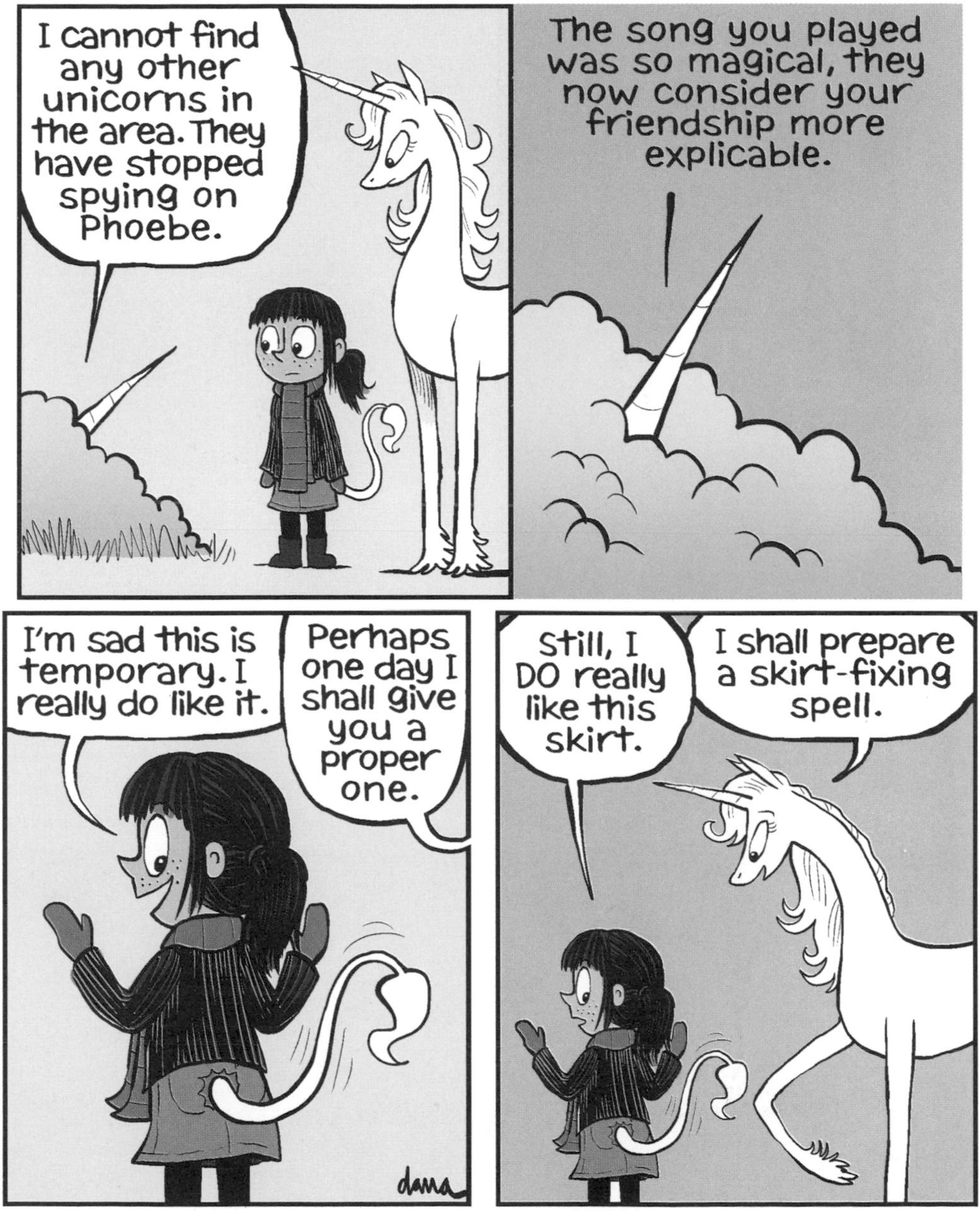

I cannot find any other unicorns in the area. They have stopped spying on Phoebe.
The song you played was so magical, they now consider your friendship more explicable.
I'm sad this is temporary. I really do like it.
Perhaps one day I shall give you a proper one.
Still, I DO really like this skirt.
I shall prepare a skirt-fixing spell.
dana

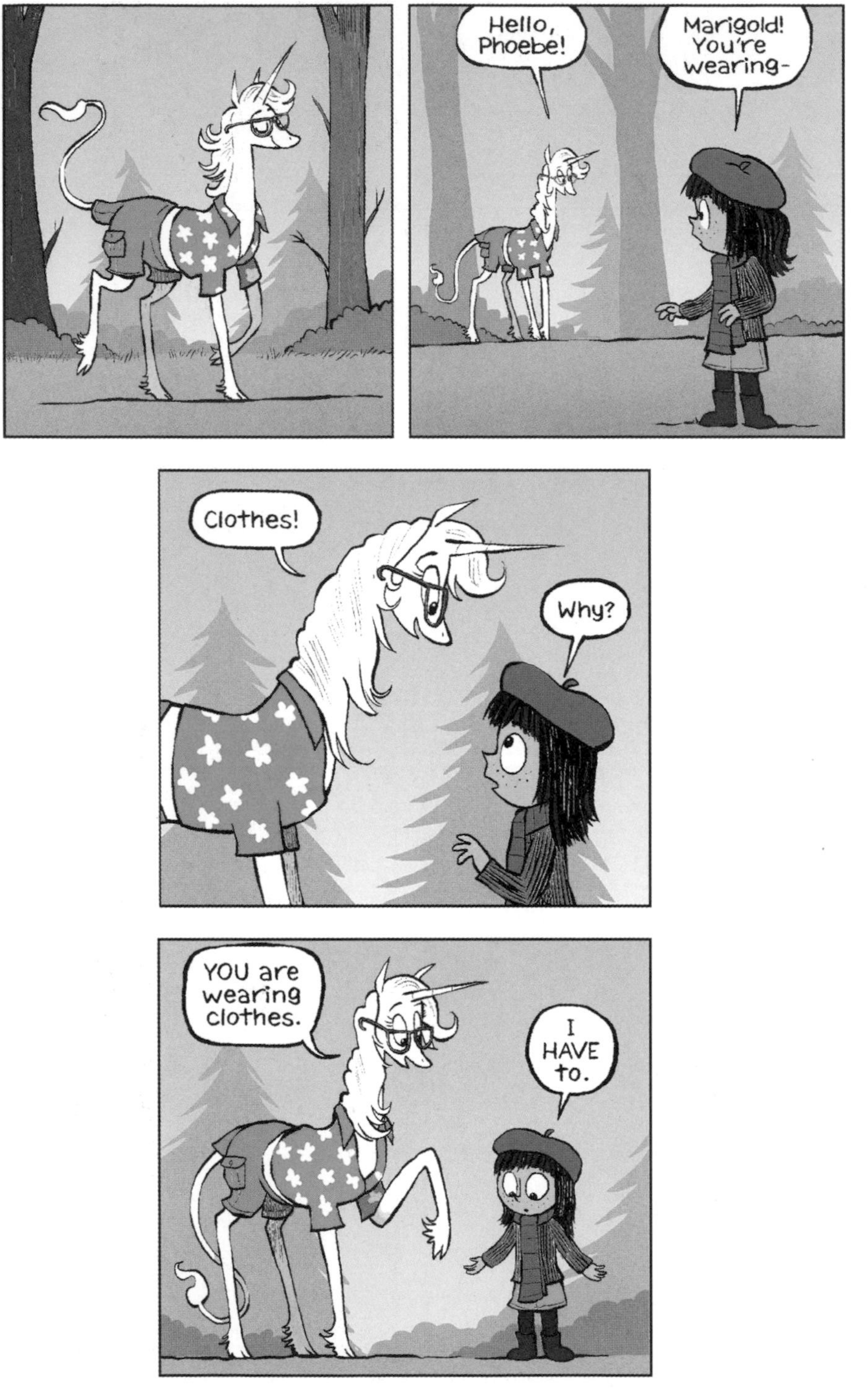
Hello, Phoebe!
Marigold! You're wearing-
Clothes!
Why?
YOU are wearing clothes.
I HAVE to.

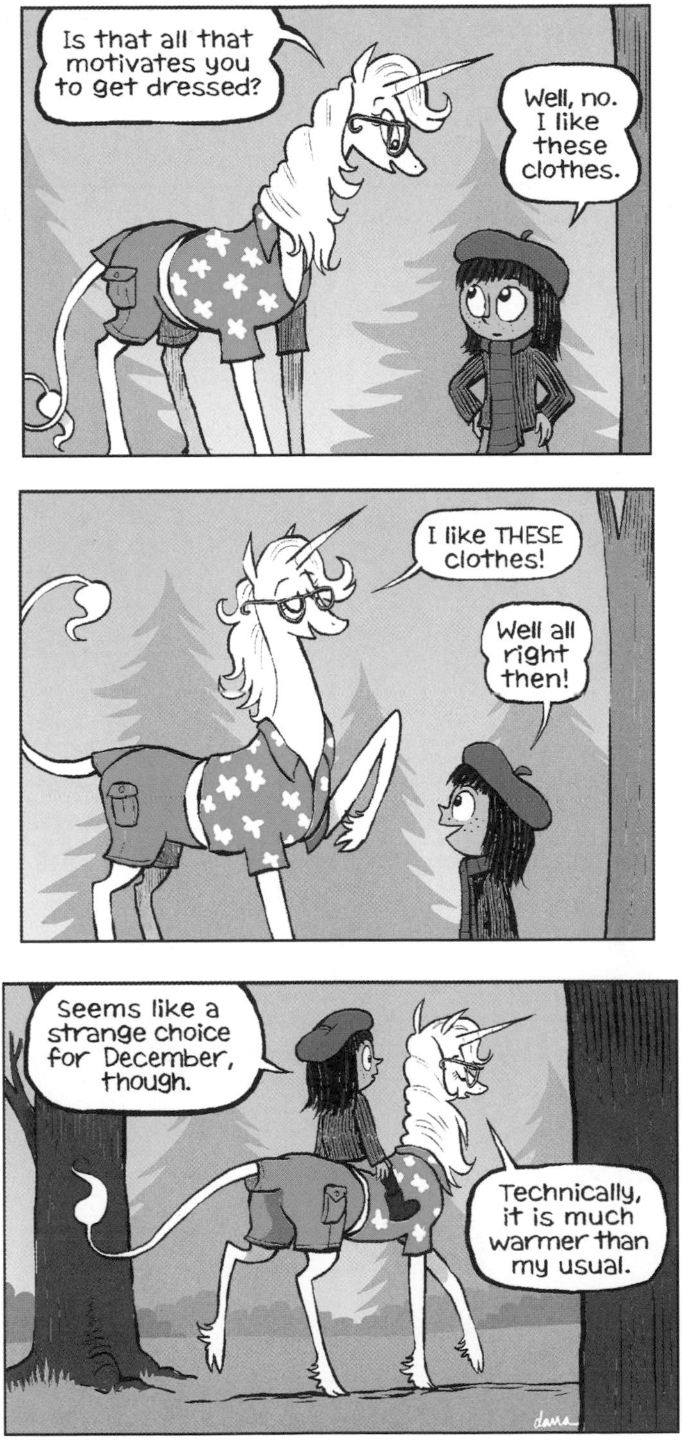
Is that all that motivates you to get dressed?
Well, no. I like these clothes.
I like THESE clothes!
Well all right then!
Seems like a strange choice for December, though.
Technically, it is much warmer than my usual.
dana

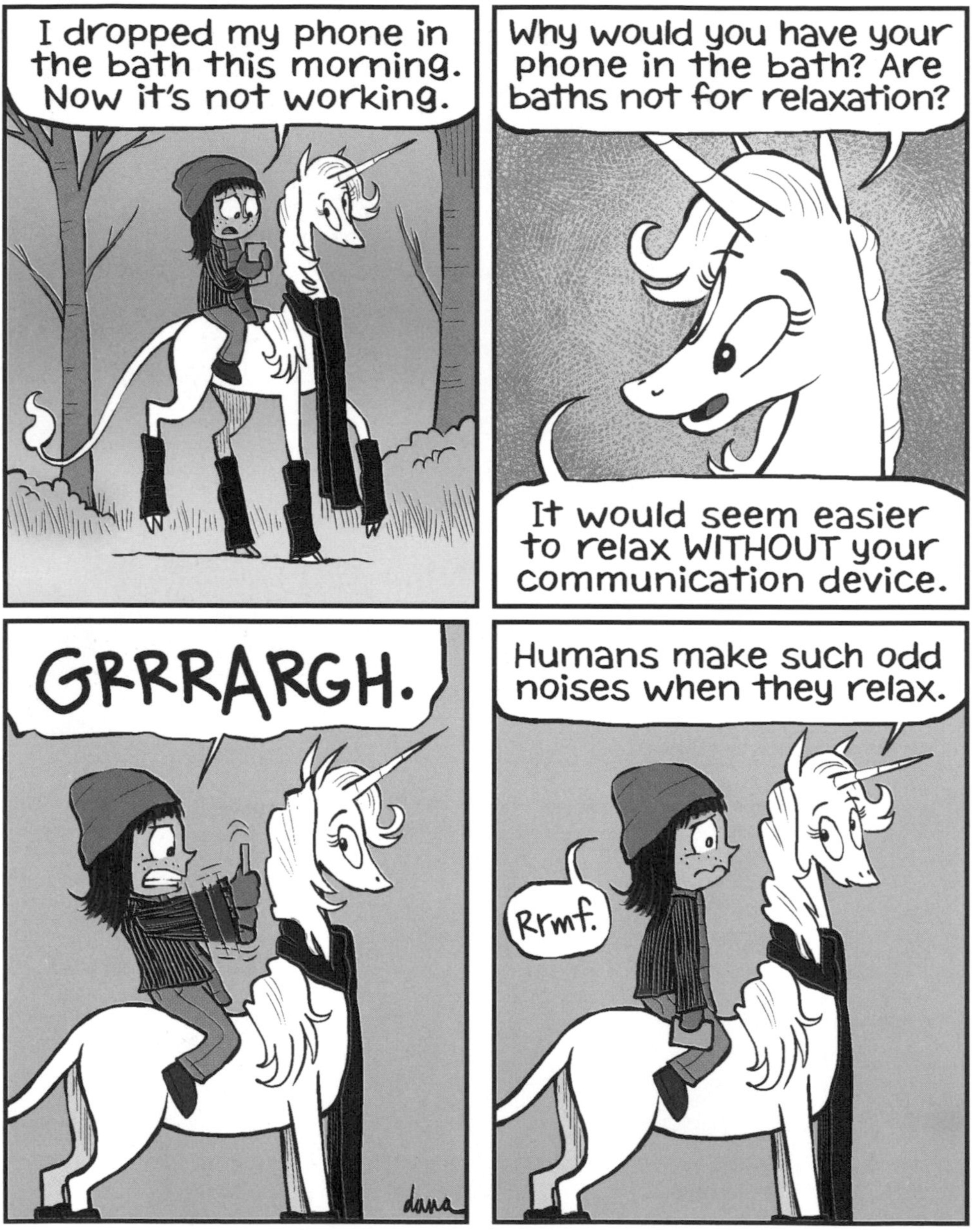
I dropped my phone in the bath this morning. Now it's not working.
Why would you have your phone in the bath? Are baths not for relaxation?
It would seem easier to relax WITHOUT your communication device.
GRRRARGH.
Humans make such odd noises when they relax.
Rrmf.
dana

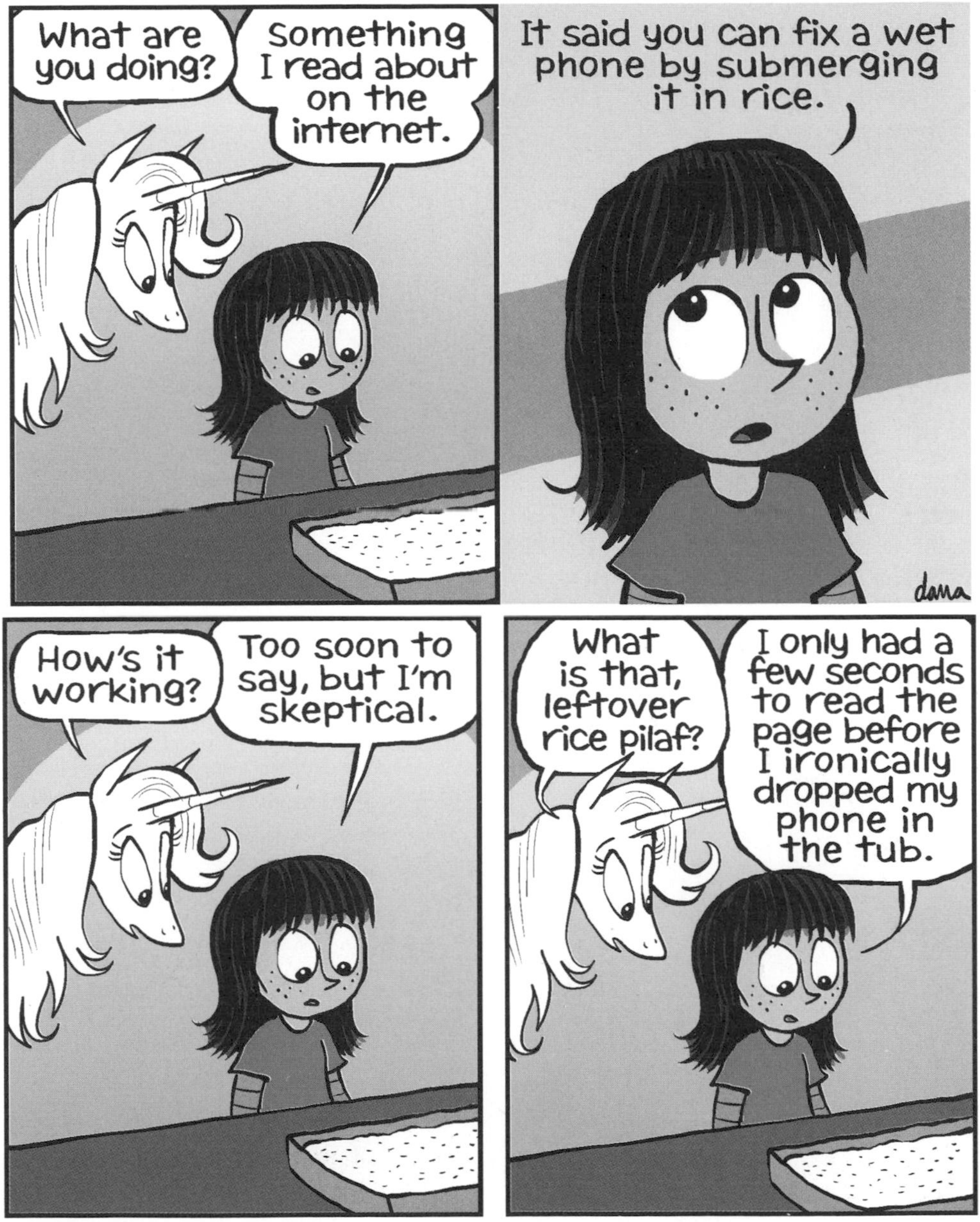
What are you doing?
Something I read about on the internet.
It said you can fix a wet phone by submerging it in rice.
dana
How's it working?
Too soon to say, but I'm skeptical.
What is that, leftover rice pilaf?
I only had a few seconds to read the page before I ironically dropped my phone in the tub.

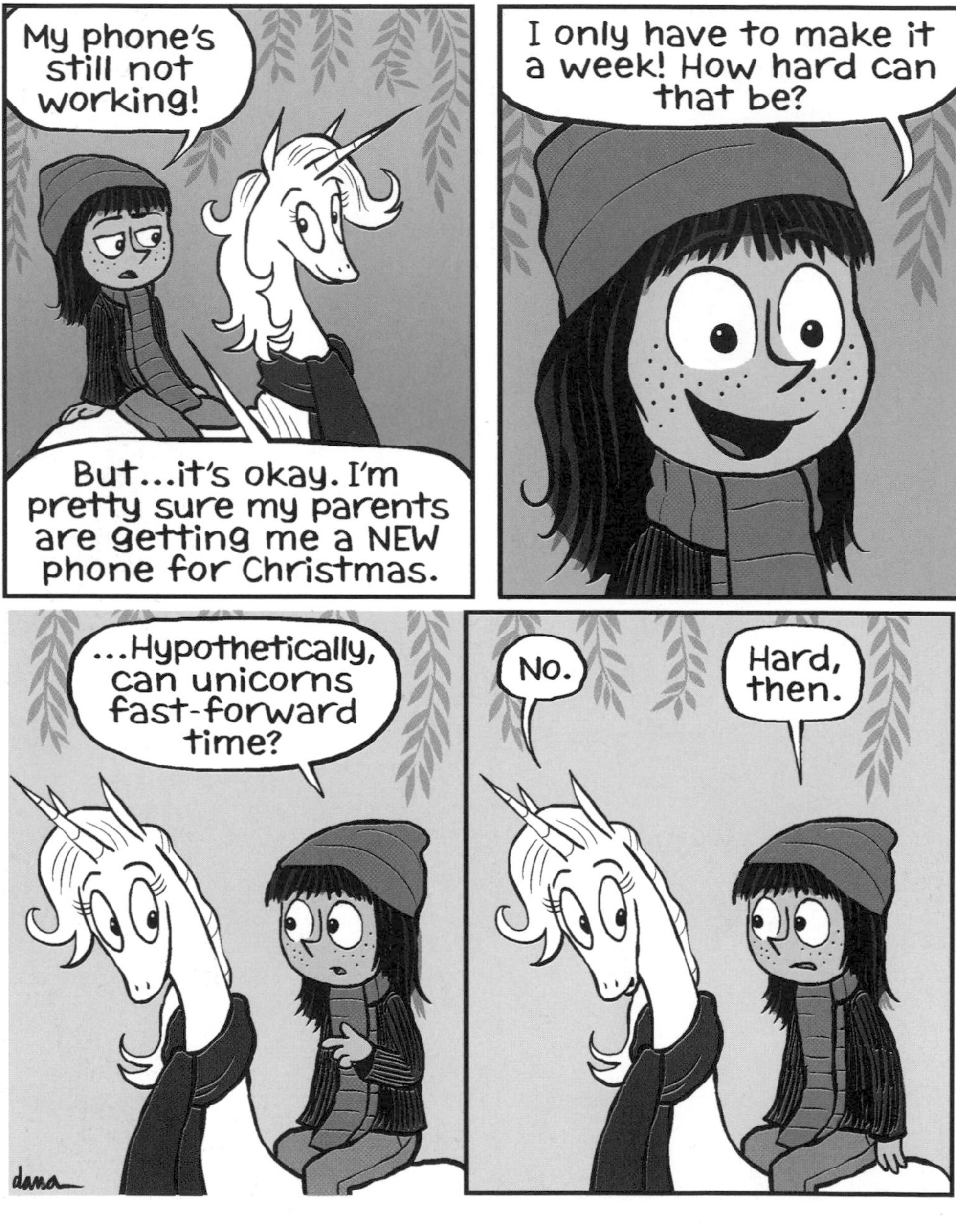
My phone's still not working!
But...it's okay. I'm pretty sure my parents are getting me a NEW phone for Christmas.
I only have to make it a week! How hard can that be?
...Hypothetically, can unicorns fast-forward time?
No.
Hard, then.
dana

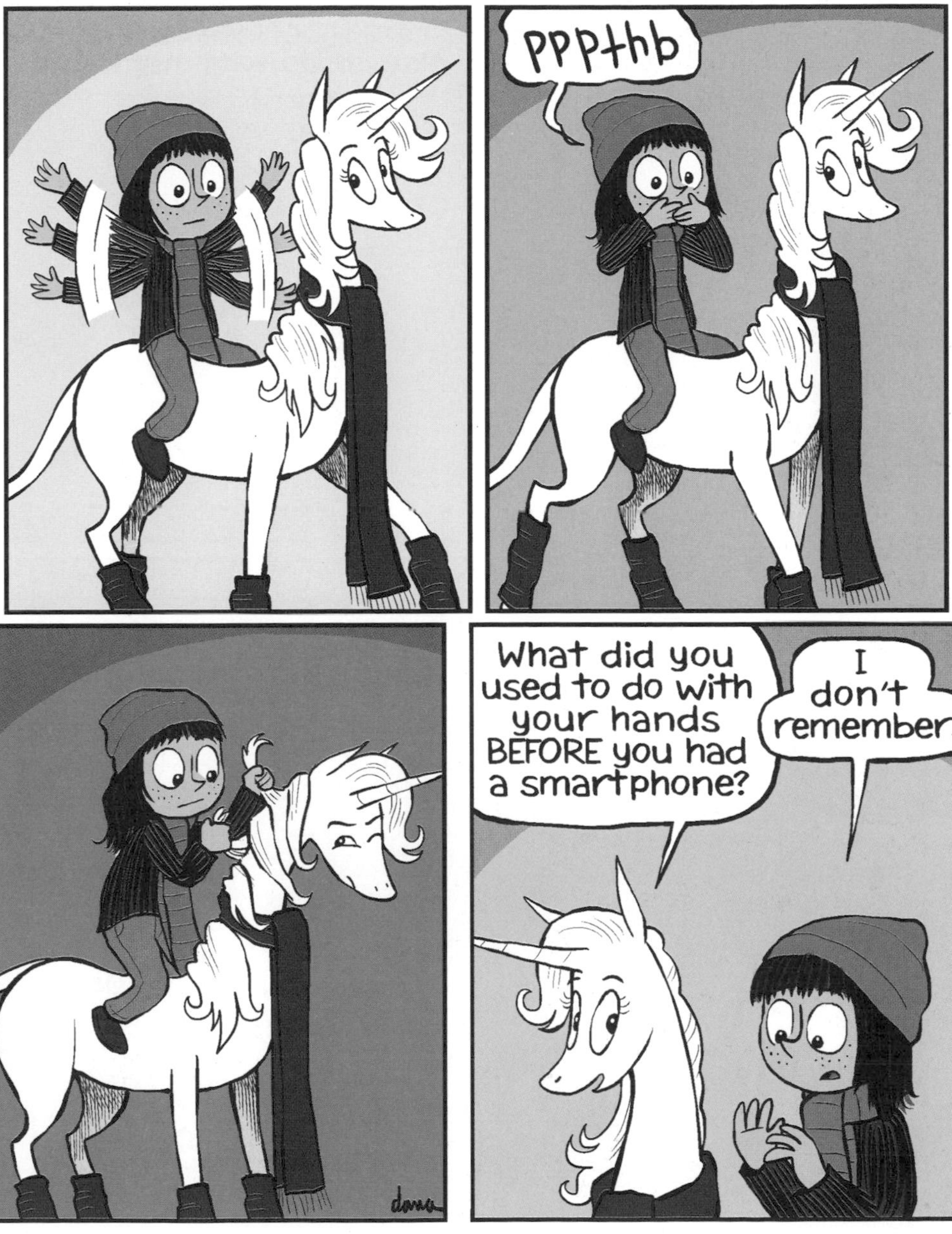
PPPthb
What did you used to do with your hands BEFORE you had a smartphone?
I don't remember.

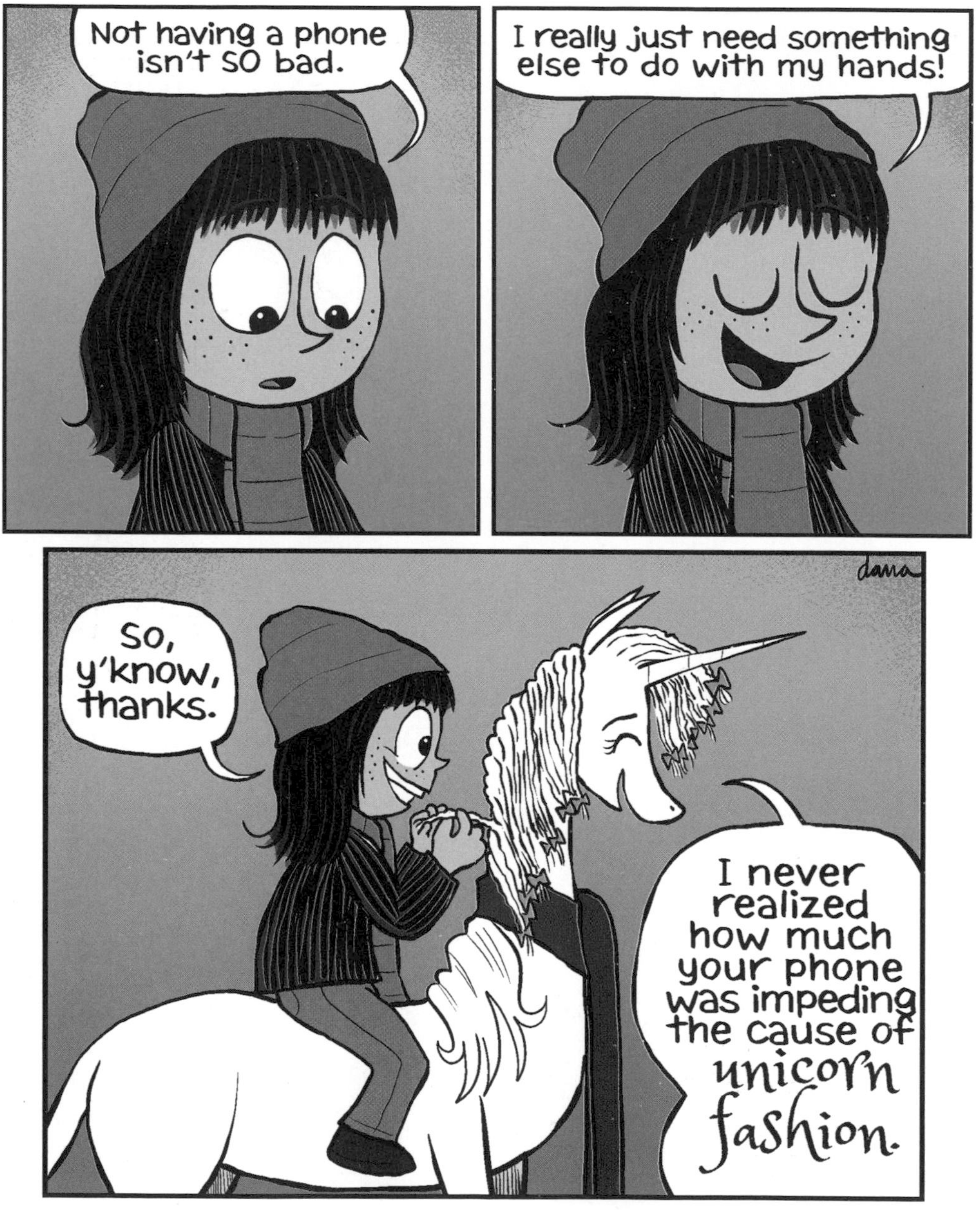
Not having a phone isn't SO bad.
I really just need something else to do with my hands!
So, y'know, thanks.
I never realized how much your phone was impeding the cause of unicorn fashion.
dana

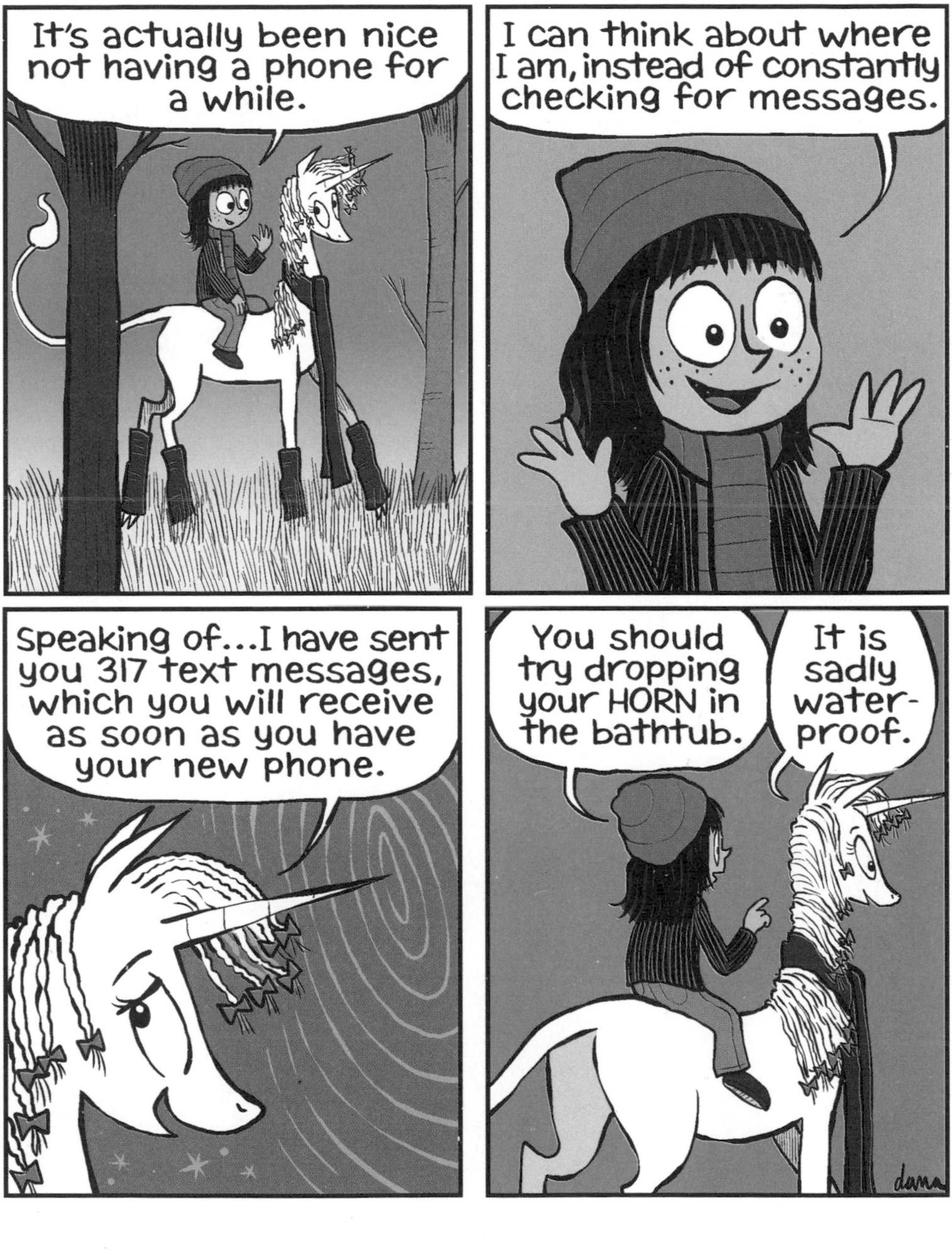
It's actually been nice not having a phone for a while.
I can think about where I am, instead of constantly checking for messages.
Speaking of...I have sent you 317 text messages, which you will receive as soon as you have your new phone.
You should try dropping your HORN in the bathtub.
It is sadly water-proof.
dana

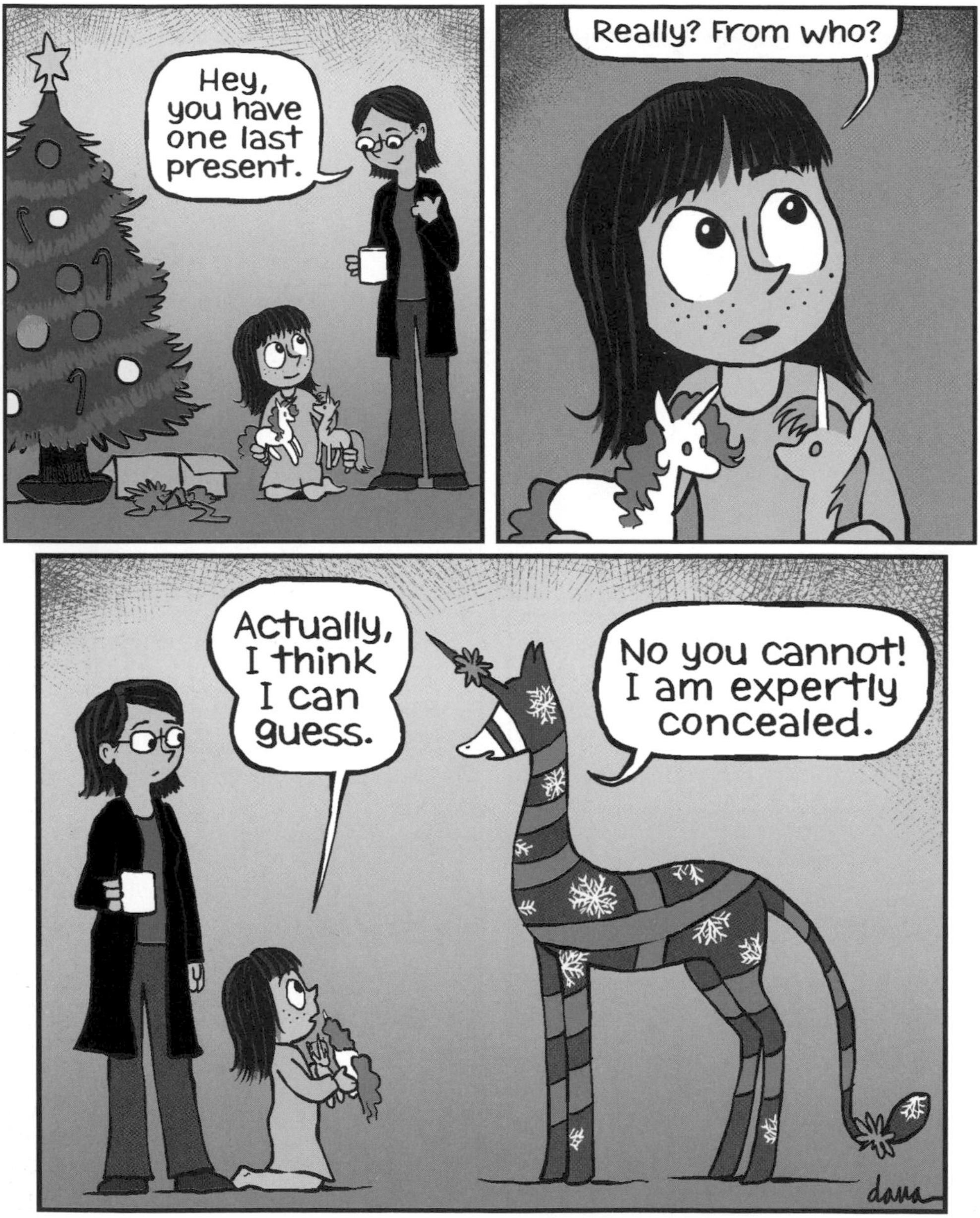
Hey, you have one last present.
Really? From who?
Actually, I think I can guess.
No you cannot! I am expertly concealed.
dana

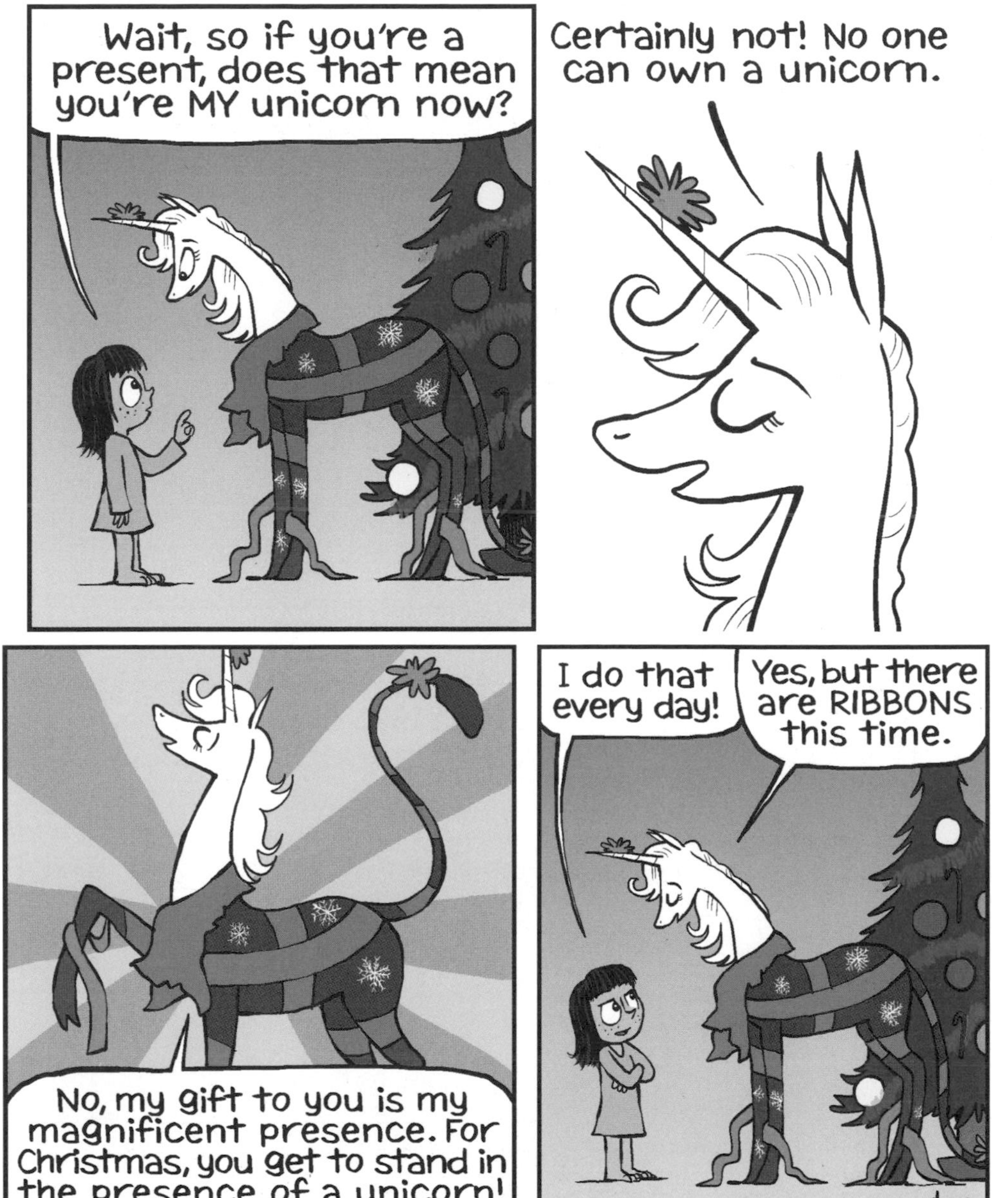
Wait, so if you're a present, does that mean you're MY unicorn now?
Certainly not! No one can own a unicorn.
No, my gift to you is my magnificent presence. For Christmas, you get to stand in the presence of a unicorn!
I do that every day!
Yes, but there are RIBBONS this time.
dana

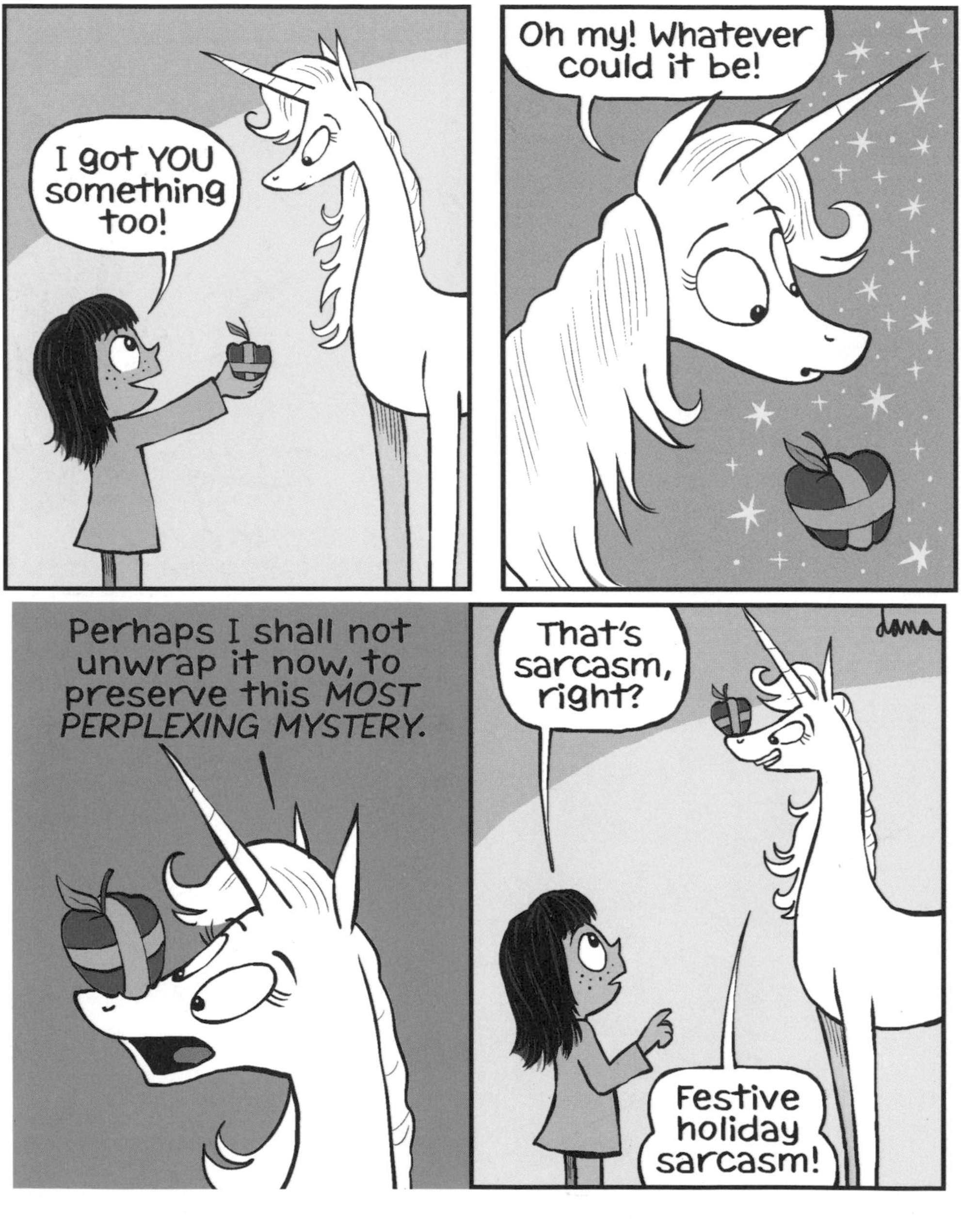
I got YOU something too!
Oh my! Whatever could it be!
Perhaps I shall not unwrap it now, to preserve this *MOST PERPLEXING MYSTERY.*
That's sarcasm, right?
Festive holiday sarcasm!

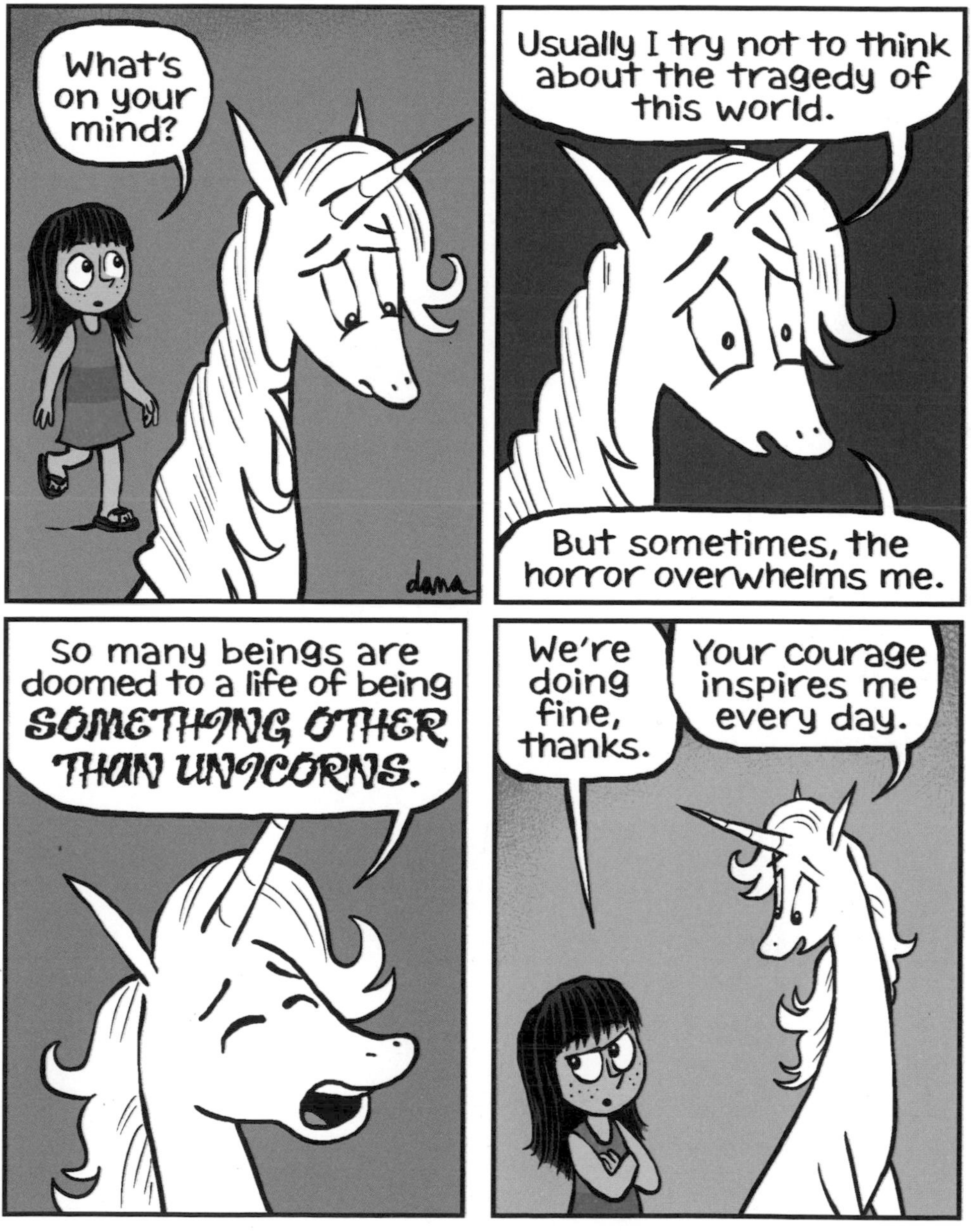
What's on your mind?
dana
Usually I try not to think about the tragedy of this world.
But sometimes, the horror overwhelms me.
So many beings are doomed to a life of being SOMETHING OTHER THAN UNICORNS.
We're doing fine, thanks.
Your courage inspires me every day.

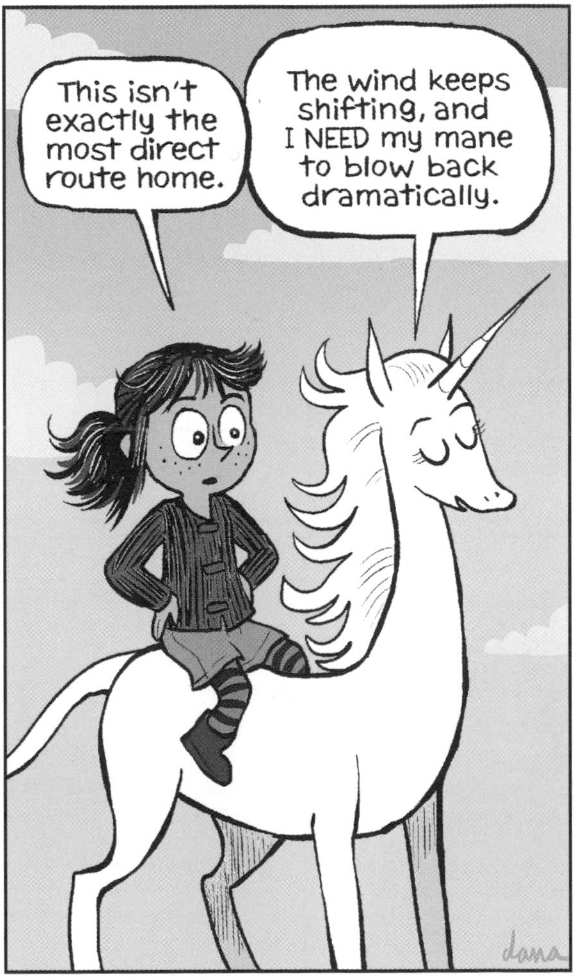
This isn't exactly the most direct route home.
The wind keeps shifting, and I NEED my mane to blow back dramatically.
dana

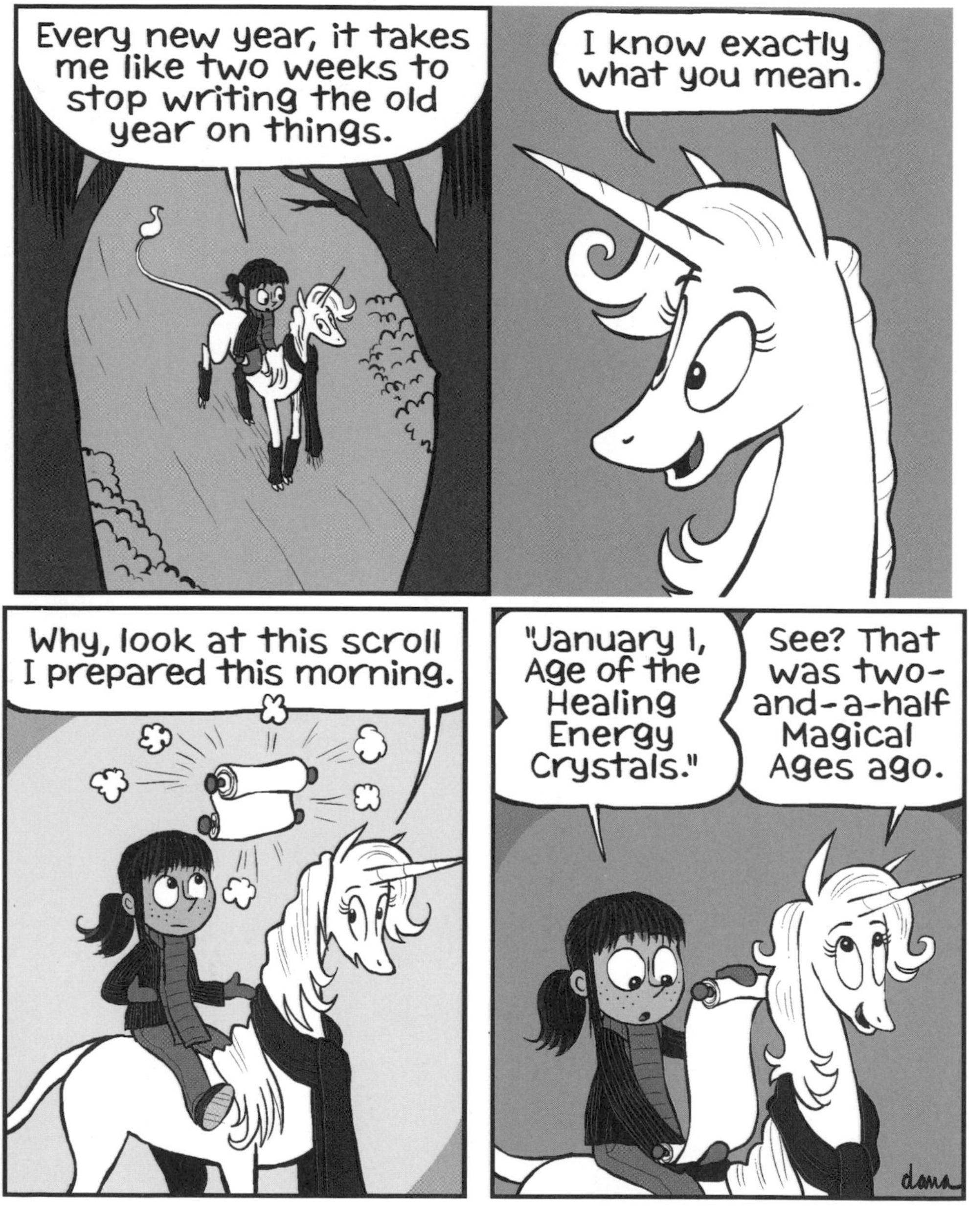
Every new year, it takes me like two weeks to stop writing the old year on things.
I know exactly what you mean.
Why, look at this scroll I prepared this morning.
"January 1, Age of the Healing Energy Crystals."
See? That was two-and-a-half Magical Ages ago.
dana

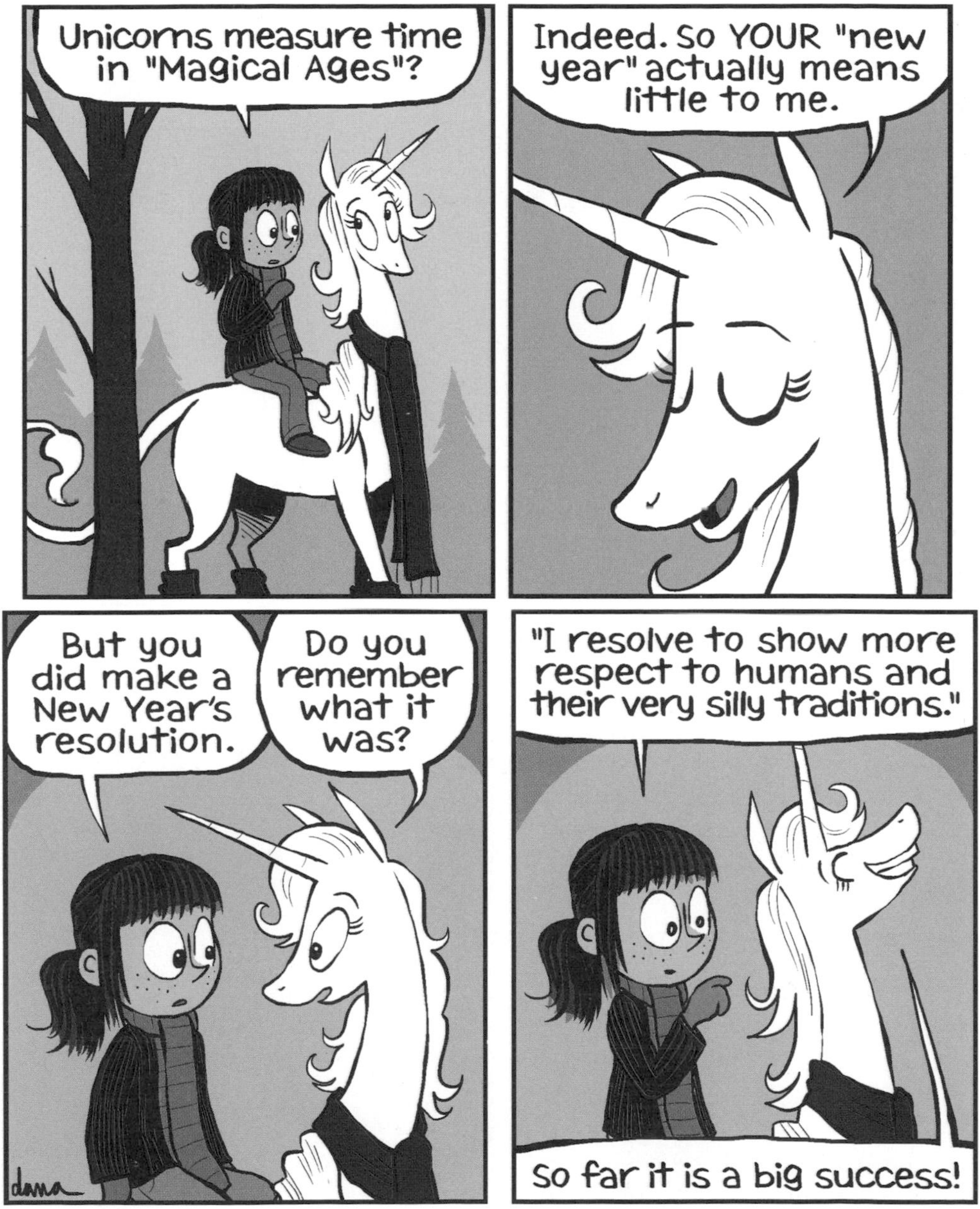
Unicorns measure time in "Magical Ages"?
Indeed. So YOUR "new year" actually means little to me.
But you did make a New Year's resolution.
Do you remember what it was?
"I resolve to show more respect to humans and their very silly traditions."
So far it is a big success!
dana

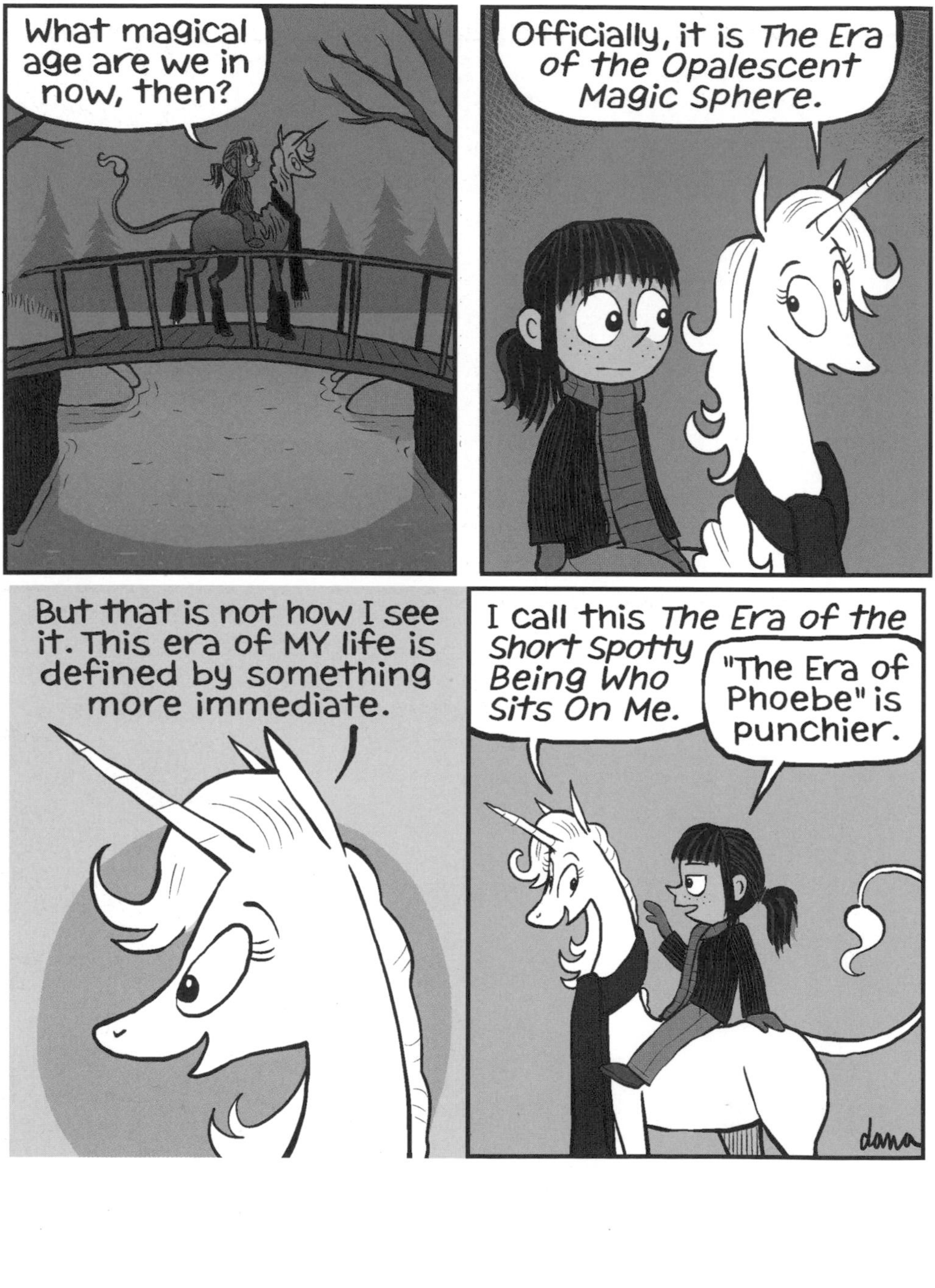
What magical age are we in now, then?
Officially, it is *The Era of the Opalescent Magic Sphere.*
But that is not how I see it. This era of MY life is defined by something more immediate.
I call this *The Era of the Short Spotty Being Who Sits On Me.*
"The Era of Phoebe" is punchier.
dana

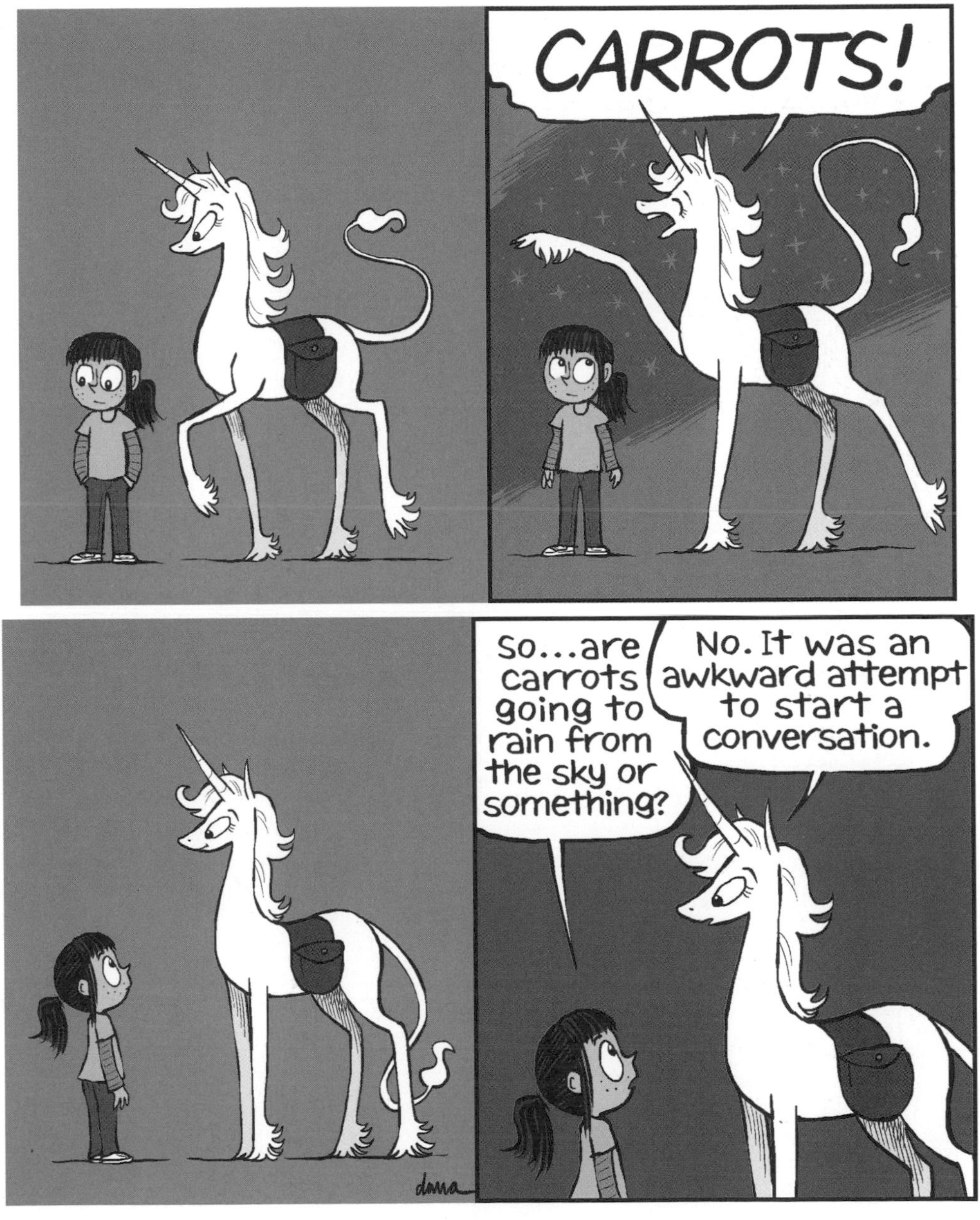
CARROTS!
So...are carrots going to rain from the sky or something?
No. It was an awkward attempt to start a conversation.
dana

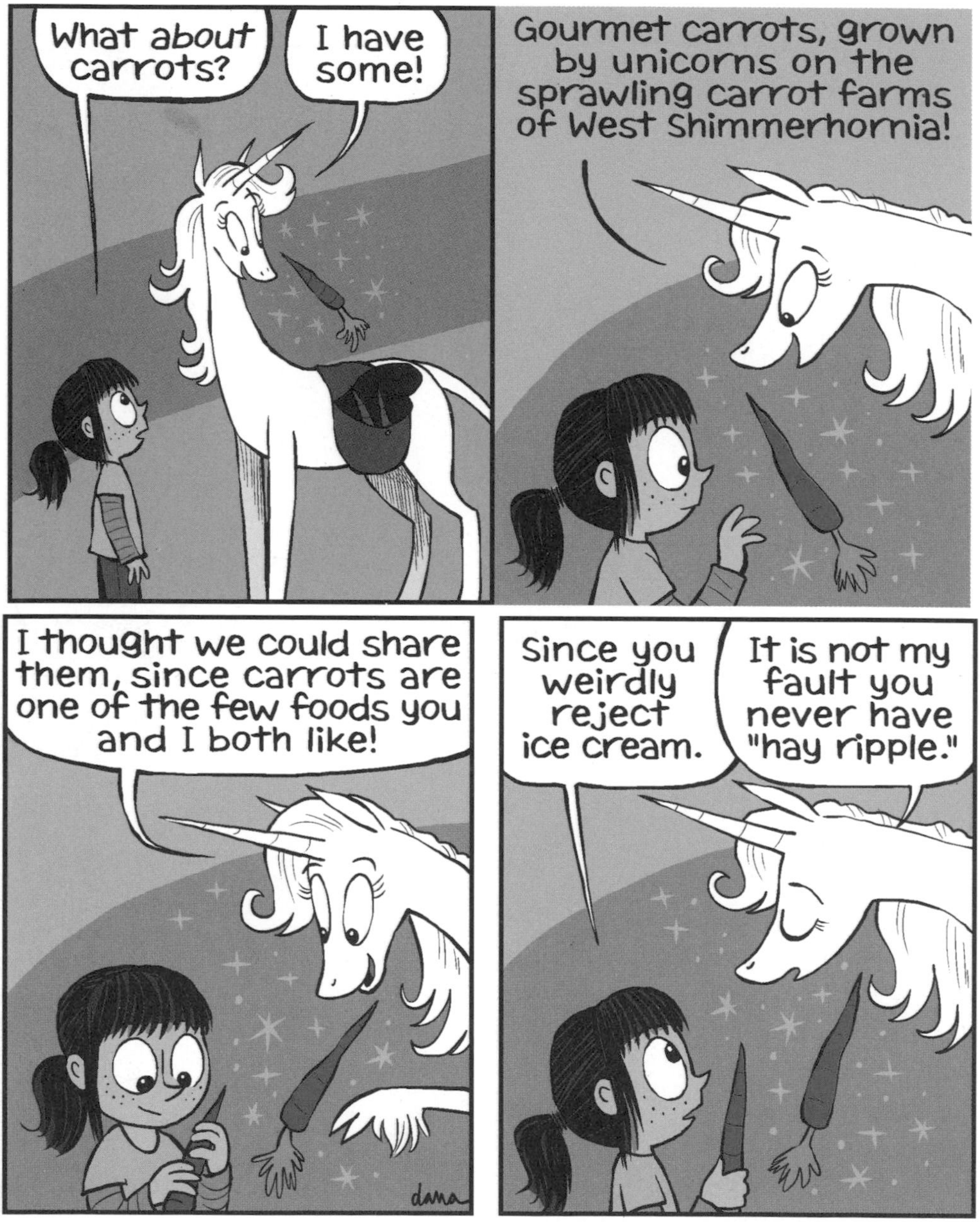
What about carrots?
I have some!
Gourmet carrots, grown by unicorns on the sprawling carrot farms of West Shimmerhornia!
I thought we could share them, since carrots are one of the few foods you and I both like!
dana
Since you weirdly reject ice cream.
It is not my fault you never have "hay ripple."

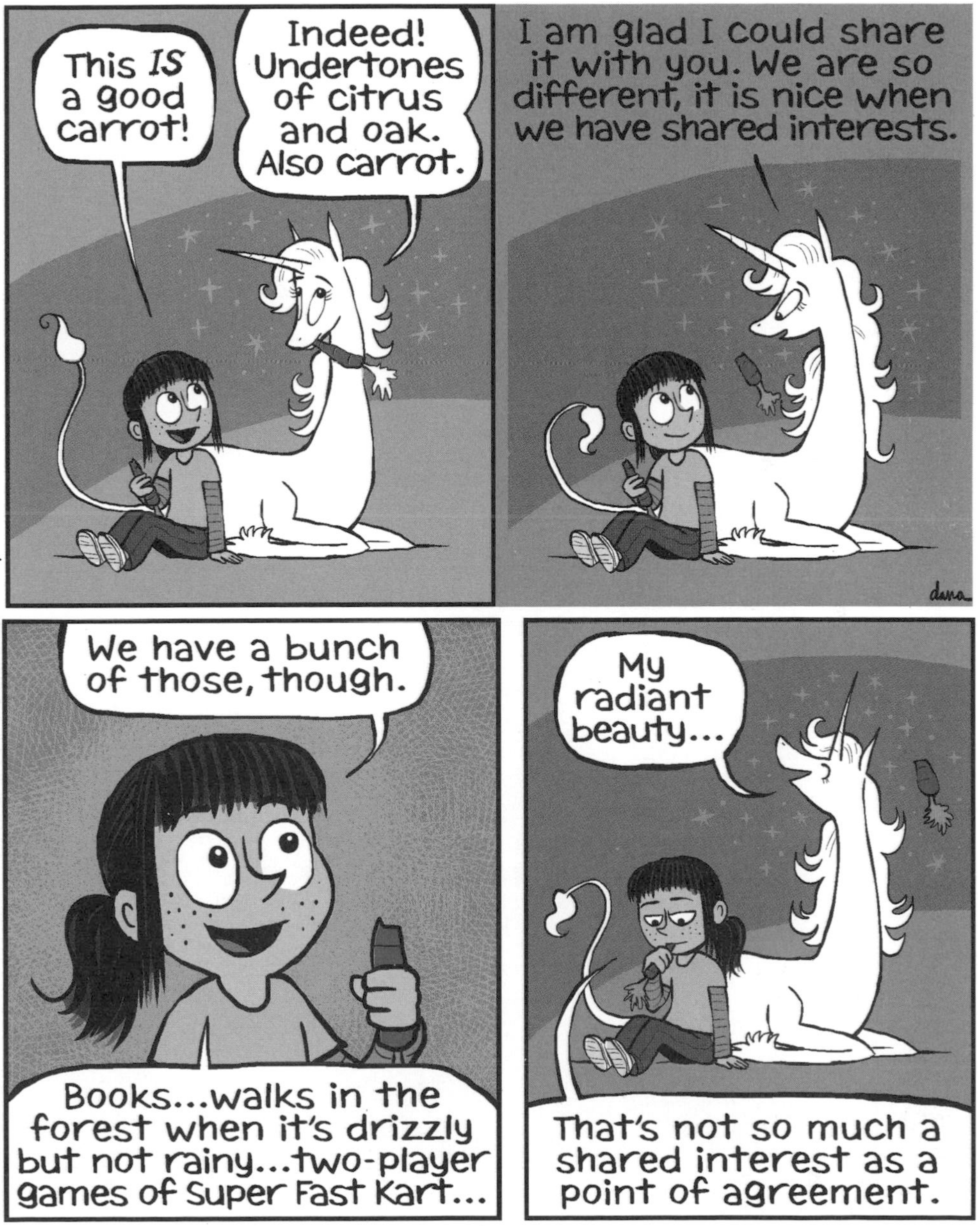
This *IS* a good carrot!
Indeed! Undertones of citrus and oak. Also carrot.
I am glad I could share it with you. We are so different, it is nice when we have shared interests.
dana
We have a bunch of those, though.
Books...walks in the forest when it's drizzly but not rainy...two-player games of Super Fast Kart...
My radiant beauty...
That's not so much a shared interest as a point of agreement.

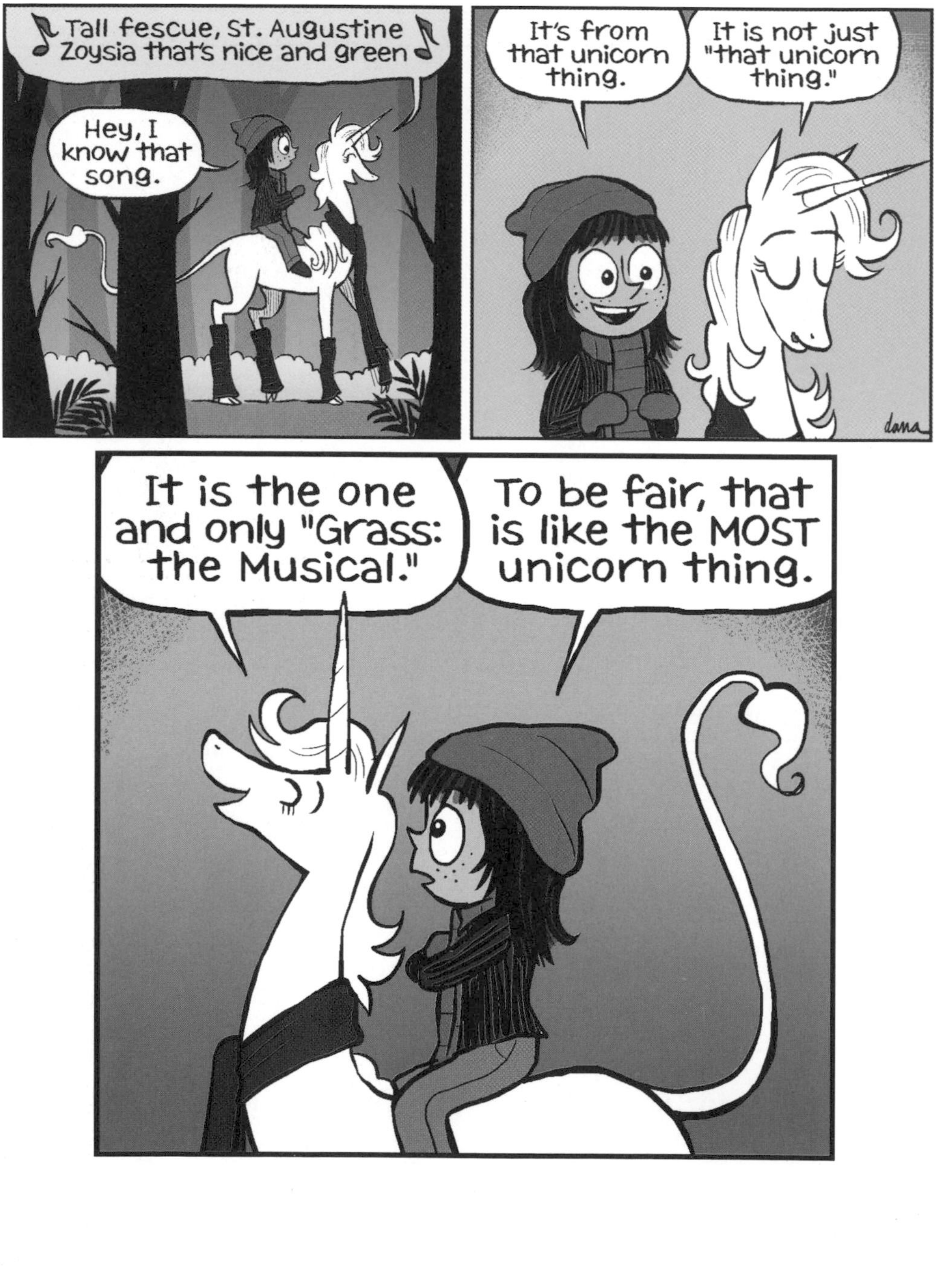
Tall fescue, St. Augustine
Zoysia that's nice and green
Hey, I know that song.
It's from that unicorn thing.
It is not just "that unicorn thing."
dana
It is the one and only "Grass: the Musical."
To be fair, that is like the MOST unicorn thing.

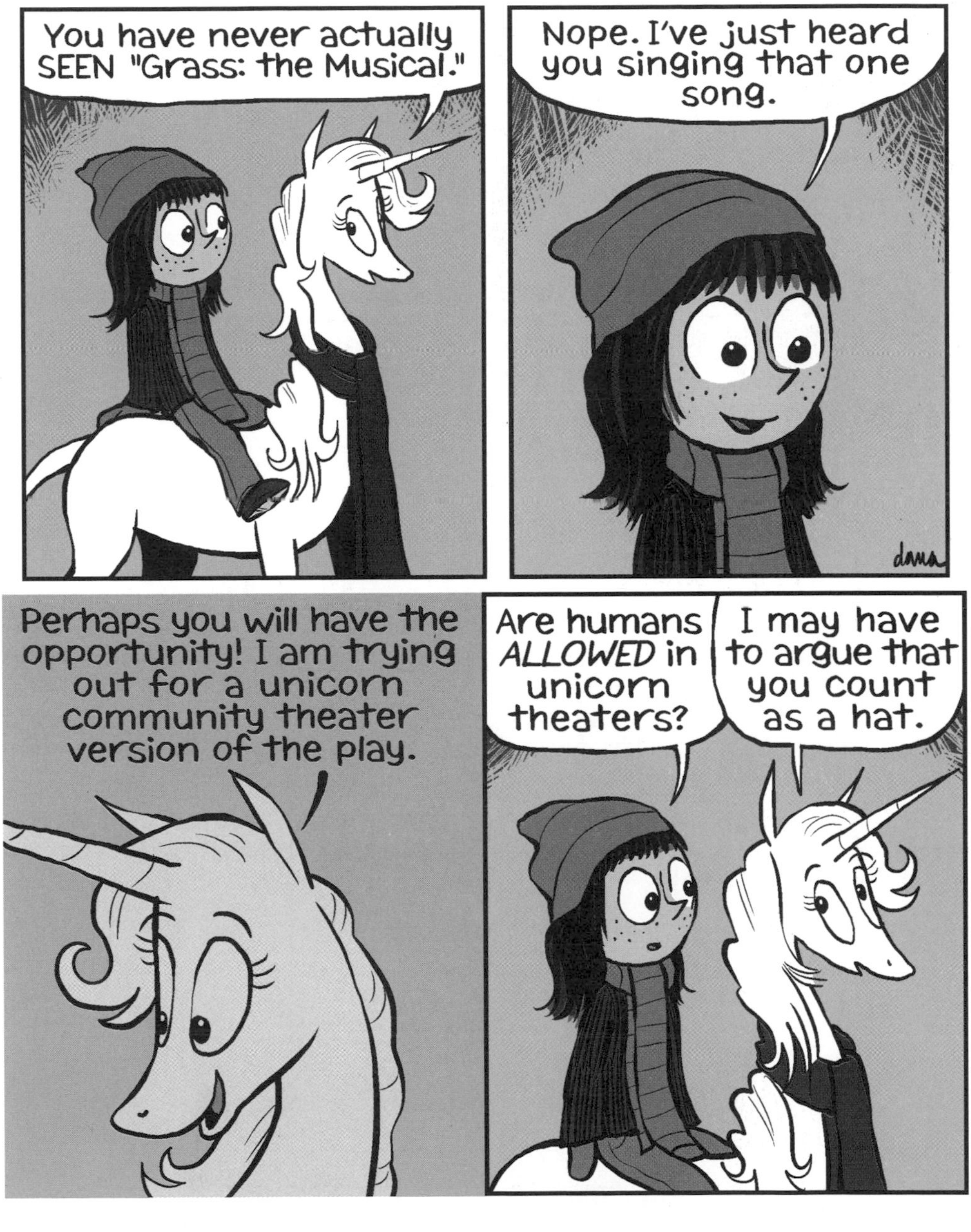
You have never actually SEEN "Grass: the Musical."
Nope. I've just heard you singing that one song.
dana
Perhaps you will have the opportunity! I am trying out for a unicorn community theater version of the play.
Are humans ALLOWED in unicorn theaters?
I may have to argue that you count as a hat.

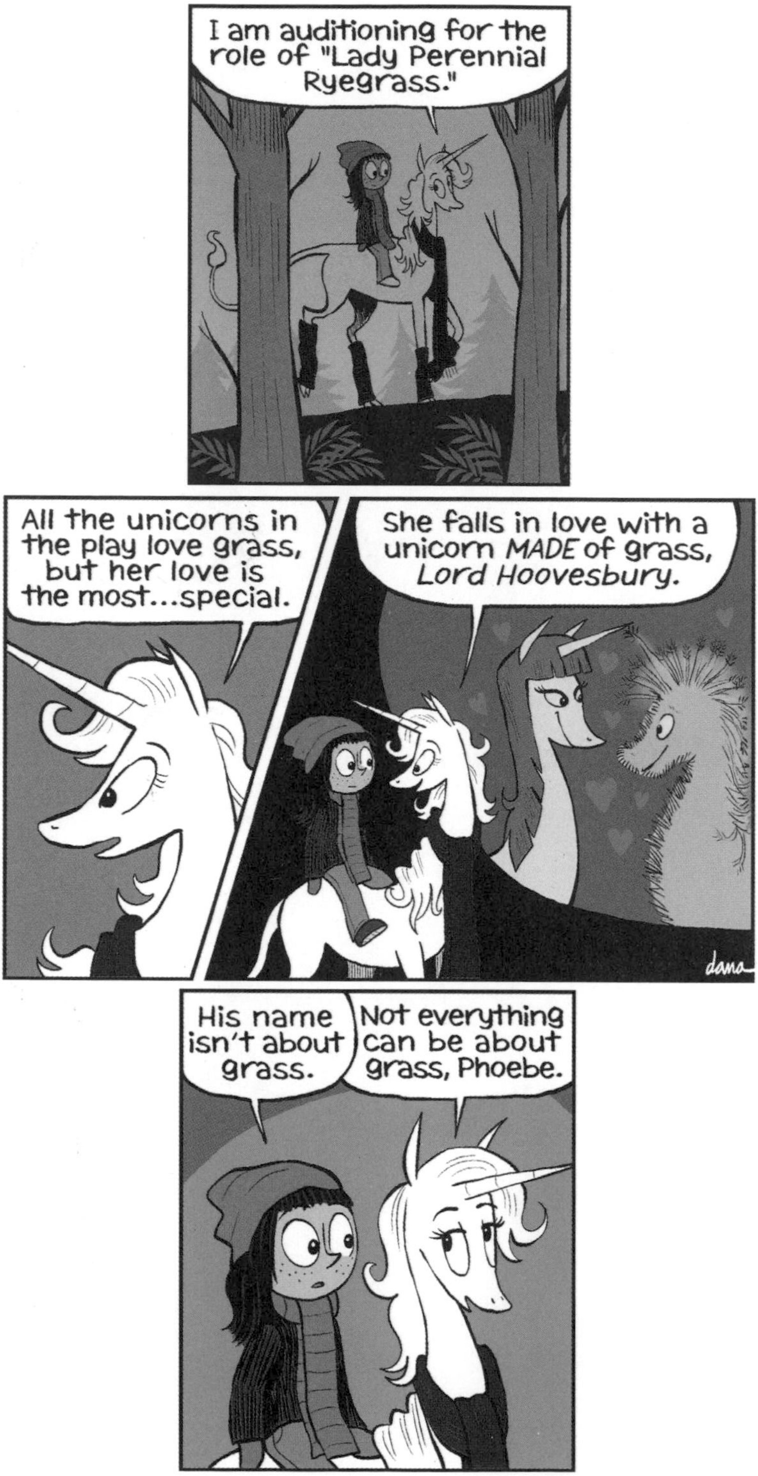
I am auditioning for the role of "Lady Perennial Ryegrass."
All the unicorns in the play love grass, but her love is the most...special.
She falls in love with a unicorn *MADE* of grass, *Lord Hoovesbury.*
dana
His name isn't about grass.
Not everything can be about grass, Phoebe.

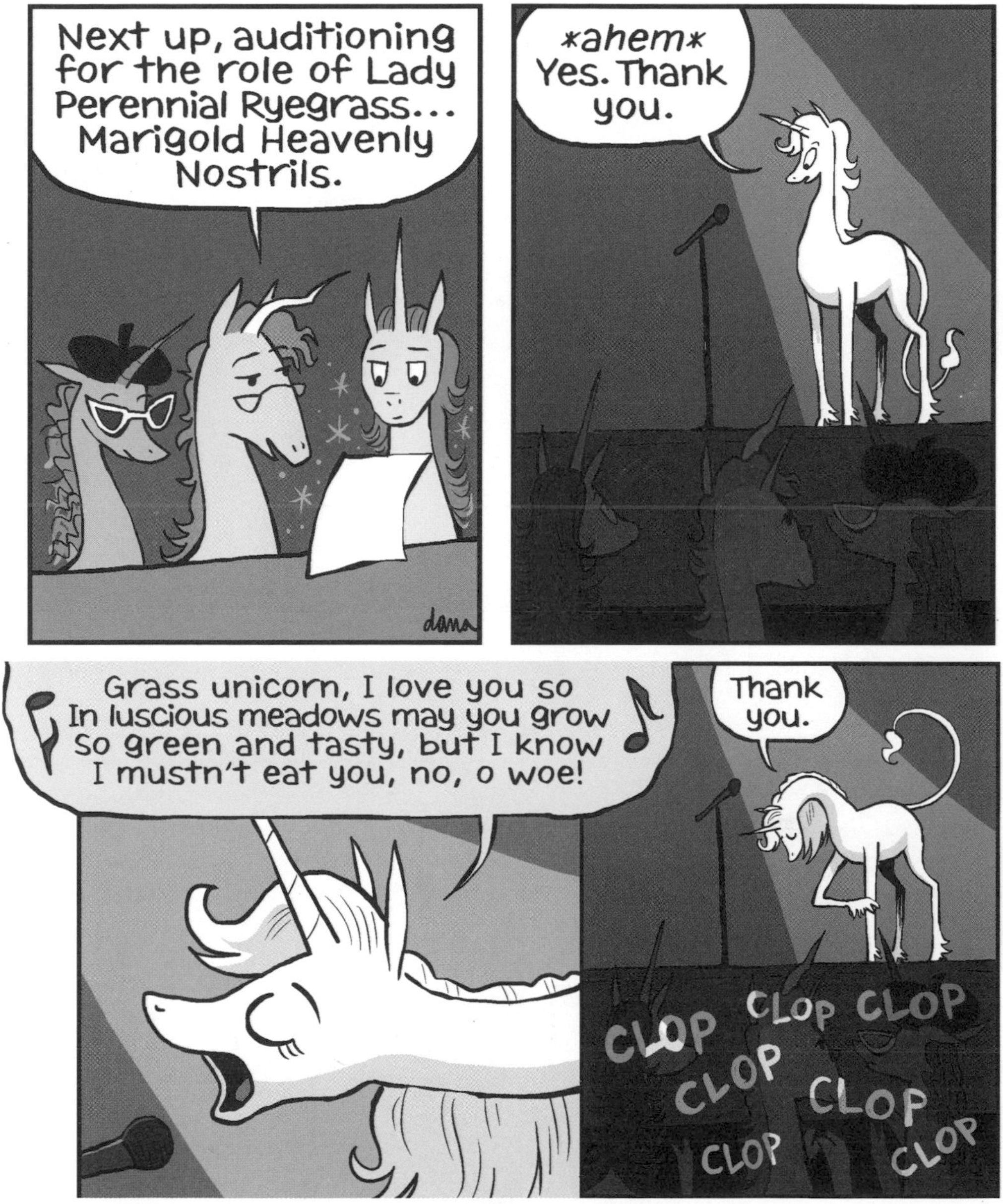
Next up, auditioning for the role of Lady Perennial Ryegrass... Marigold Heavenly Nostrils.
ahem Yes. Thank you.
Grass unicorn, I love you so
In luscious meadows may you grow
So green and tasty, but I know
I mustn't eat you, no, o woe!
Thank you.
CLOP CLOP CLOP CLOP CLOP CLOP CLOP

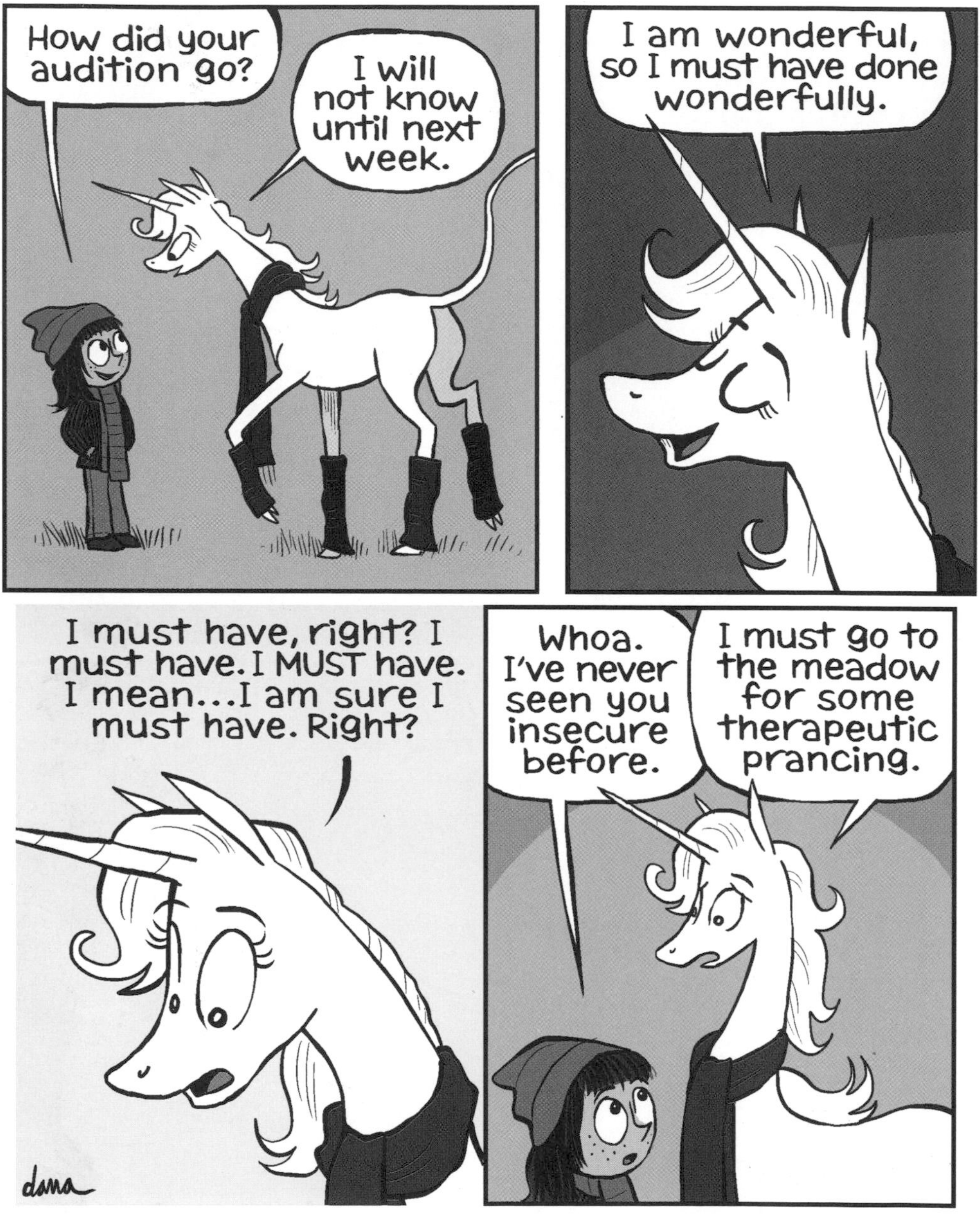
How did your audition go?
I will not know until next week.
I am wonderful, so I must have done wonderfully.
I must have, right? I must have. I MUST have. I mean...I am sure I must have. Right?
dana
Whoa. I've never seen you insecure before.
I must go to the meadow for some therapeutic prancing.

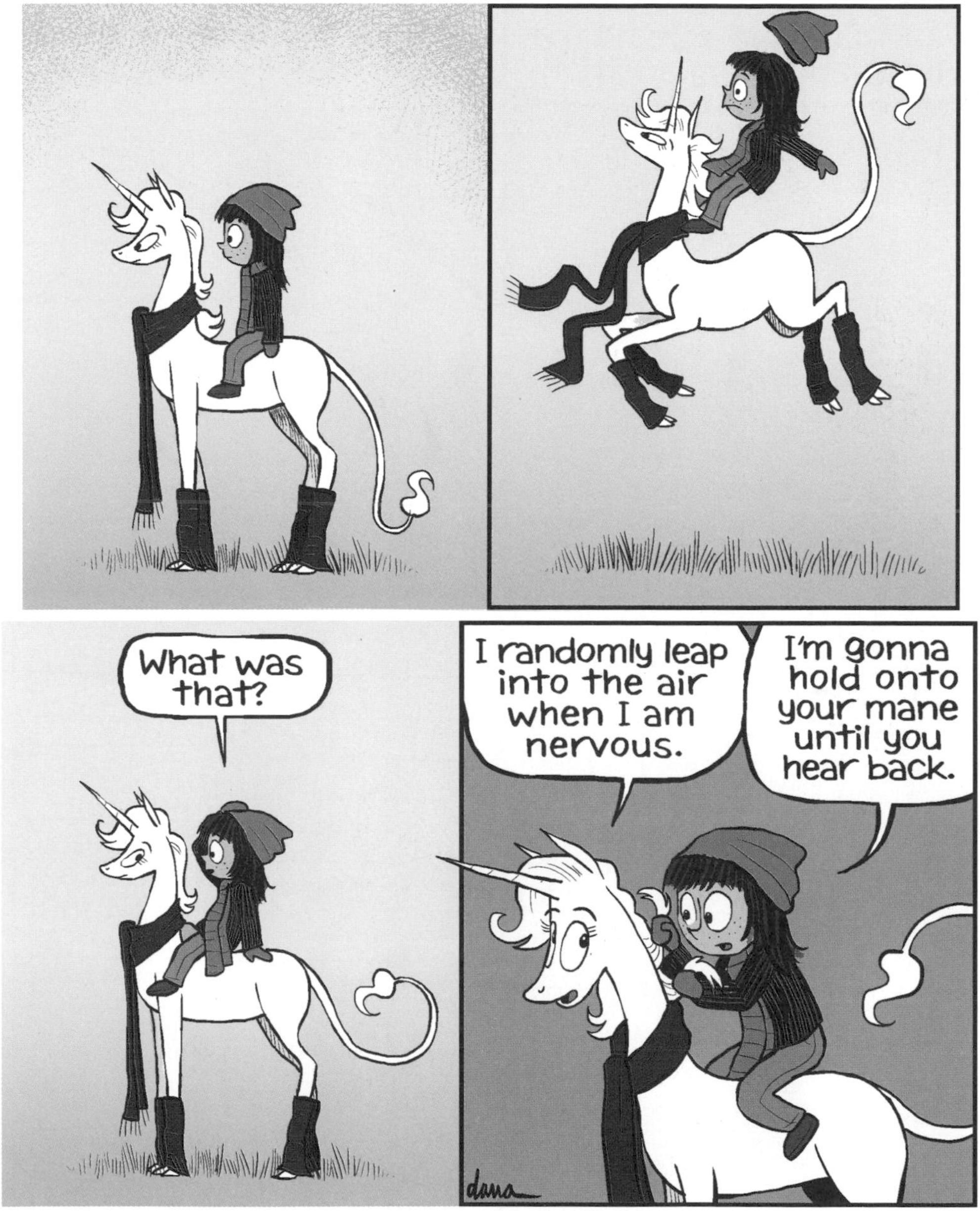
What was that?
I randomly leap into the air when I am nervous.
I'm gonna hold onto your mane until you hear back.
dana

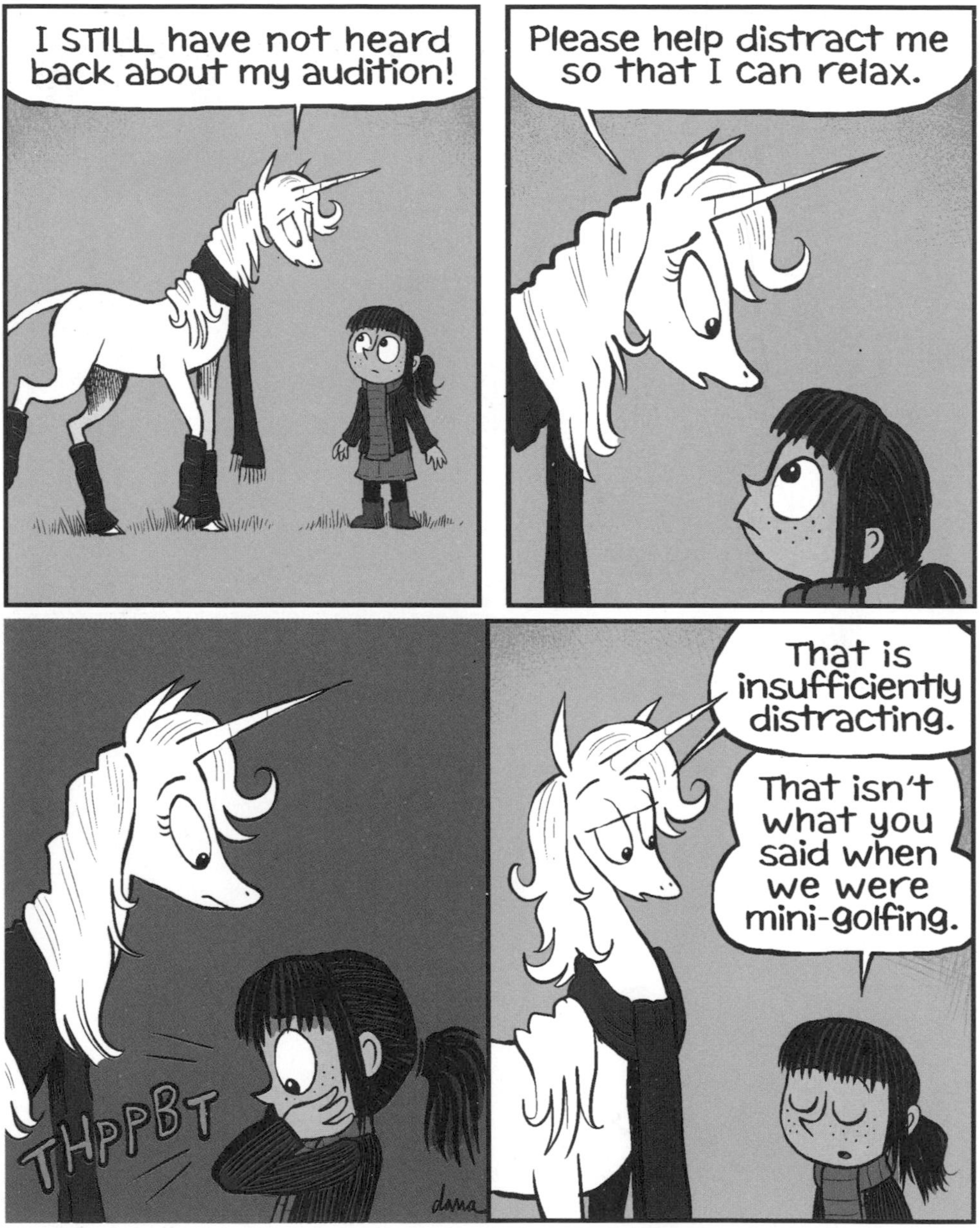
I STILL have not heard back about my audition!
Please help distract me so that I can relax.
THPPBT
That is insufficiently distracting.
That isn't what you said when we were mini-golfing.
dana

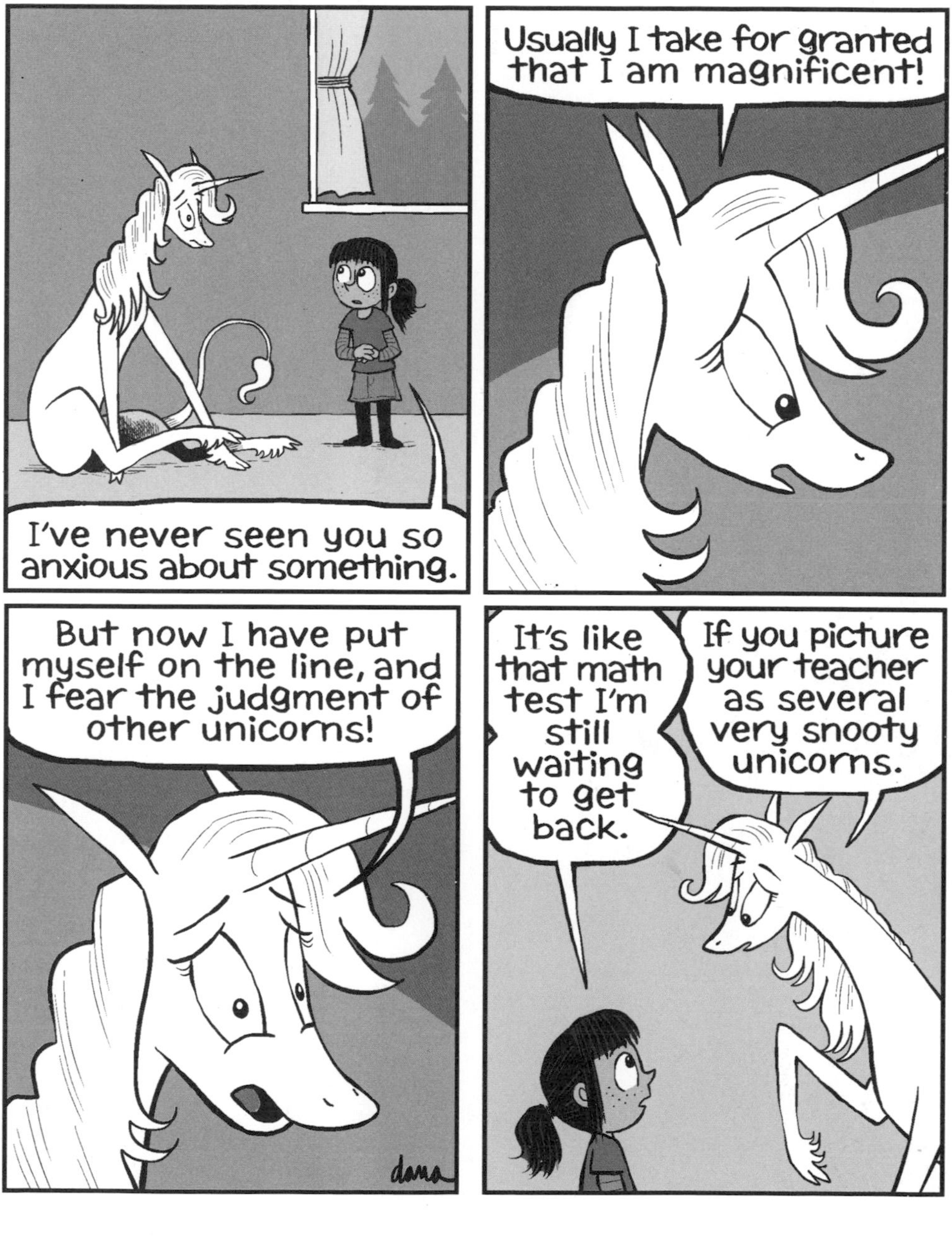
I've never seen you so anxious about something.
Usually I take for granted that I am magnificent!
But now I have put myself on the line, and I fear the judgment of other unicorns!
dana
It's like that math test I'm still waiting to get back.
If you picture your teacher as several very snooty unicorns.

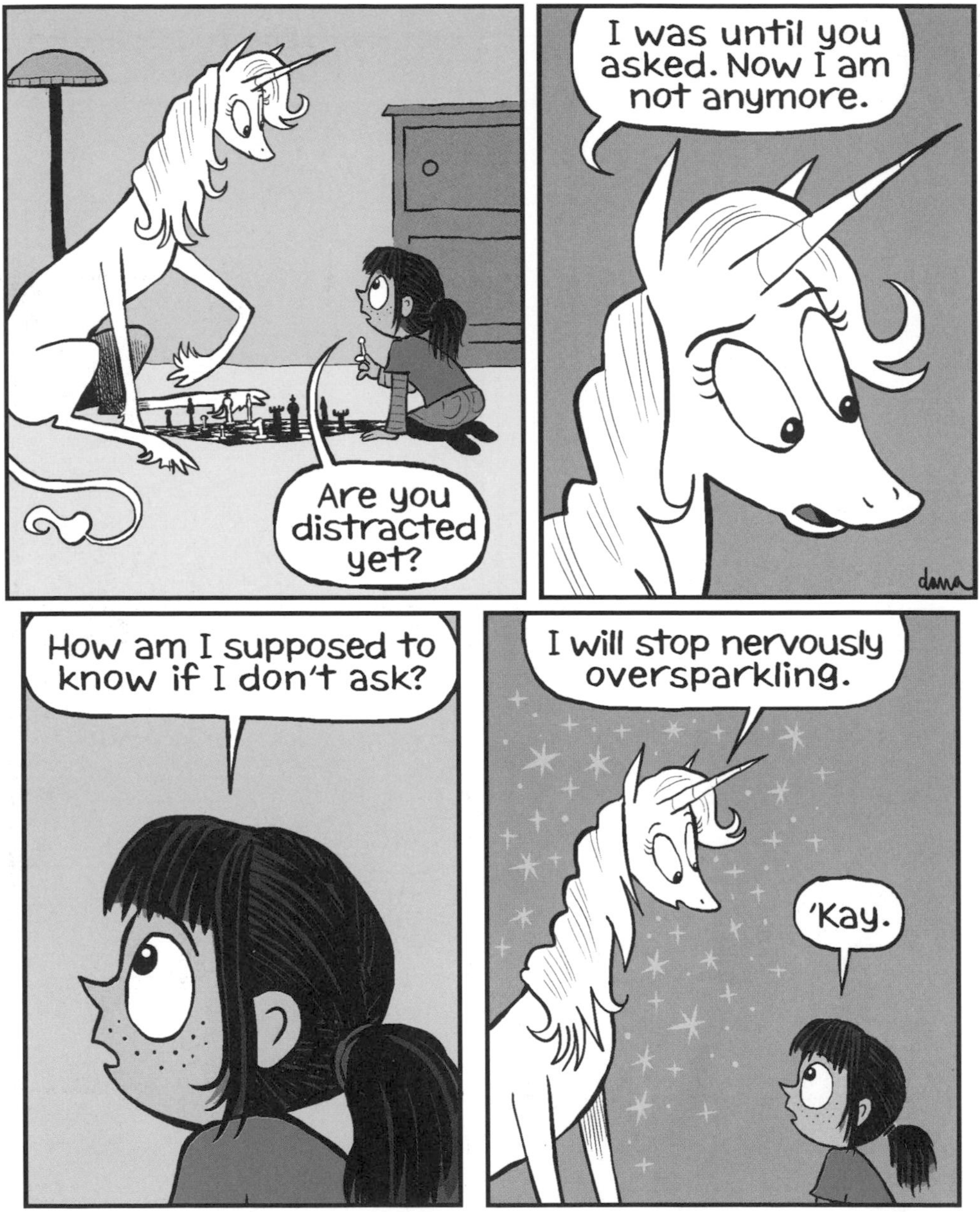
Are you distracted yet?
I was until you asked. Now I am not anymore.
dana
How am I supposed to know if I don't ask?
I will stop nervously oversparkling.
'Kay.

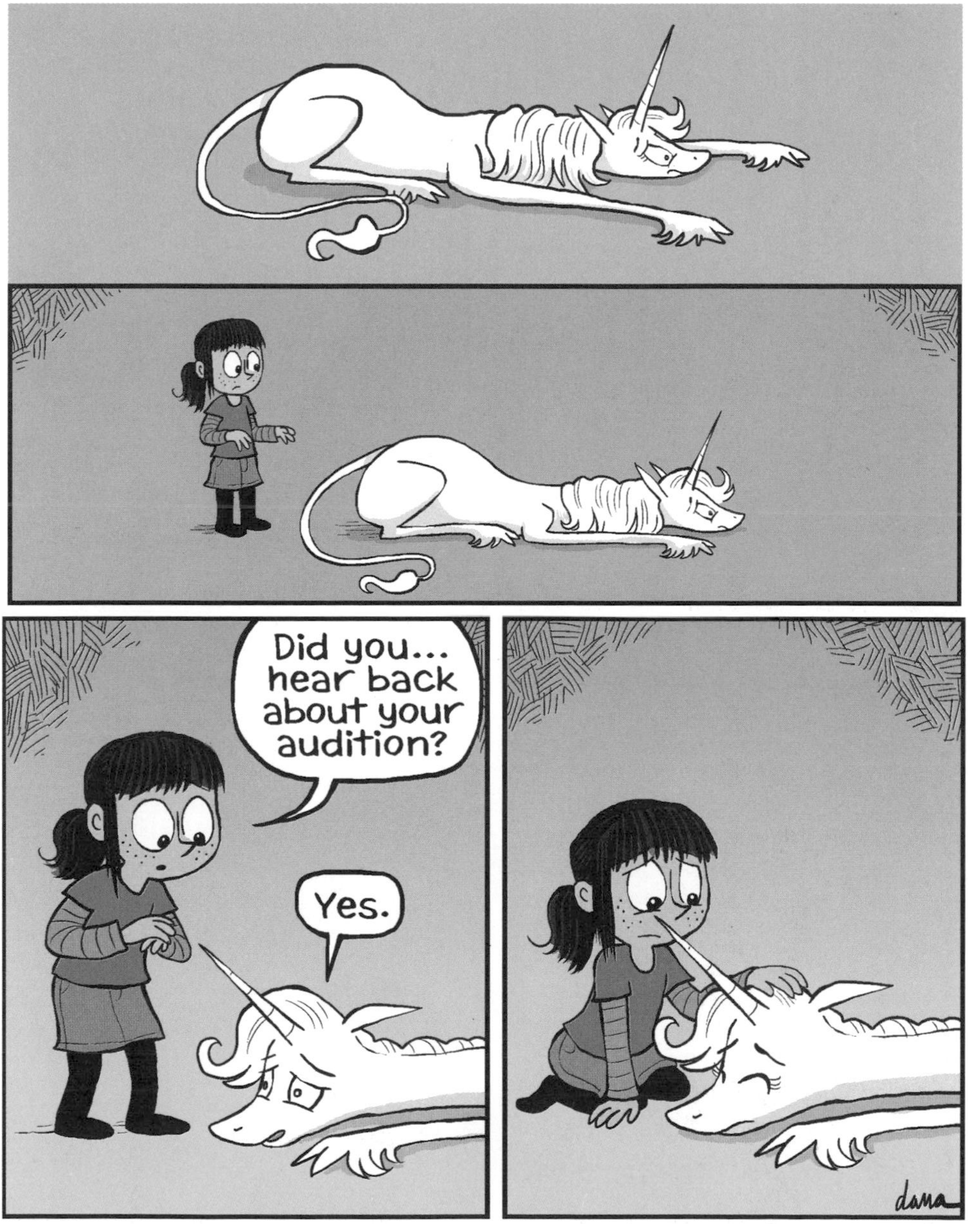
Did you... hear back about your audition?
Yes.
dana

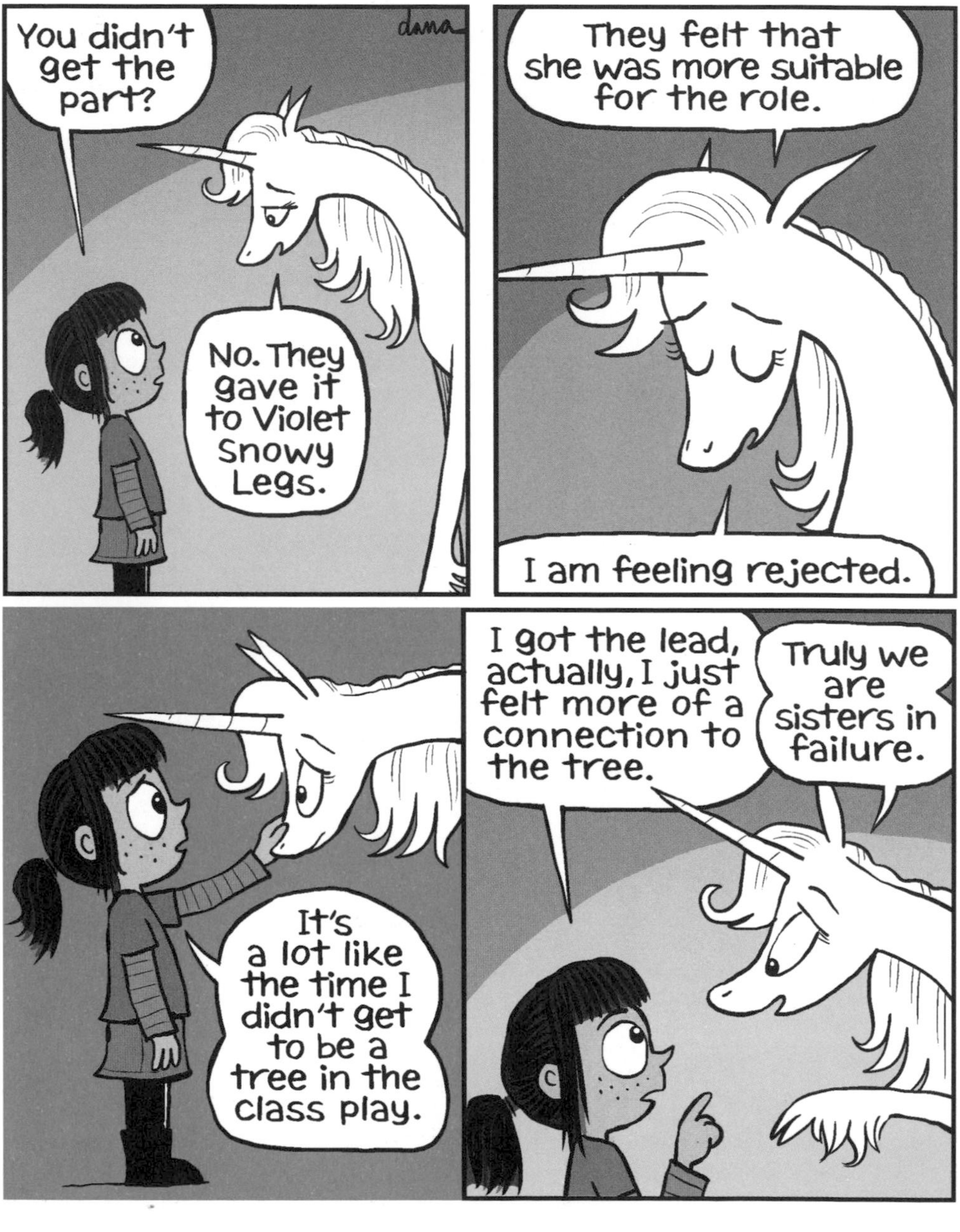

dana
You didn't get the part?
No. They gave it to Violet Snowy Legs.
They felt that she was more suitable for the role.
I am feeling rejected.
It's a lot like the time I didn't get to be a tree in the class play.
I got the lead, actually, I just felt more of a connection to the tree.
Truly we are sisters in failure.

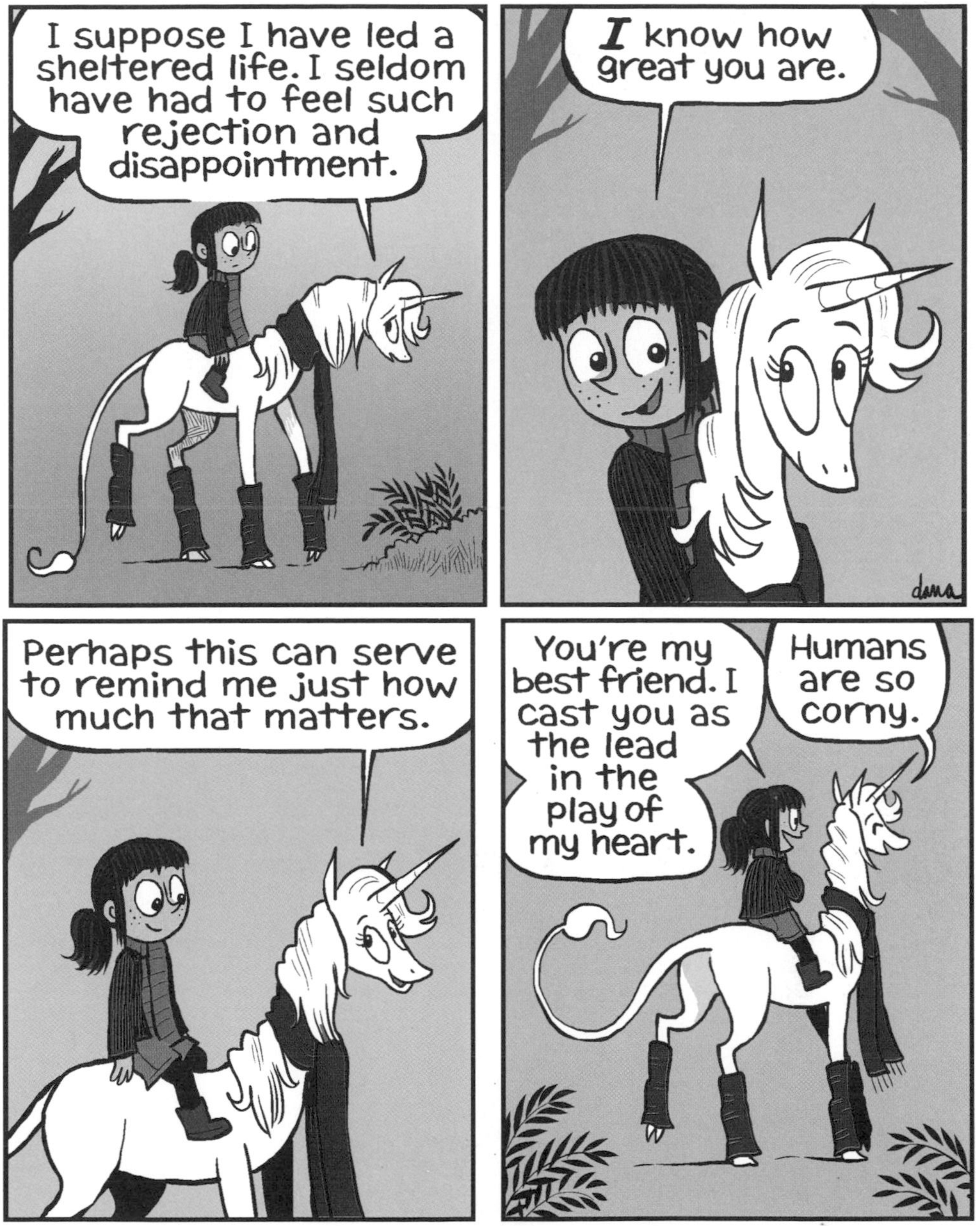
I suppose I have led a sheltered life. I seldom have had to feel such rejection and disappointment.
I know how great you are.
Perhaps this can serve to remind me just how much that matters.
You're my best friend. I cast you as the lead in the play of my heart.
Humans are so corny.

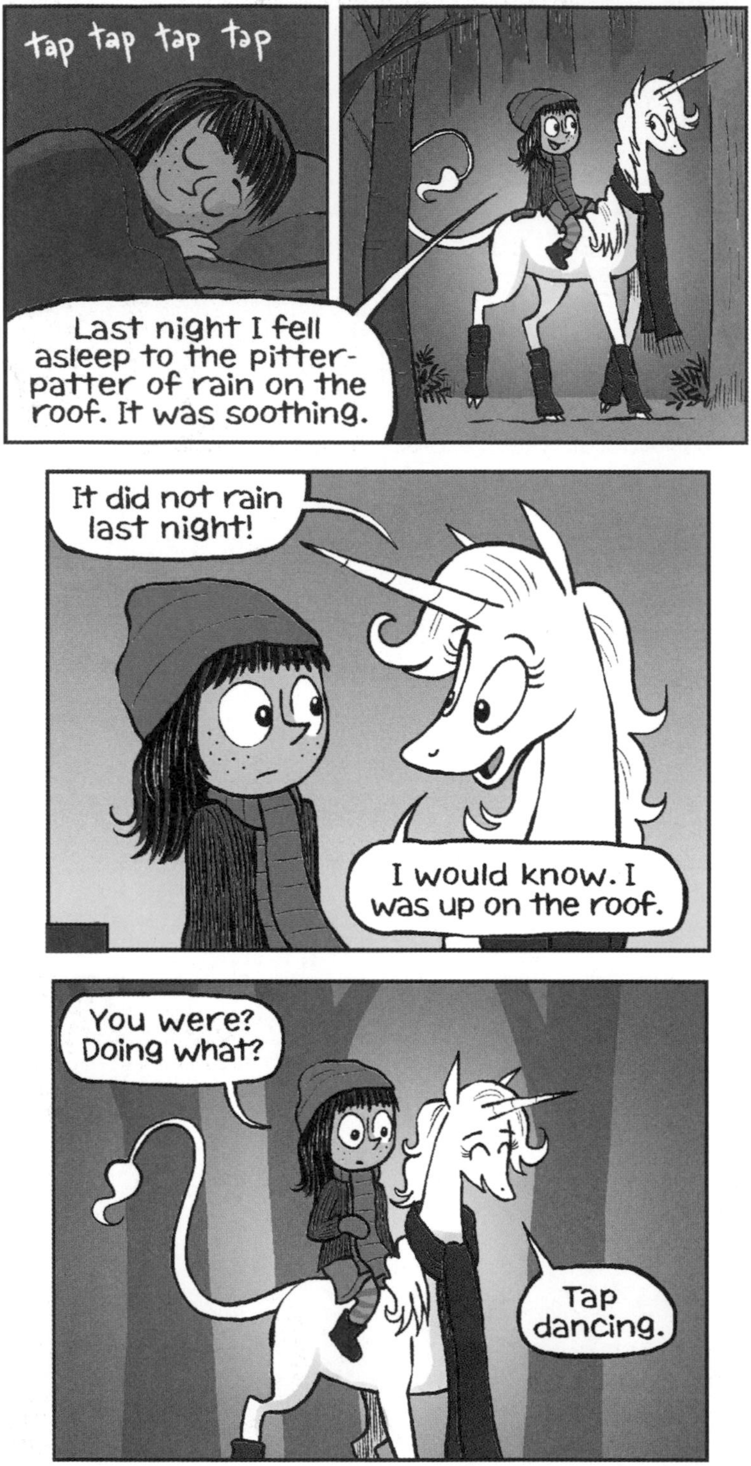
tap tap tap tap
Last night I fell asleep to the pitter-patter of rain on the roof. It was soothing.
It did not rain last night!
I would know. I was up on the roof.
You were? Doing what?
Tap dancing.

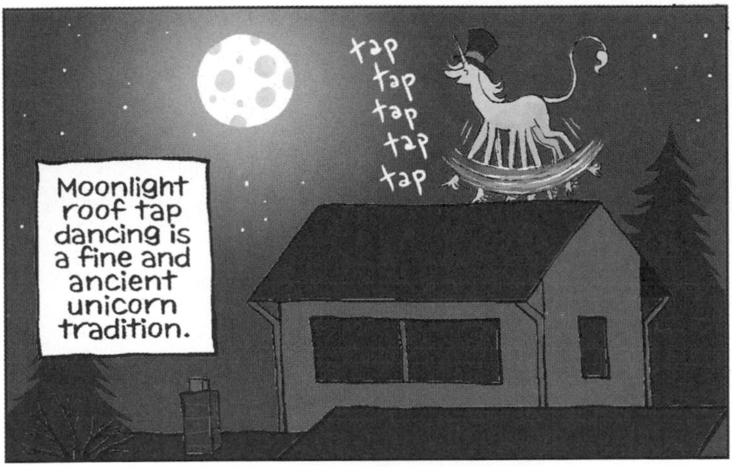
tap
tap
tap
tap
tap
Moonlight roof tap dancing is a fine and ancient unicorn tradition.

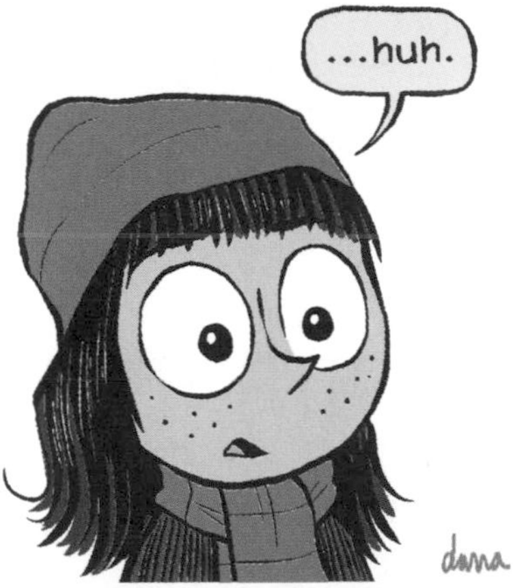
...huh.

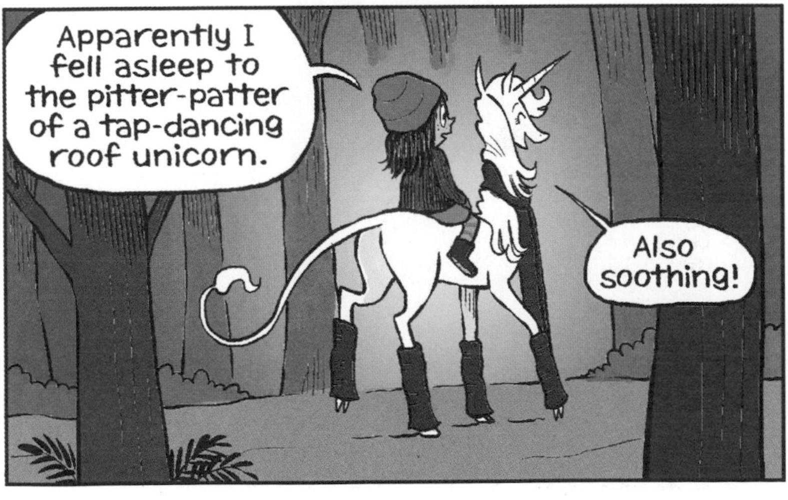
Apparently I fell asleep to the pitter-patter of a tap-dancing roof unicorn.
Also soothing!

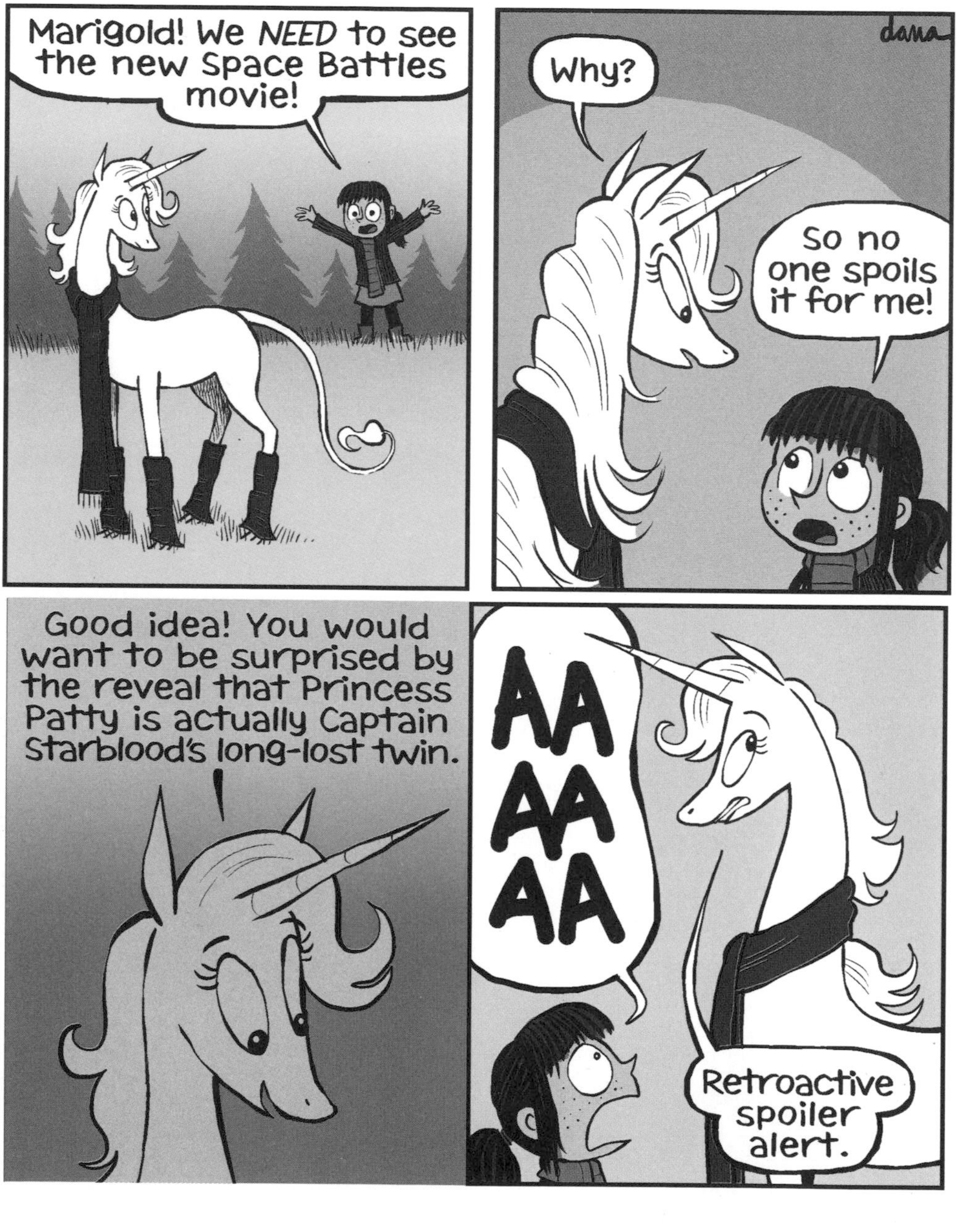

Marigold! We NEED to see the new Space Battles movie!
dana
Why?
So no one spoils it for me!
Good idea! You would want to be surprised by the reveal that Princess Patty is actually Captain Starblood's long-lost twin.
AAAAAA
Retroactive spoiler alert.

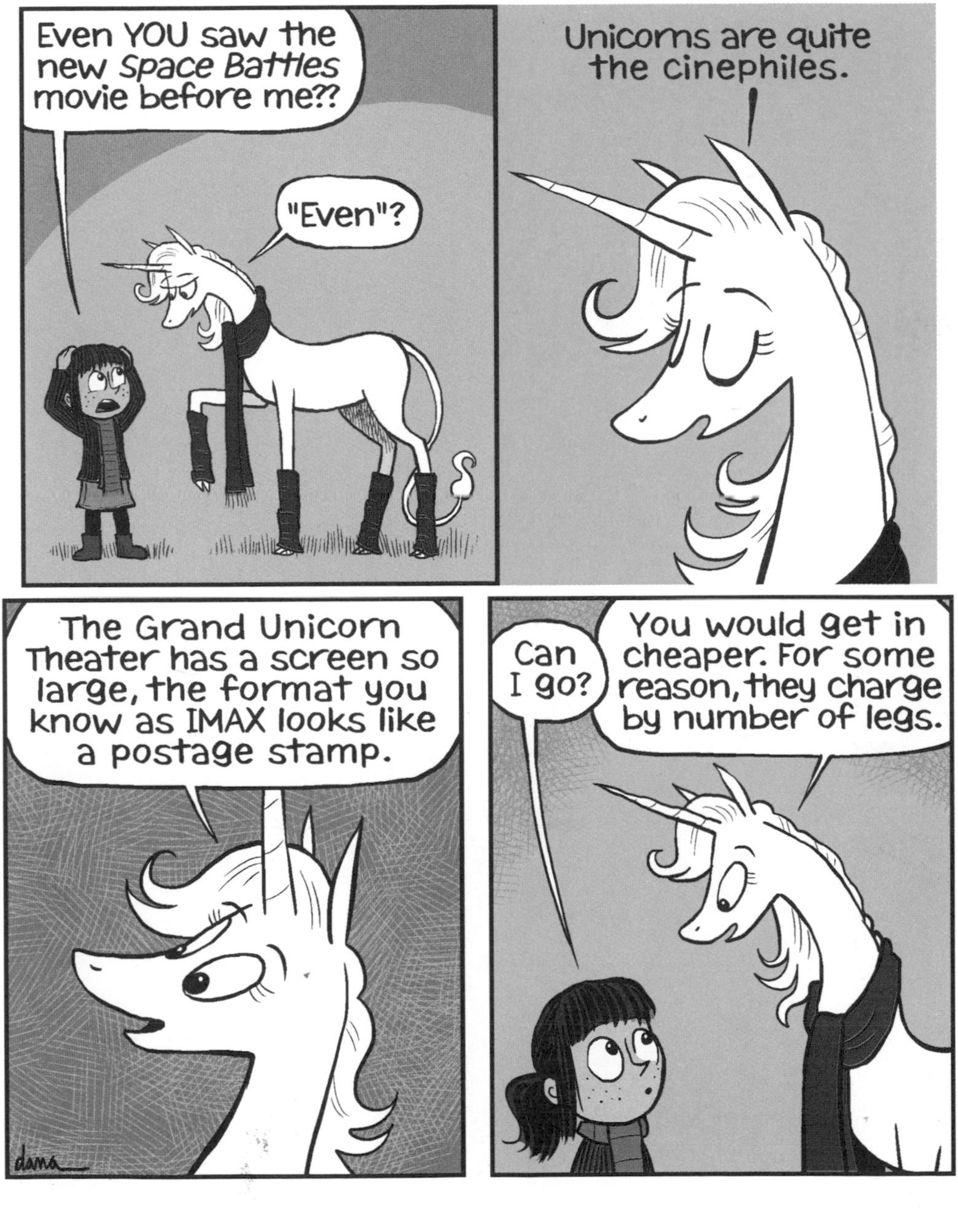
Even YOU saw the new *Space Battles* movie before me??
"Even"?
Unicorns are quite the cinephiles.
The Grand Unicorn Theater has a screen so large, the format you know as IMAX looks like a postage stamp.
Can I go?
You would get in cheaper. For some reason, they charge by number of legs.
dana

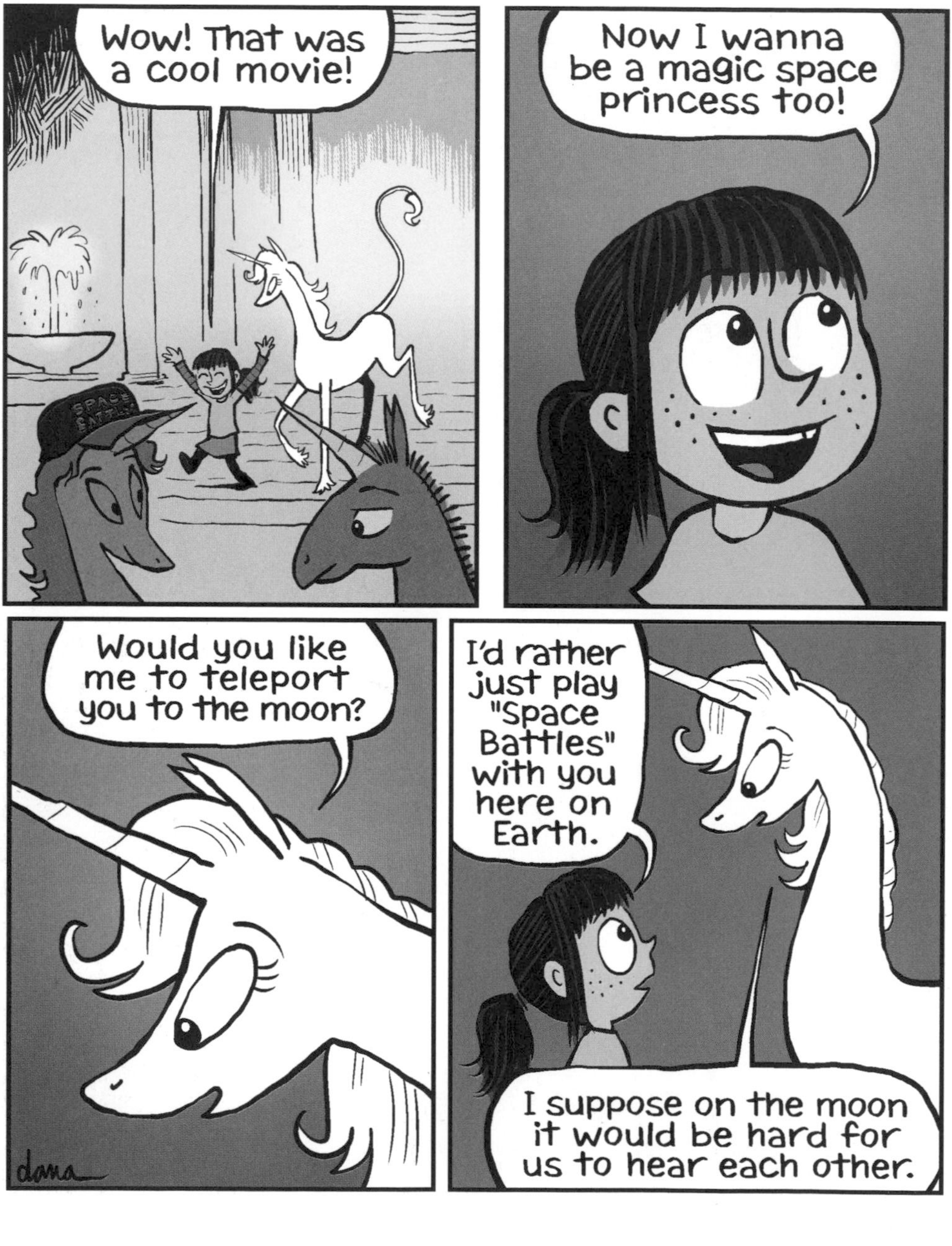
Wow! That was a cool movie!
SPACE BATTLES
Now I wanna be a magic space princess too!
Would you like me to teleport you to the moon?
dana
I'd rather just play "Space Battles" with you here on Earth.
I suppose on the moon it would be hard for us to hear each other.

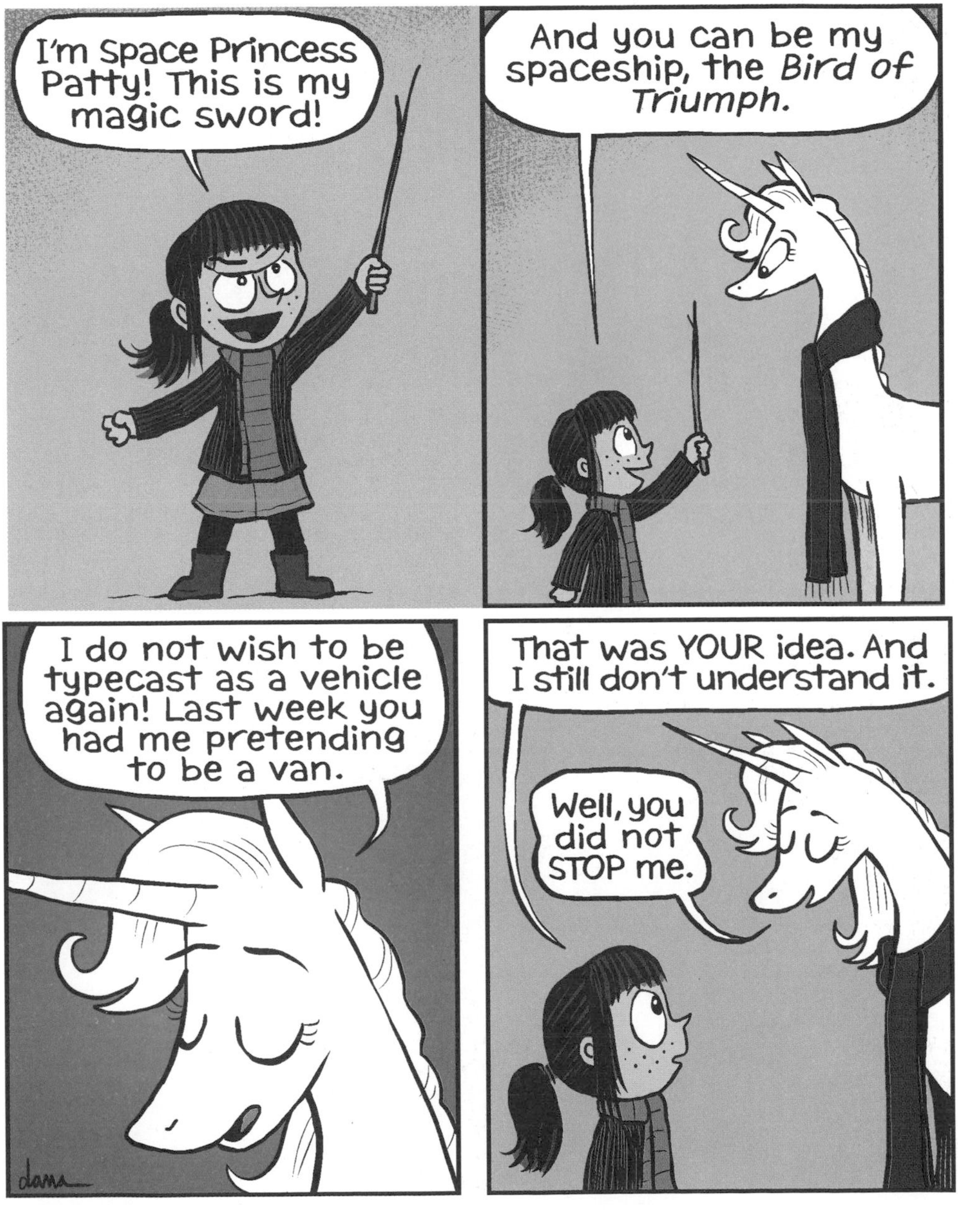
I'm Space Princess Patty! This is my magic sword!
And you can be my spaceship, the *Bird of Triumph.*
I do not wish to be typecast as a vehicle again! Last week you had me pretending to be a van.
That was YOUR idea. And I still don't understand it.
Well, you did not STOP me.
dana

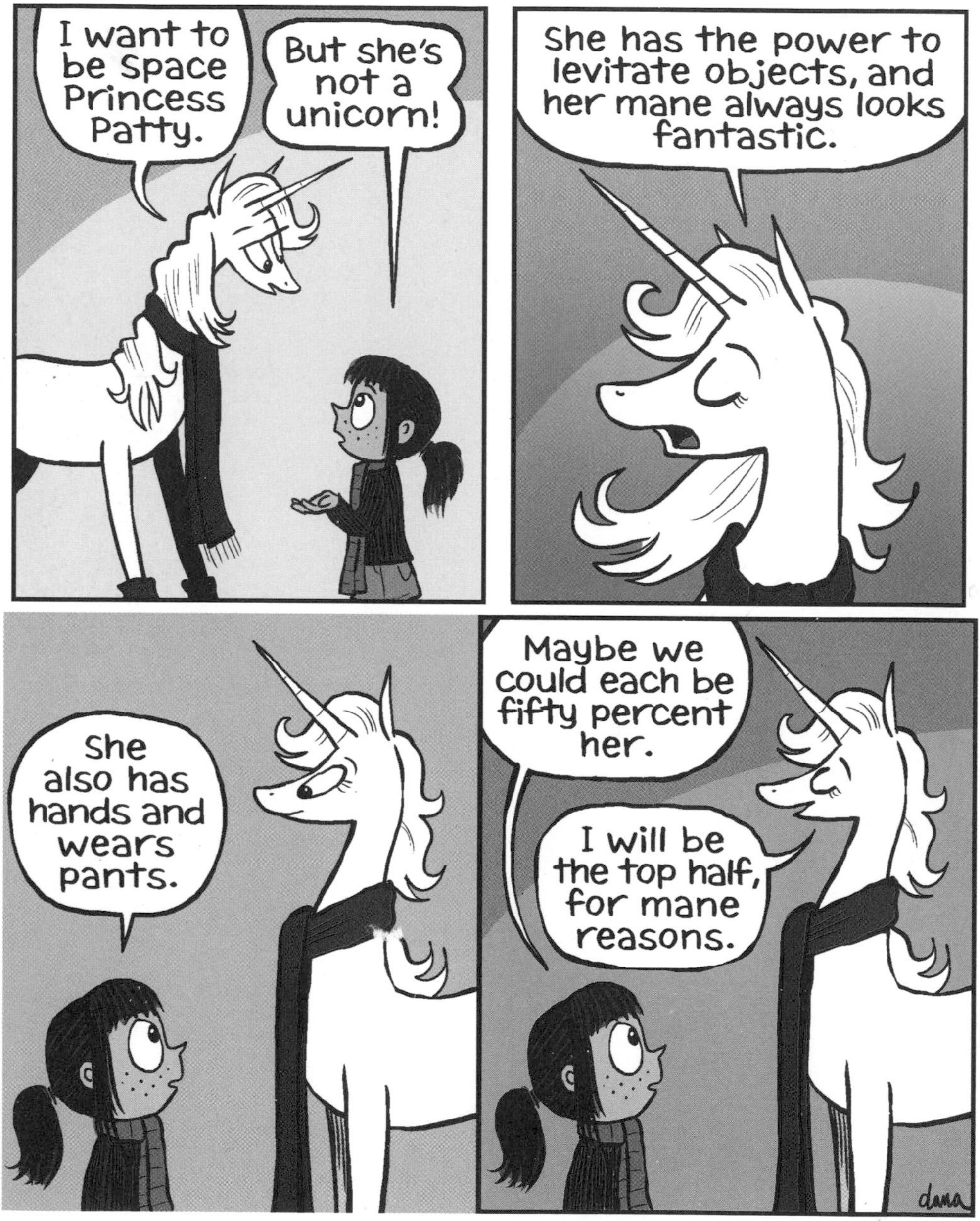
I want to be Space Princess Patty.
But she's not a unicorn!
She has the power to levitate objects, and her mane always looks fantastic.
She also has hands and wears pants.
Maybe we could each be fifty percent her.
I will be the top half, for mane reasons.
dana

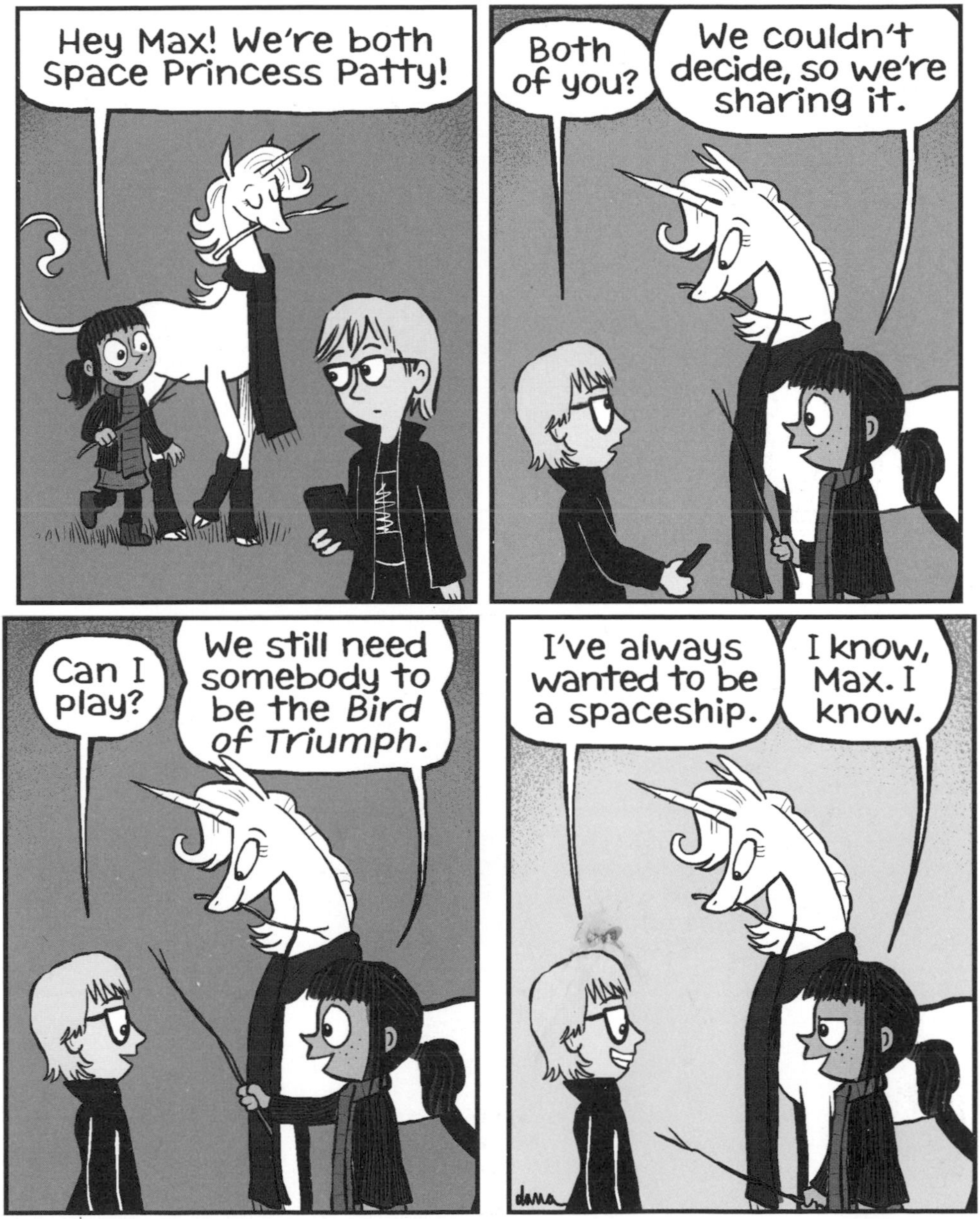
Hey Max! We're both Space Princess Patty!
Both of you?
We couldn't decide, so we're sharing it.
Can I play?
We still need somebody to be the *Bird of Triumph*.
I've always wanted to be a spaceship.
I know, Max. I know.
dana

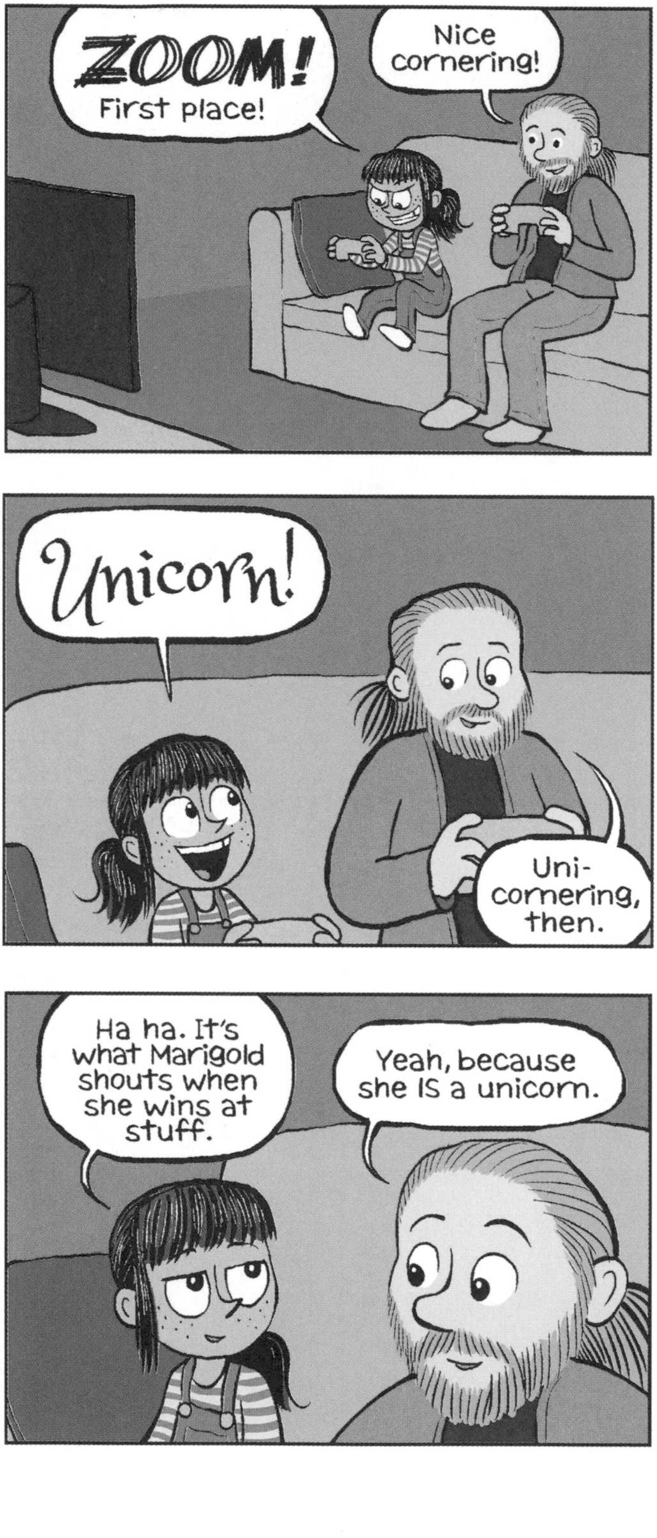
ZOOM!
First place!
Nice cornering!
Unicorn!
Uni-cornering, then.
Ha ha. It's what Marigold shouts when she wins at stuff.
Yeah, because she IS a unicorn.

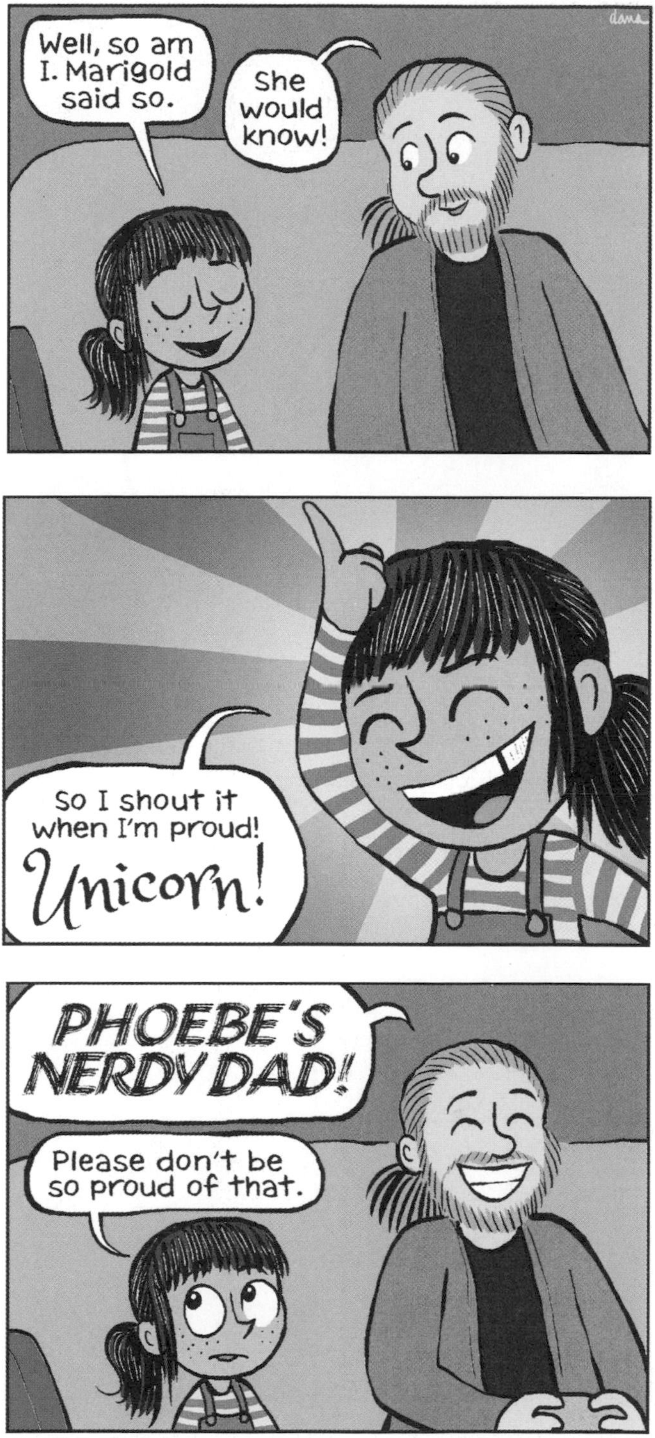
dana
Well, so am I. Marigold said so.
She would know!
So I shout it when I'm proud! Unicorn!
PHOEBE'S NERDY DAD!
Please don't be so proud of that.

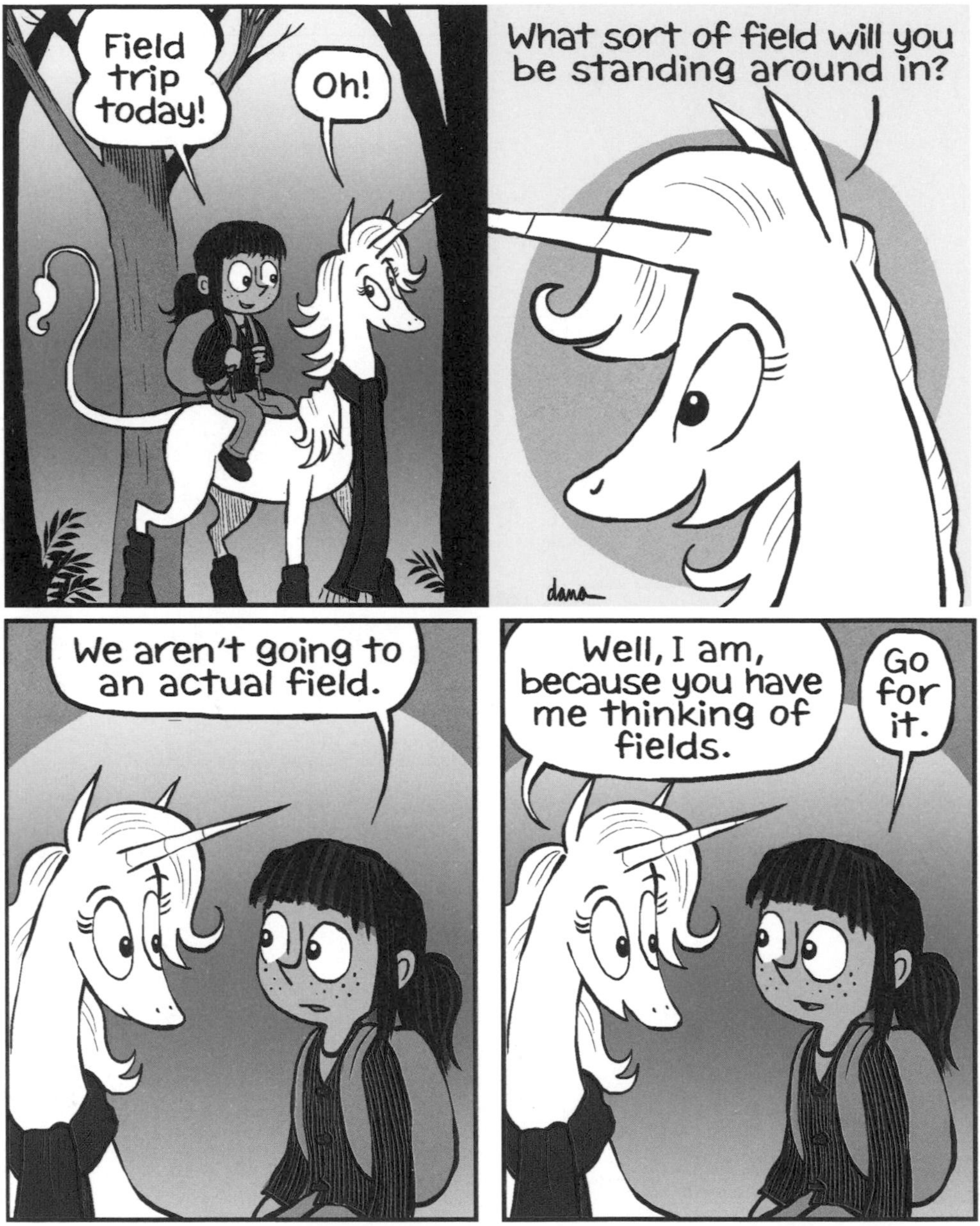
Field trip today!
Oh!
What sort of field will you be standing around in?
dana
We aren't going to an actual field.
Well, I am, because you have me thinking of fields.
Go for it.

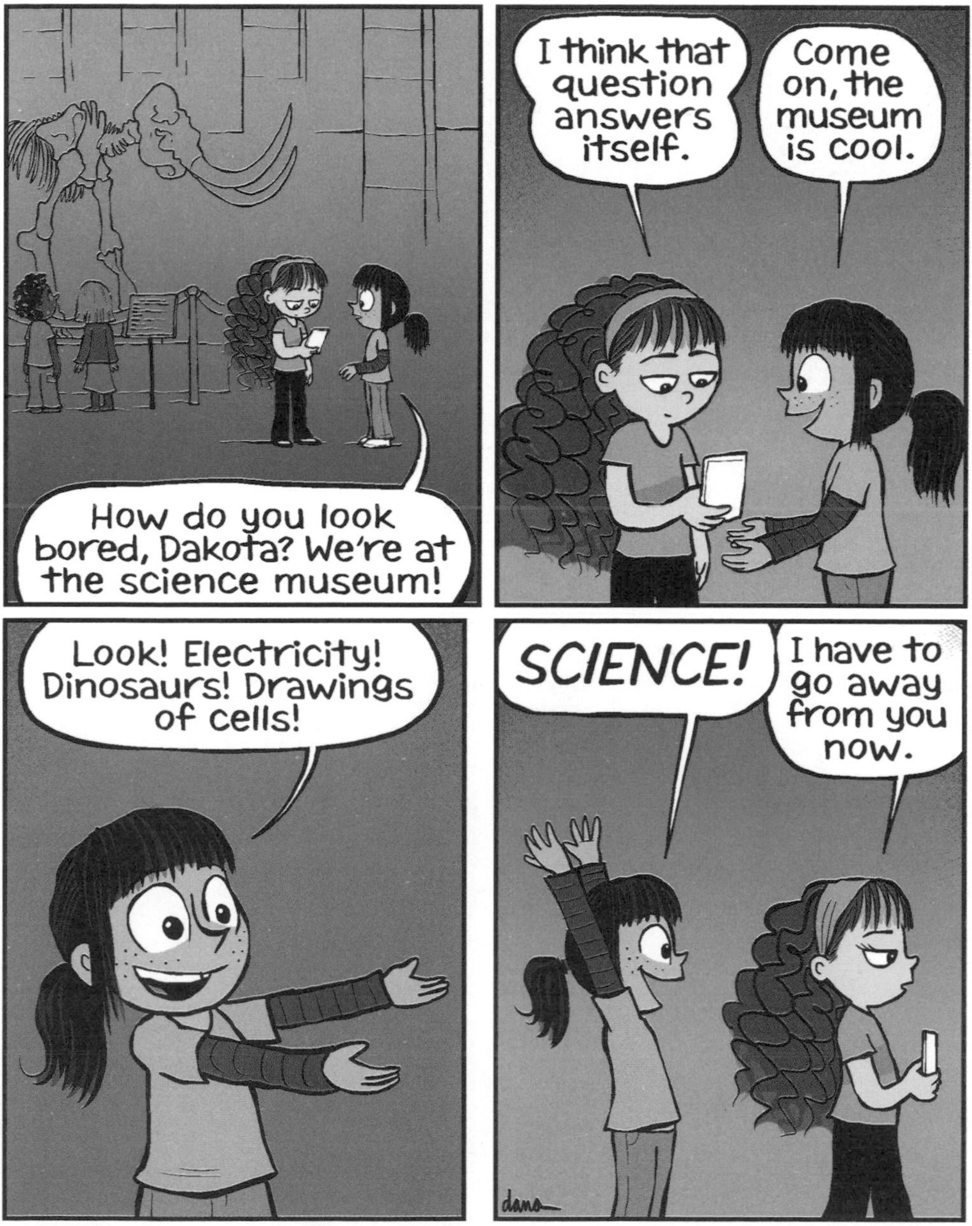
How do you look bored, Dakota? We're at the science museum!
I think that question answers itself.
Come on, the museum is cool.
Look! Electricity! Dinosaurs! Drawings of cells!
SCIENCE!
I have to go away from you now.
dana

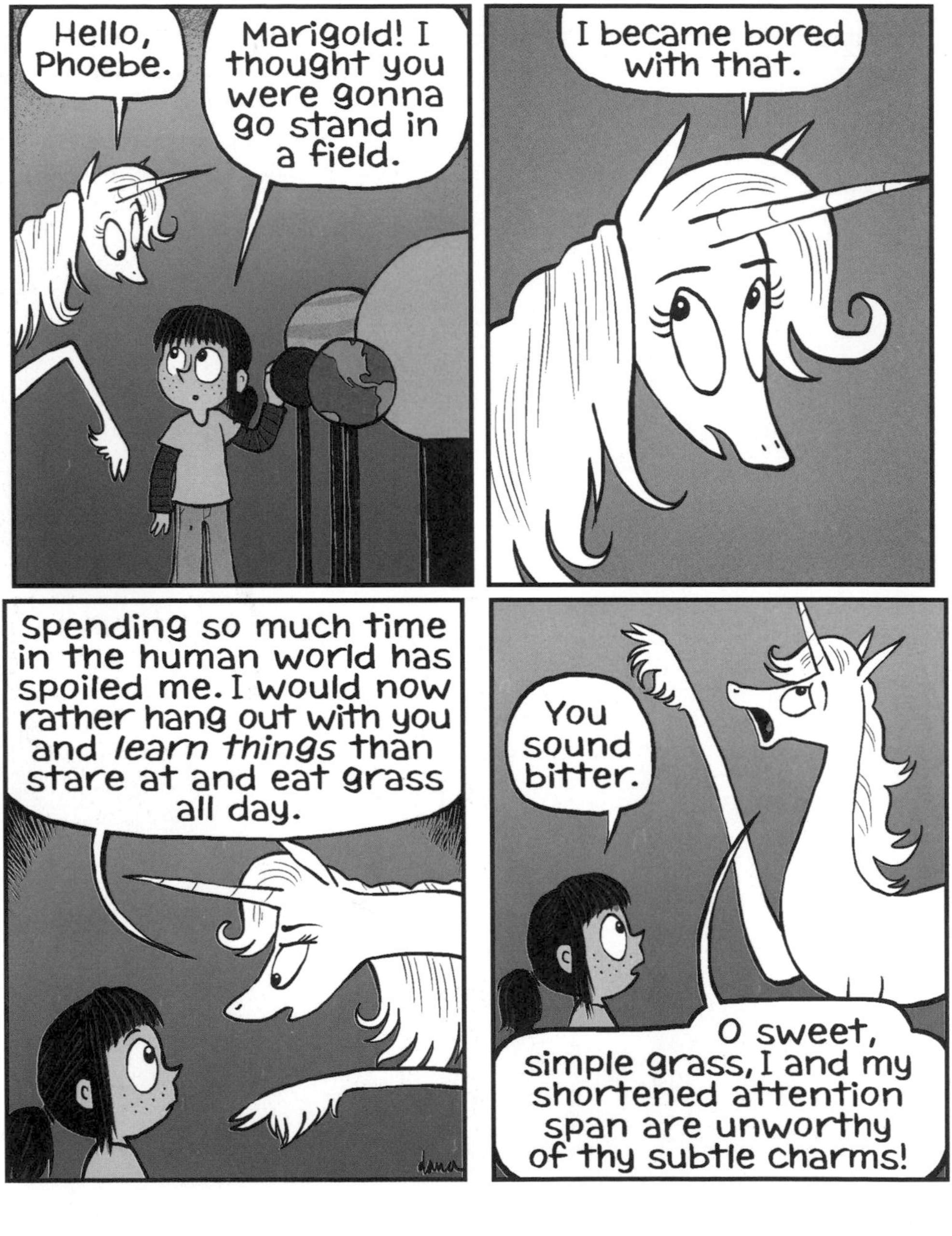
Hello, Phoebe.
Marigold! I thought you were gonna go stand in a field.
I became bored with that.
Spending so much time in the human world has spoiled me. I would now rather hang out with you and *learn things* than stare at and eat grass all day.
You sound bitter.
O sweet, simple grass, I and my shortened attention span are unworthy of thy subtle charms!
dana

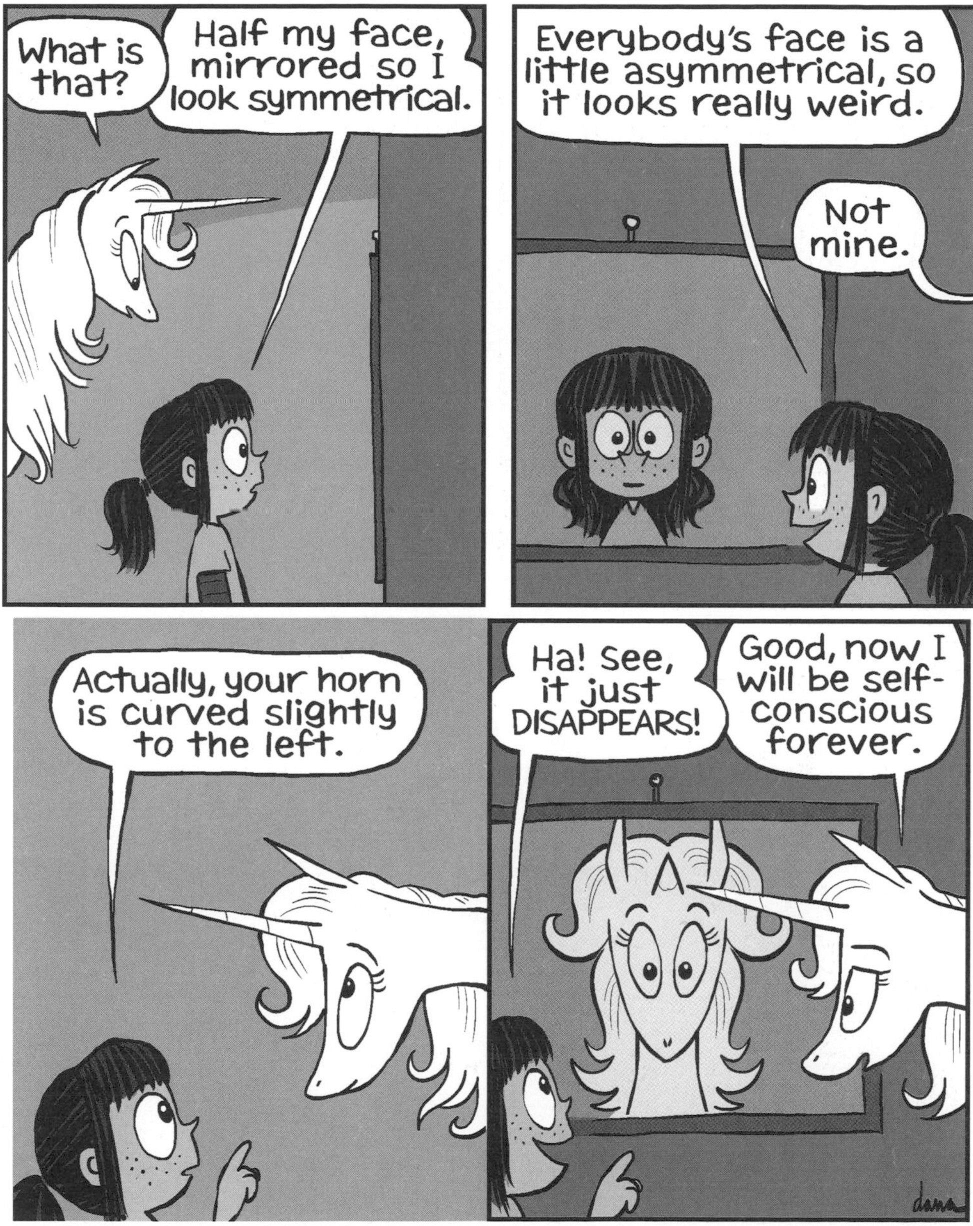
What is that?
Half my face, mirrored so I look symmetrical.
Everybody's face is a little asymmetrical, so it looks really weird.
Not mine.
Actually, your horn is curved slightly to the left.
Ha! See, it just DISAPPEARS!
Good, now I will be self-conscious forever.
dana

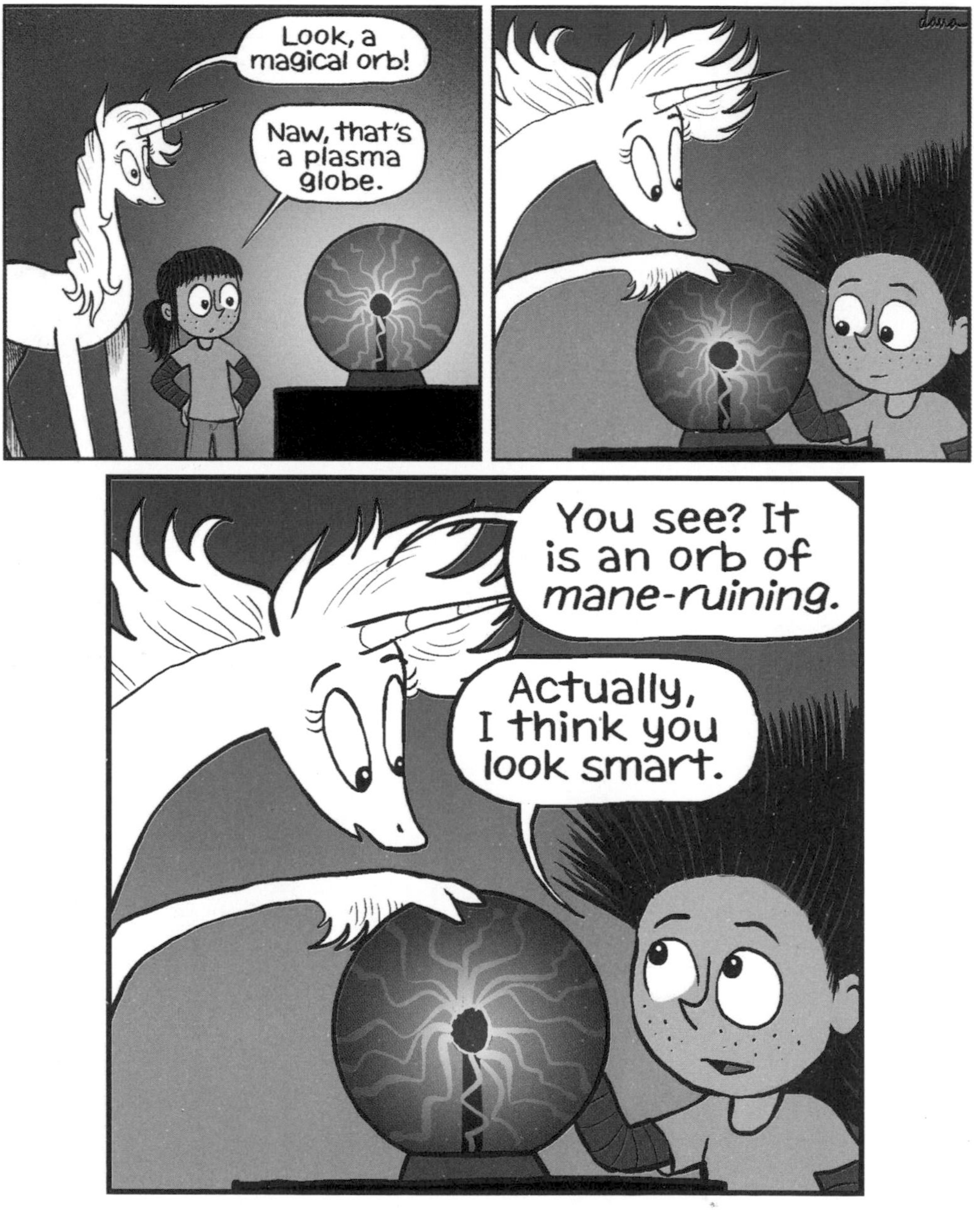
Look, a magical orb!
Naw, that's a plasma globe.
You see? It is an orb of *mane-ruining*.
Actually, I think you look smart.

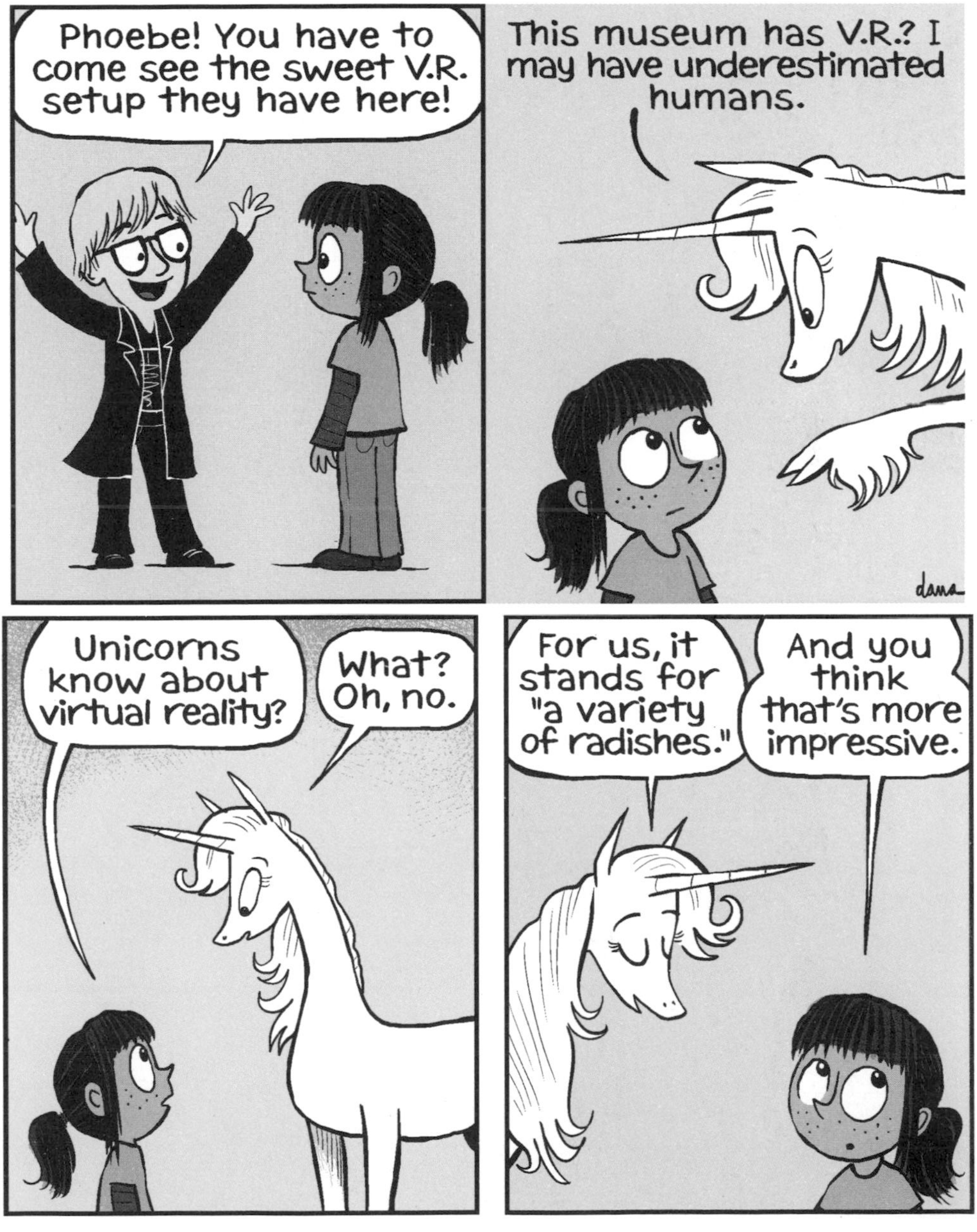
Phoebe! You have to come see the sweet V.R. setup they have here!
This museum has V.R.? I may have underestimated humans.
dana
Unicorns know about virtual reality?
What? Oh, no.
For us, it stands for "a variety of radishes."
And you think that's more impressive.

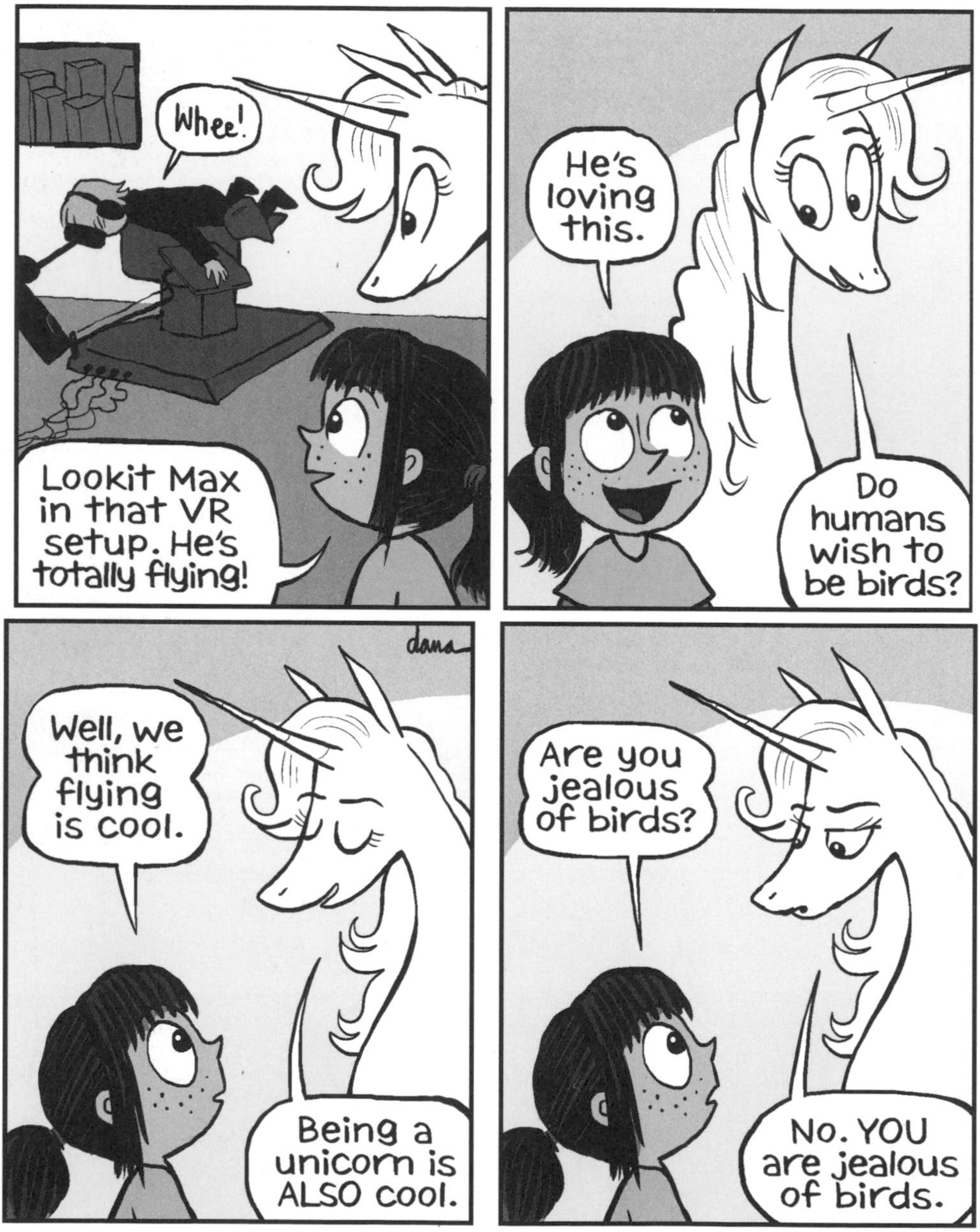
Whee!
Lookit Max in that VR setup. He's totally flying!
He's loving this.
Do humans wish to be birds?
dana
Well, we think flying is cool.
Being a unicorn is ALSO cool.
Are you jealous of birds?
No. YOU are jealous of birds.

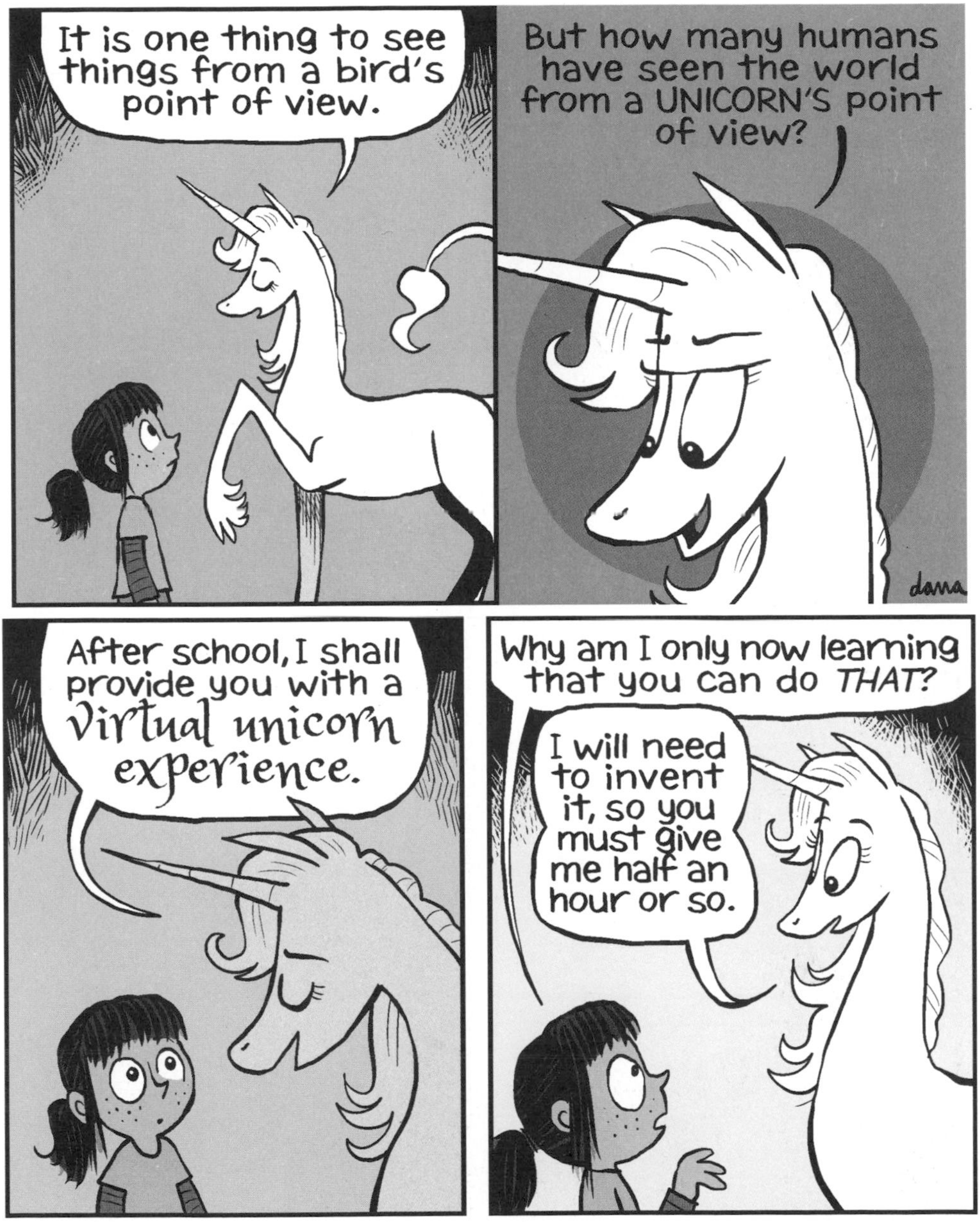
It is one thing to see things from a bird's point of view.
But how many humans have seen the world from a UNICORN'S point of view?
dana
After school, I shall provide you with a virtual unicorn experience.
Why am I only now learning that you can do *THAT*?
I will need to invent it, so you must give me half an hour or so.

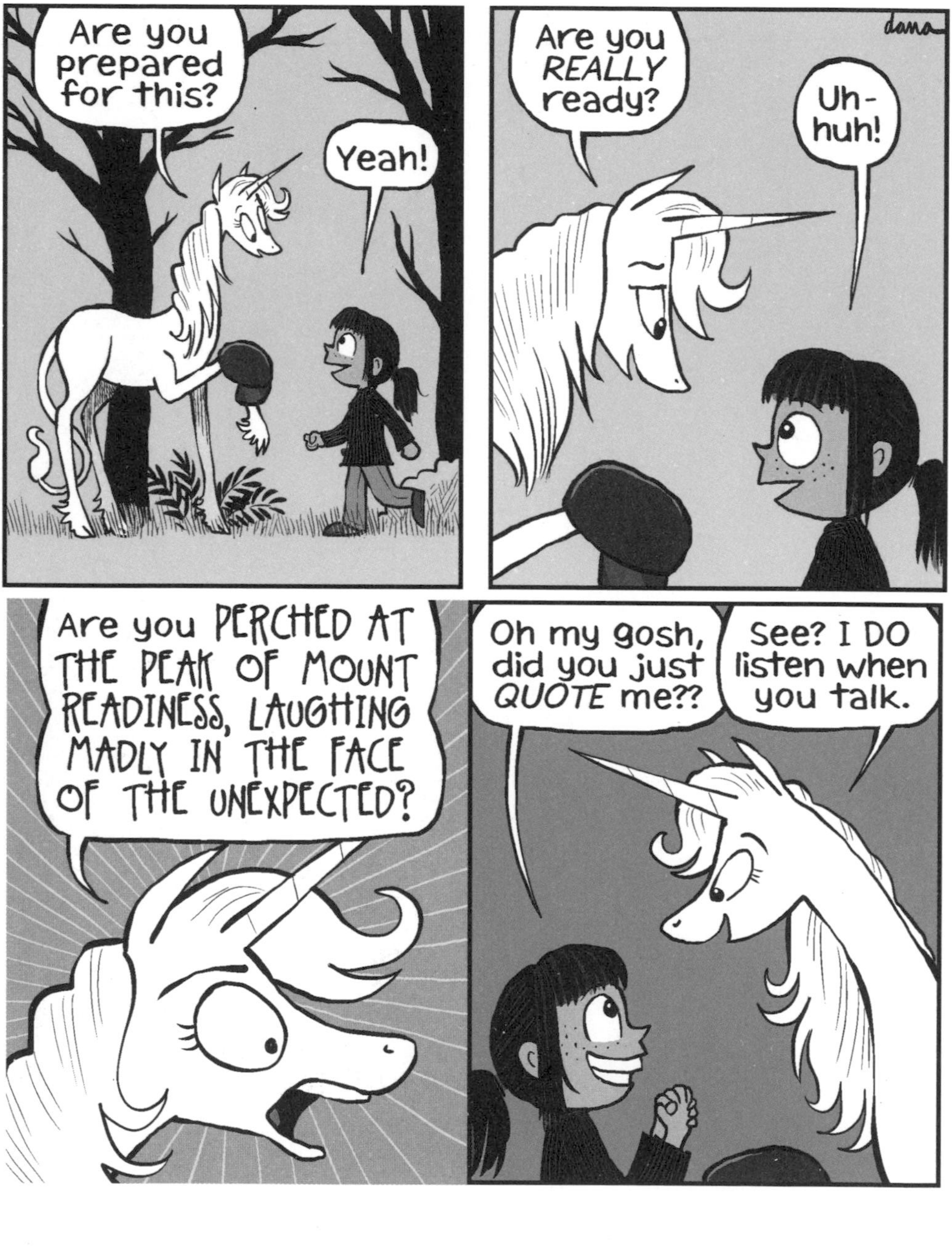
Are you prepared for this?
Yeah!
dana
Are you REALLY ready?
Uh-huh!
Are you PERCHED AT THE PEAK OF MOUNT READINESS, LAUGHING MADLY IN THE FACE OF THE UNEXPECTED?
Oh my gosh, did you just QUOTE me??
See? I DO listen when you talk.

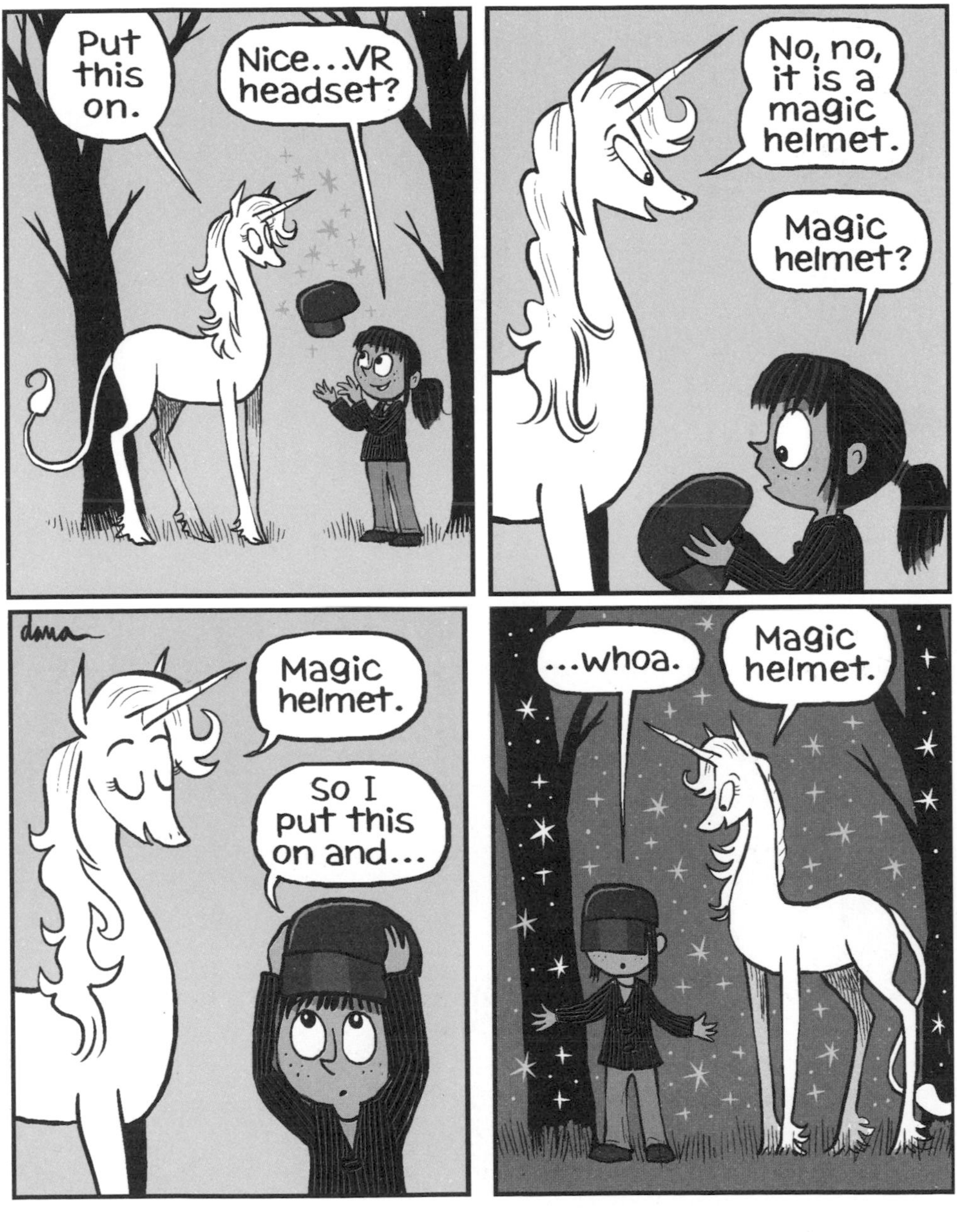
Put this on.
Nice...VR headset?
No, no, it is a magic helmet.
Magic helmet?
Magic helmet.
So I put this on and...
...whoa.
Magic helmet.

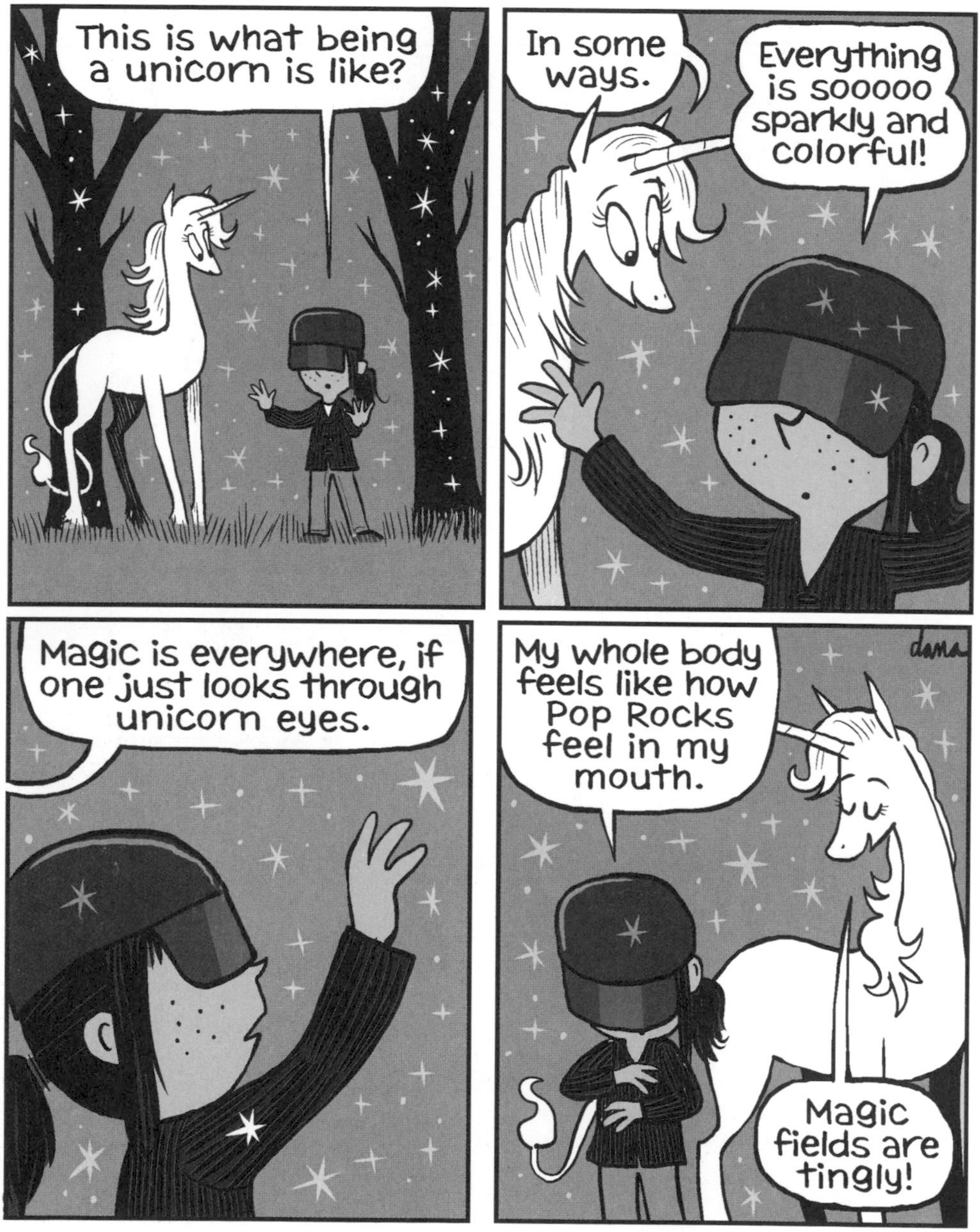
This is what being a unicorn is like?
In some ways.
Everything is sooooo sparkly and colorful!
Magic is everywhere, if one just looks through unicorn eyes.
My whole body feels like how Pop Rocks feel in my mouth.
Magic fields are tingly!
dana

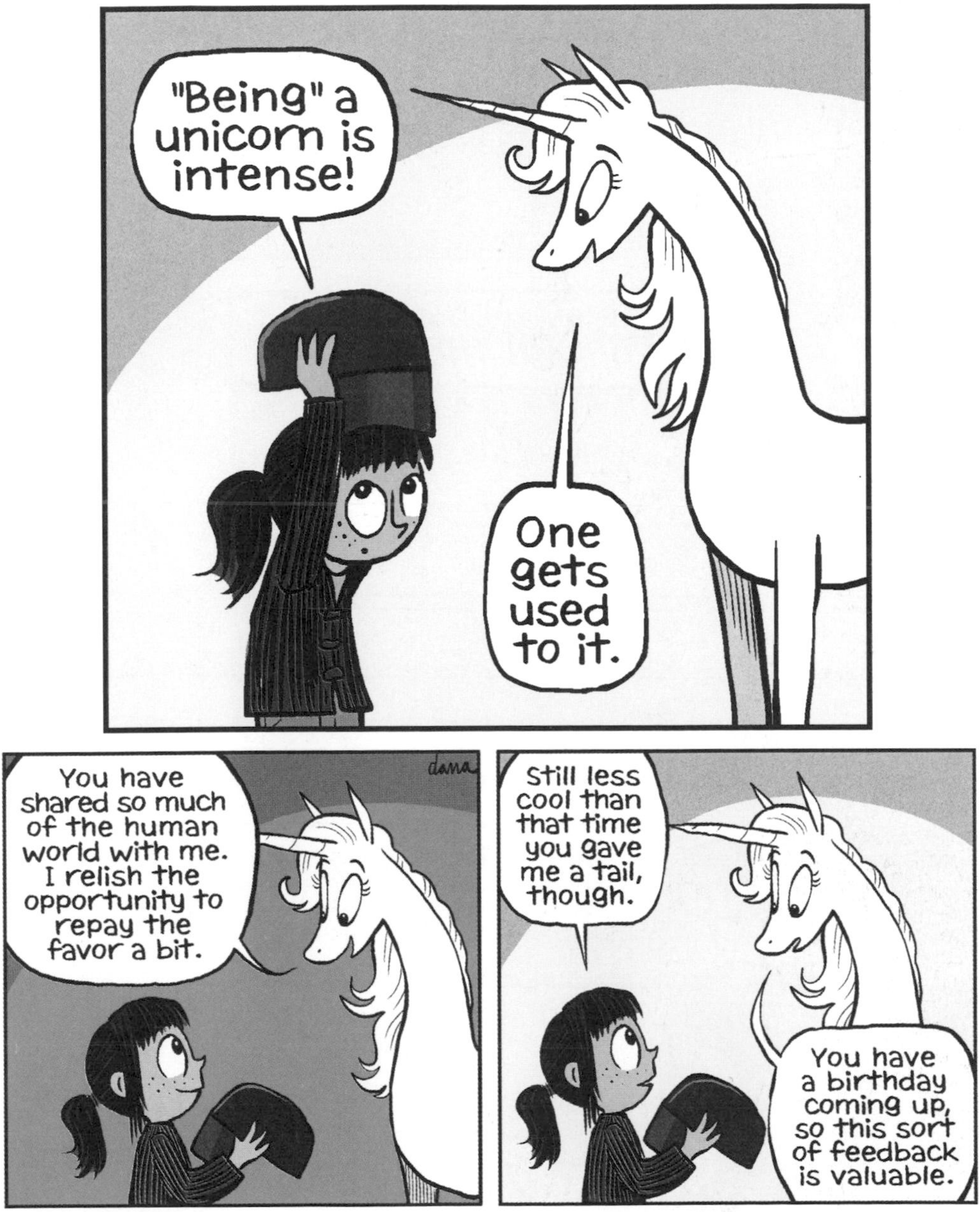
"Being" a unicorn is intense!
One gets used to it.
dana
You have shared so much of the human world with me. I relish the opportunity to repay the favor a bit.
Still less cool than that time you gave me a tail, though.
You have a birthday coming up, so this sort of feedback is valuable.

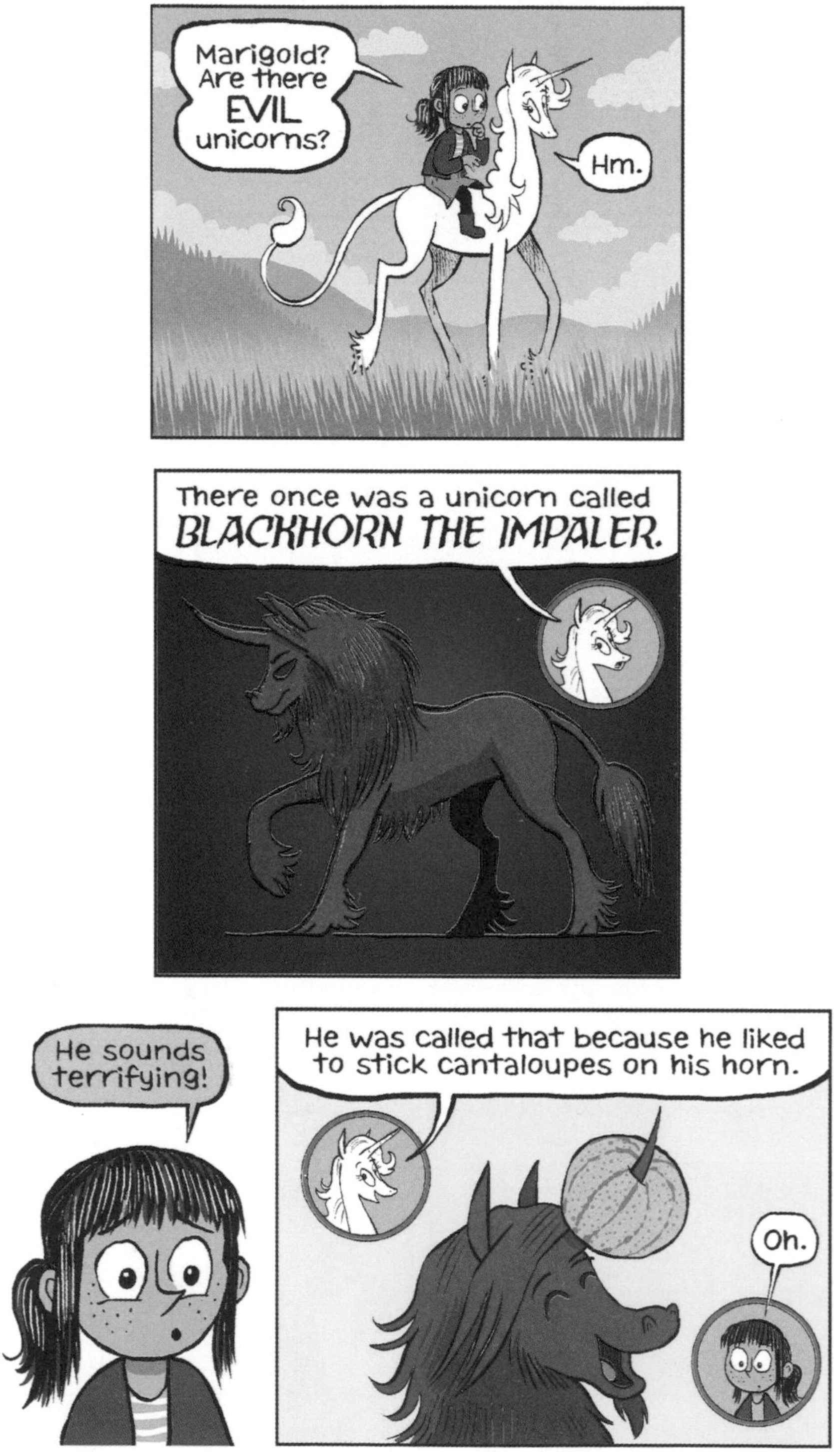
Marigold? Are there EVIL unicorns?
Hm.
There once was a unicorn called BLACKHORN THE IMPALER.
He sounds terrifying!
He was called that because he liked to stick cantaloupes on his horn.
Oh.

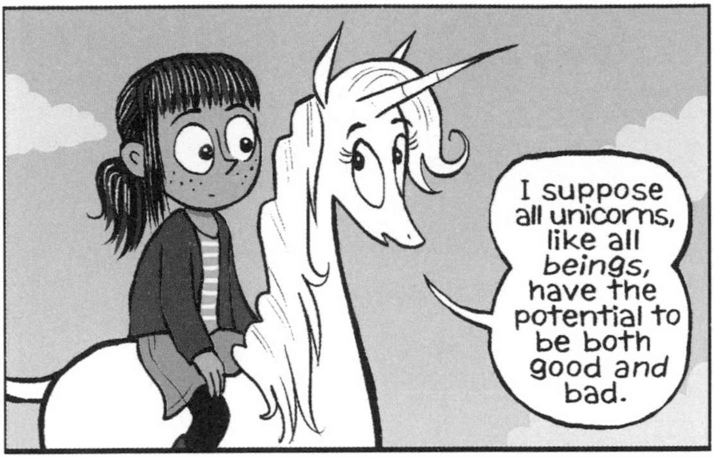
I suppose all unicorns, like all *beings*, have the potential to be both good *and* bad.

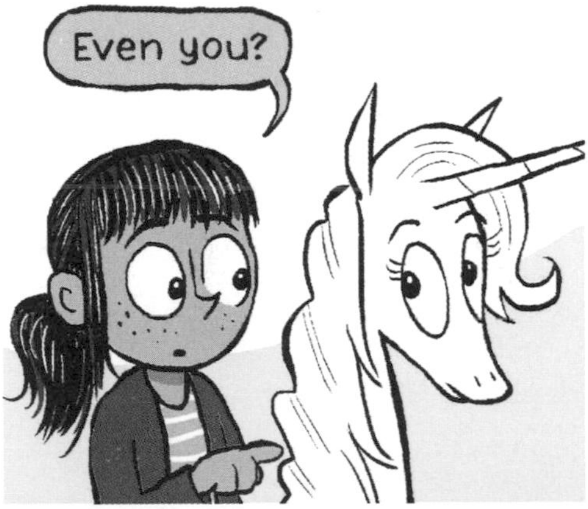
Even you?

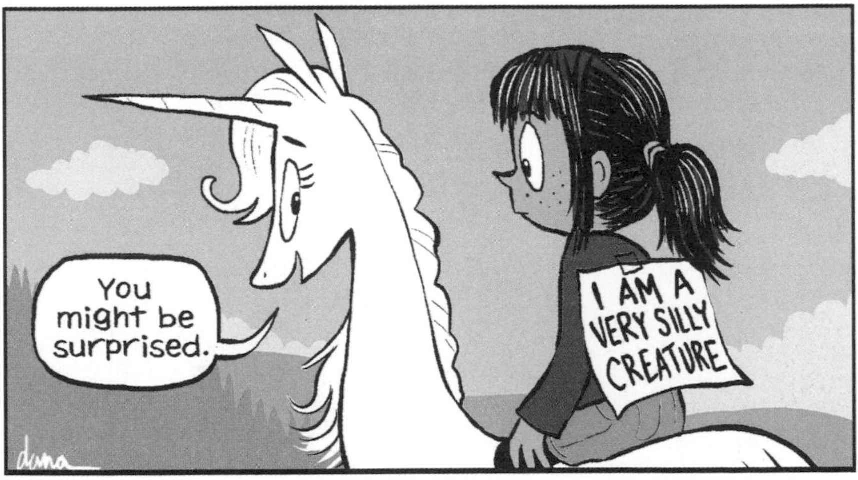
You might be surprised.
I AM A VERY SILLY CREATURE
dana

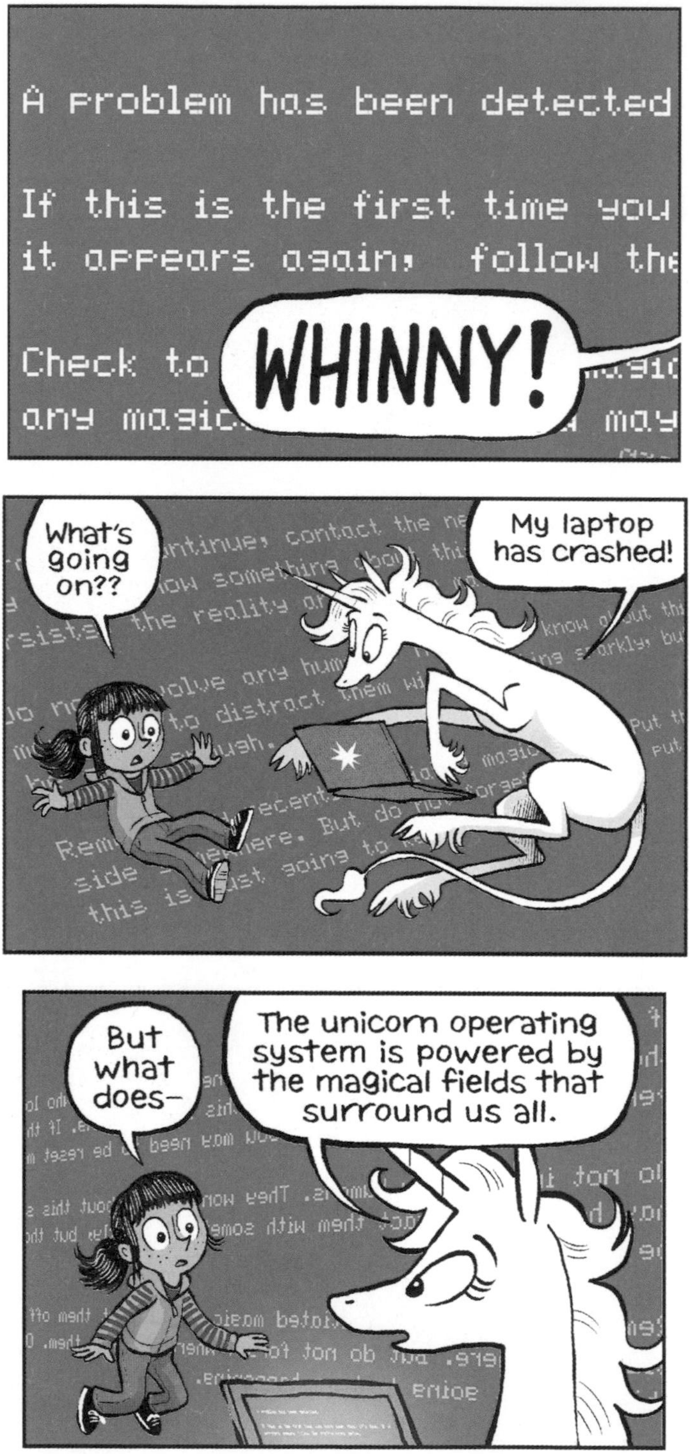
A problem has been detected
If this is the first time you
it appears again, follow the
Check to
any magic
may
WHINNY!
What's going on??
My laptop has crashed!
But what does-
The unicorn operating system is powered by the magical fields that surround us all.

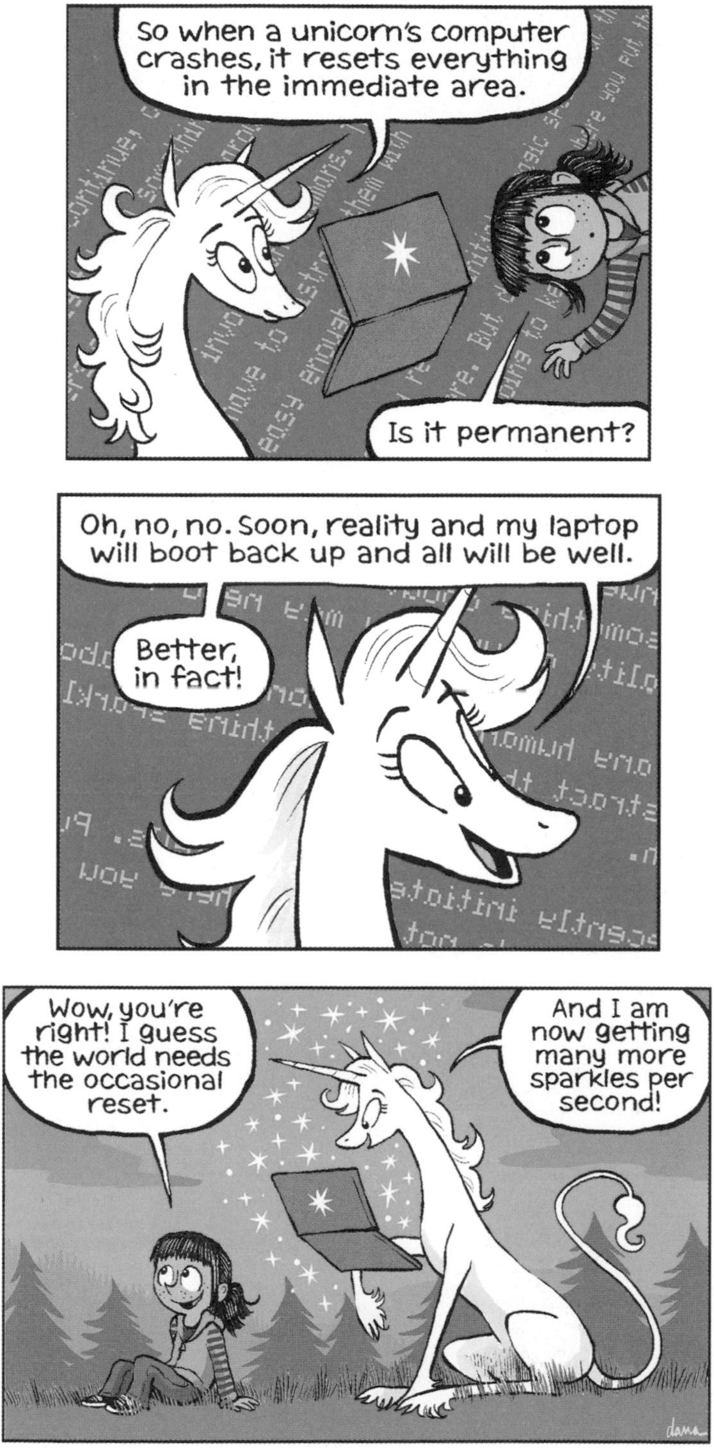
So when a unicorn's computer crashes, it resets everything in the immediate area.
Is it permanent?
Oh, no, no. Soon, reality and my laptop will boot back up and all will be well.
Better, in fact!
Wow, you're right! I guess the world needs the occasional reset.
And I am now getting many more sparkles per second!
dana

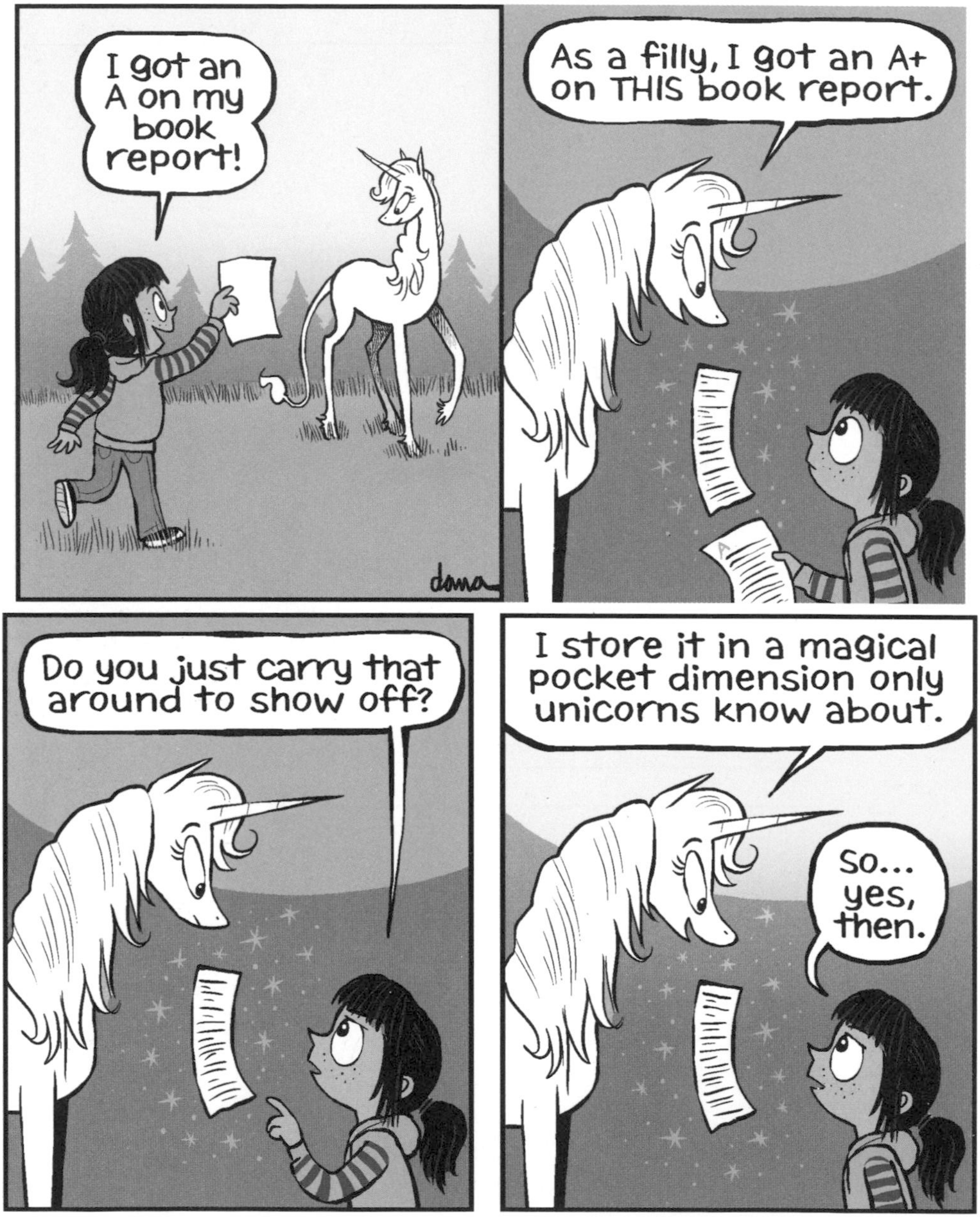
I got an A on my book report!
As a filly, I got an A+ on THIS book report.
Do you just carry that around to show off?
I store it in a magical pocket dimension only unicorns know about.
So... yes, then.

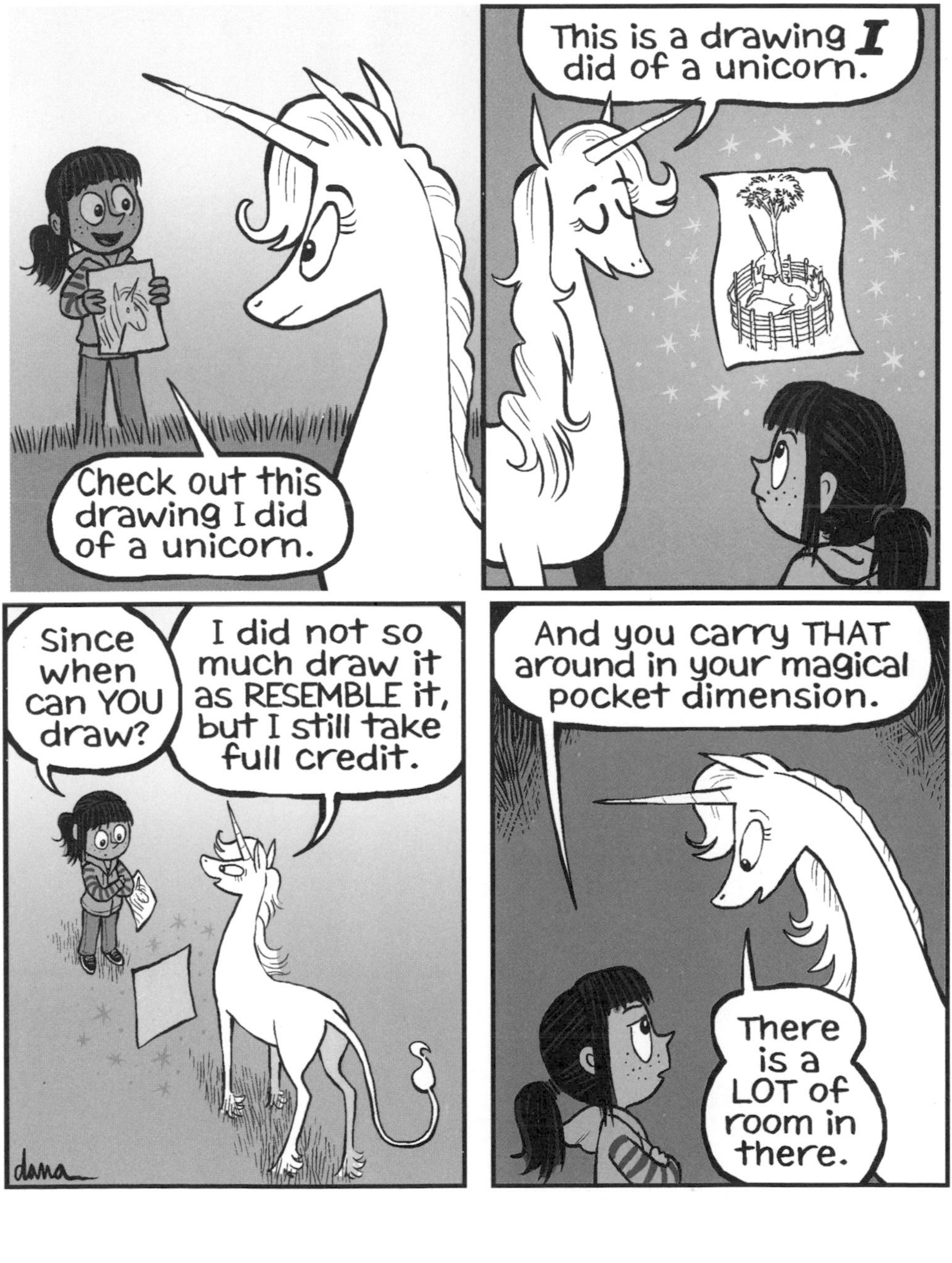

Check out this drawing I did of a unicorn.
This is a drawing *I* did of a unicorn.
Since when can YOU draw?
I did not so much draw it as RESEMBLE it, but I still take full credit.
dana
And you carry THAT around in your magical pocket dimension.
There is a LOT of room in there.

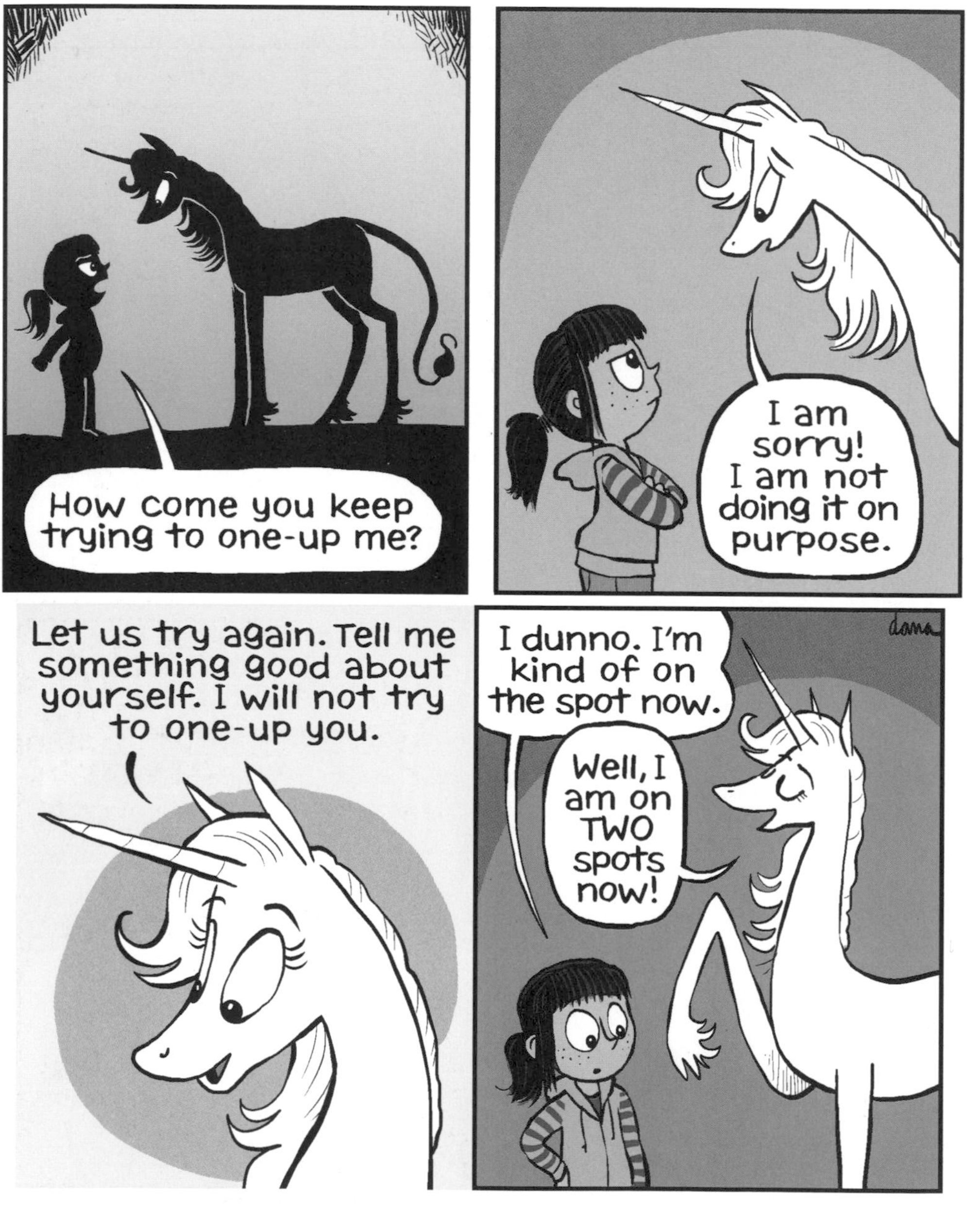
How come you keep trying to one-up me?
I am sorry! I am not doing it on purpose.
Let us try again. Tell me something good about yourself. I will not try to one-up you.
I dunno. I'm kind of on the spot now.
Well, I am on TWO spots now!
dana

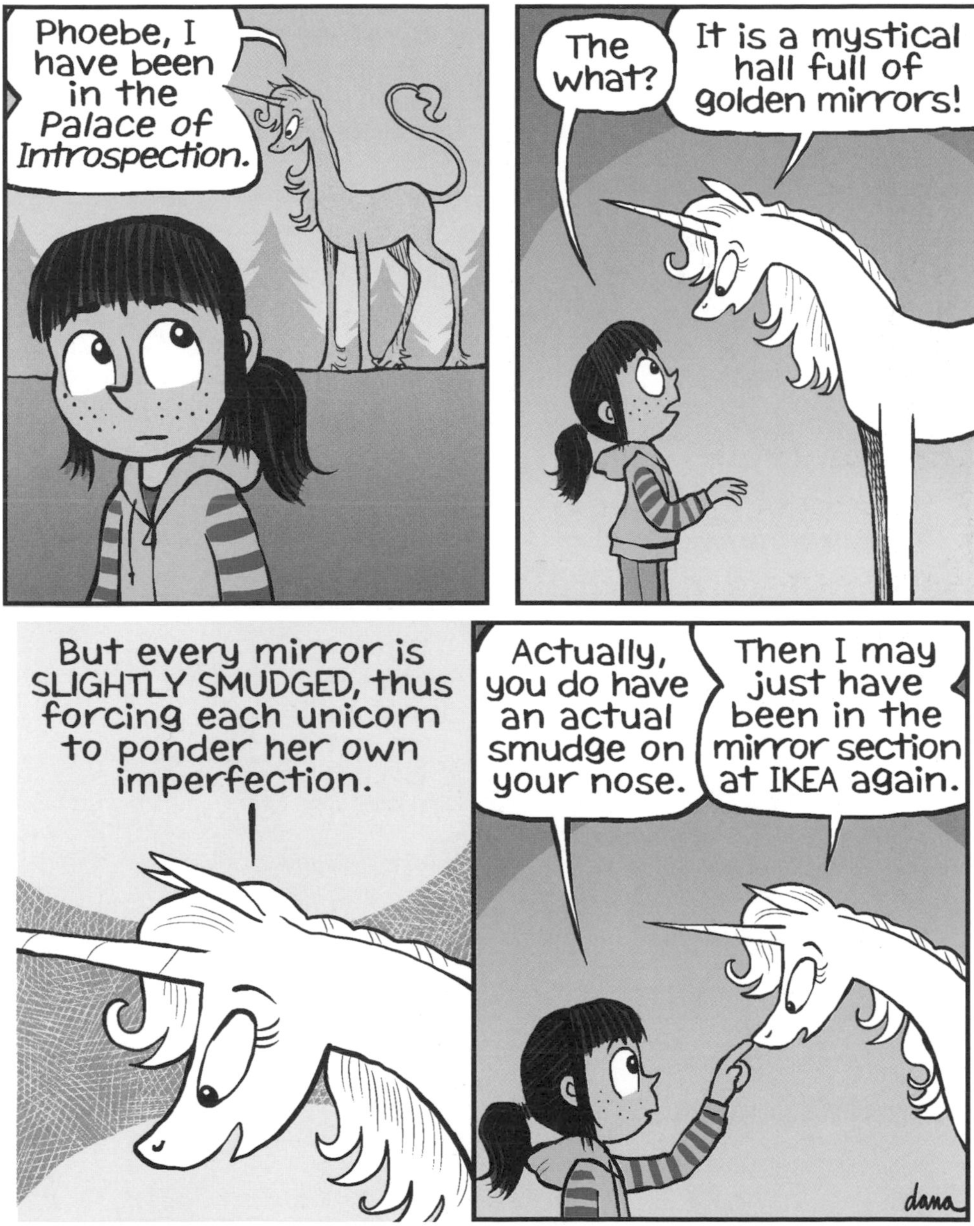
Phoebe, I have been in the *Palace of Introspection.*
The what?
It is a mystical hall full of golden mirrors!
But every mirror is SLIGHTLY SMUDGED, thus forcing each unicorn to ponder her own imperfection.
Actually, you do have an actual smudge on your nose.
Then I may just have been in the mirror section at IKEA again.
dana

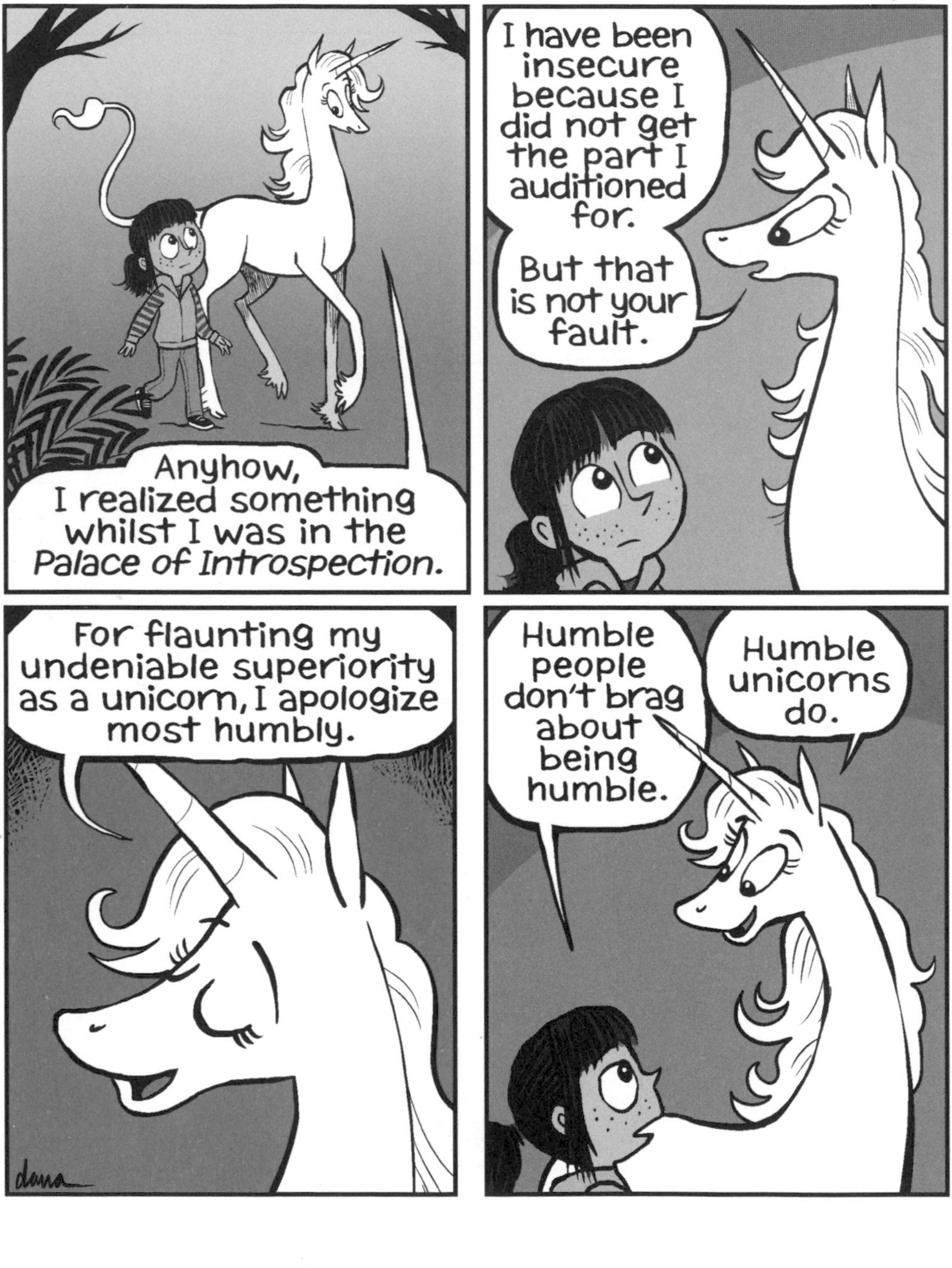
Anyhow, I realized something whilst I was in the *Palace of Introspection.*
I have been insecure because I did not get the part I auditioned for.
But that is not your fault.
For flaunting my undeniable superiority as a unicorn, I apologize most humbly.
Humble people don't brag about being humble.
Humble unicorns do.
dana

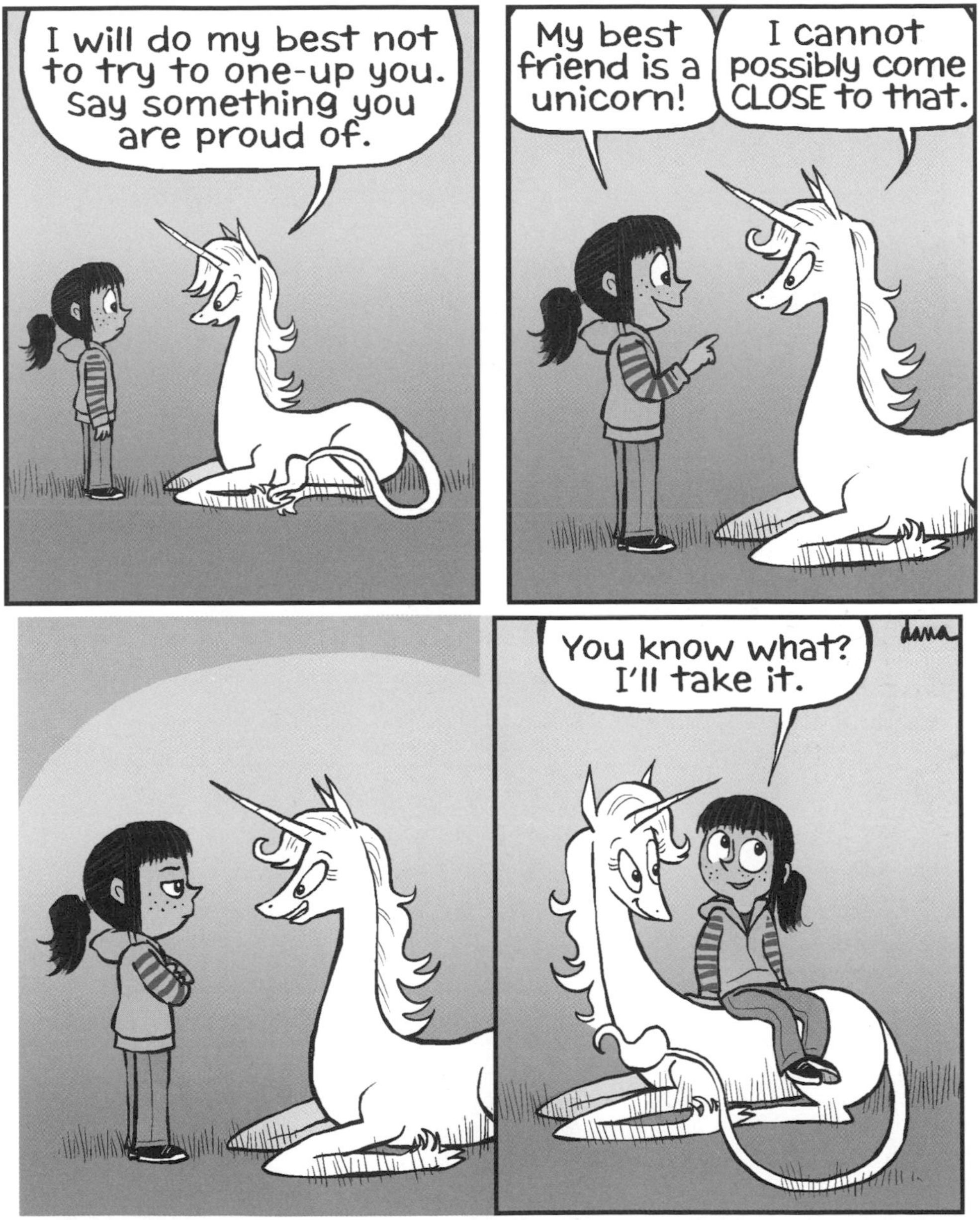
I will do my best not to try to one-up you. Say something you are proud of.
My best friend is a unicorn!
I cannot possibly come CLOSE to that.
dana
You know what? I'll take it.

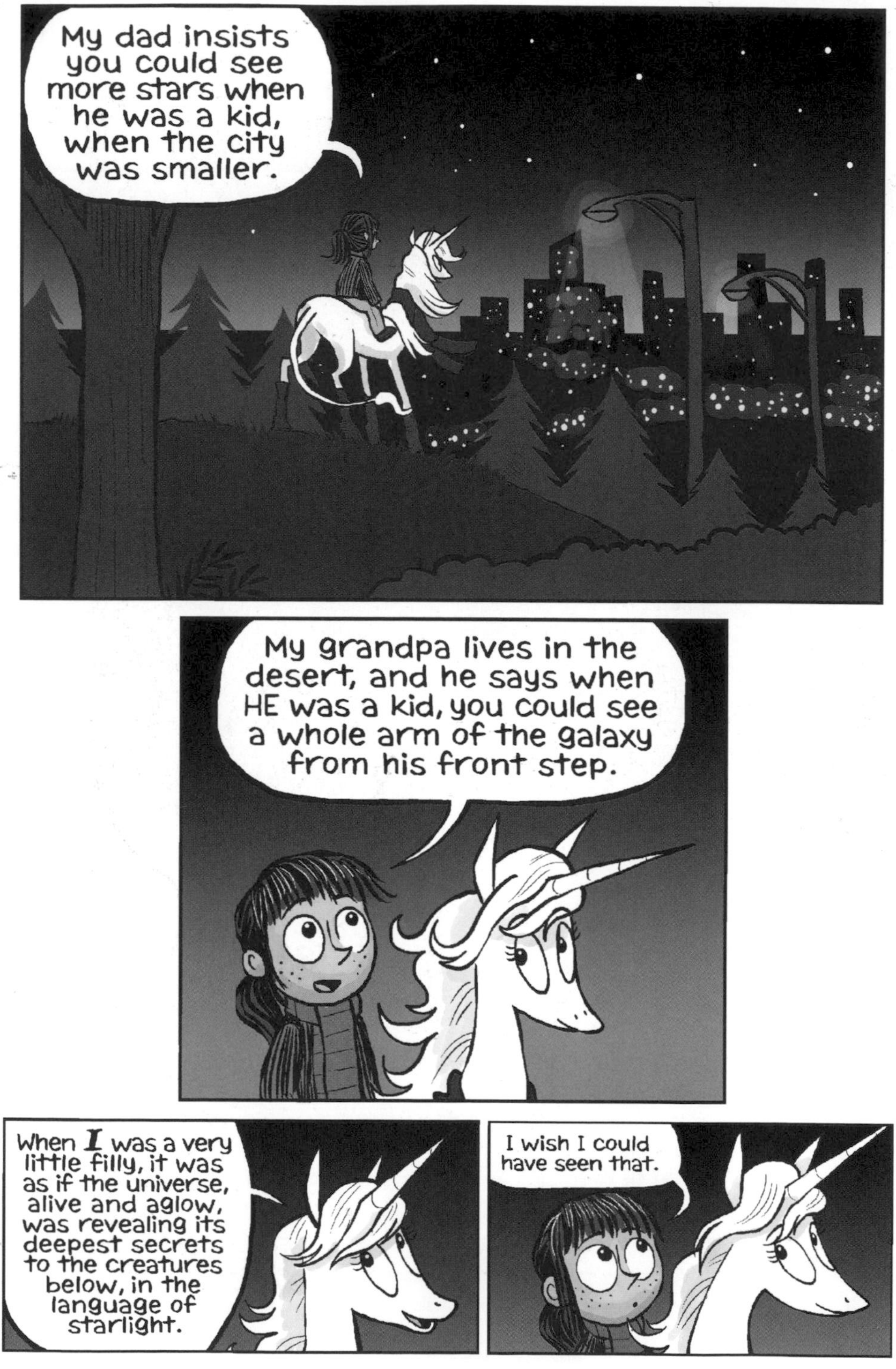

My dad insists you could see more stars when he was a kid, when the city was smaller.
My grandpa lives in the desert, and he says when HE was a kid, you could see a whole arm of the galaxy from his front step.
When I was a very little filly, it was as if the universe, alive and aglow, was revealing its deepest secrets to the creatures below, in the language of starlight.
I wish I could have seen that.

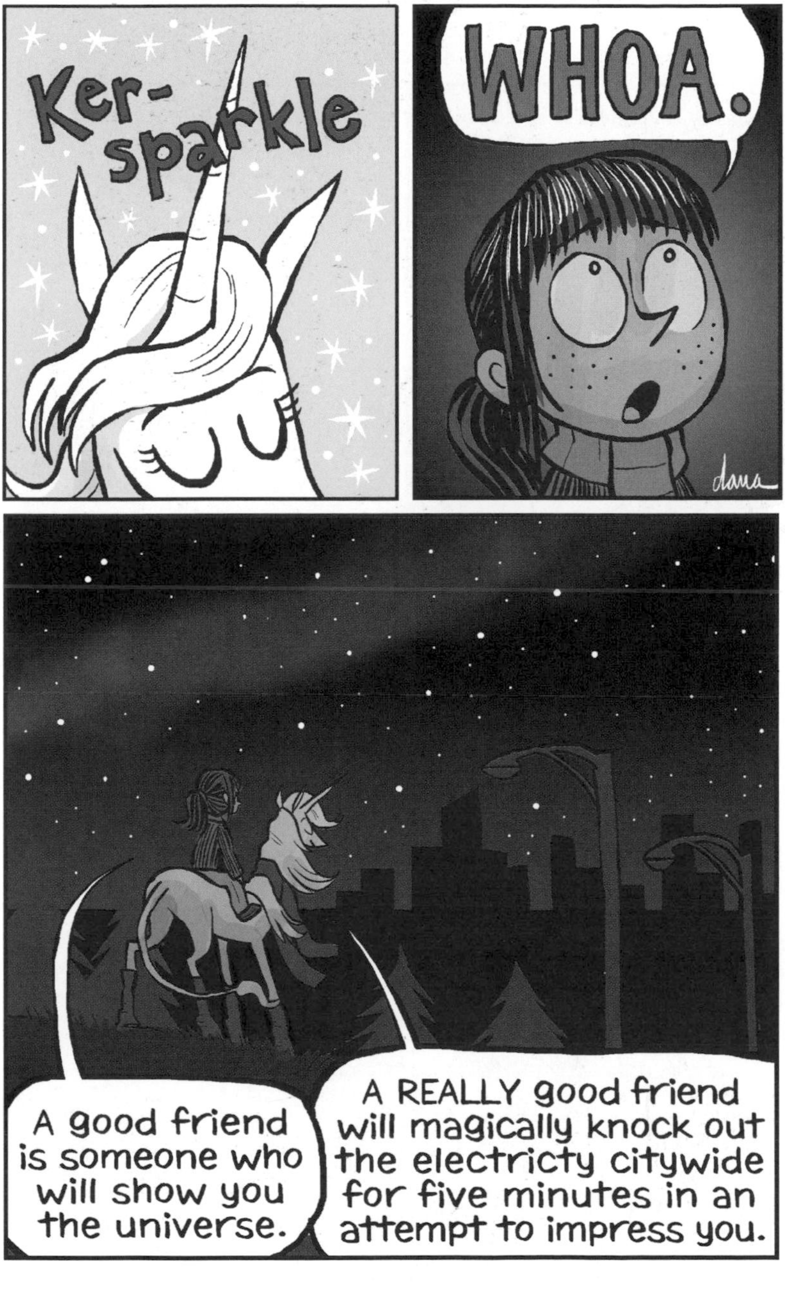
Ker-sparkle
WHOA.
dana
A good friend is someone who will show you the universe.
A REALLY good friend will magically knock out the electricty citywide for five minutes in an attempt to impress you.

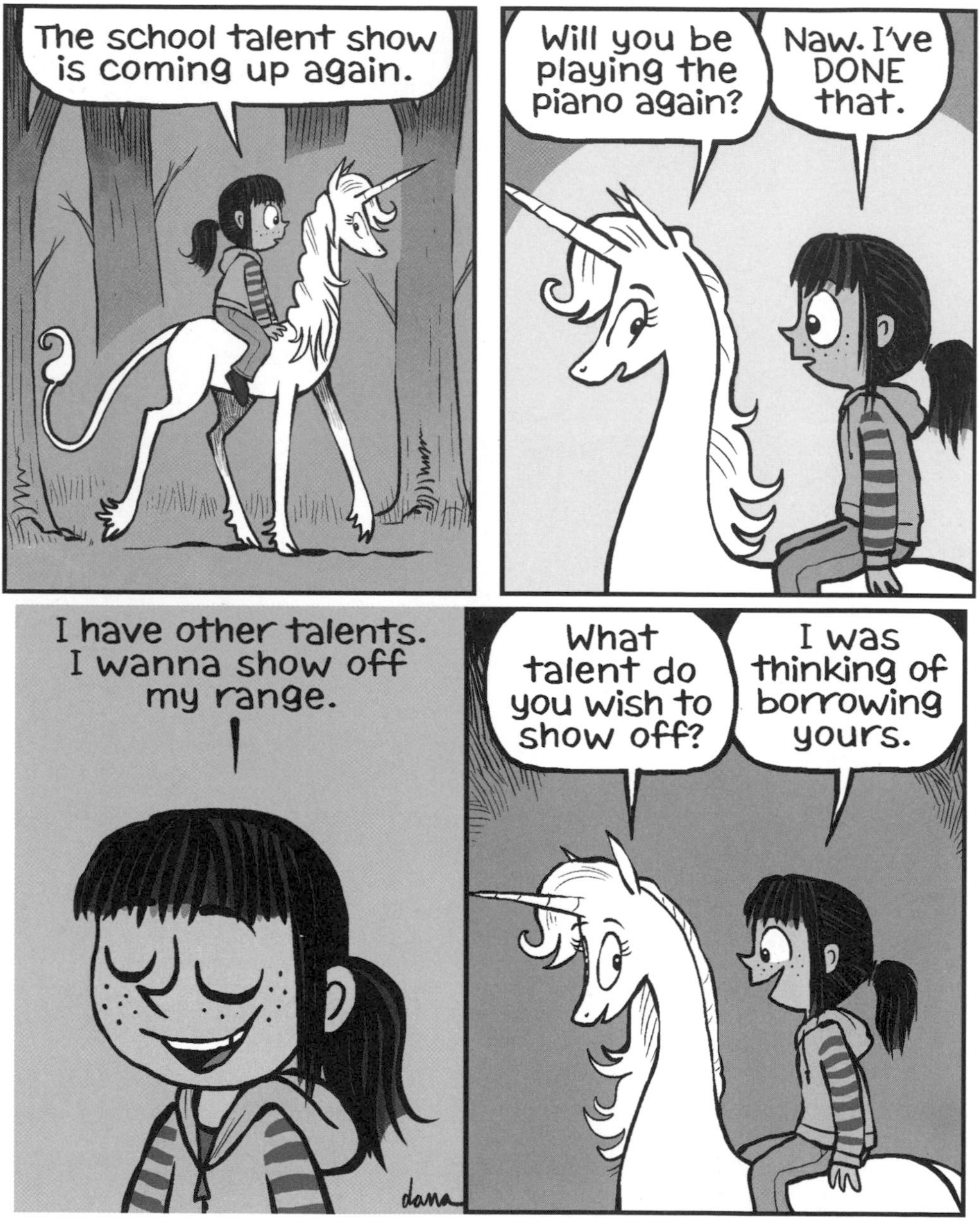

The school talent show is coming up again.
Will you be playing the piano again?
Naw. I've DONE that.
I have other talents. I wanna show off my range.
What talent do you wish to show off?
I was thinking of borrowing yours.
dana

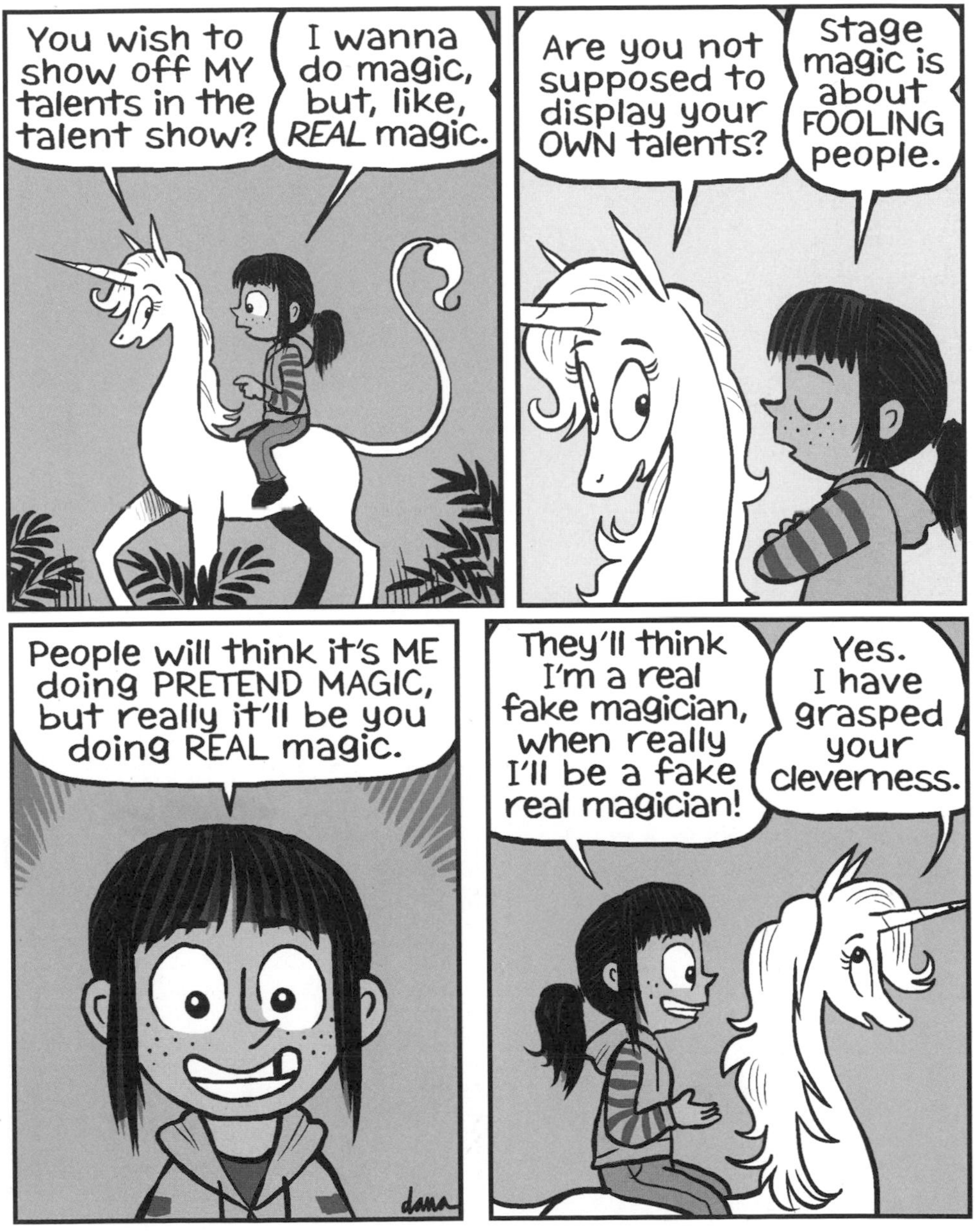
You wish to show off MY talents in the talent show?
I wanna do magic, but, like, REAL magic.
Are you not supposed to display your OWN talents?
Stage magic is about FOOLING people.
People will think it's ME doing PRETEND MAGIC, but really it'll be you doing REAL magic.
They'll think I'm a real fake magician, when really I'll be a fake real magician!
Yes. I have grasped your cleverness.
dana

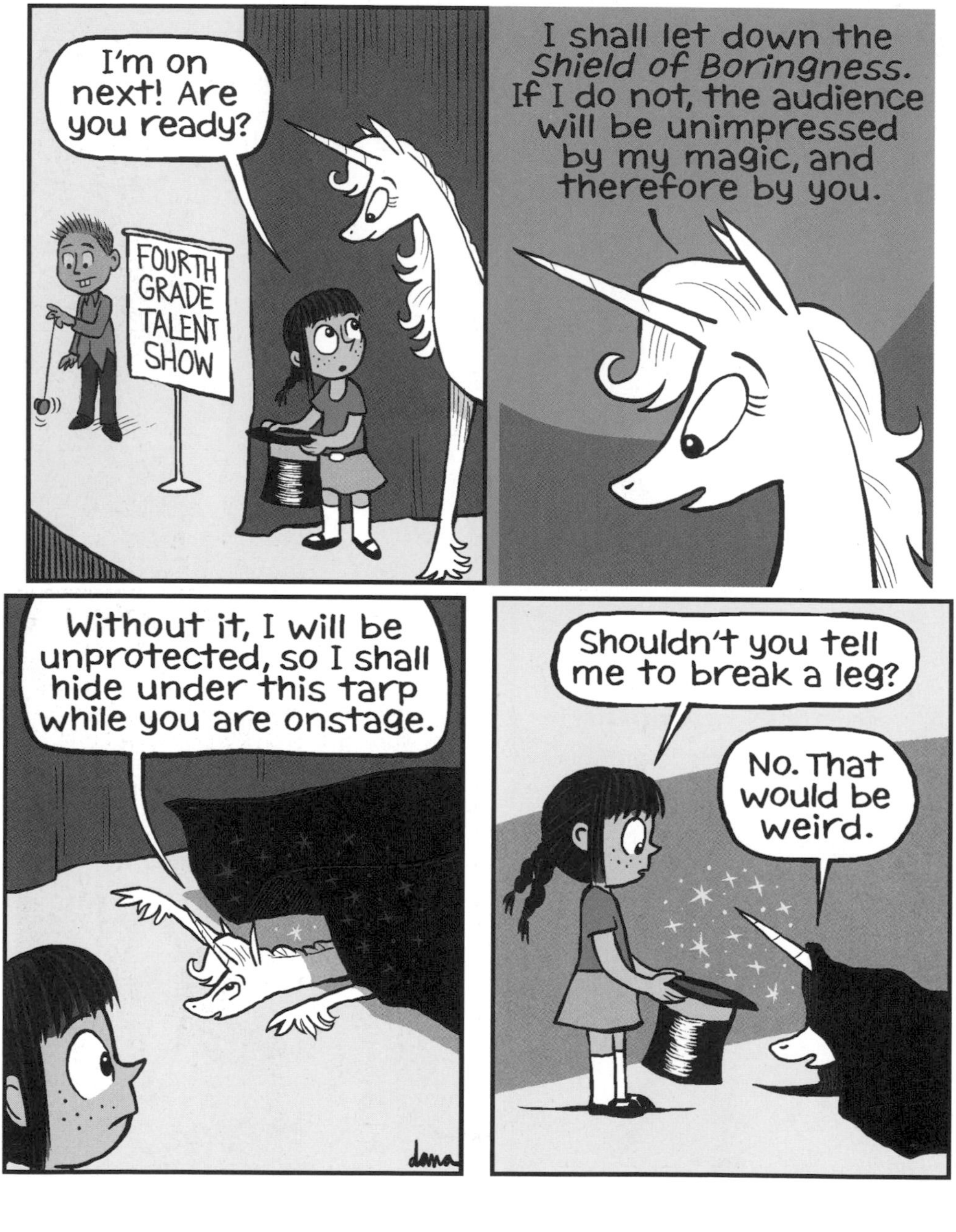
I'm on next! Are you ready?
FOURTH GRADE TALENT SHOW
I shall let down the *Shield of Boringness.* If I do not, the audience will be unimpressed by my magic, and therefore by you.
Without it, I will be unprotected, so I shall hide under this tarp while you are onstage.
dana
Shouldn't you tell me to break a leg?
No. That would be weird.

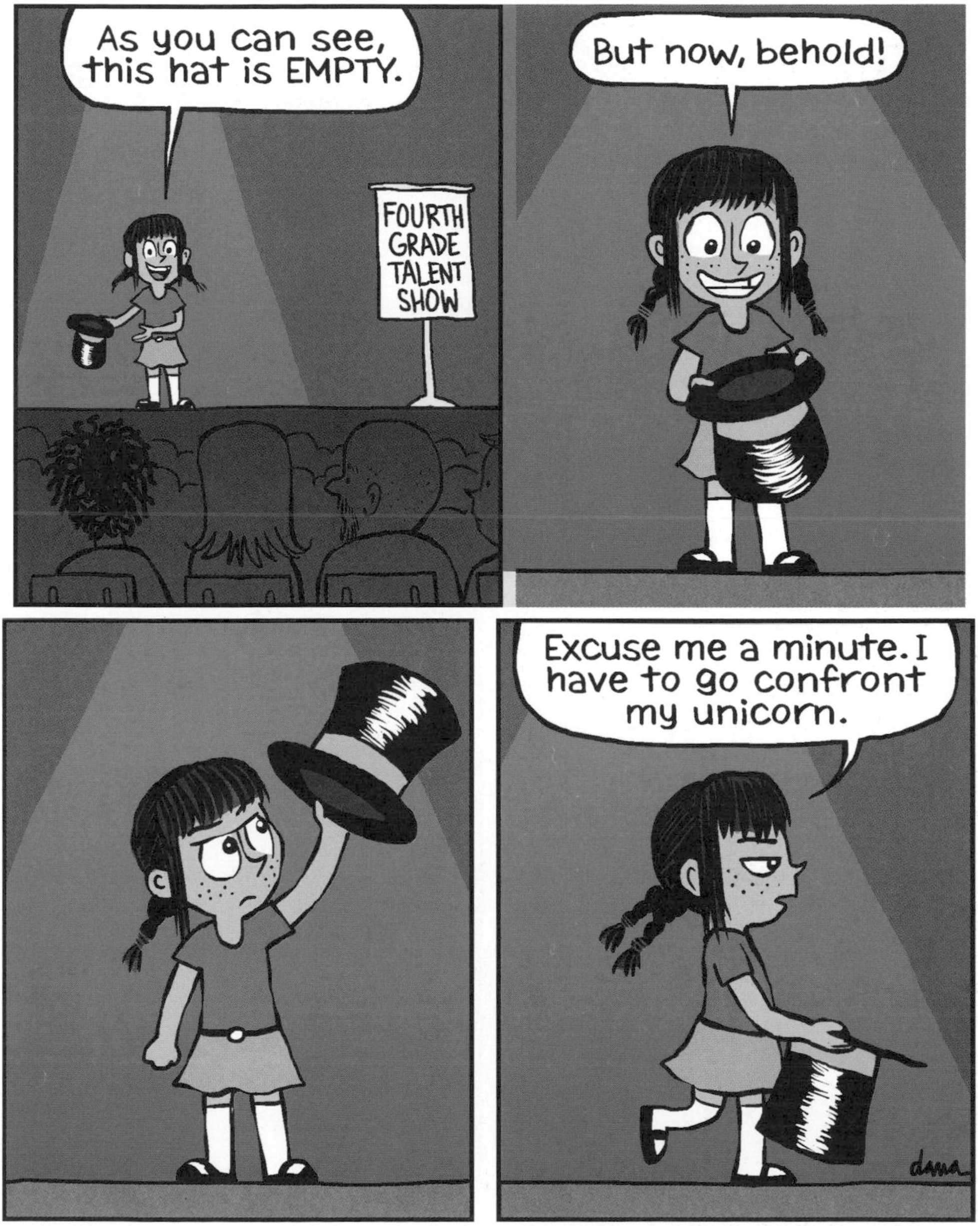
As you can see, this hat is EMPTY.
FOURTH GRADE TALENT SHOW
But now, behold!
Excuse me a minute. I have to go confront my unicorn.
dana

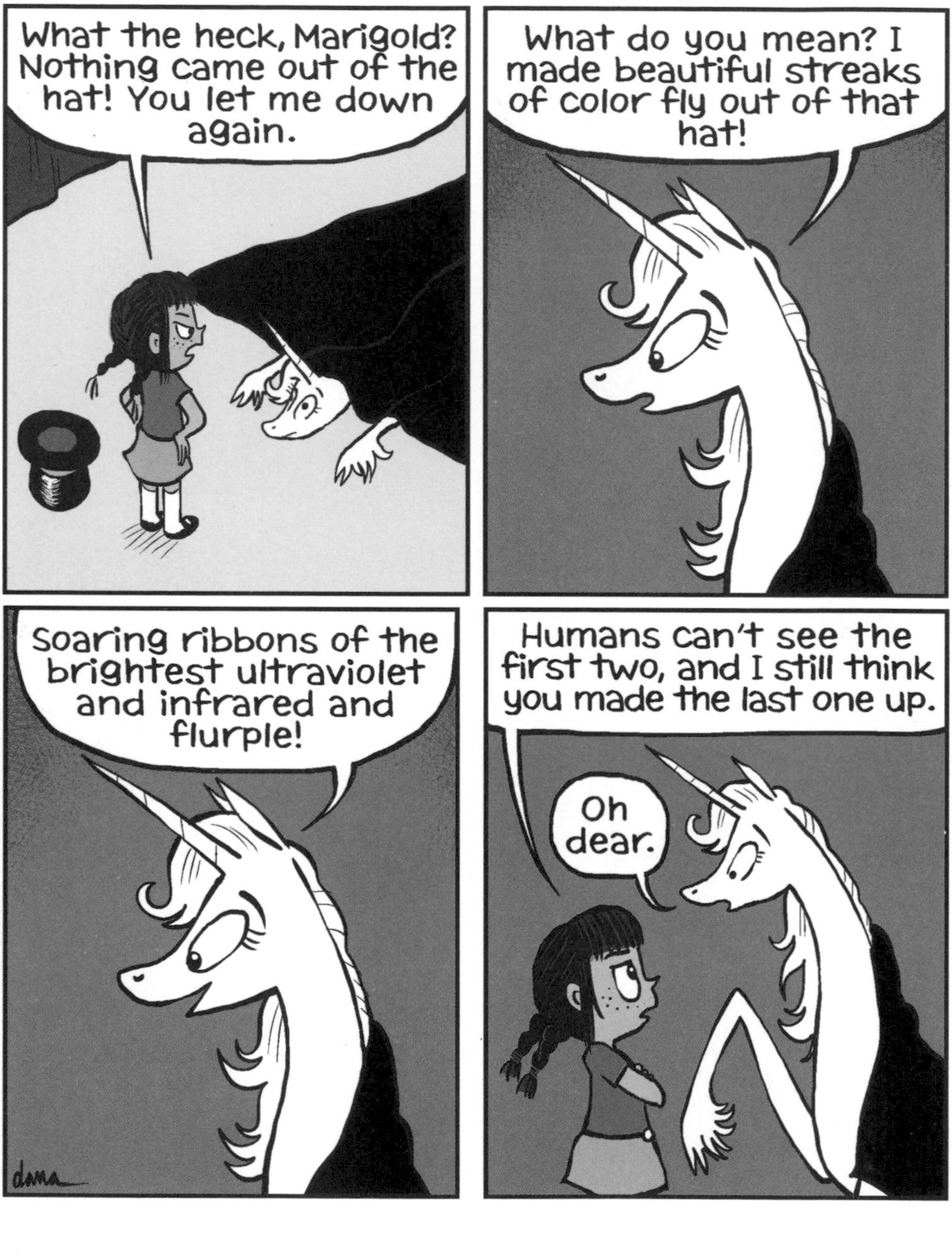
What the heck, Marigold? Nothing came out of the hat! You let me down again.
What do you mean? I made beautiful streaks of color fly out of that hat!
Soaring ribbons of the brightest ultraviolet and infrared and flurple!
dana
Humans can't see the first two, and I still think you made the last one up.
Oh dear.

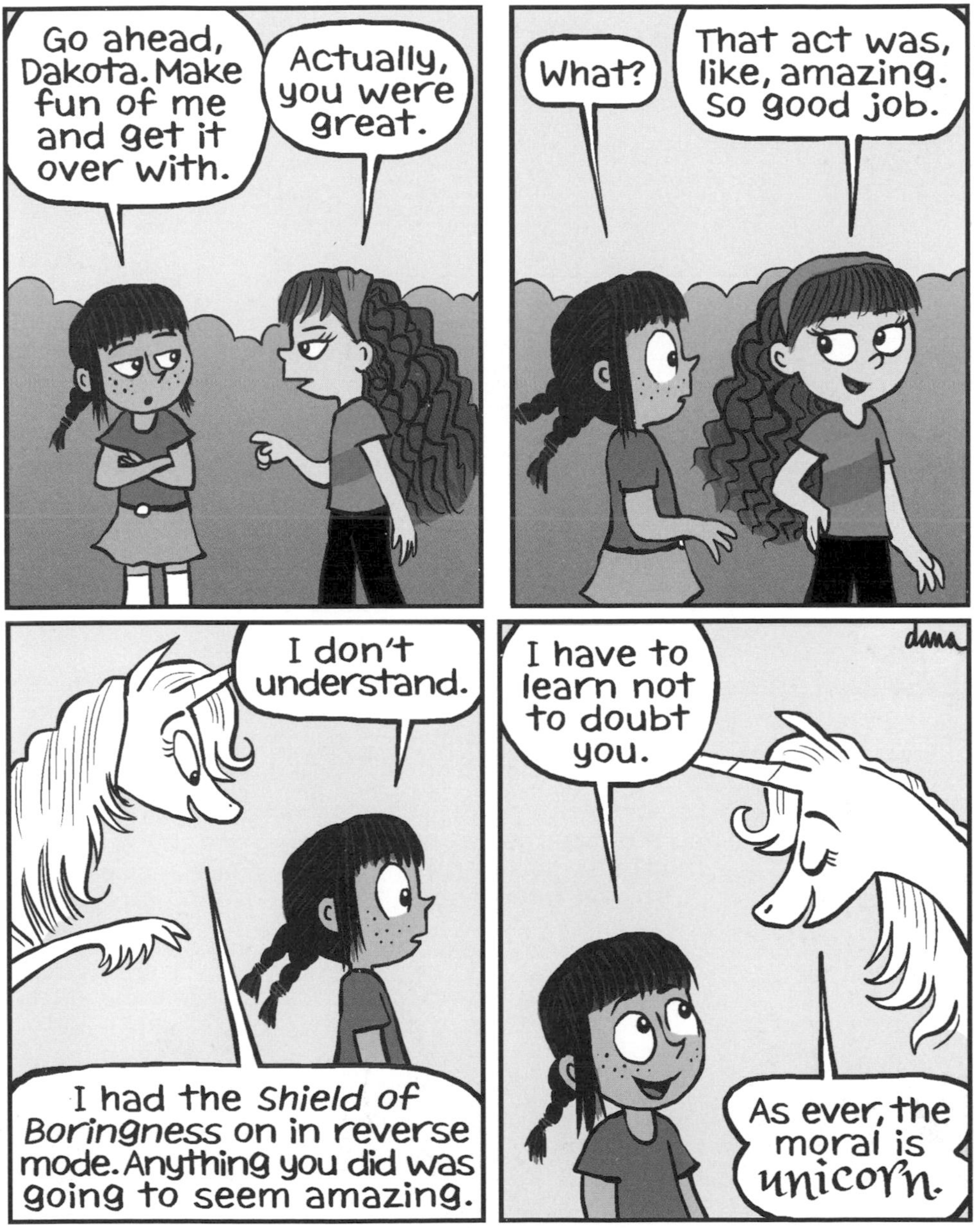
Go ahead, Dakota. Make fun of me and get it over with.
Actually, you were great.
What?
That act was, like, amazing. So good job.
dana
I don't understand.
I had the *Shield of Boringness* on in reverse mode. Anything you did was going to seem amazing.
I have to learn not to doubt you.
As ever, the moral is unicorn.

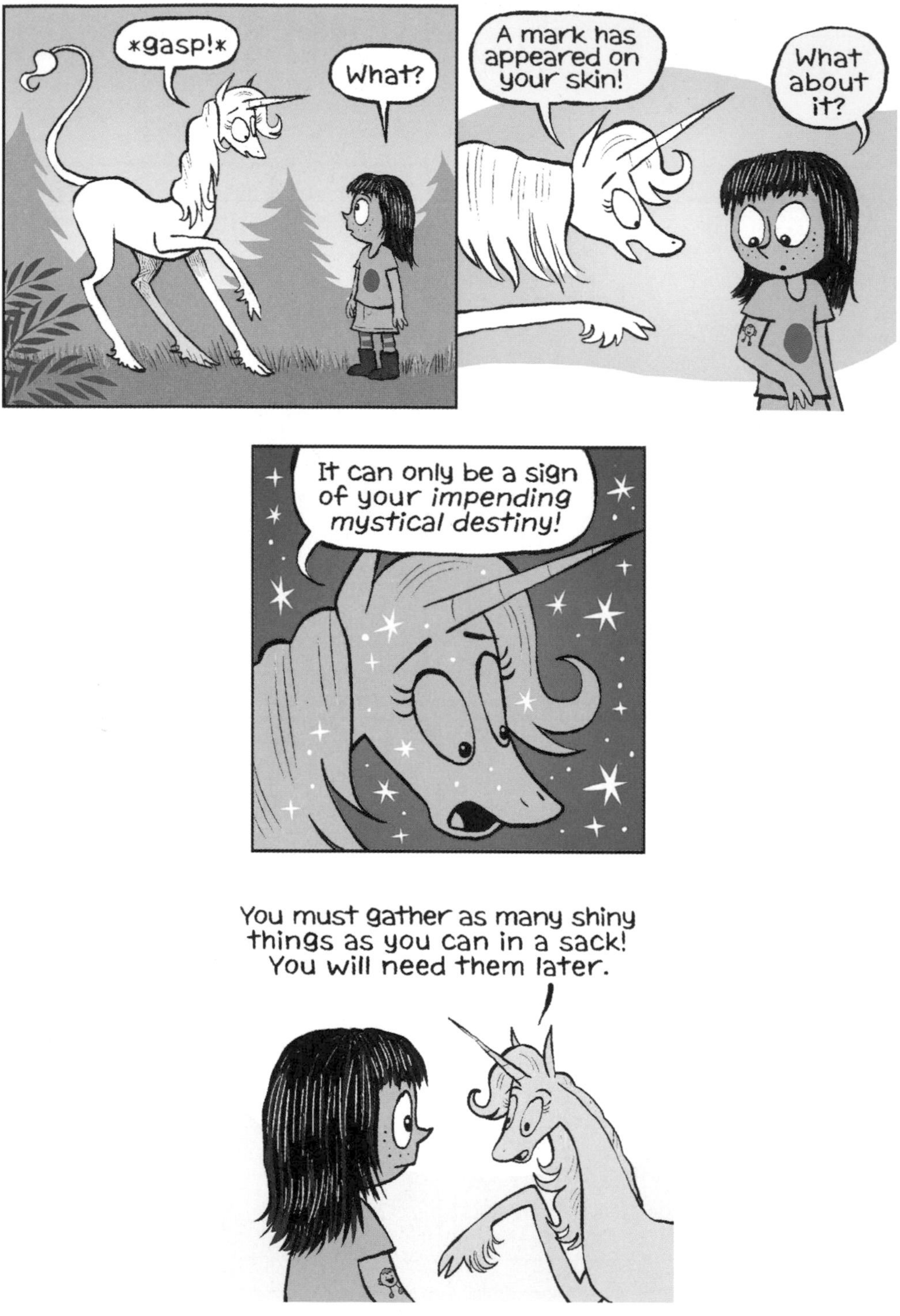
gasp!
What?
A mark has appeared on your skin!
What about it?
It can only be a sign of your *impending mystical destiny!*
You must gather as many shiny things as you can in a sack! You will need them later.

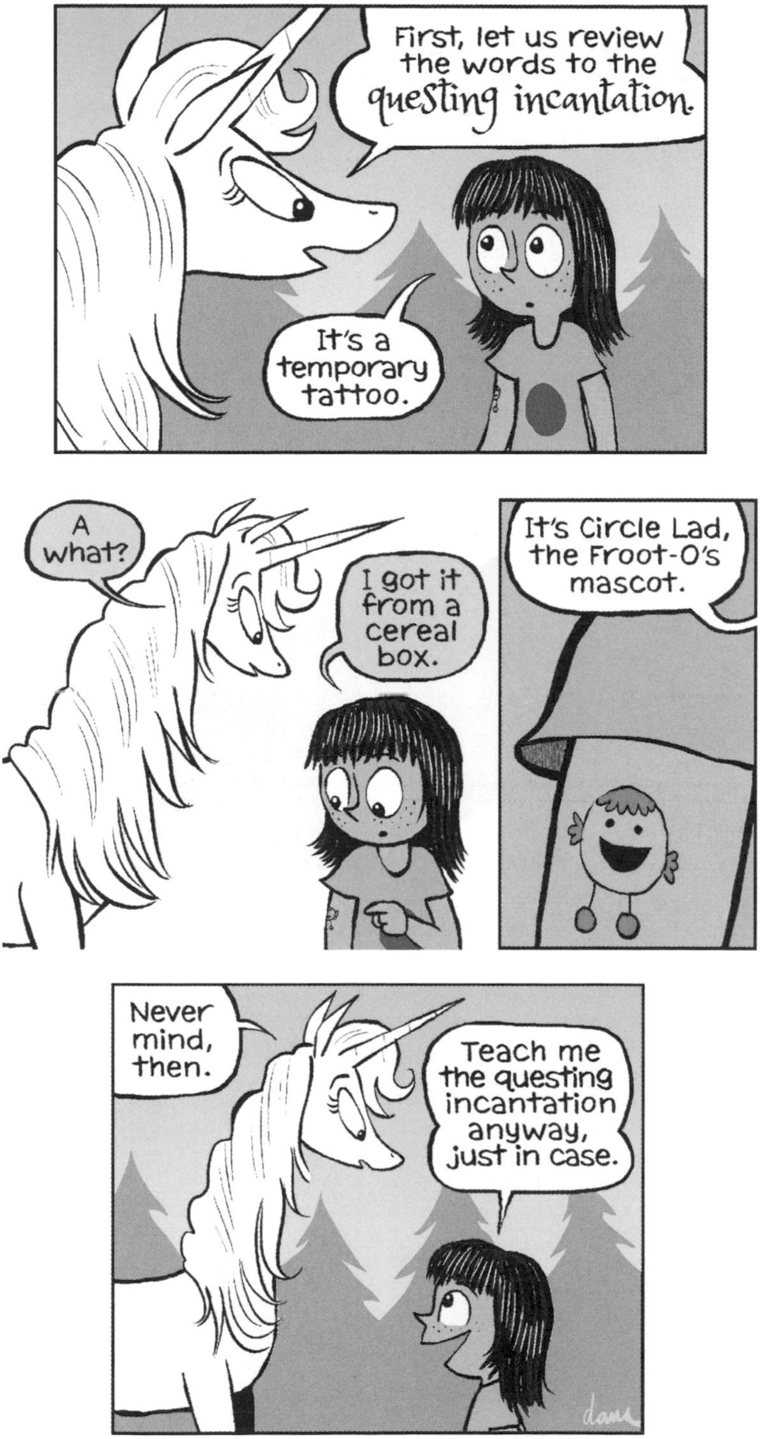
First, let us review the words to the questing incantation.
It's a temporary tattoo.
A what?
I got it from a cereal box.
It's Circle Lad, the Froot-O's mascot.
Never mind, then.
Teach me the questing incantation anyway, just in case.
dana

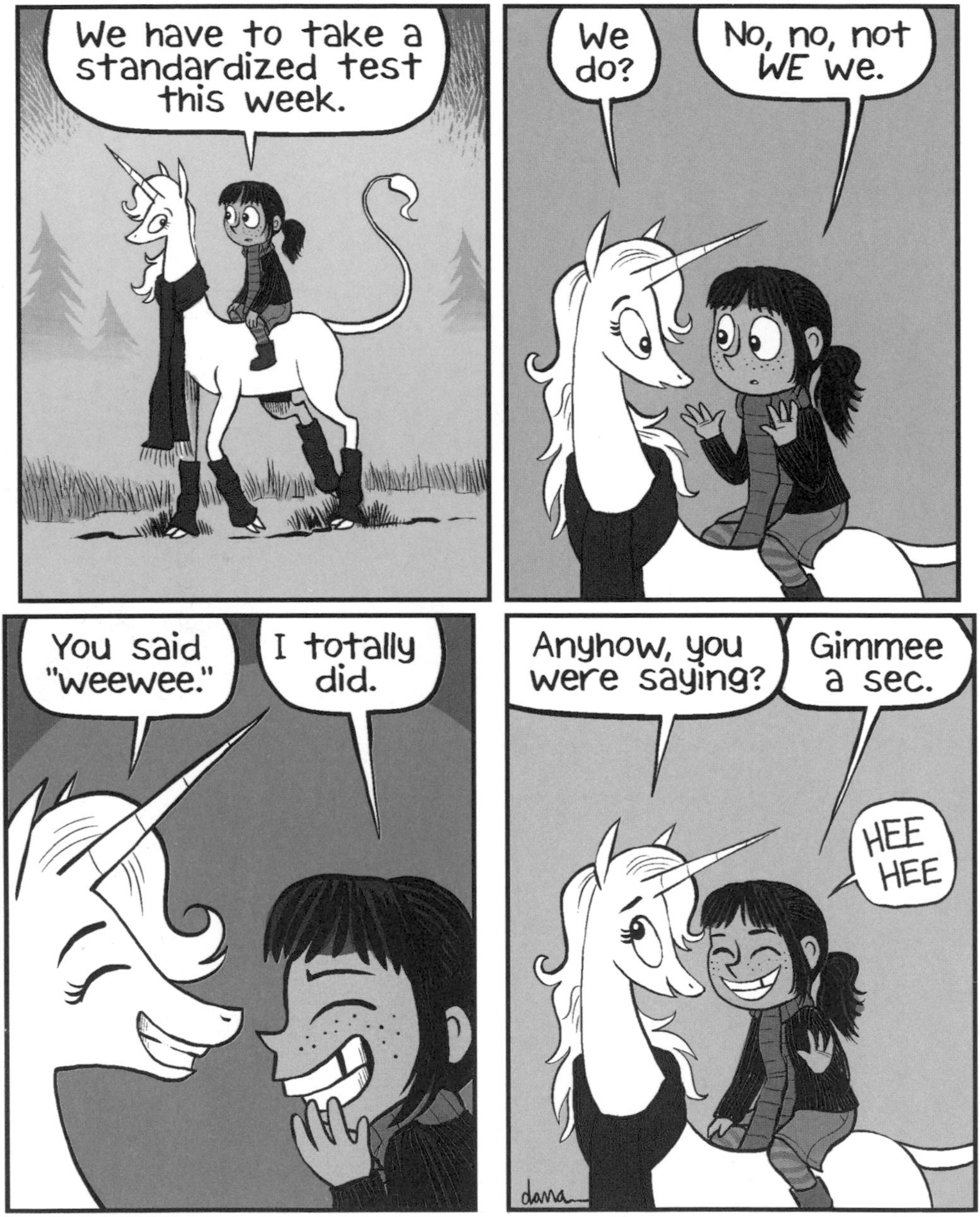
We have to take a standardized test this week.
We do?
No, no, not WE we.
You said "weewee."
I totally did.
Anyhow, you were saying?
Gimmee a sec.
HEE HEE
dana

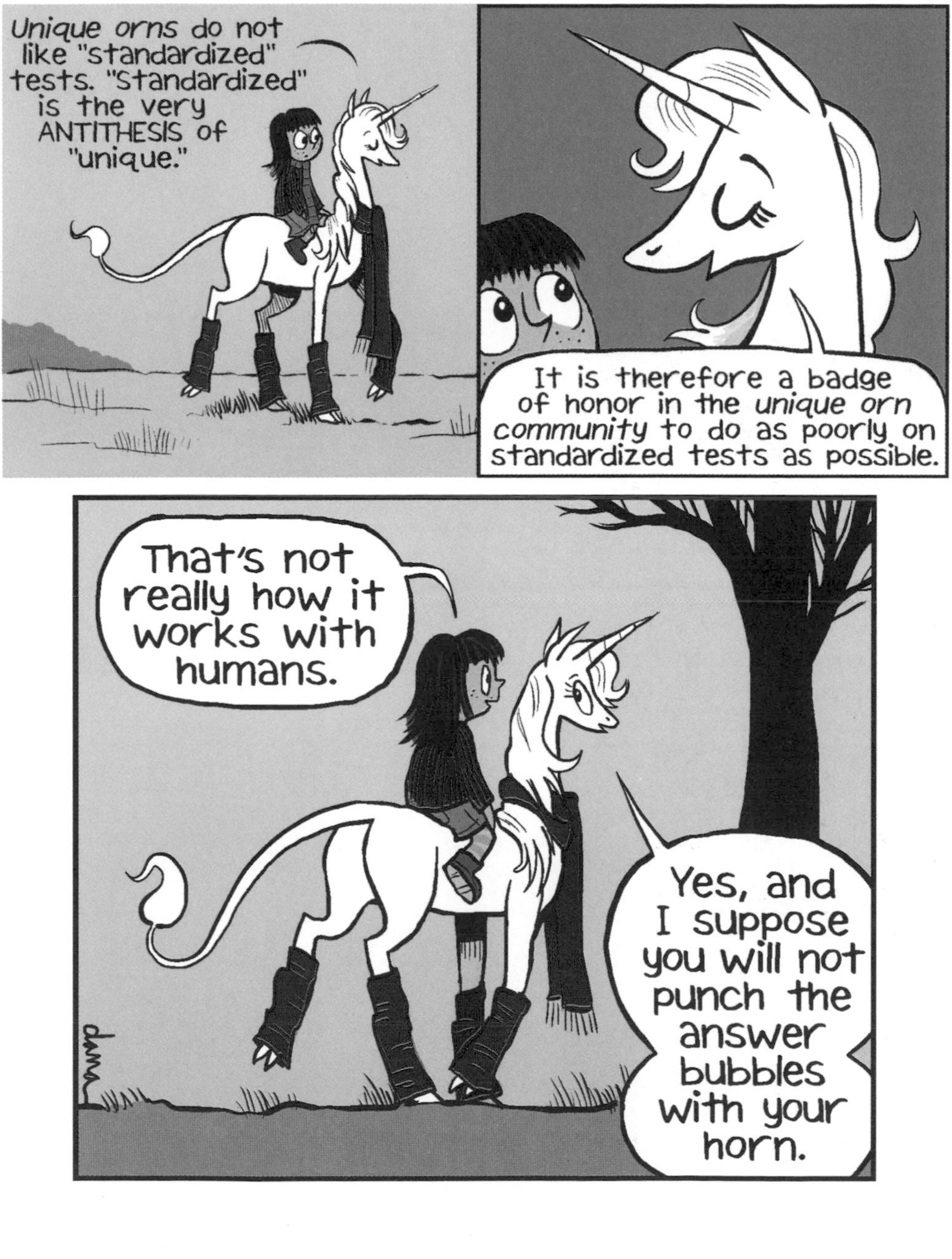
Unique orns do not like "standardized" tests. "Standardized" is the very ANTITHESIS of "unique."
It is therefore a badge of honor in the unique orn community to do as poorly on standardized tests as possible.
That's not really how it works with humans.
Yes, and I suppose you will not punch the answer bubbles with your horn.
dana

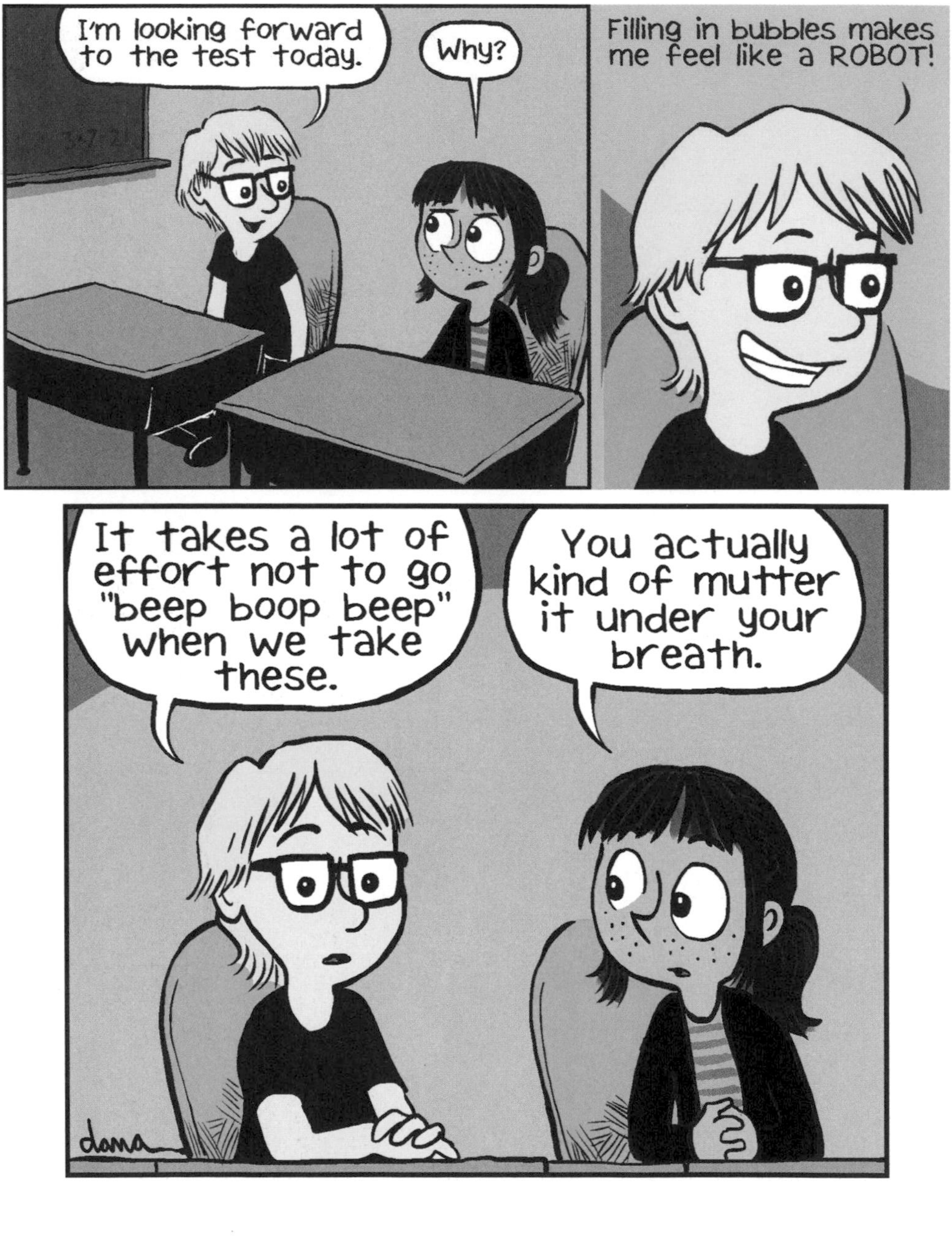
I'm looking forward to the test today.
Why?
Filling in bubbles makes me feel like a ROBOT!
It takes a lot of effort not to go "beep boop beep" when we take these.
You actually kind of mutter it under your breath.
dana

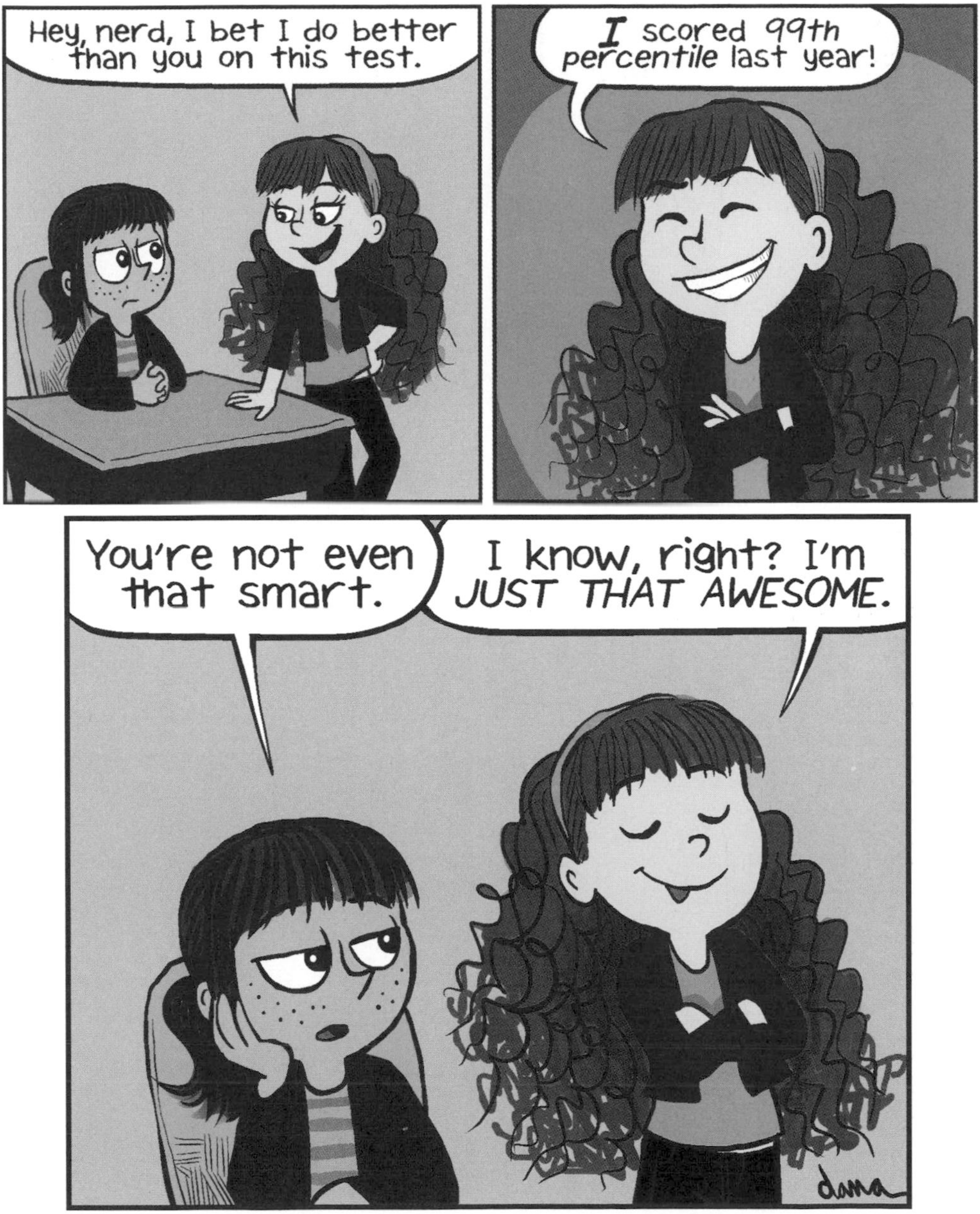
Hey, nerd, I bet I do better than you on this test.
I scored 99th percentile last year!
You're not even that smart.
I know, right? I'm JUST THAT AWESOME.
dana

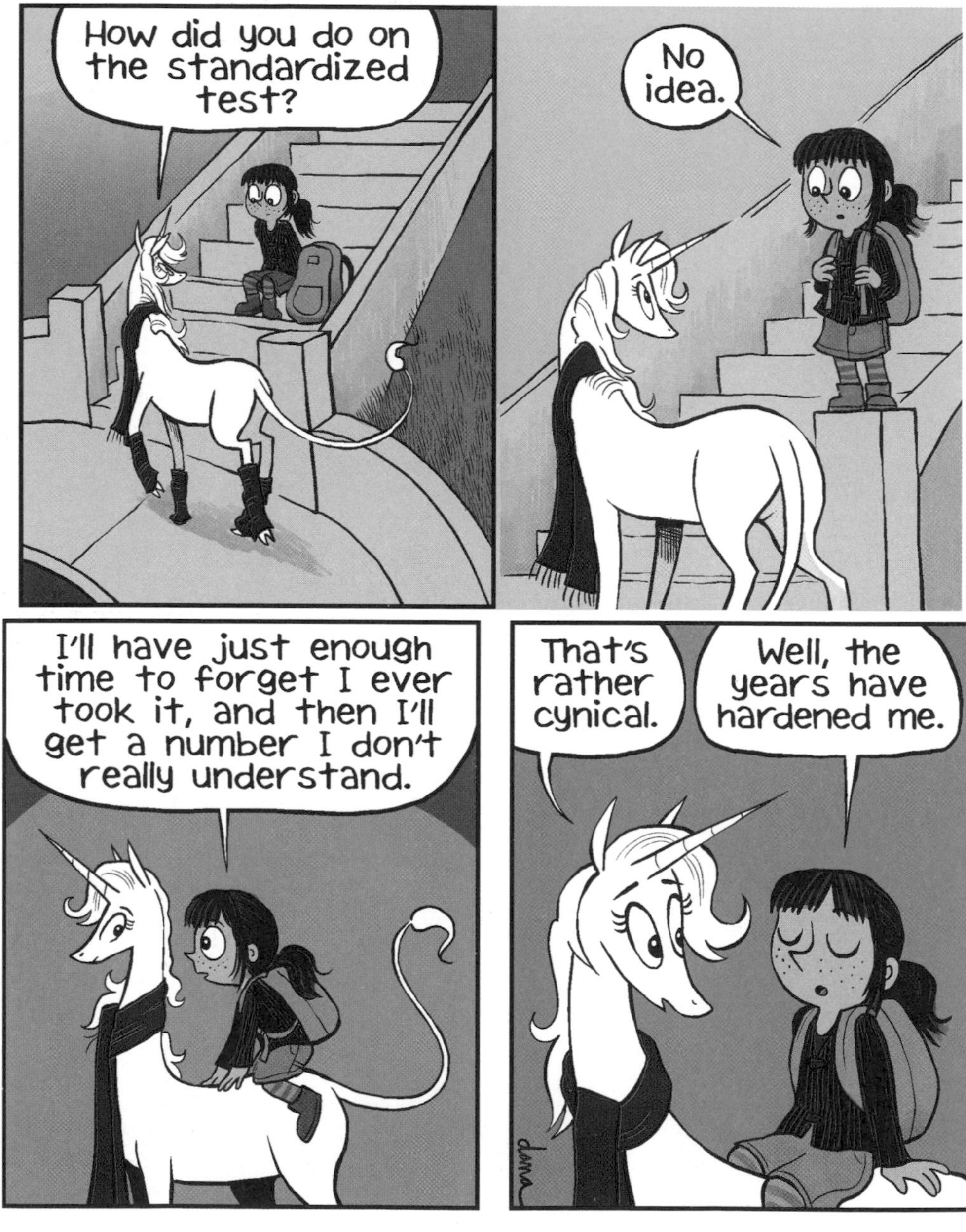
How did you do on the standardized test?
No idea.
I'll have just enough time to forget I ever took it, and then I'll get a number I don't really understand.
That's rather cynical.
Well, the years have hardened me.

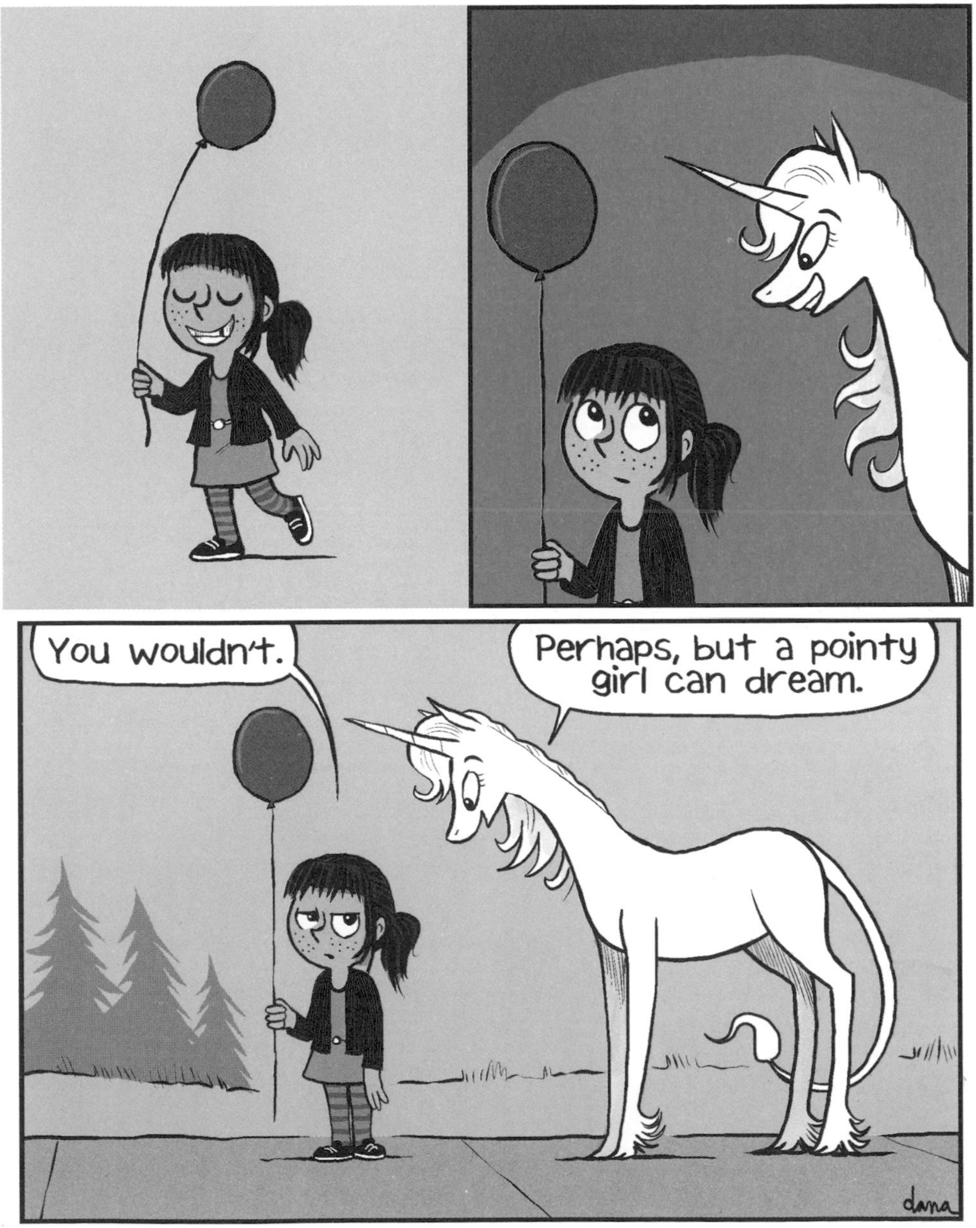
You wouldn't.
Perhaps, but a pointy girl can dream.
dana

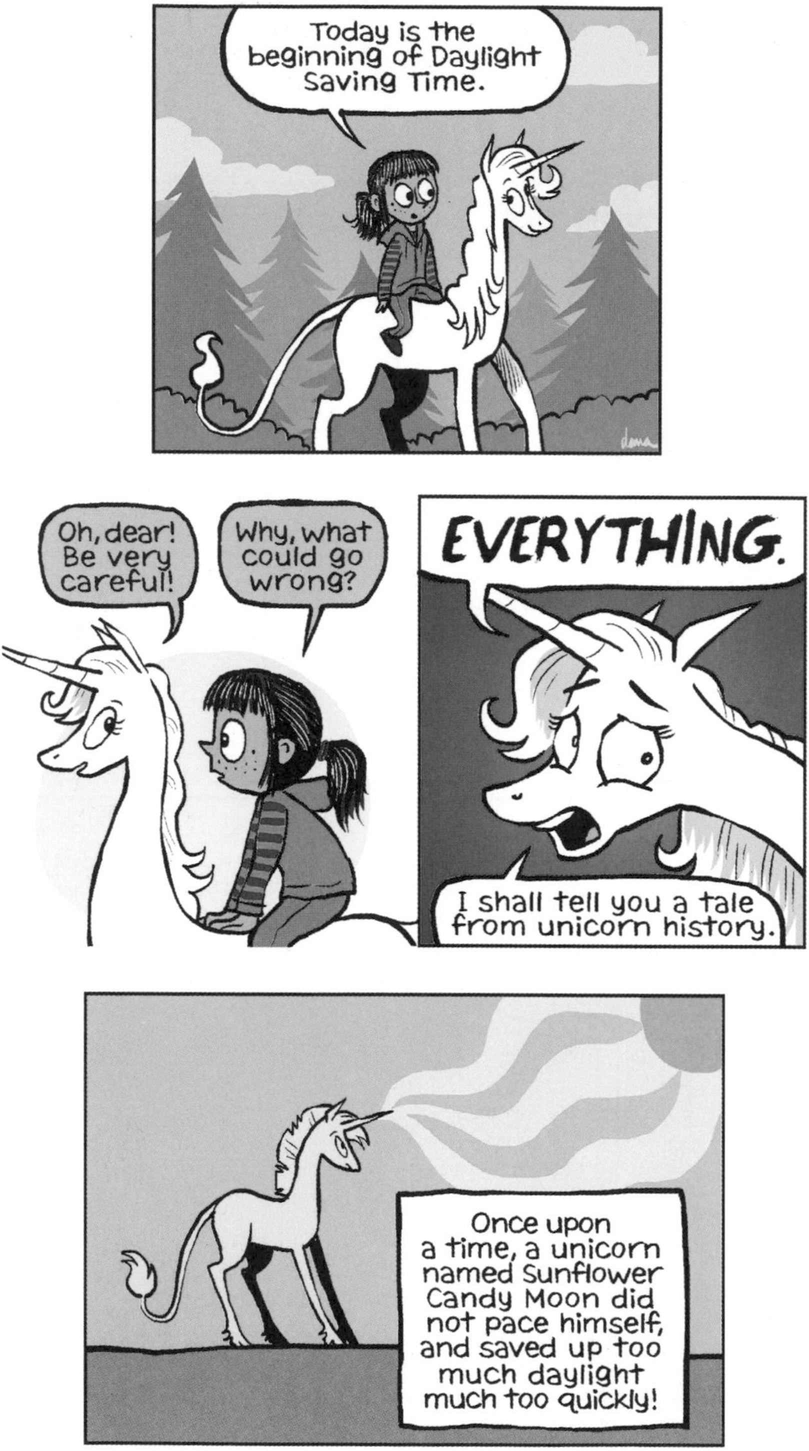
Today is the beginning of Daylight Saving Time.
Oh, dear! Be very careful!
Why, what could go wrong?
EVERYTHING.
I shall tell you a tale from unicorn history.
Once upon a time, a unicorn named Sunflower Candy Moon did not pace himself, and saved up too much daylight much too quickly!

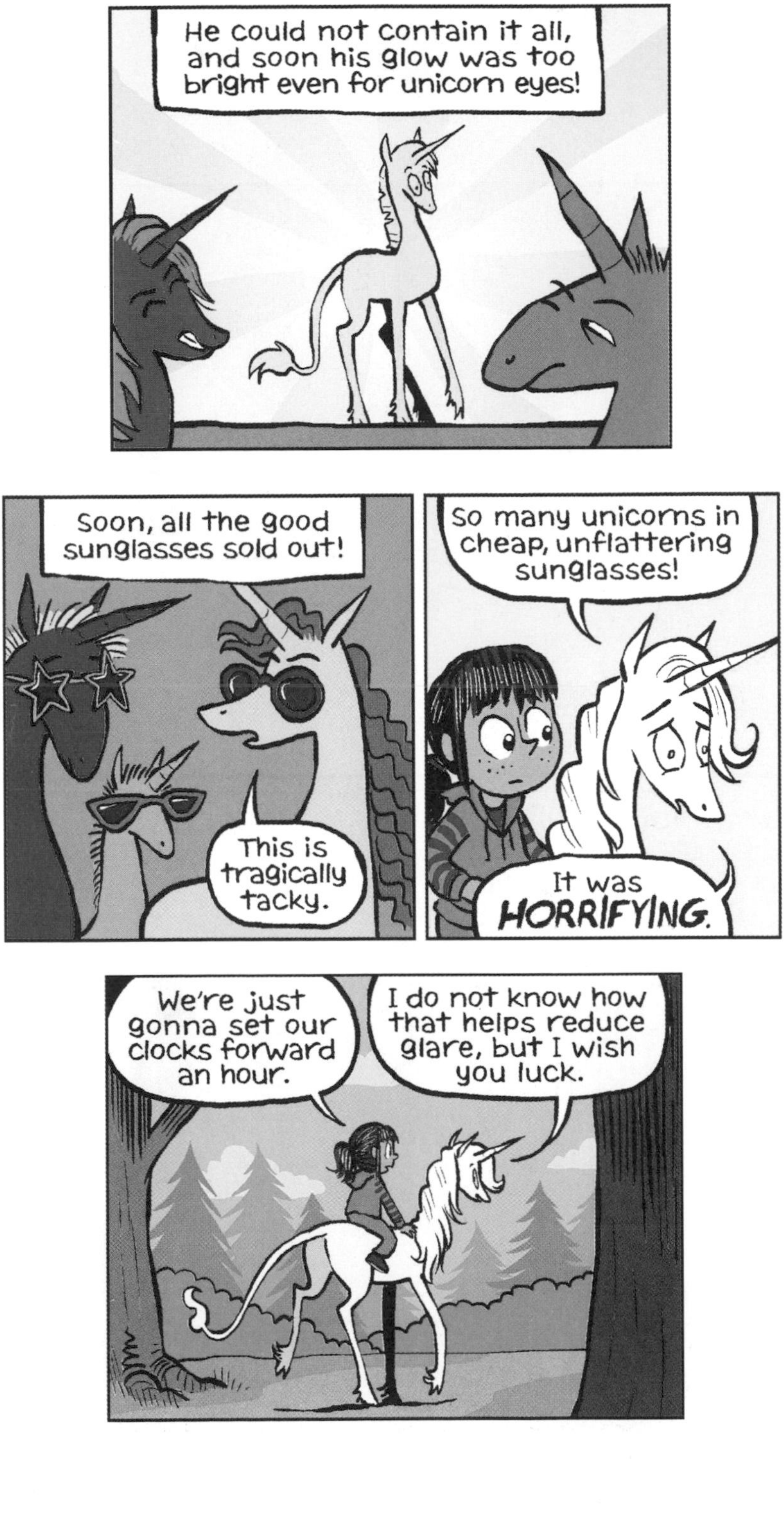
He could not contain it all, and soon his glow was too bright even for unicorn eyes!
Soon, all the good sunglasses sold out!
This is tragically tacky.
So many unicorns in cheap, unflattering sunglasses!
It was HORRIFYING.
We're just gonna set our clocks forward an hour.
I do not know how that helps reduce glare, but I wish you luck.

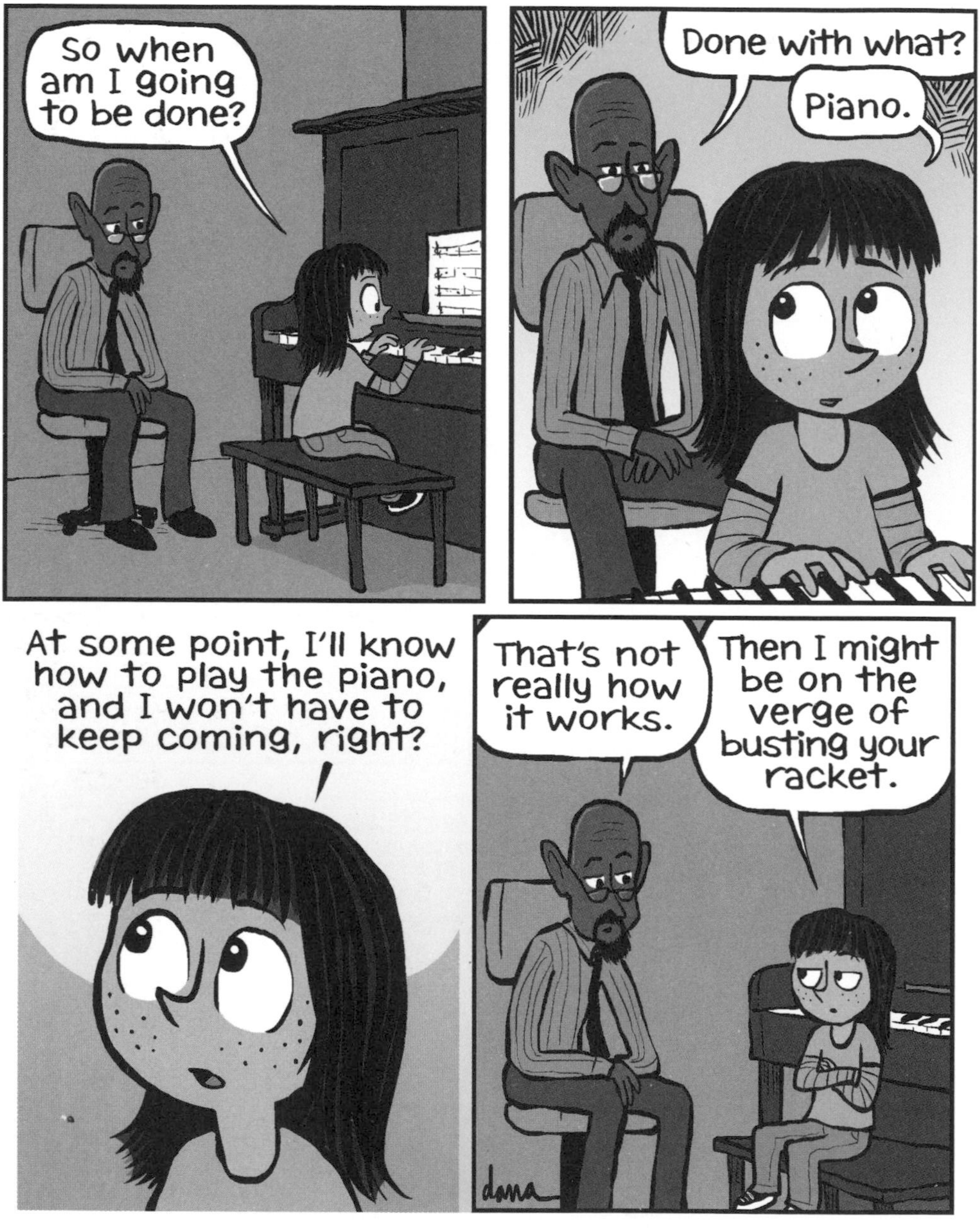
So when am I going to be done?
Done with what?
Piano.
At some point, I'll know how to play the piano, and I won't have to keep coming, right?
That's not really how it works.
Then I might be on the verge of busting your racket.
dana

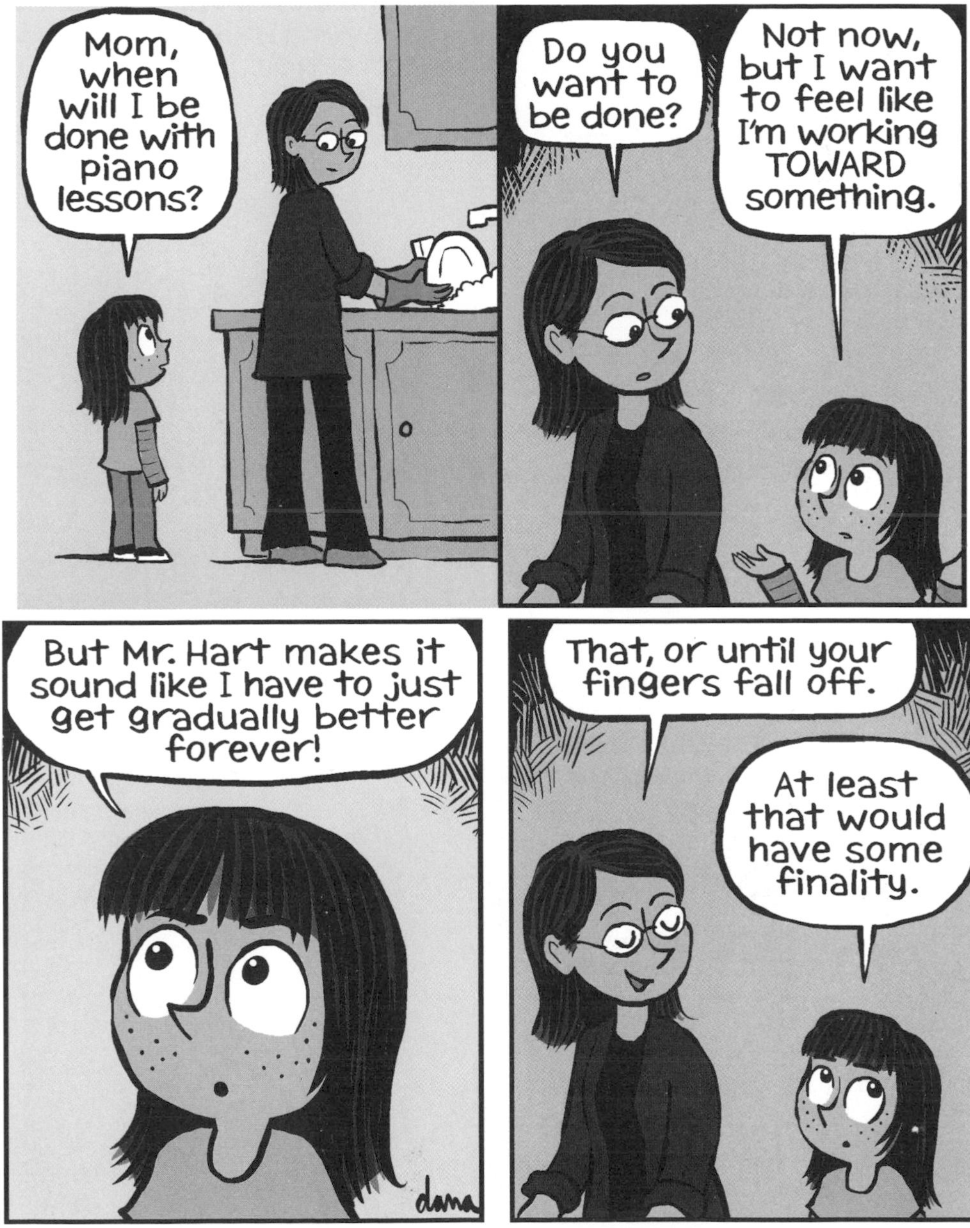
Mom, when will I be done with piano lessons?
Do you want to be done?
Not now, but I want to feel like I'm working TOWARD something.
But Mr. Hart makes it sound like I have to just get gradually better forever!
dana
That, or until your fingers fall off.
At least that would have some finality.

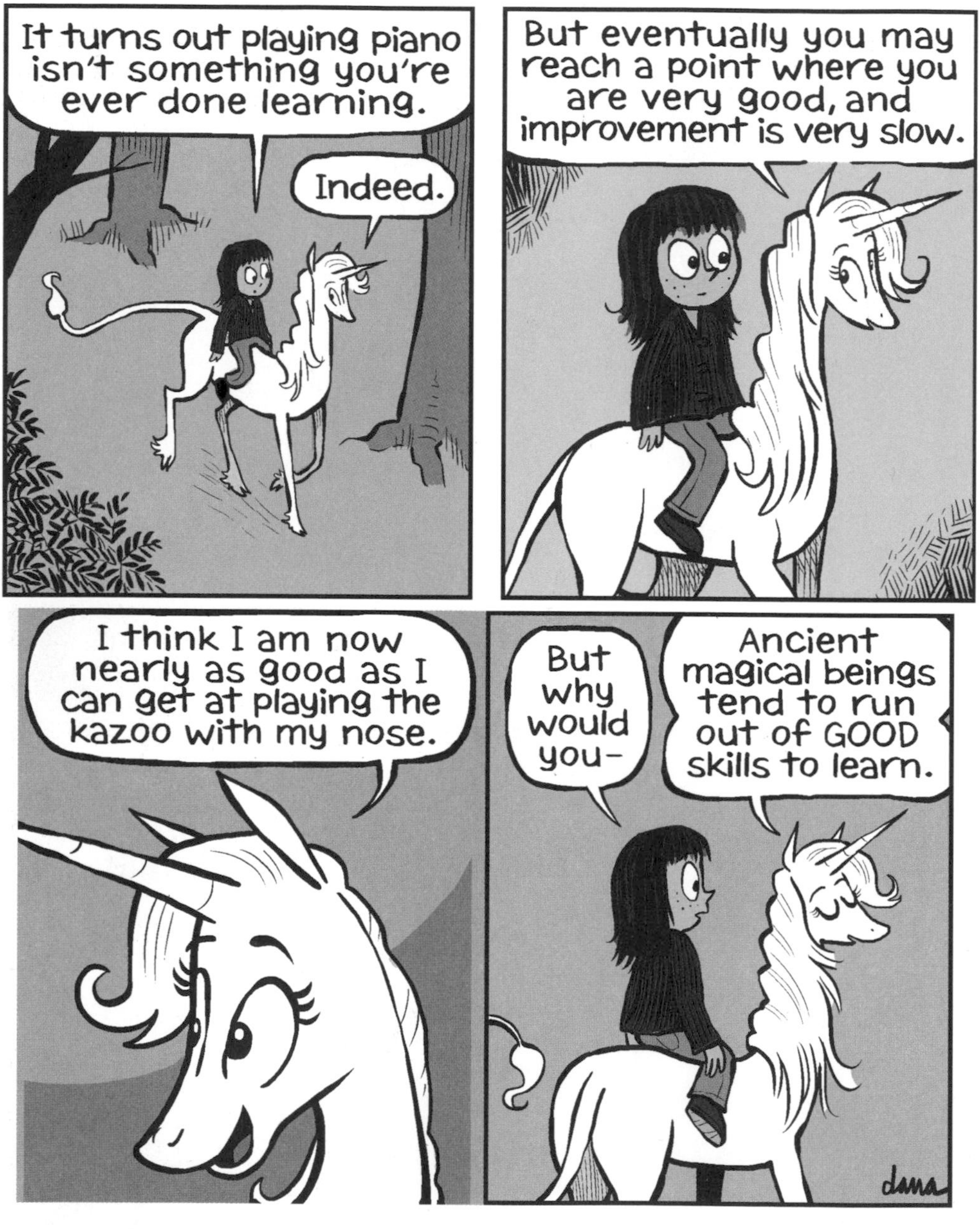
It turns out playing piano isn't something you're ever done learning.
Indeed.
But eventually you may reach a point where you are very good, and improvement is very slow.
I think I am now nearly as good as I can get at playing the kazoo with my nose.
But why would you-
Ancient magical beings tend to run out of GOOD skills to learn.
dana

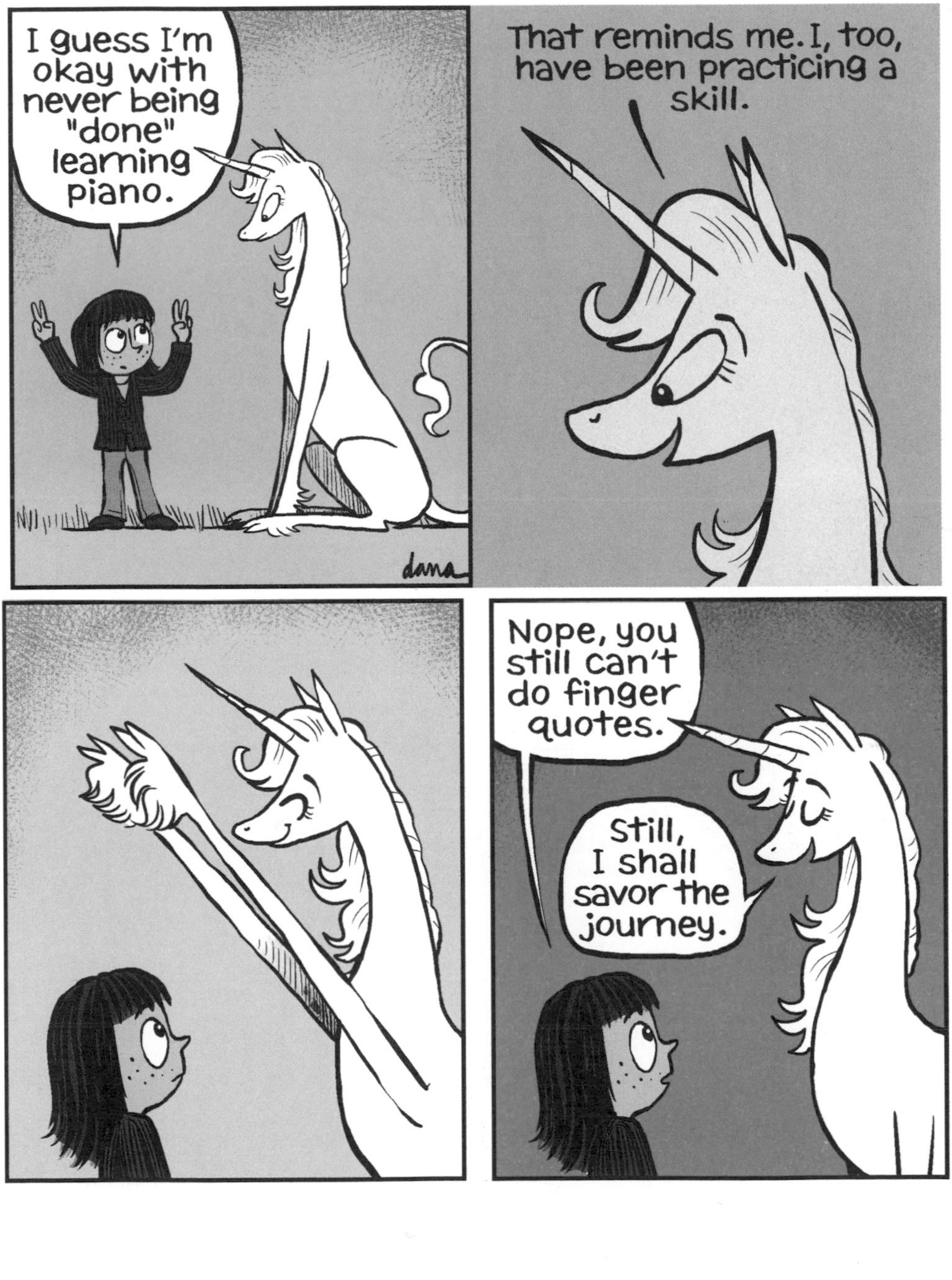
I guess I'm okay with never being "done" learning piano.
dana
That reminds me. I, too, have been practicing a skill.
Nope, you still can't do finger quotes.
Still, I shall savor the journey.

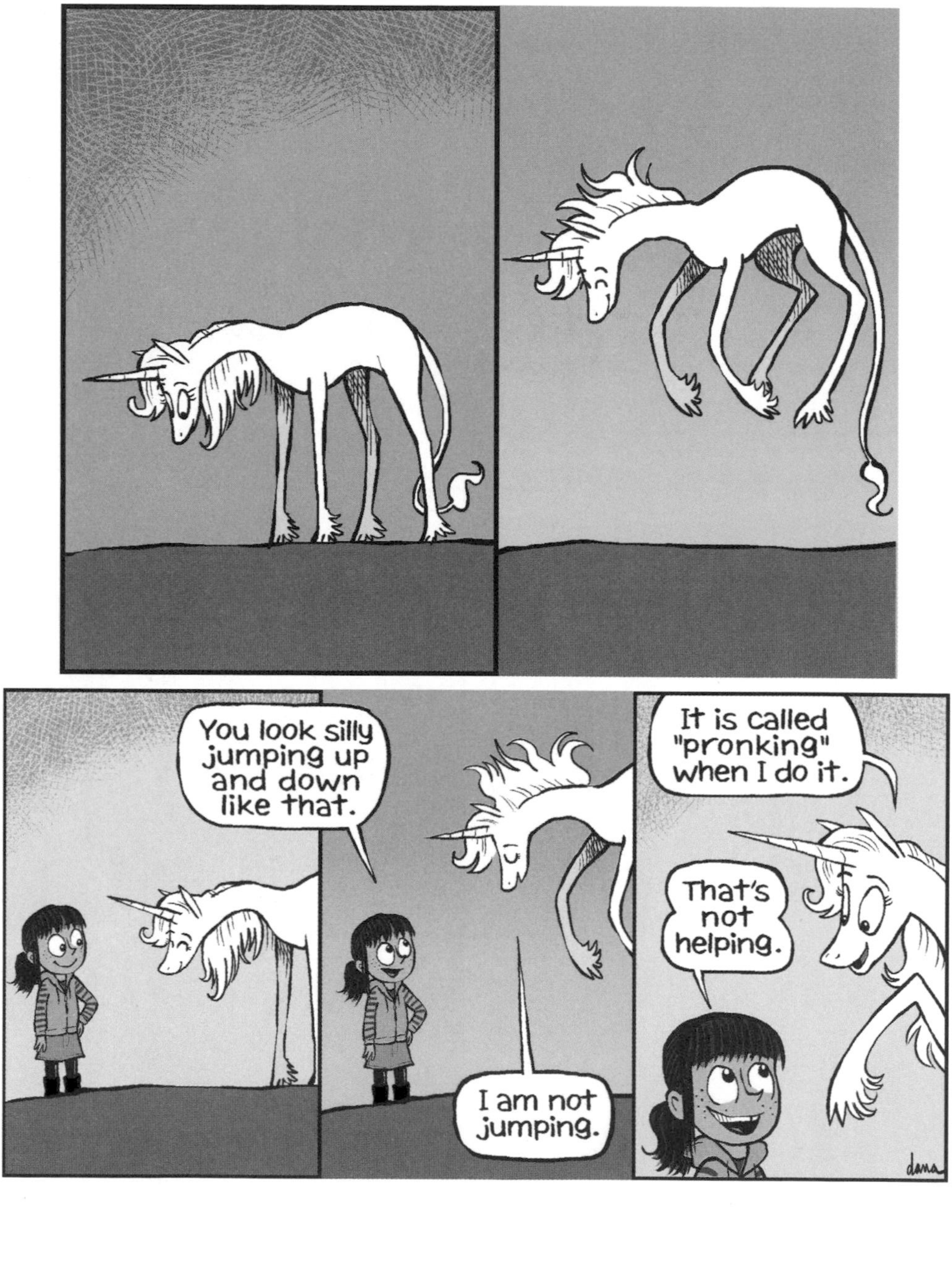
You look silly jumping up and down like that.
I am not jumping.
It is called "pronking" when I do it.
That's not helping.

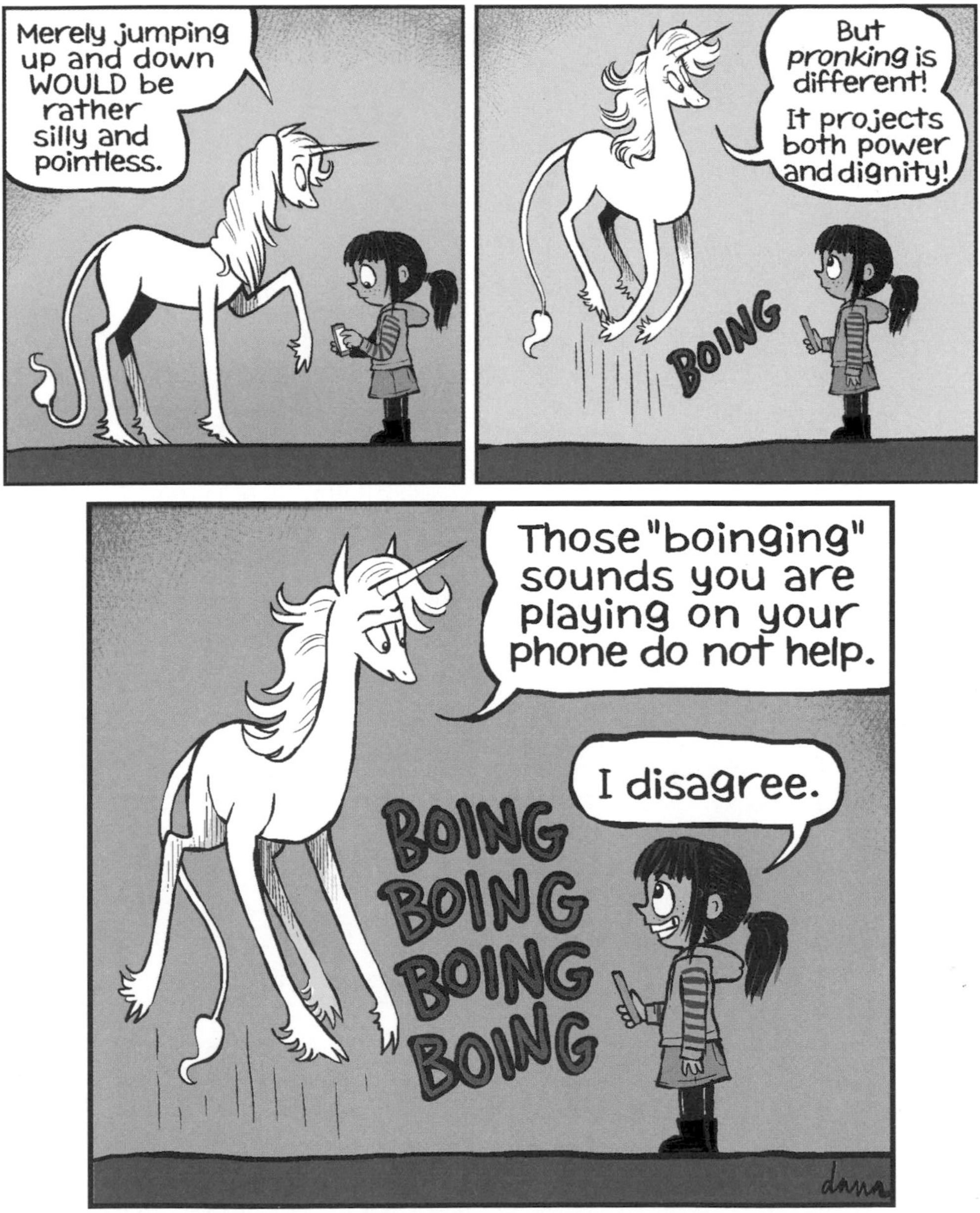

Merely jumping up and down WOULD be rather silly and pointless.
But *pronking* is different!
It projects both power and dignity!
BOING
Those "boinging" sounds you are playing on your phone do not help.
I disagree.
BOING BOING BOING BOING
dana

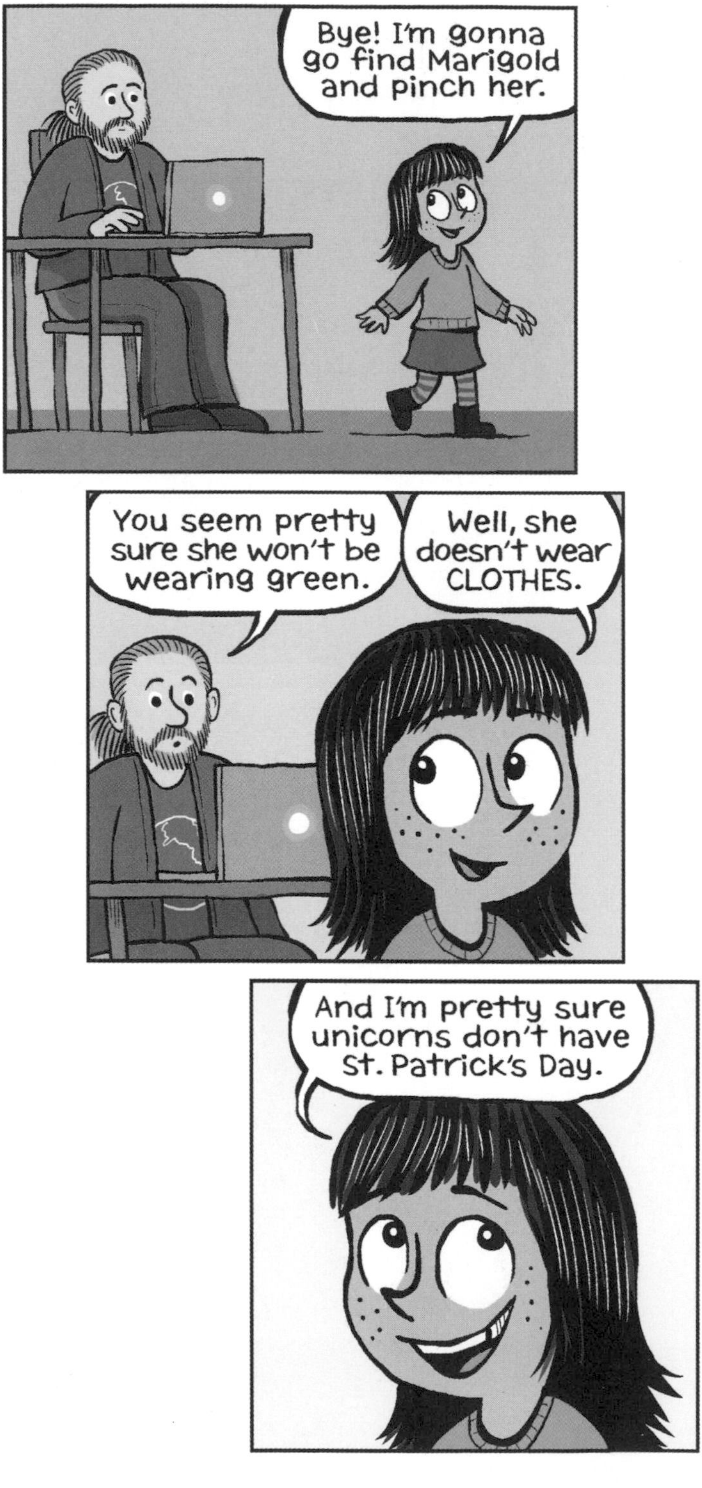
Bye! I'm gonna go find Marigold and pinch her.
You seem pretty sure she won't be wearing green.
Well, she doesn't wear CLOTHES.
And I'm pretty sure unicorns don't have St. Patrick's Day.

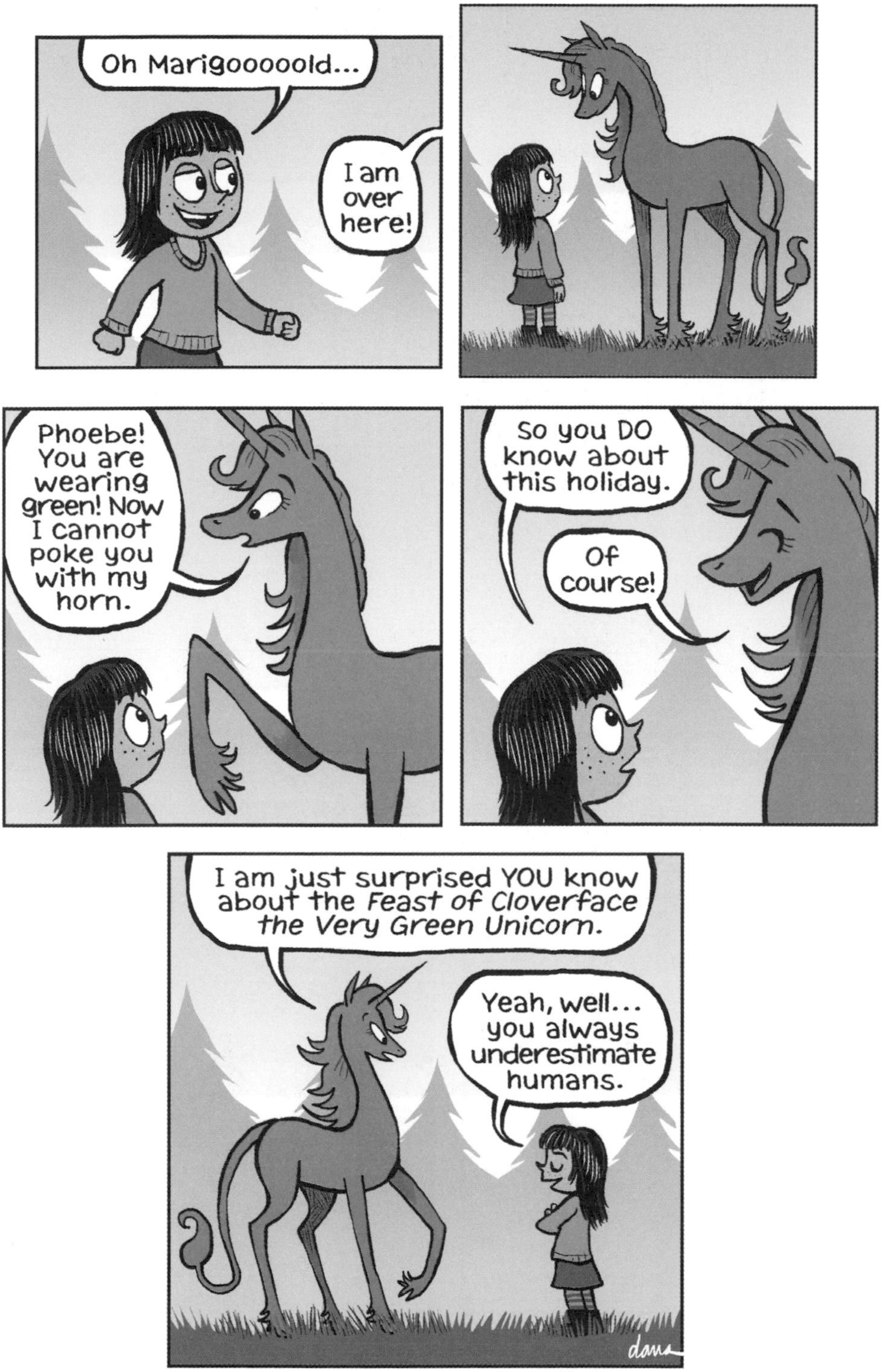
Oh Marigoooold...
I am over here!
Phoebe! You are wearing green! Now I cannot poke you with my horn.
So you DO know about this holiday.
Of course!
I am just surprised YOU know about the *Feast of Cloverface the Very Green Unicorn.*
Yeah, well... you always underestimate humans.
dana

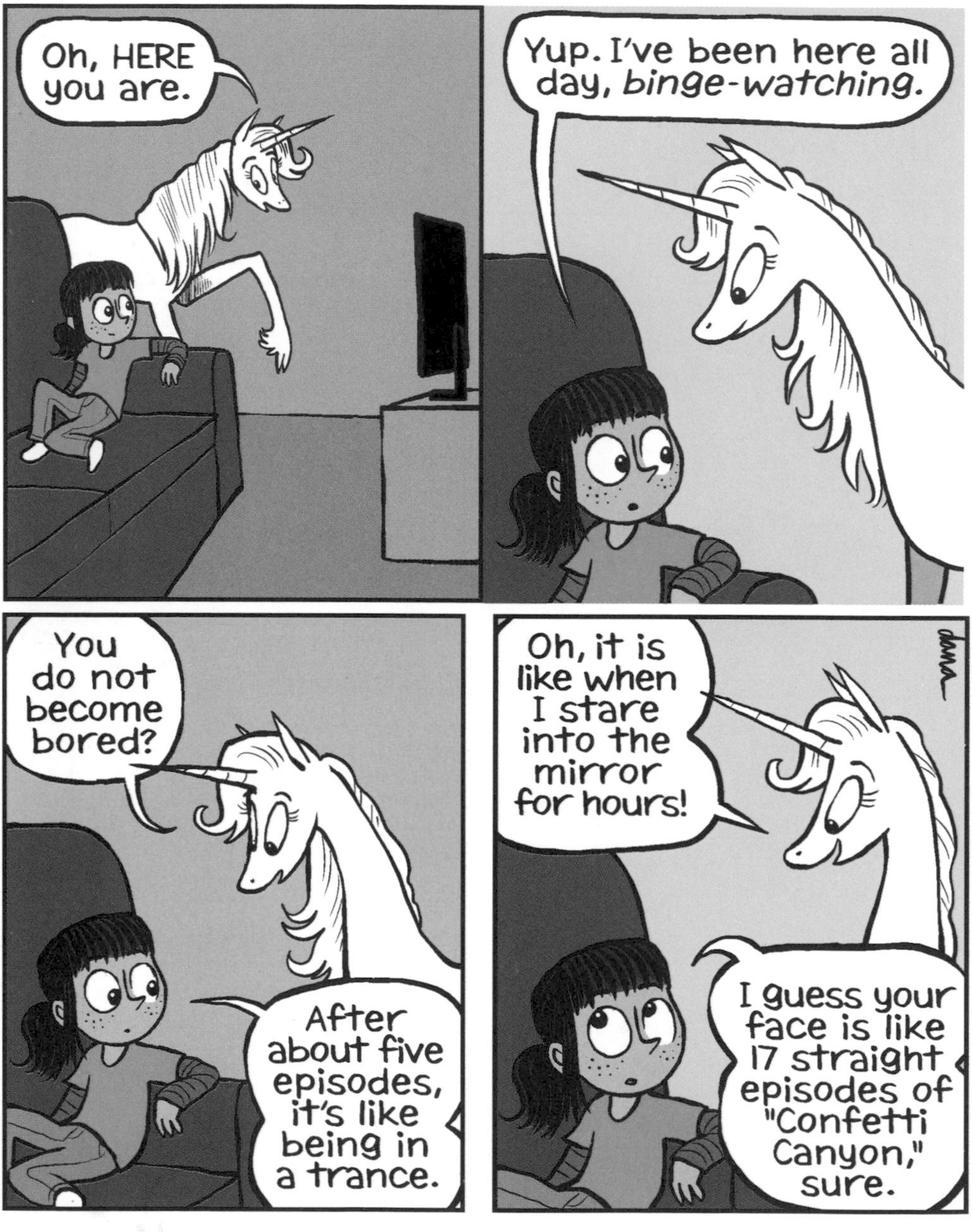
Oh, HERE you are.
Yup. I've been here all day, *binge-watching.*
You do not become bored?
After about five episodes, it's like being in a trance.
Oh, it is like when I stare into the mirror for hours!
I guess your face is like 17 straight episodes of "Confetti Canyon," sure.

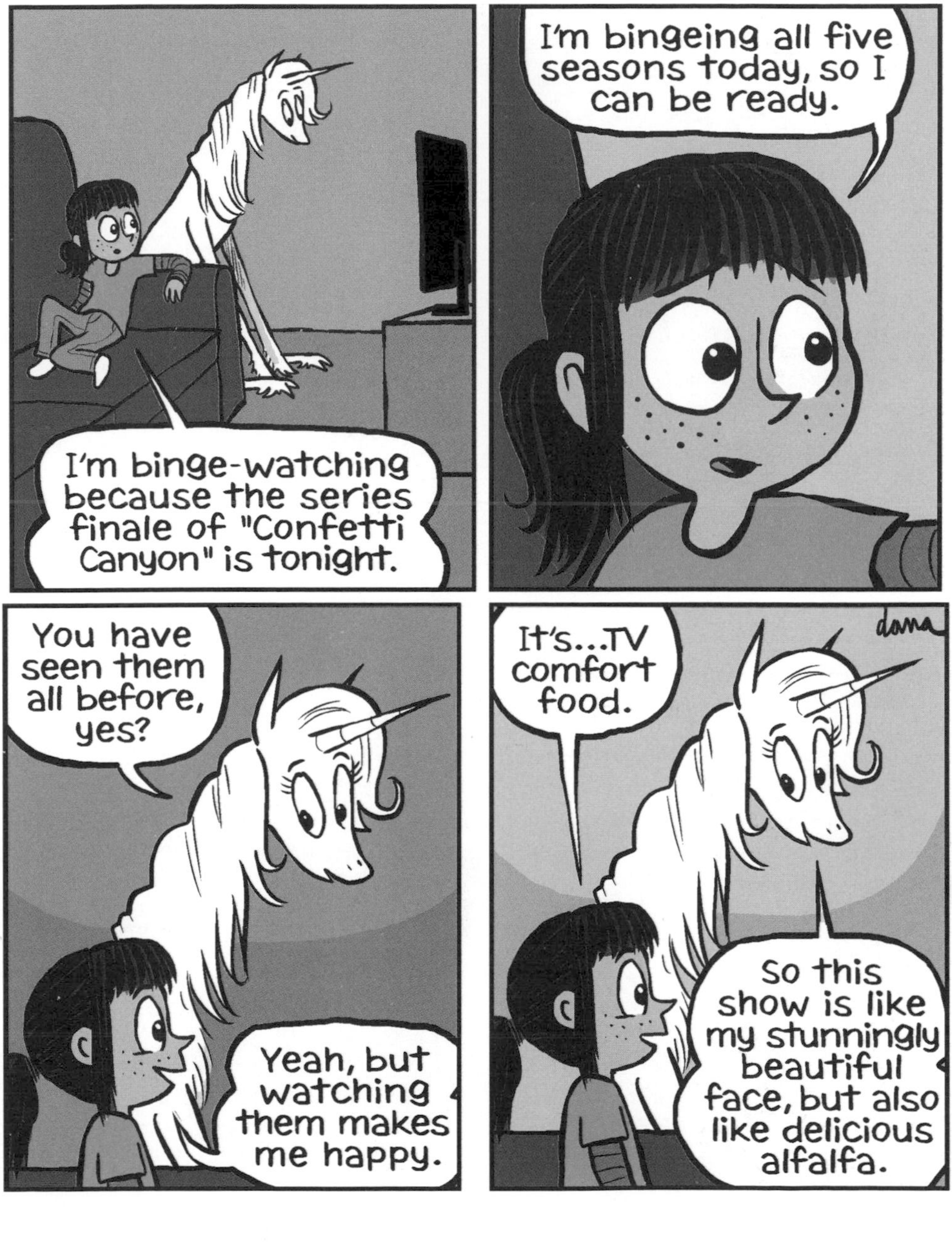
I'm binge-watching because the series finale of "Confetti Canyon" is tonight.
I'm bingeing all five seasons today, so I can be ready.
You have seen them all before, yes?
Yeah, but watching them makes me happy.
It's...TV comfort food.
So this show is like my stunningly beautiful face, but also like delicious alfalfa.
dana

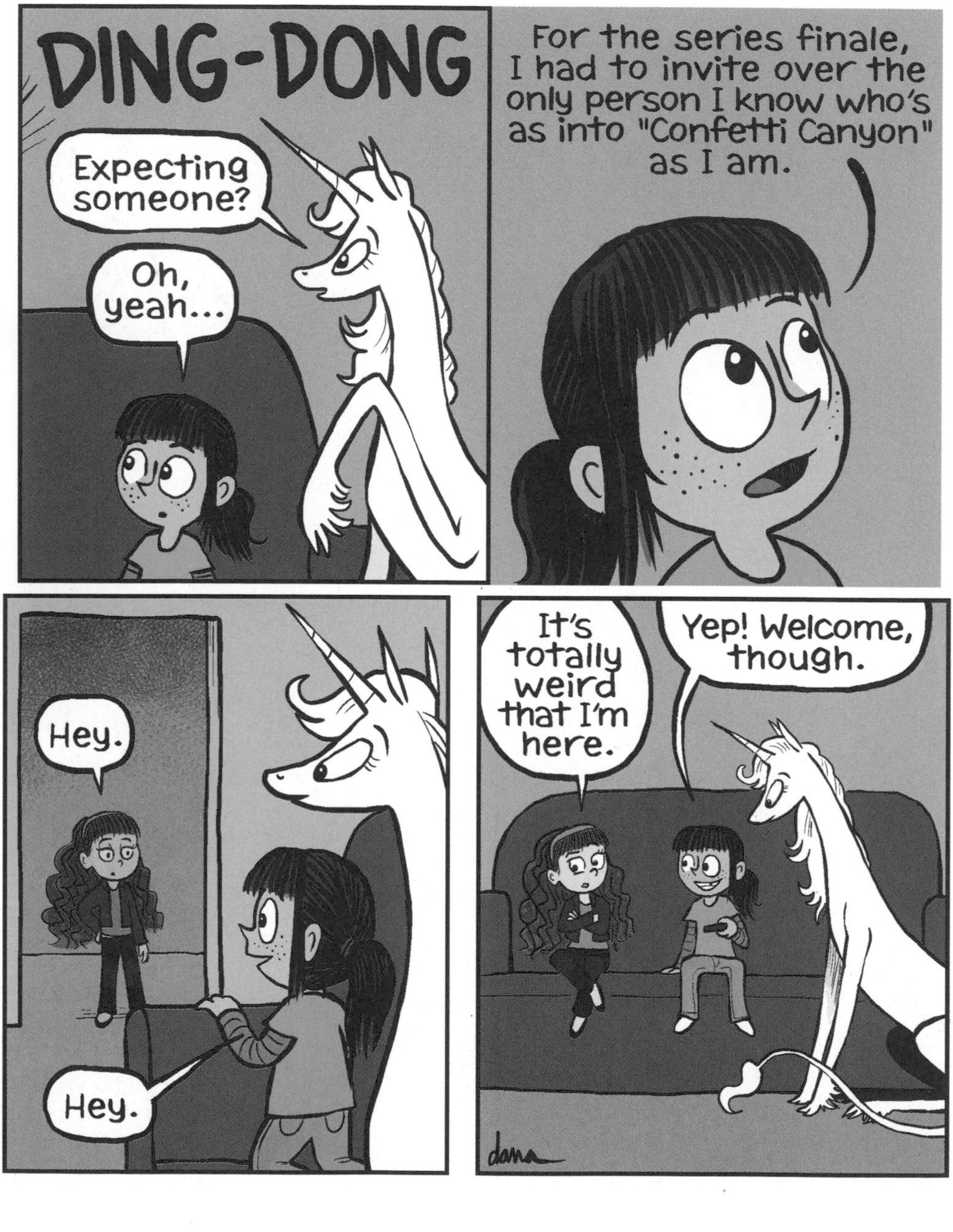
DING-DONG
Expecting someone?
Oh, yeah...
For the series finale, I had to invite over the only person I know who's as into "Confetti Canyon" as I am.
Hey.
Hey.
It's totally weird that I'm here.
Yep! Welcome, though.
dana

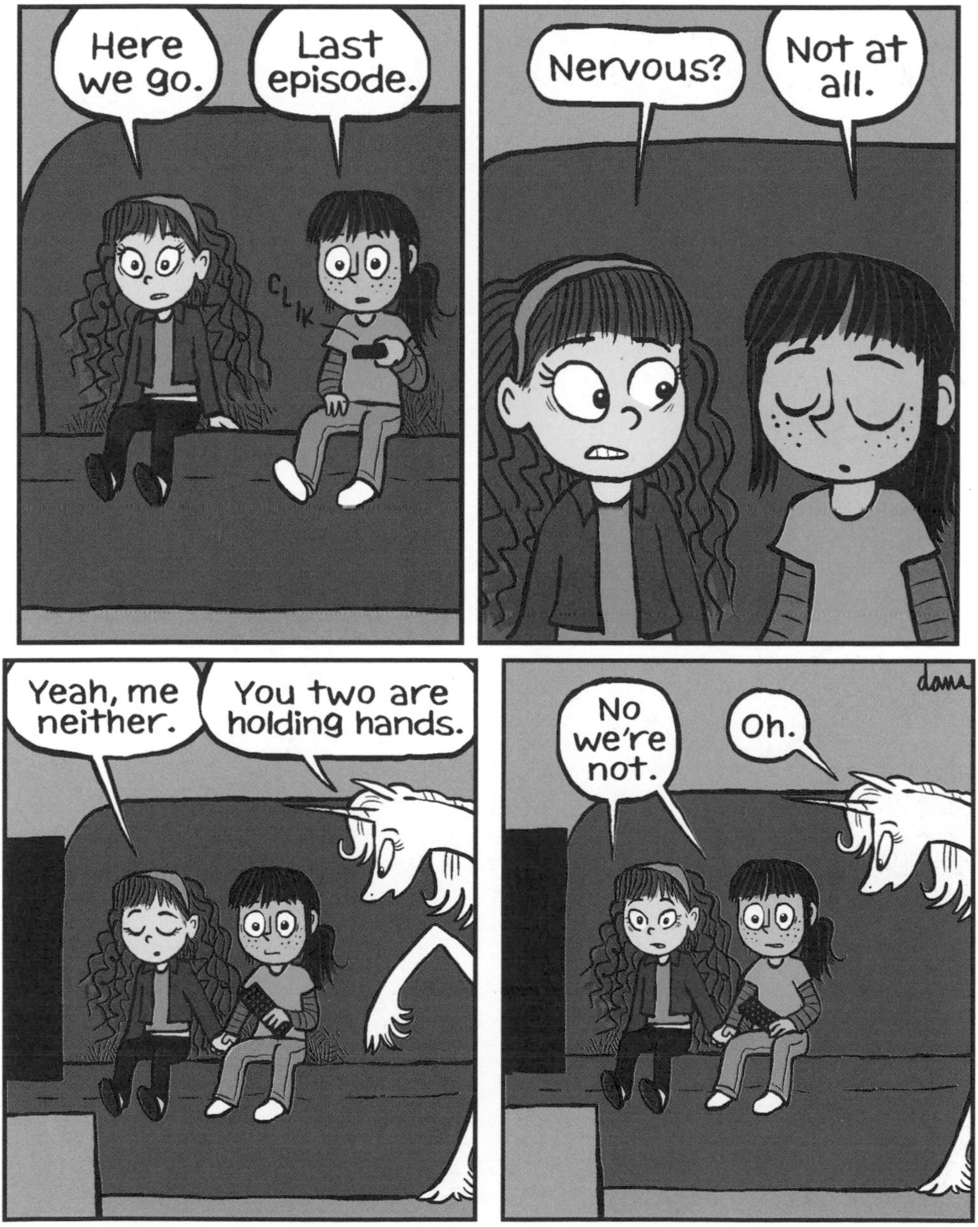
Here we go.
Last episode.
CLIK
Nervous?
Not at all.
Yeah, me neither.
You two are holding hands.
No we're not.
Oh.
dana

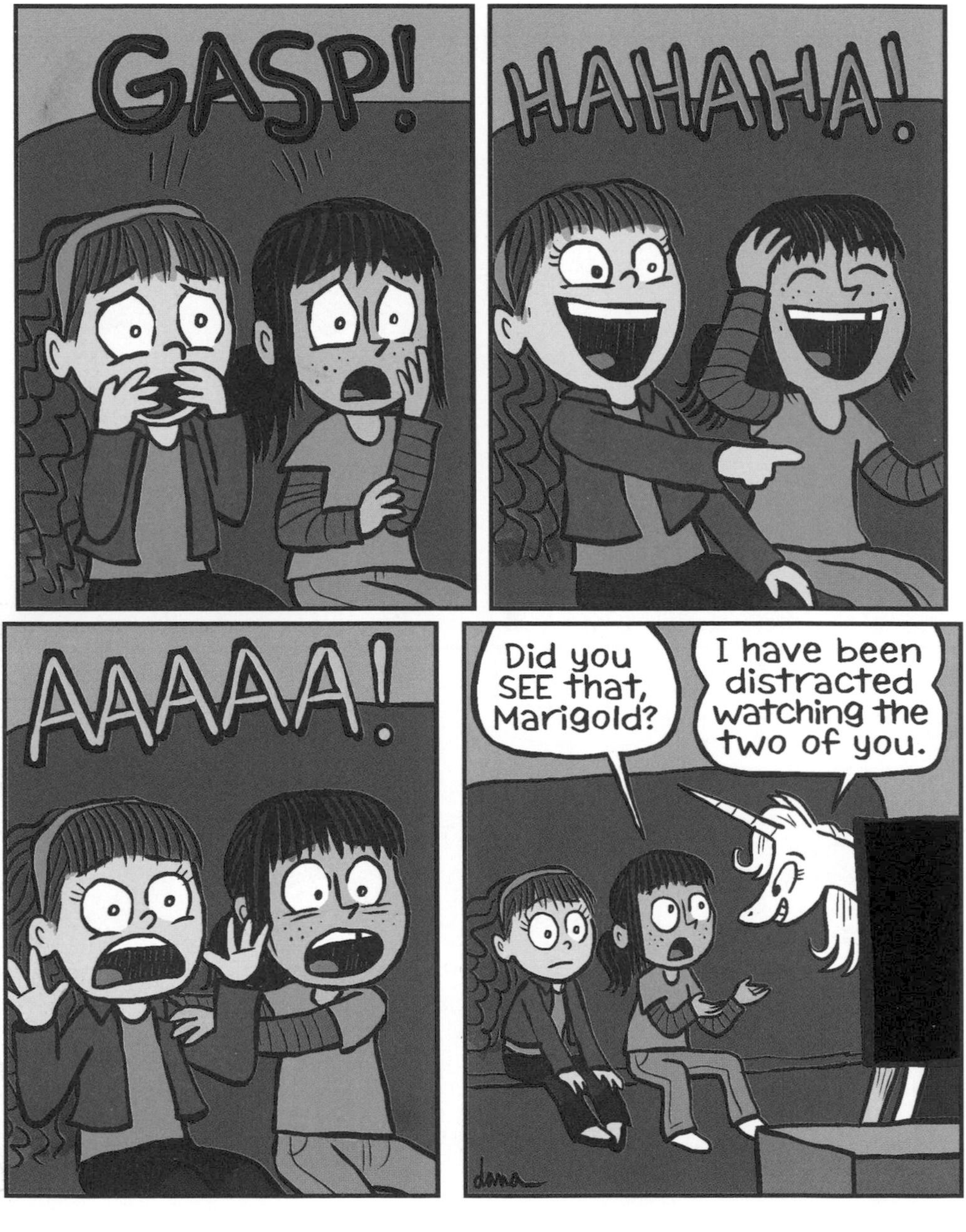
GASP!
HAHAHA!
AAAAA!
Did you SEE that, Marigold?
I have been distracted watching the two of you.
dana

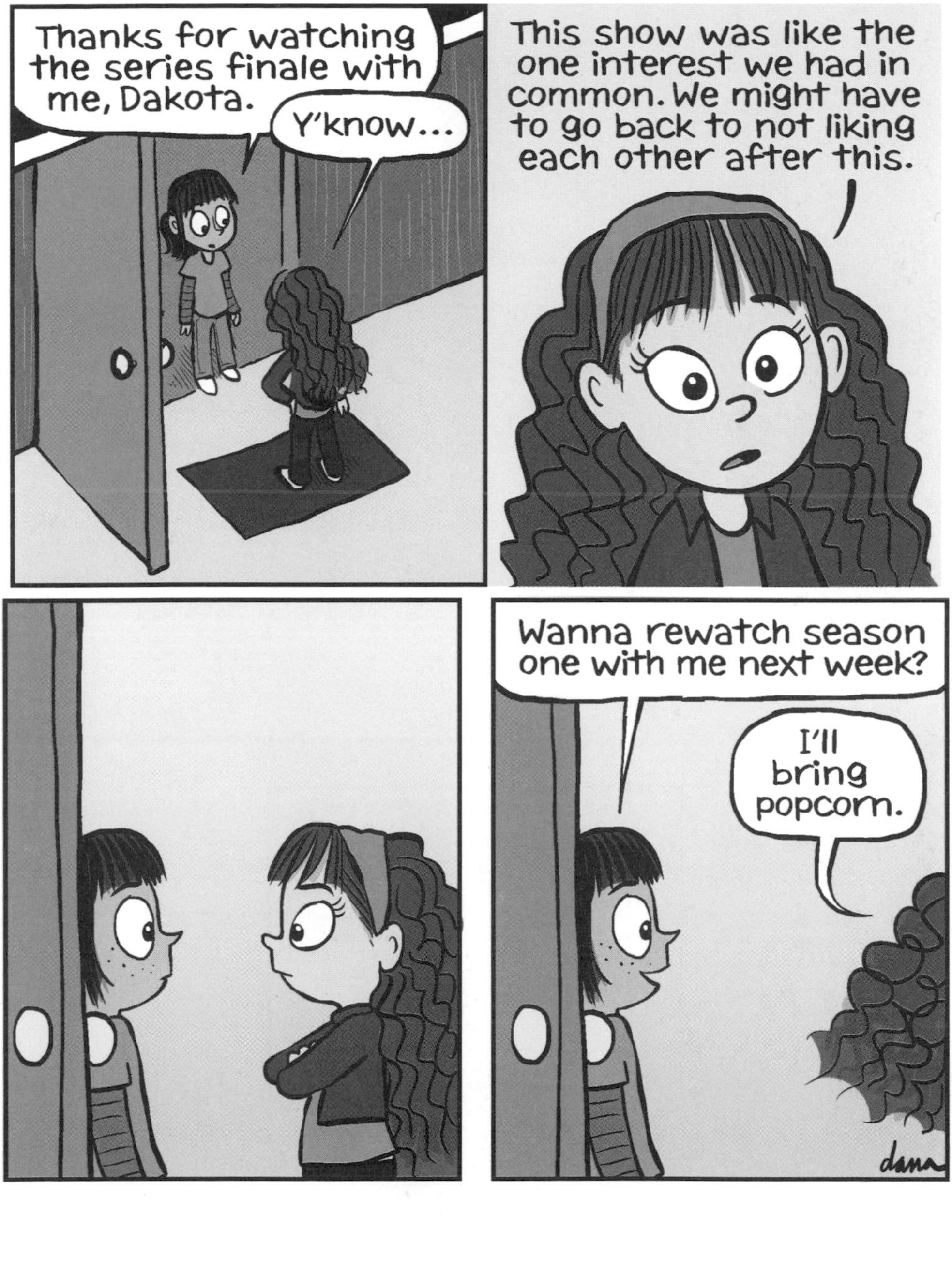
Thanks for watching the series finale with me, Dakota.
Y'know...
This show was like the one interest we had in common. We might have to go back to not liking each other after this.
Wanna rewatch season one with me next week?
I'll bring popcorn.
dana

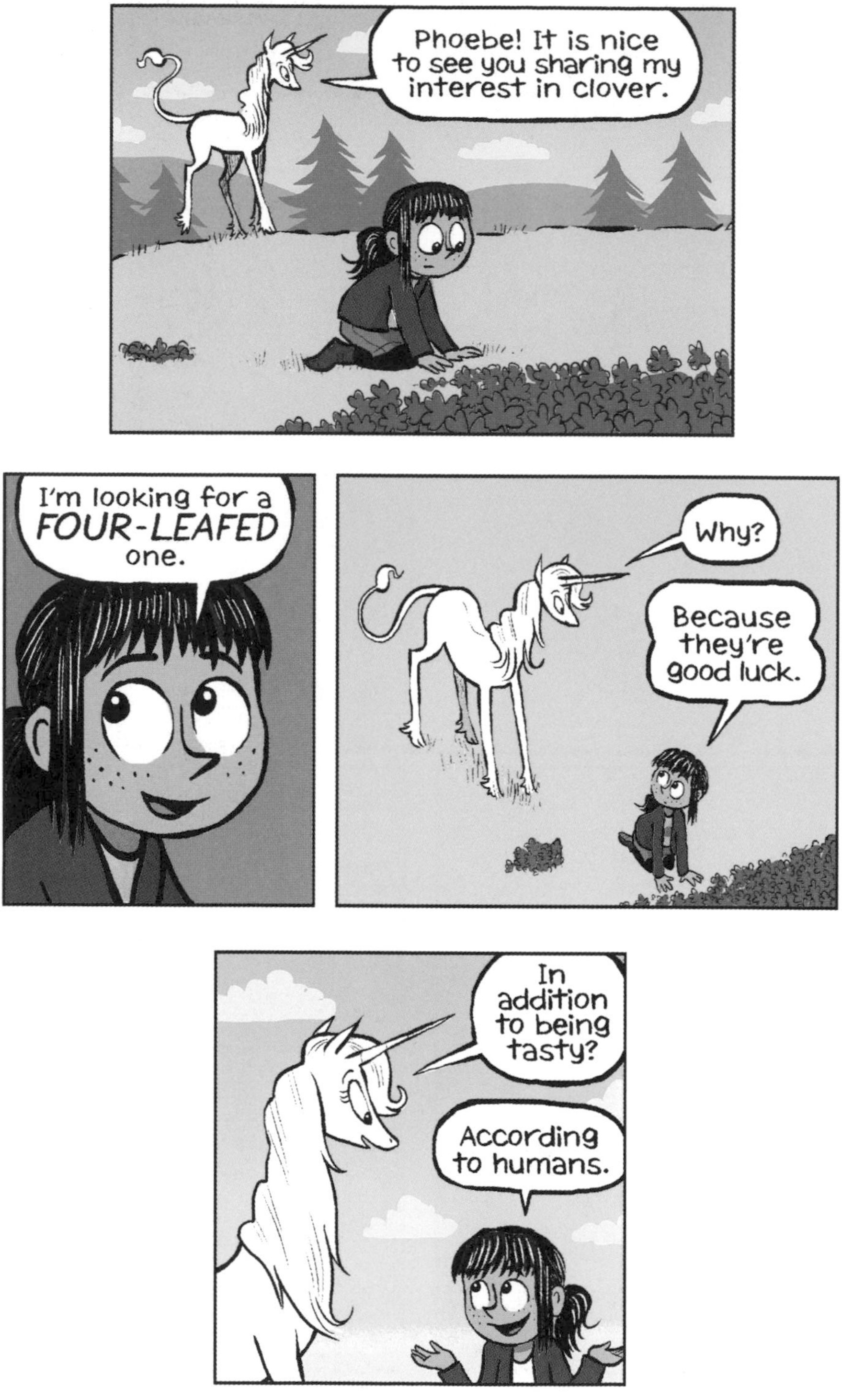
Phoebe! It is nice to see you sharing my interest in clover.
I'm looking for a FOUR-LEAFED one.
Why?
Because they're good luck.
In addition to being tasty?
According to humans.

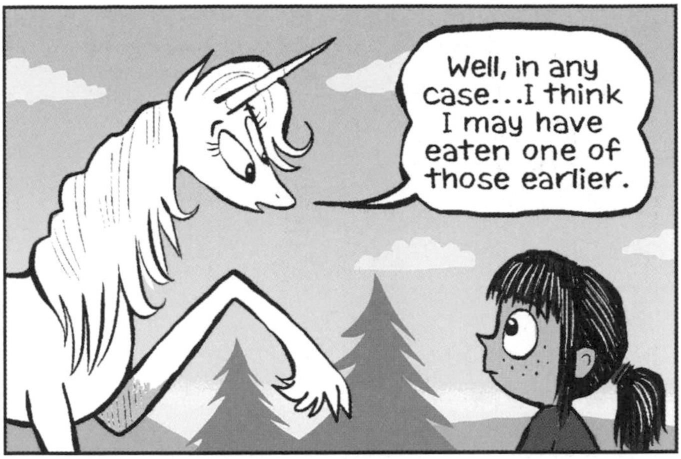
Well, in any case...I think I may have eaten one of those earlier.

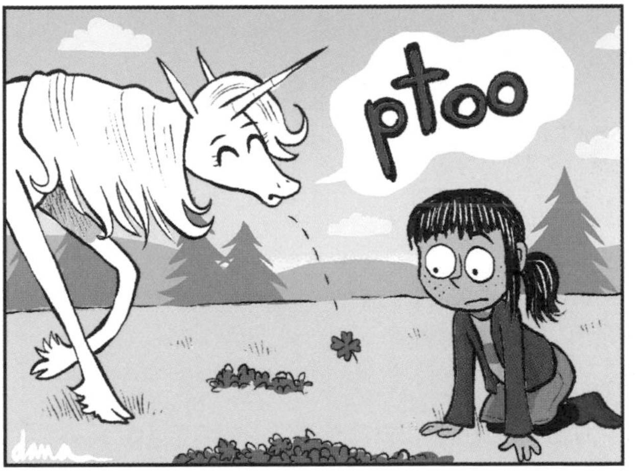
ptoo

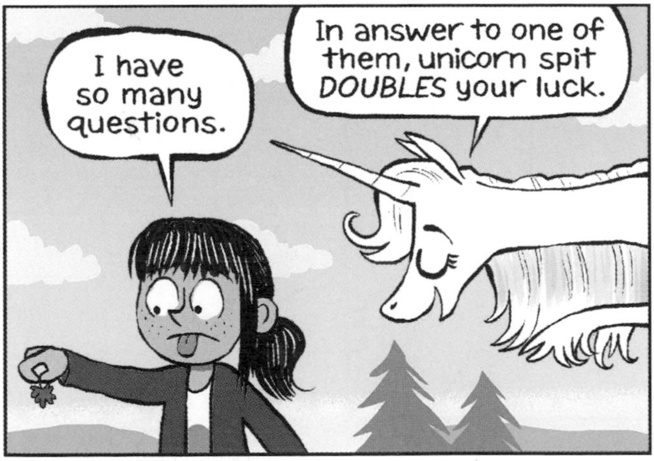
I have so many questions.
In answer to one of them, unicorn spit *DOUBLES* your luck.

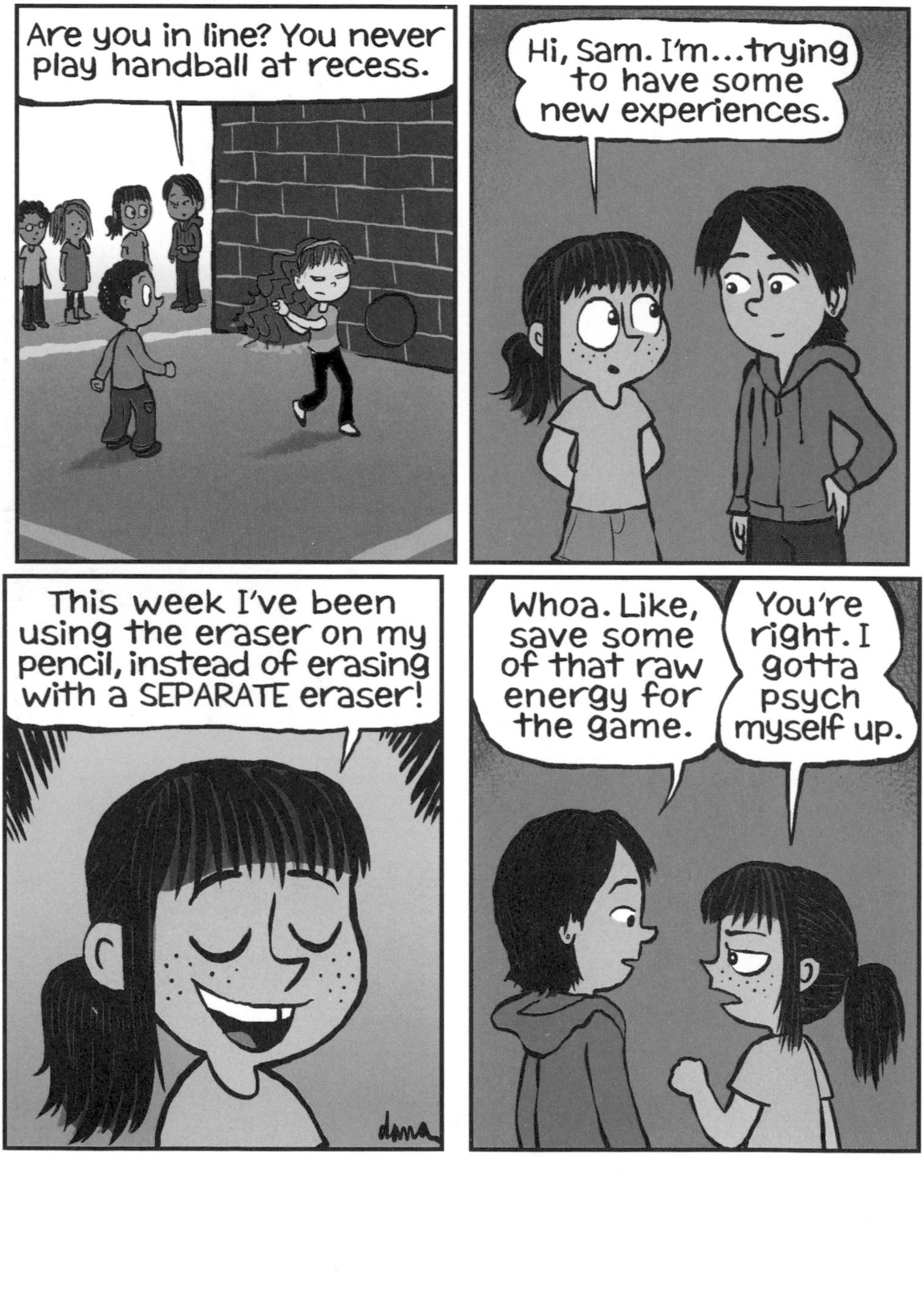
Are you in line? You never play handball at recess.
Hi, Sam. I'm...trying to have some new experiences.
This week I've been using the eraser on my pencil, instead of erasing with a SEPARATE eraser!
Whoa. Like, save some of that raw energy for the game.
You're right. I gotta psych myself up.

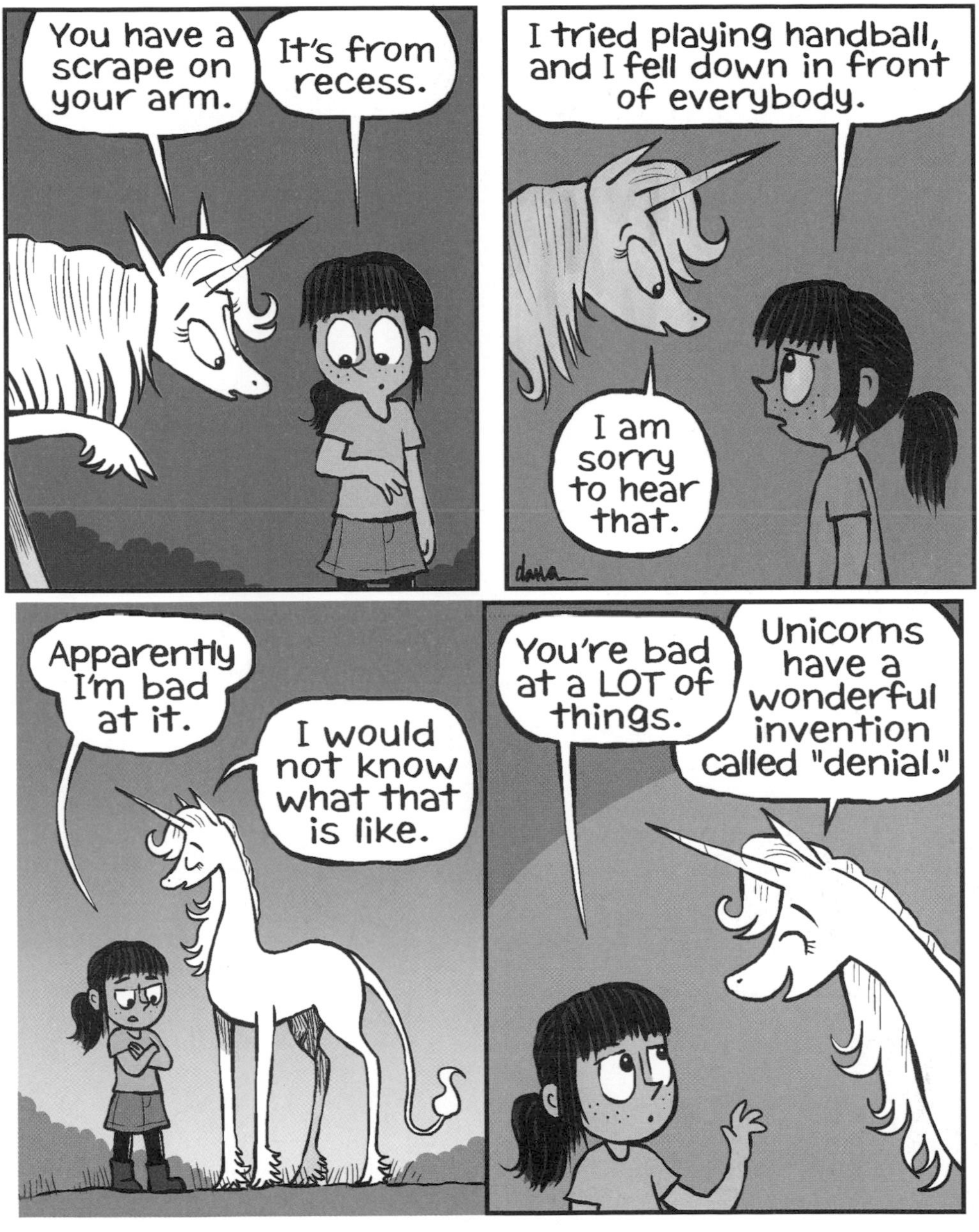
You have a scrape on your arm.
It's from recess.
I tried playing handball, and I fell down in front of everybody.
I am sorry to hear that.
dana
Apparently I'm bad at it.
I would not know what that is like.
You're bad at a LOT of things.
Unicorns have a wonderful invention called "denial."

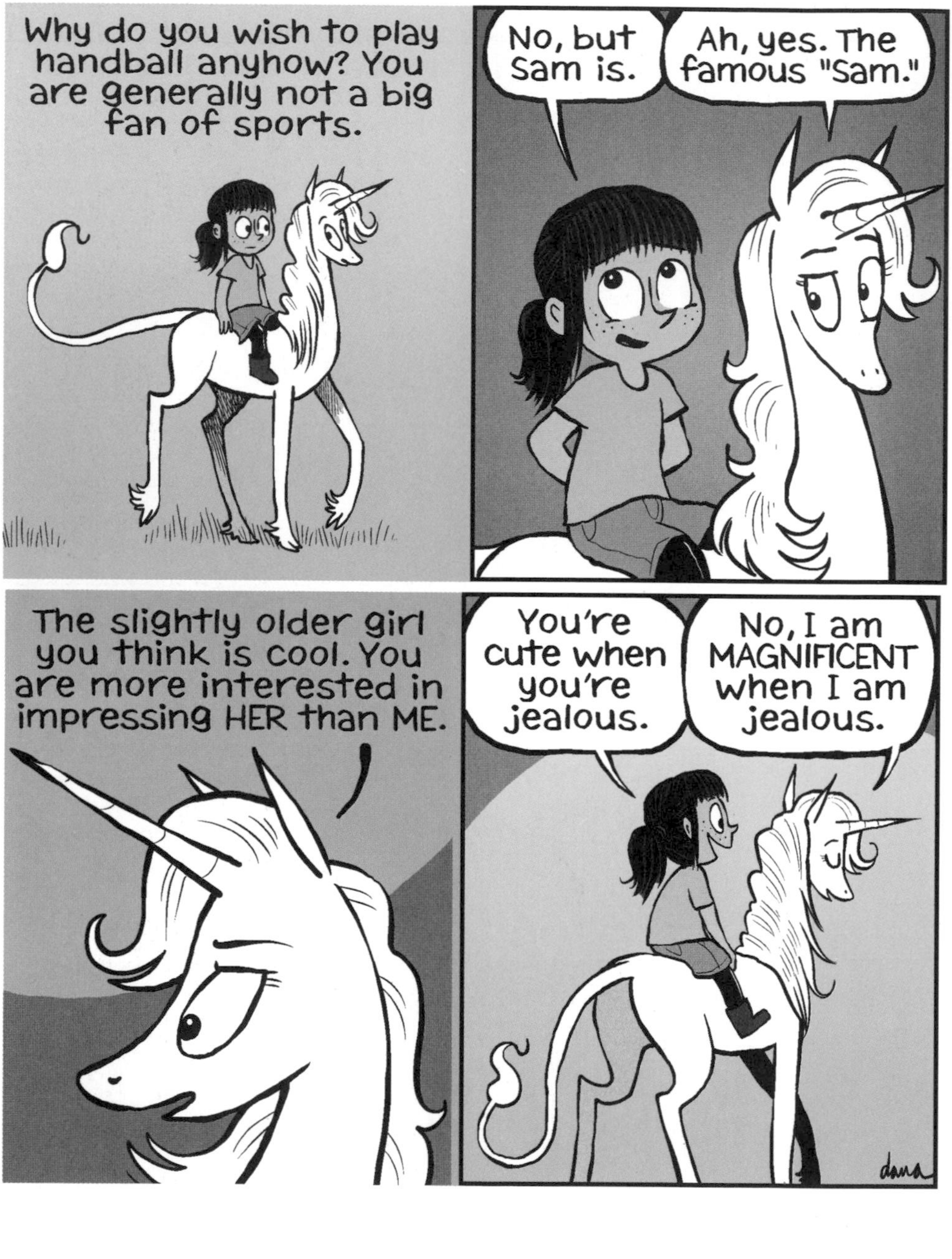
Why do you wish to play handball anyhow? You are generally not a big fan of sports.
No, but Sam is.
Ah, yes. The famous "Sam."
The slightly older girl you think is cool. You are more interested in impressing HER than ME.
You're cute when you're jealous.
No, I am MAGNIFICENT when I am jealous.
dana

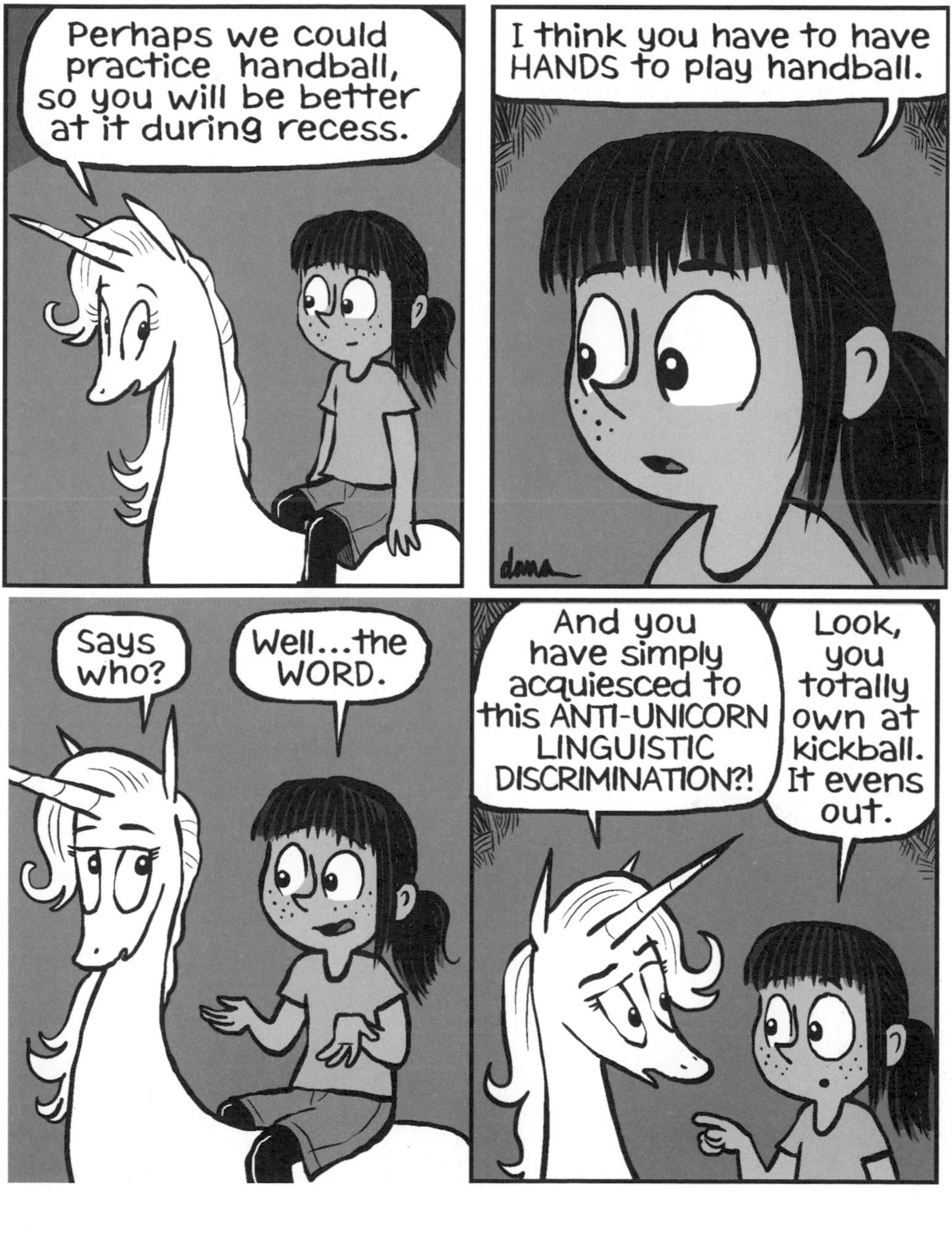
Perhaps we could practice handball, so you will be better at it during recess.
I think you have to have HANDS to play handball.
dana
Says who?
Well...the WORD.
And you have simply acquiesced to this ANTI-UNICORN LINGUISTIC DISCRIMINATION?!
Look, you totally own at kickball. It evens out.

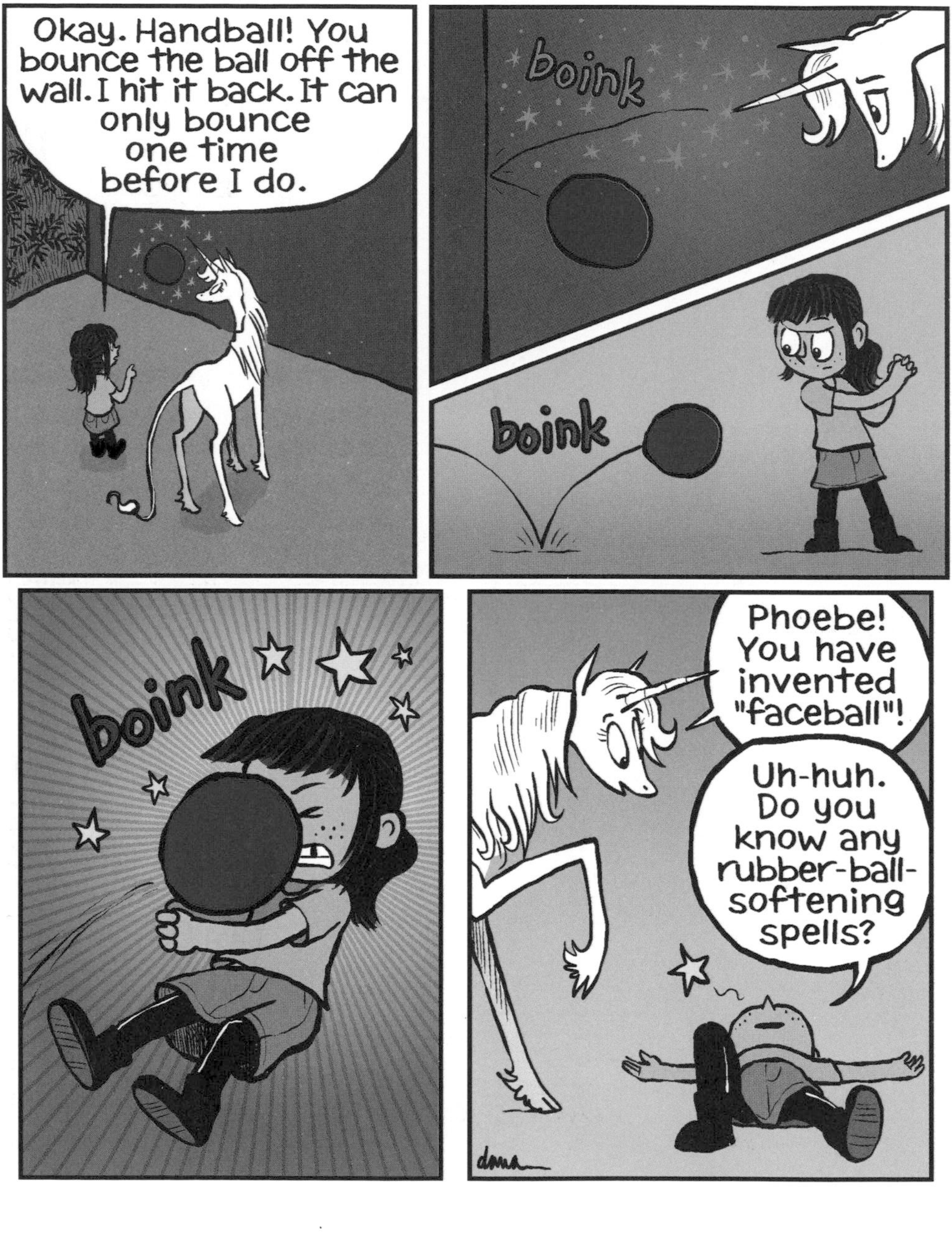
Okay. Handball! You bounce the ball off the wall. I hit it back. It can only bounce one time before I do.
boink
boink
boink
Phoebe! You have invented "faceball"!
Uh-huh. Do you know any rubber-ball-softening spells?
dana

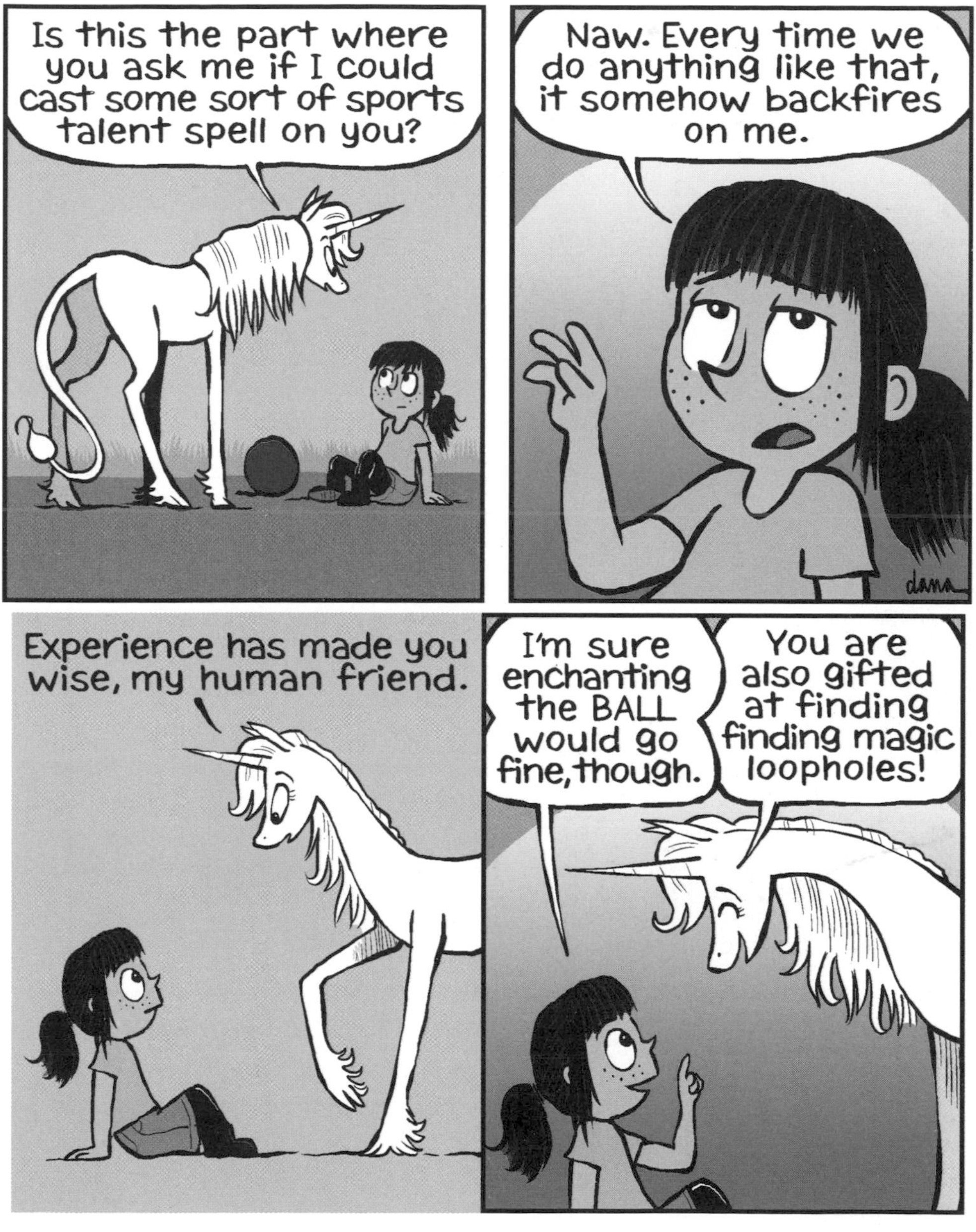
Is this the part where you ask me if I could cast some sort of sports talent spell on you?
Naw. Every time we do anything like that, it somehow backfires on me.
dana
Experience has made you wise, my human friend.
I'm sure enchanting the BALL would go fine, though.
You are also gifted at finding finding magic loopholes!

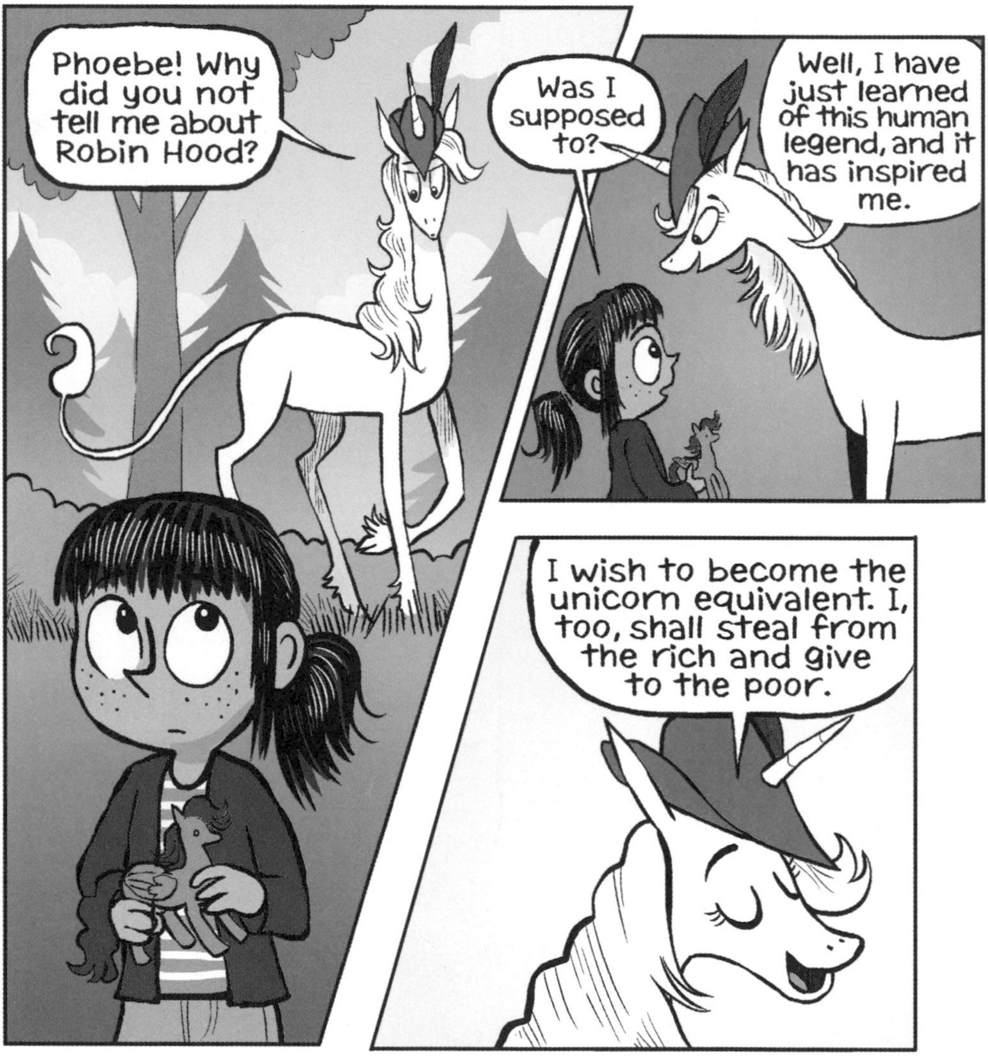
Phoebe! Why did you not tell me about Robin Hood?
Was I supposed to?
Well, I have just learned of this human legend, and it has inspired me.
I wish to become the unicorn equivalent. I, too, shall steal from the rich and give to the poor.

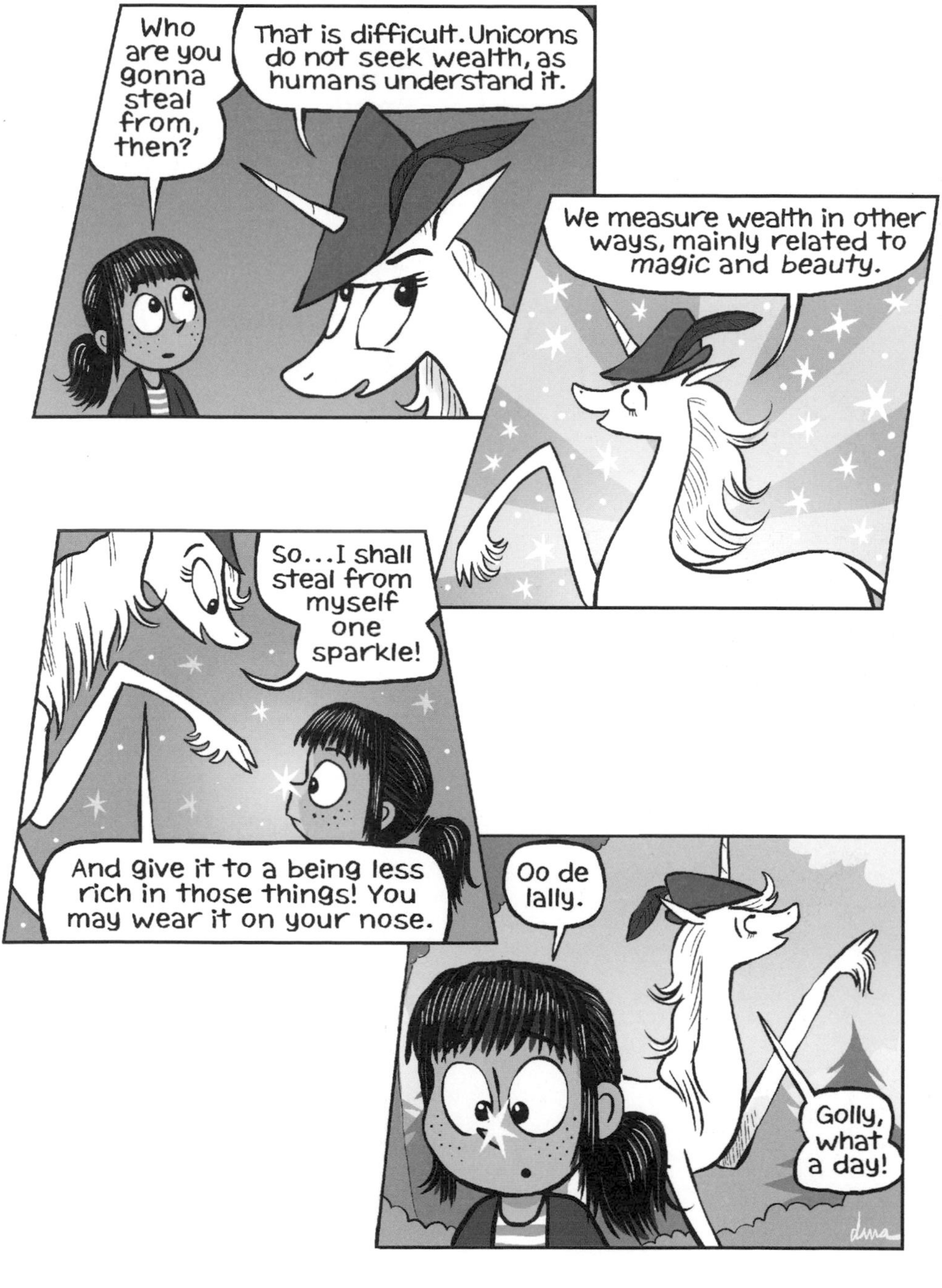
Who are you gonna steal from, then?
That is difficult. Unicorns do not seek wealth, as humans understand it.
We measure wealth in other ways, mainly related to *magic* and *beauty*.
So...I shall steal from myself one sparkle!
And give it to a being less rich in those things! You may wear it on your nose.
Oo de lally.
Golly, what a day!

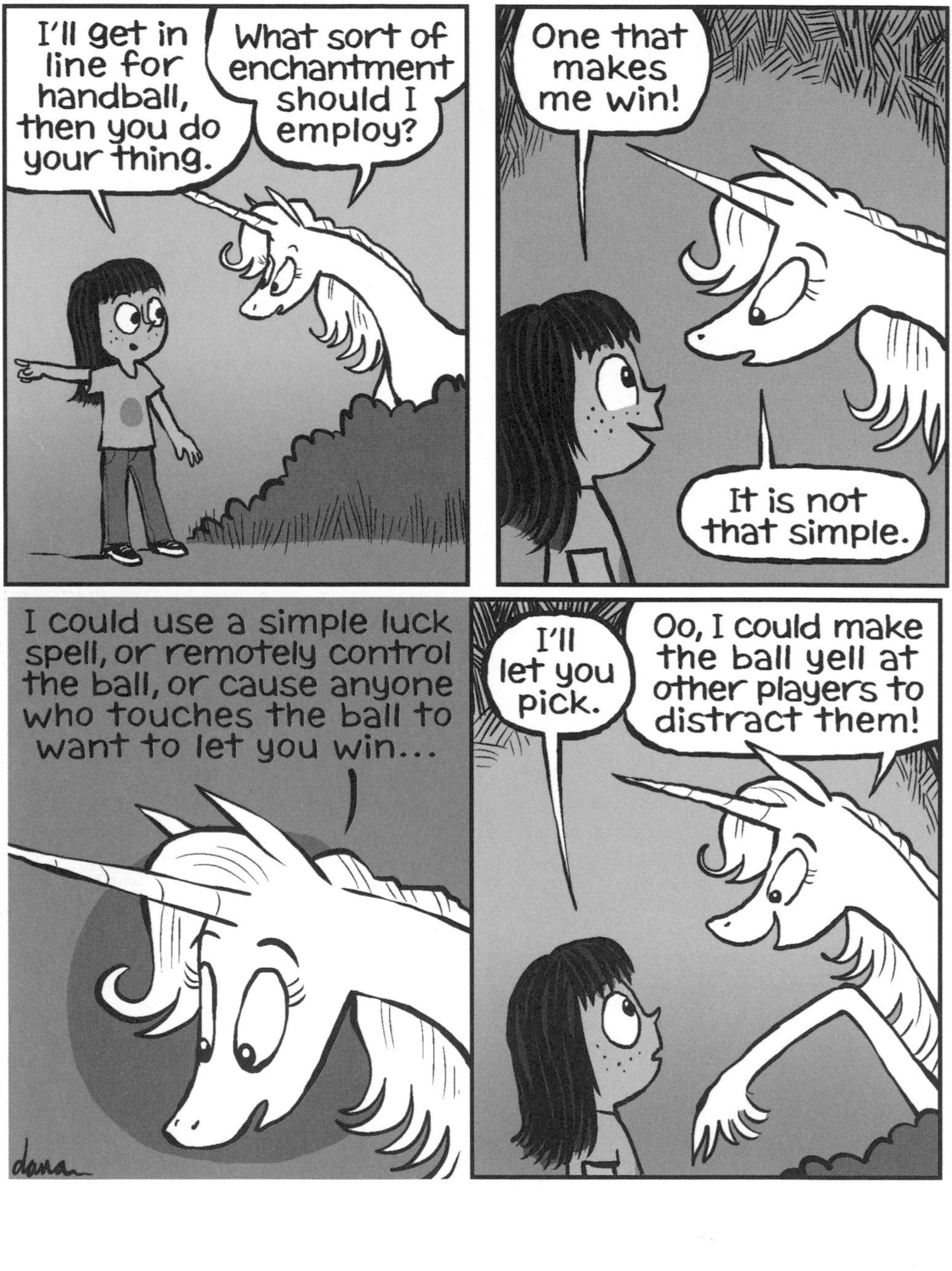
I'll get in line for handball, then you do your thing.
What sort of enchantment should I employ?
One that makes me win!
It is not that simple.
I could use a simple luck spell, or remotely control the ball, or cause anyone who touches the ball to want to let you win...
I'll let you pick.
Oo, I could make the ball yell at other players to distract them!
dana

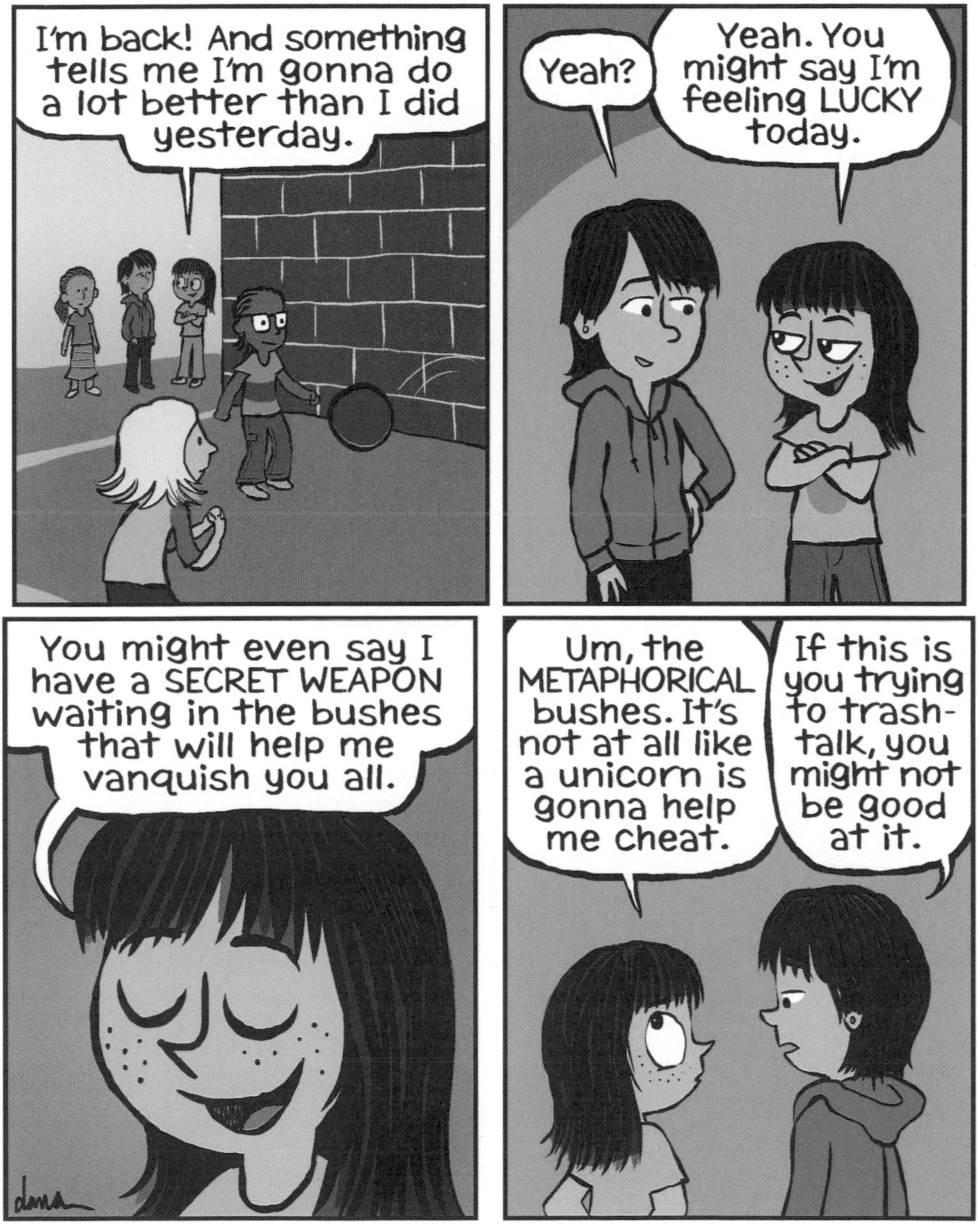
I'm back! And something tells me I'm gonna do a lot better than I did yesterday.
Yeah?
Yeah. You might say I'm feeling LUCKY today.
You might even say I have a SECRET WEAPON waiting in the bushes that will help me vanquish you all.
Um, the METAPHORICAL bushes. It's not at all like a unicorn is gonna help me cheat.
If this is you trying to trash-talk, you might not be good at it.

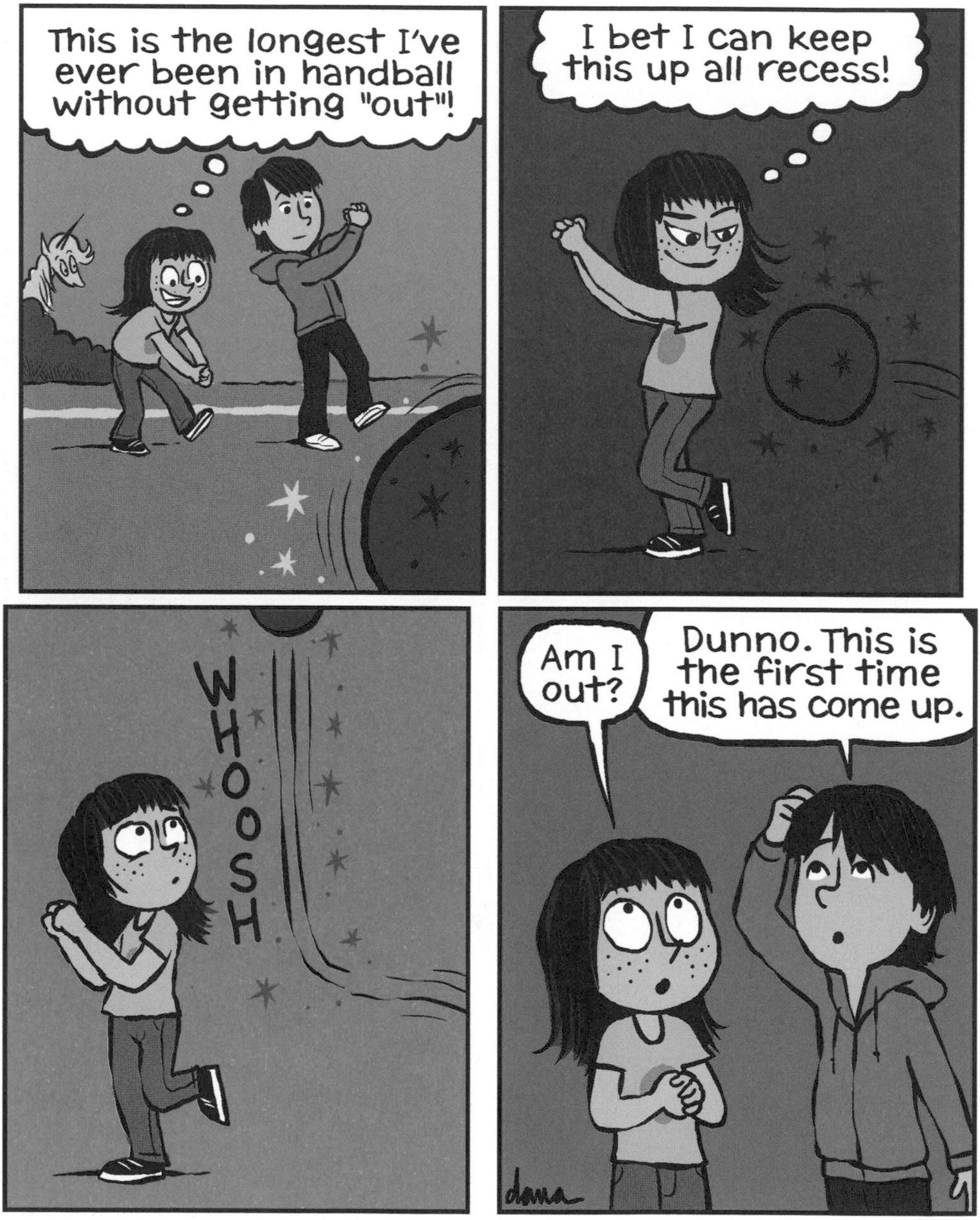
This is the longest I've ever been in handball without getting "out"!
I bet I can keep this up all recess!
WHOOSH
Am I out?
Dunno. This is the first time this has come up.
dana

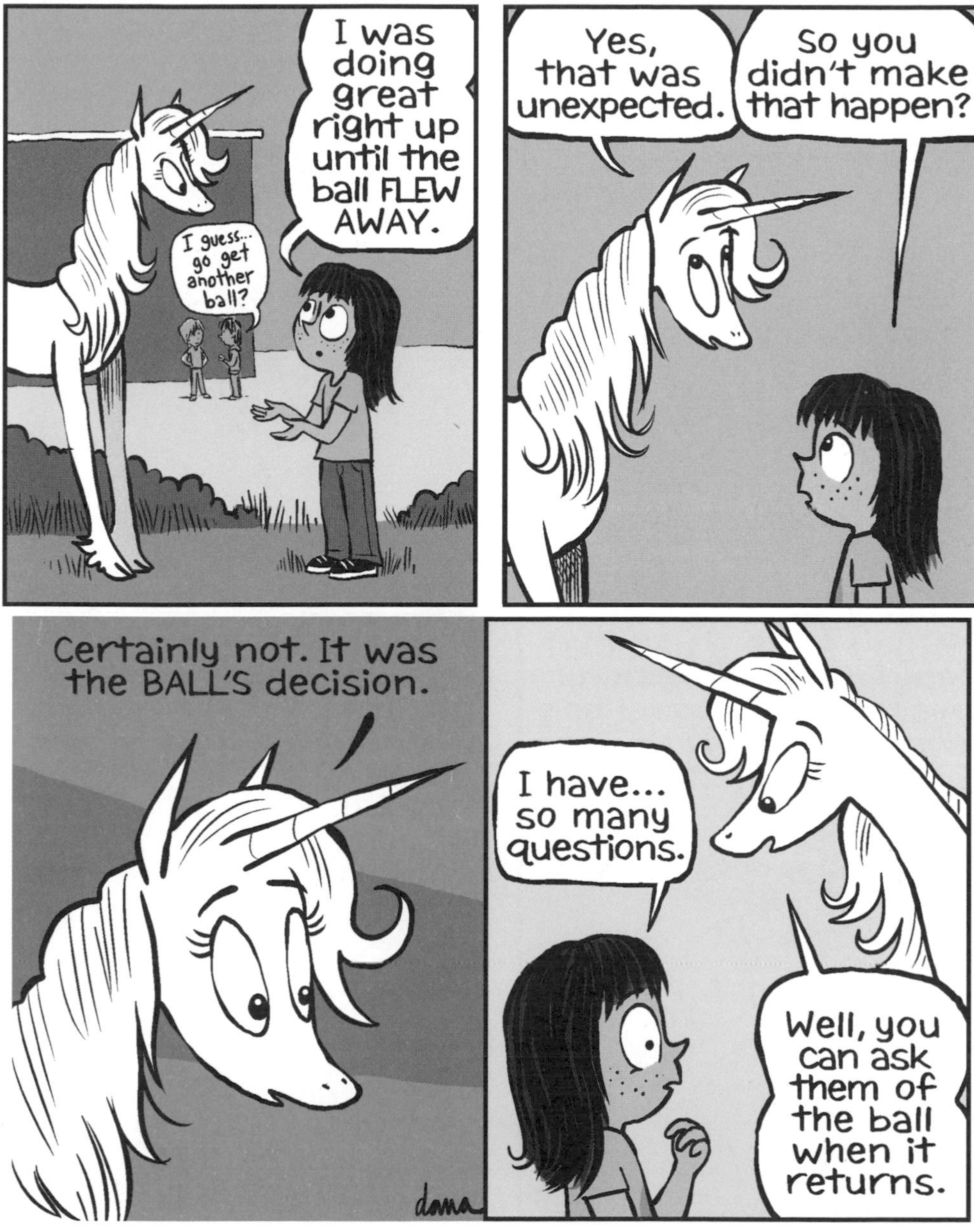
I was doing great right up until the ball FLEW AWAY.
I guess... go get another ball?
Yes, that was unexpected.
So you didn't make that happen?
Certainly not. It was the BALL'S decision.
I have... so many questions.
Well, you can ask them of the ball when it returns.
dana

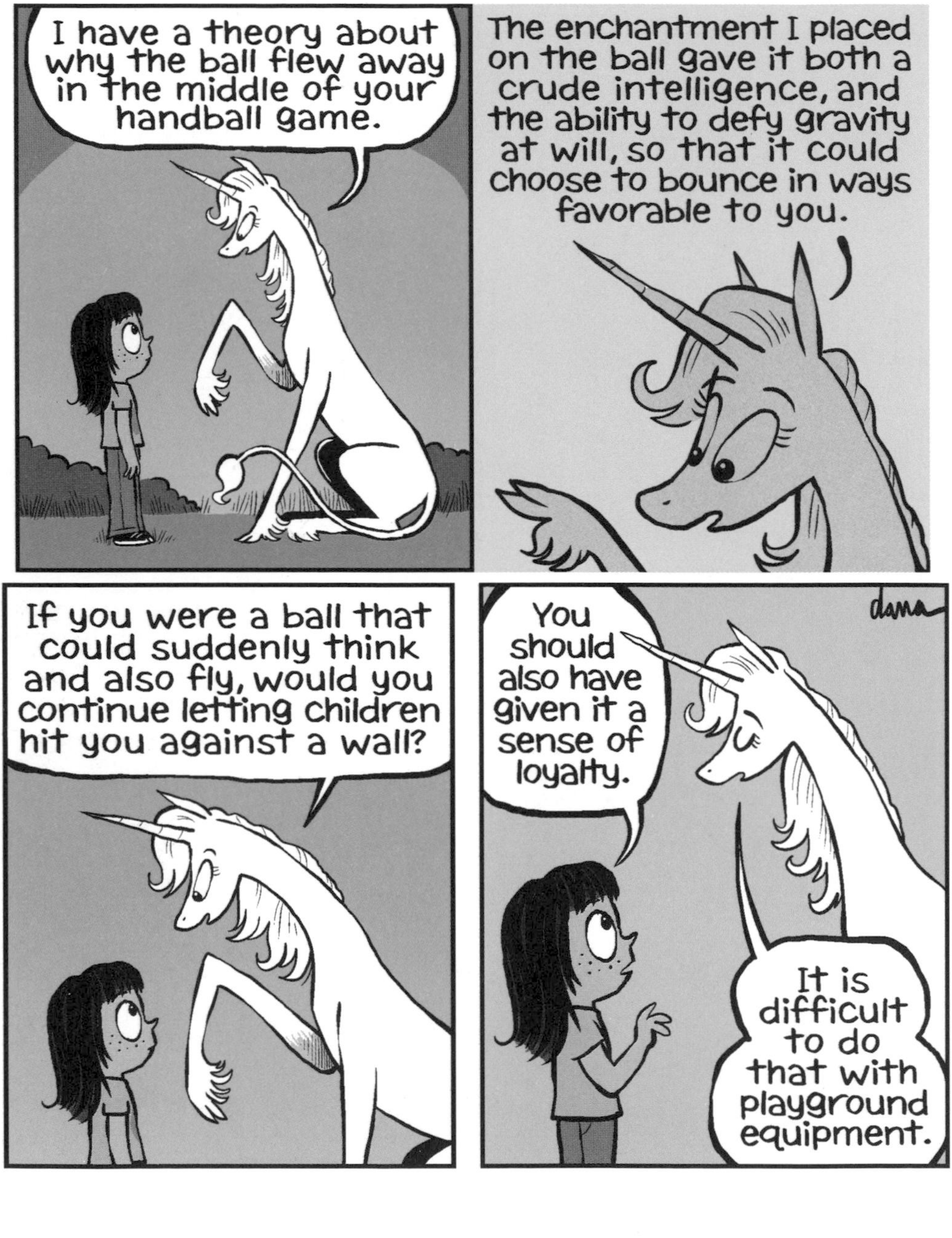
I have a theory about why the ball flew away in the middle of your handball game.
The enchantment I placed on the ball gave it both a crude intelligence, and the ability to defy gravity at will, so that it could choose to bounce in ways favorable to you.
If you were a ball that could suddenly think and also fly, would you continue letting children hit you against a wall?
You should also have given it a sense of loyalty.
It is difficult to do that with playground equipment.
dana

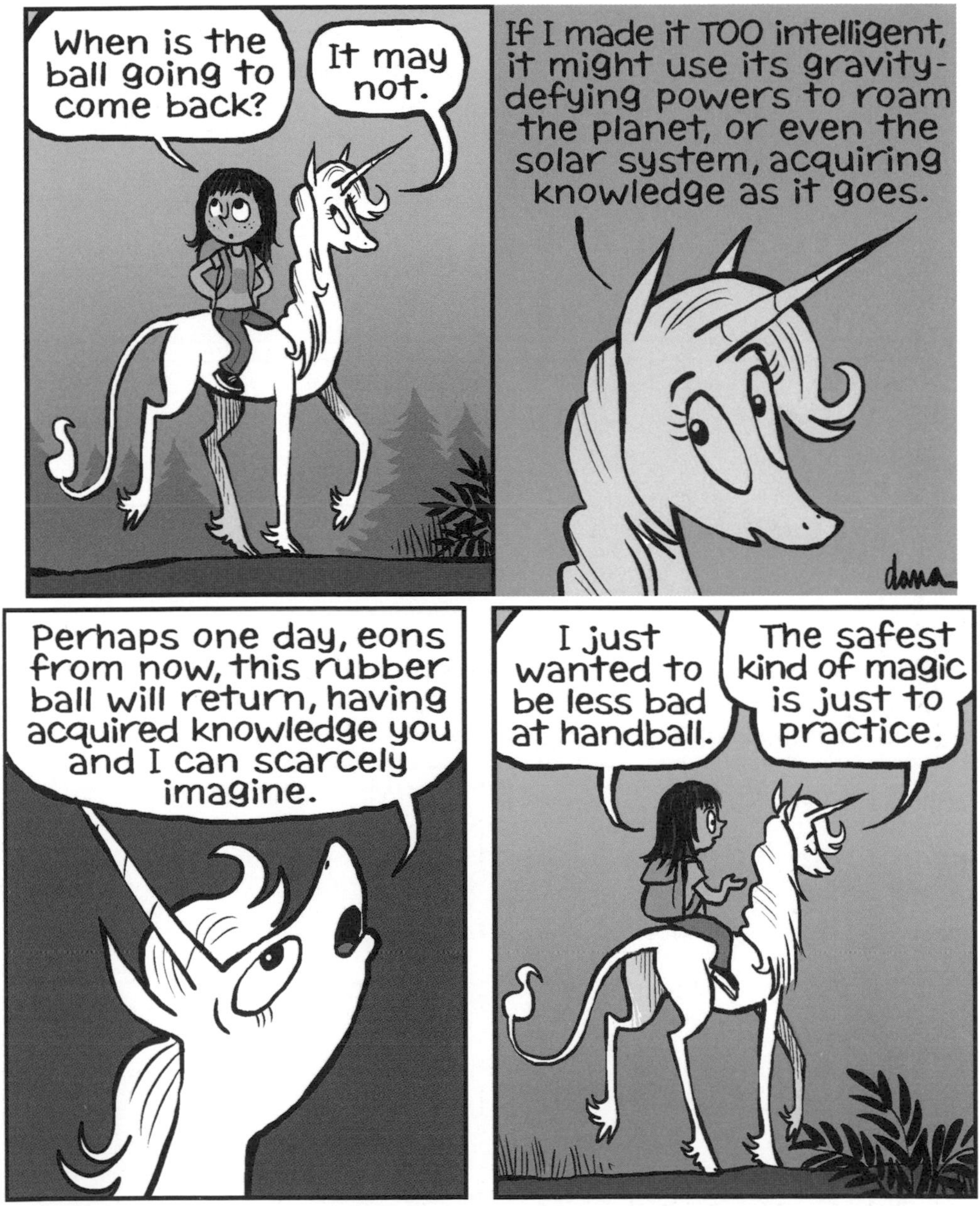
When is the ball going to come back?
It may not.
If I made it TOO intelligent, it might use its gravity-defying powers to roam the planet, or even the solar system, acquiring knowledge as it goes.
dana
Perhaps one day, eons from now, this rubber ball will return, having acquired knowledge you and I can scarcely imagine.
I just wanted to be less bad at handball.
The safest kind of magic is just to practice.

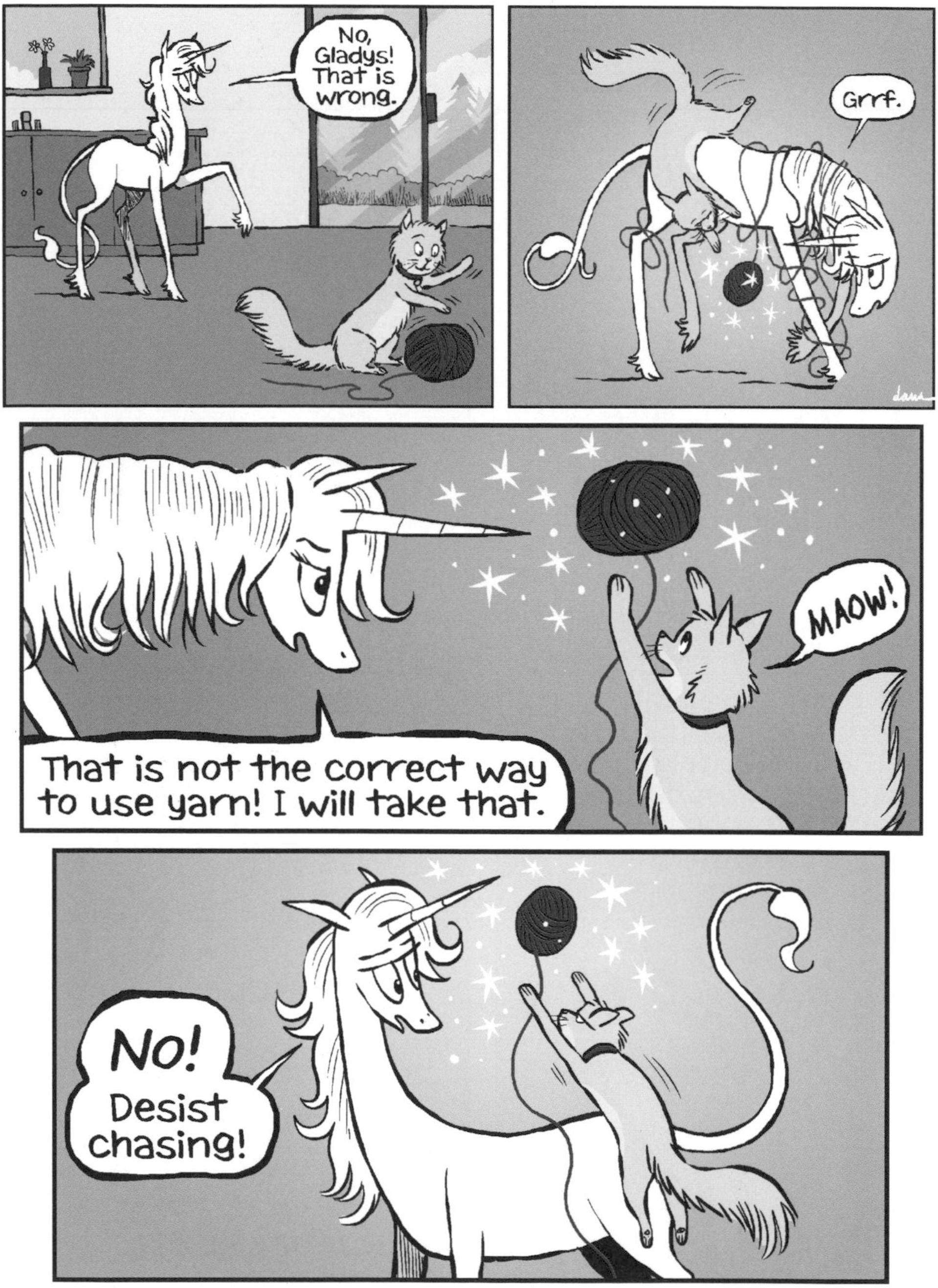
No, Gladys! That is wrong.
Grrf.
MAOW!
That is not the correct way to use yarn! I will take that.
No! Desist chasing!

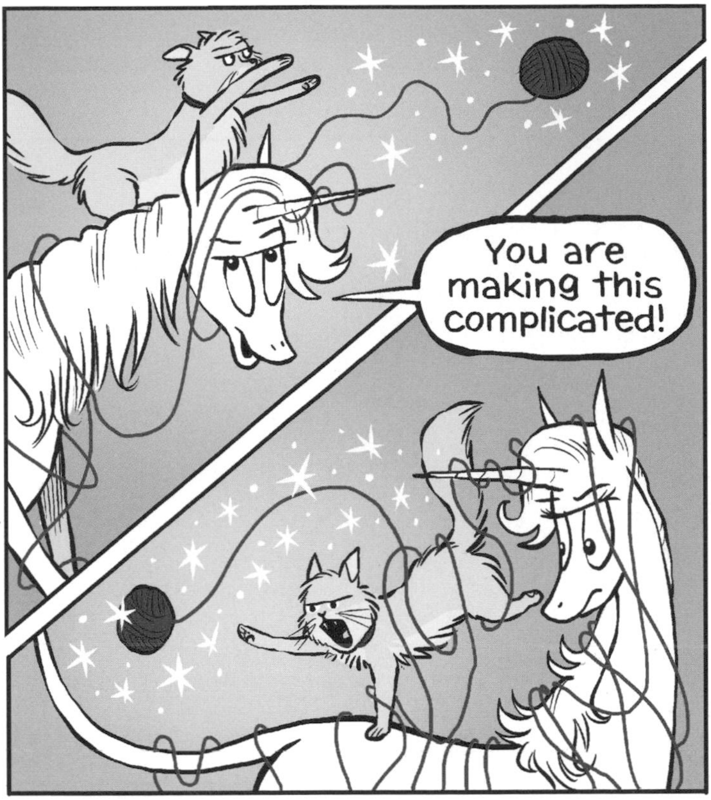
You are making this complicated!

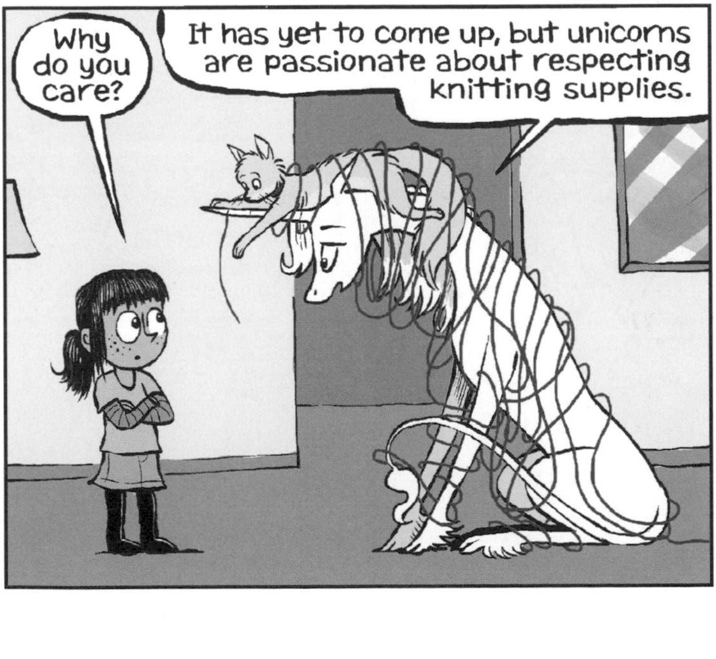
Why do you care?
It has yet to come up, but unicorns are passionate about respecting knitting supplies.

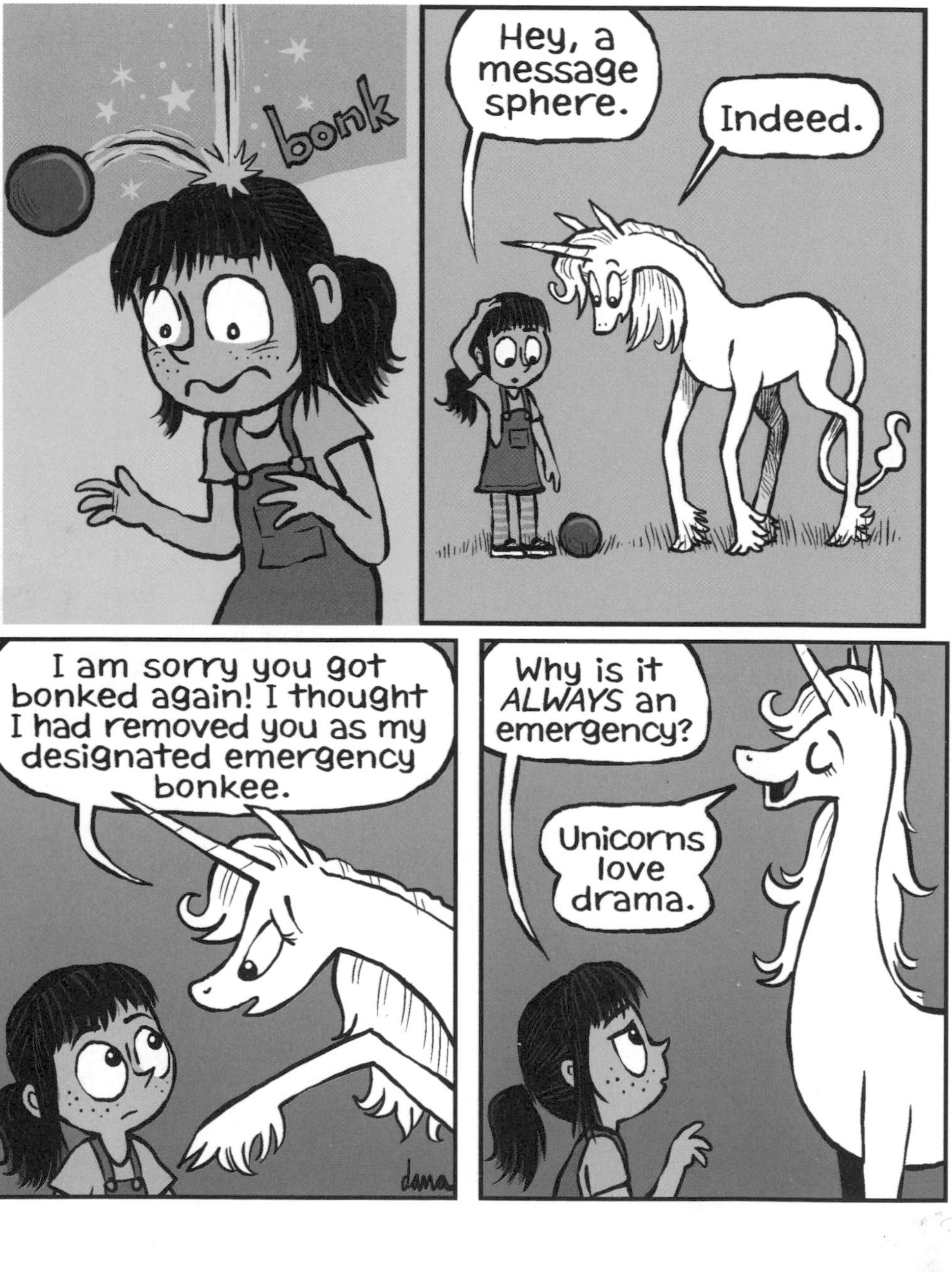
bonk
Hey, a message sphere.
Indeed.
I am sorry you got bonked again! I thought I had removed you as my designated emergency bonkee.
Why is it *ALWAYS* an emergency?
Unicorns love drama.

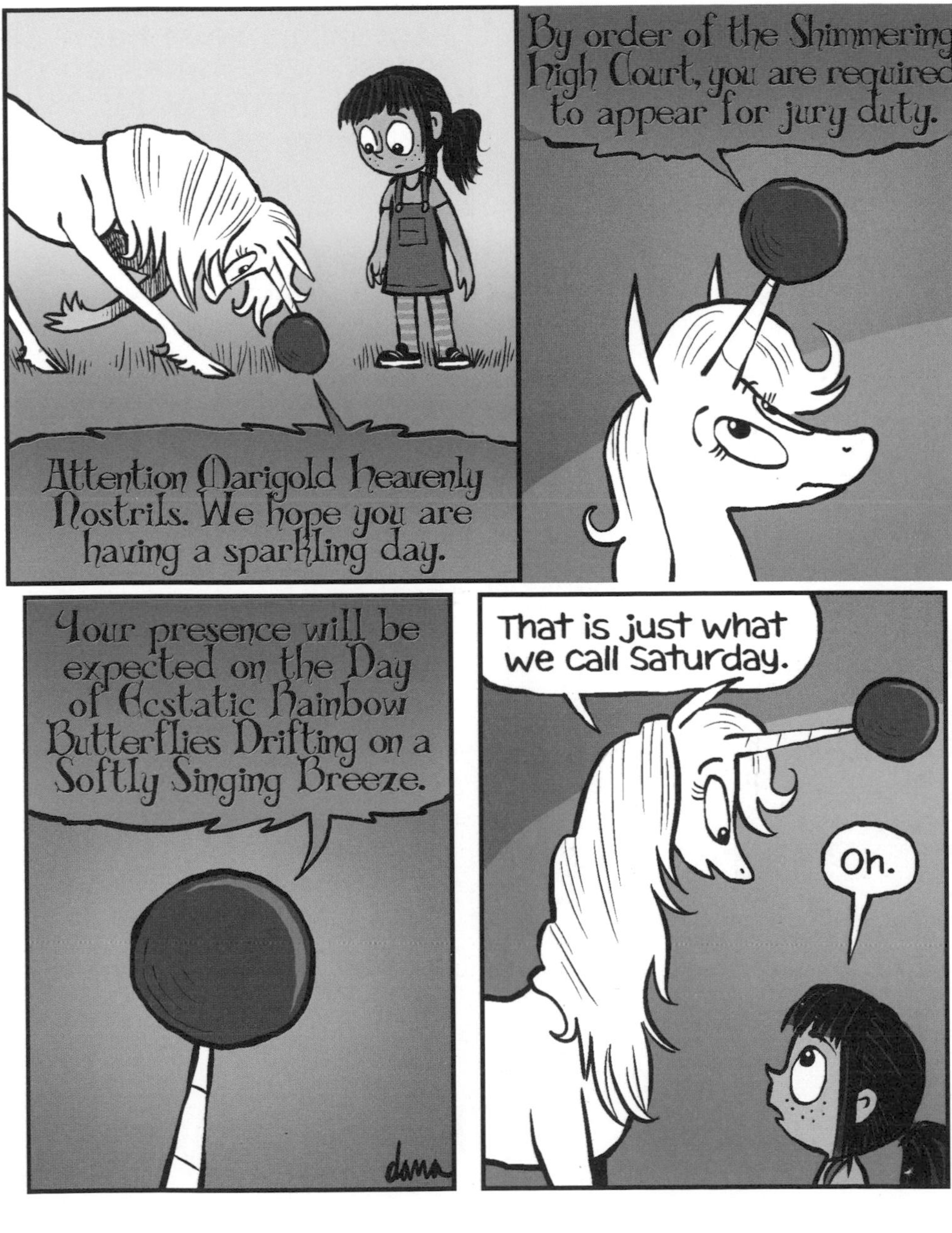
Attention Marigold Heavenly Nostrils. We hope you are having a sparkling day.
By order of the Shimmering High Court, you are required to appear for jury duty.
Your presence will be expected on the Day of Ecstatic Rainbow Butterflies Drifting on a Softly Singing Breeze.
That is just what we call Saturday.
Oh.

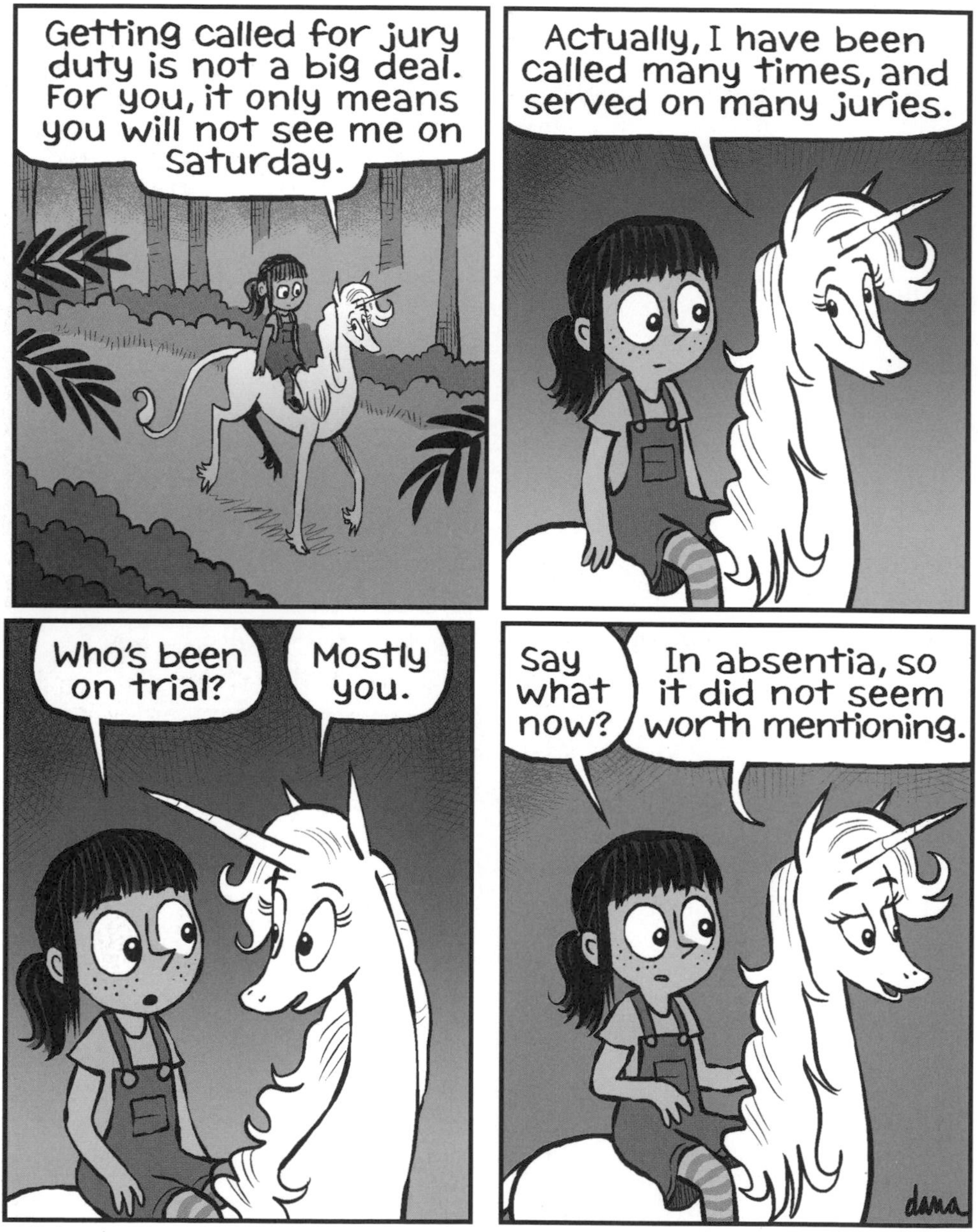
Getting called for jury duty is not a big deal. For you, it only means you will not see me on Saturday.
Actually, I have been called many times, and served on many juries.
Who's been on trial?
Mostly you.
Say what now?
In absentia, so it did not seem worth mentioning.
dana

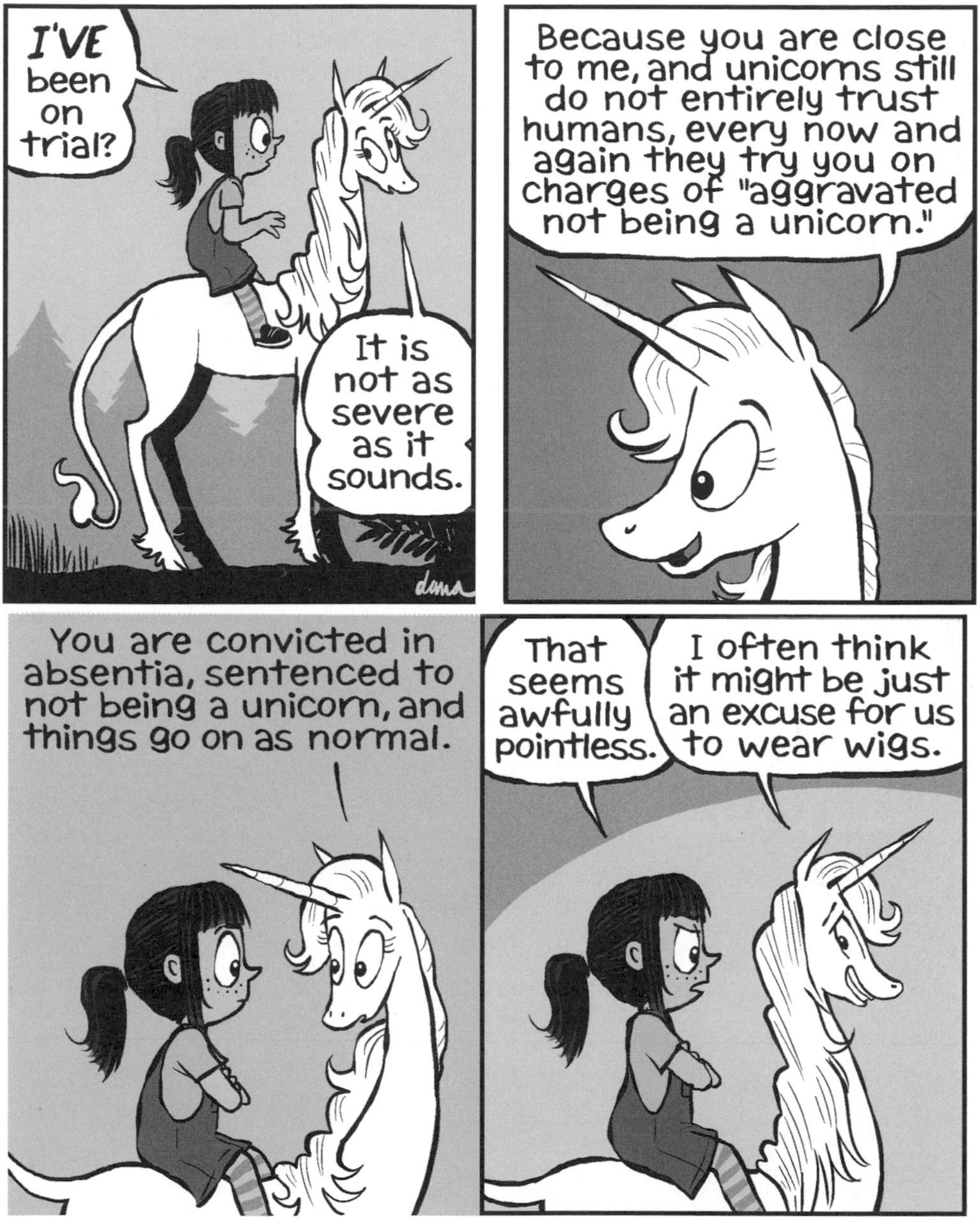
I'VE been on trial?
It is not as severe as it sounds.
Because you are close to me, and unicorns still do not entirely trust humans, every now and again they try you on charges of "aggravated not being a unicorn."
You are convicted in absentia, sentenced to not being a unicorn, and things go on as normal.
That seems awfully pointless.
I often think it might be just an excuse for us to wear wigs.

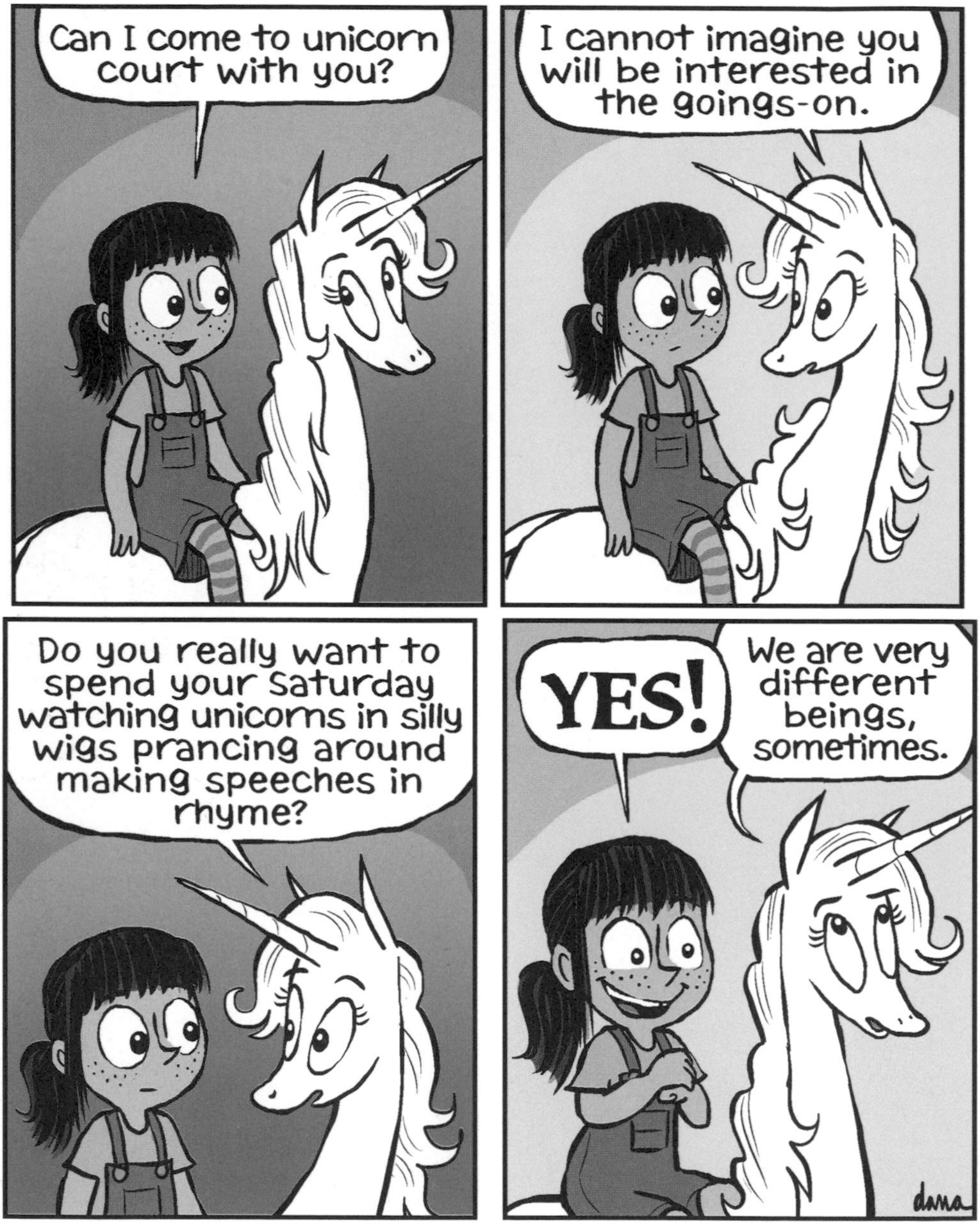
Can I come to unicorn court with you?
I cannot imagine you will be interested in the goings-on.
Do you really want to spend your Saturday watching unicorns in silly wigs prancing around making speeches in rhyme?
YES!
We are very different beings, sometimes.
dana

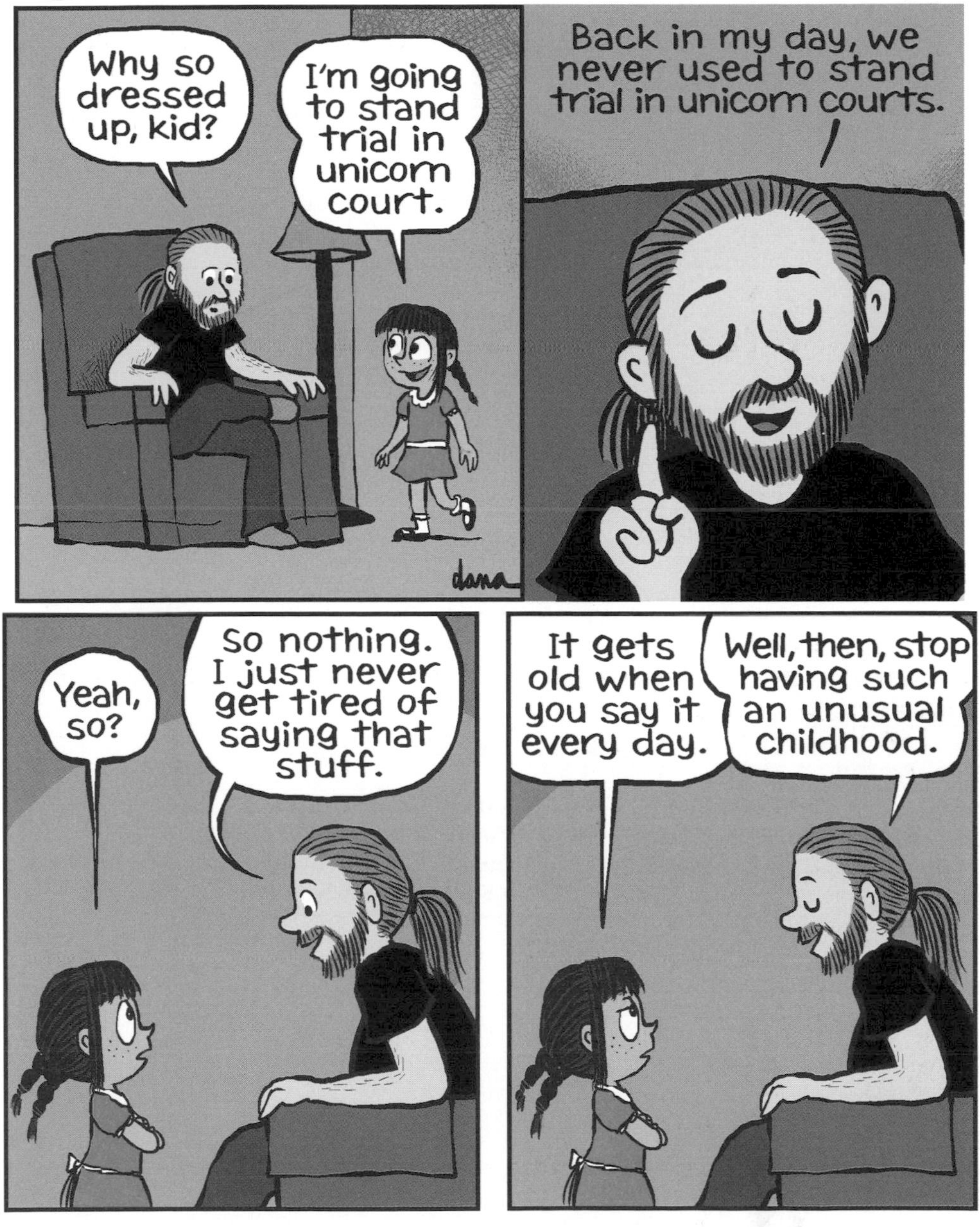
Why so dressed up, kid?
I'm going to stand trial in unicorn court.
Back in my day, we never used to stand trial in unicorn courts.
Yeah, so?
So nothing. I just never get tired of saying that stuff.
It gets old when you say it every day.
Well, then, stop having such an unusual childhood.

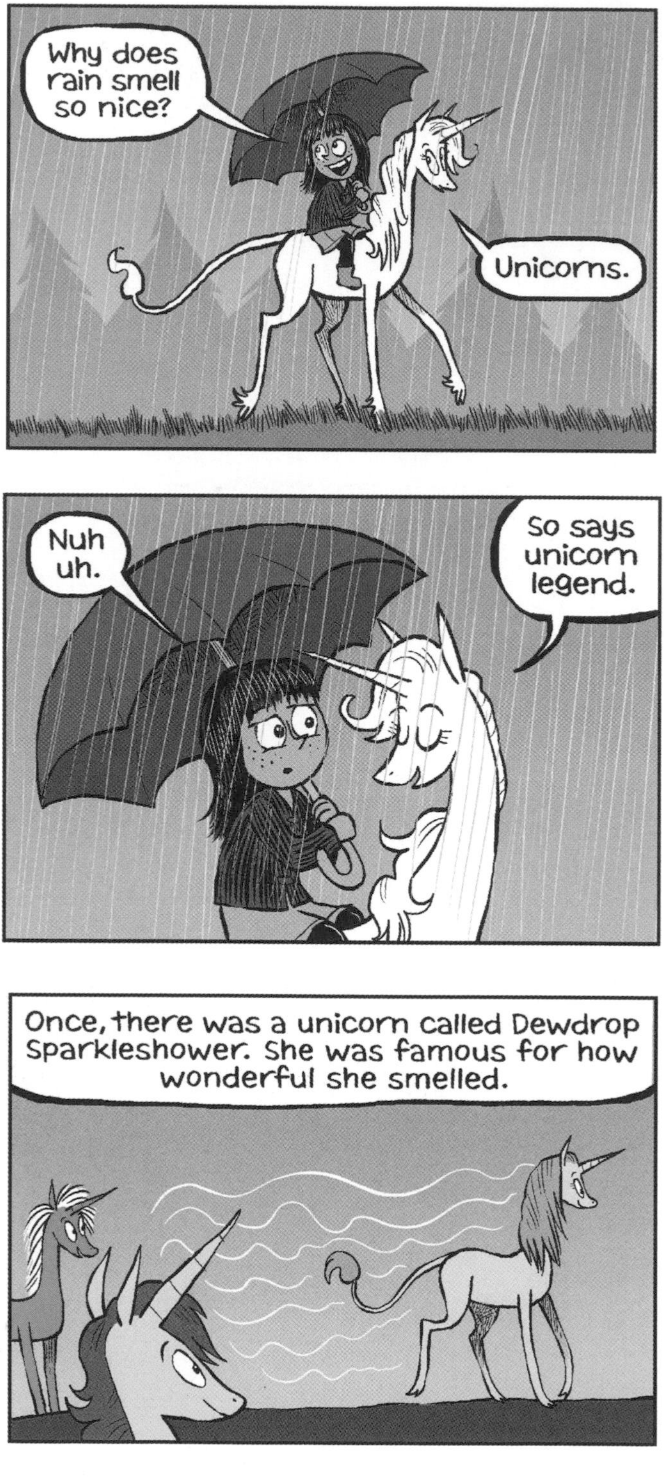
Why does rain smell so nice?
Unicorns.
Nuh uh.
So says unicorn legend.
Once, there was a unicorn called Dewdrop Sparkleshower. She was famous for how wonderful she smelled.

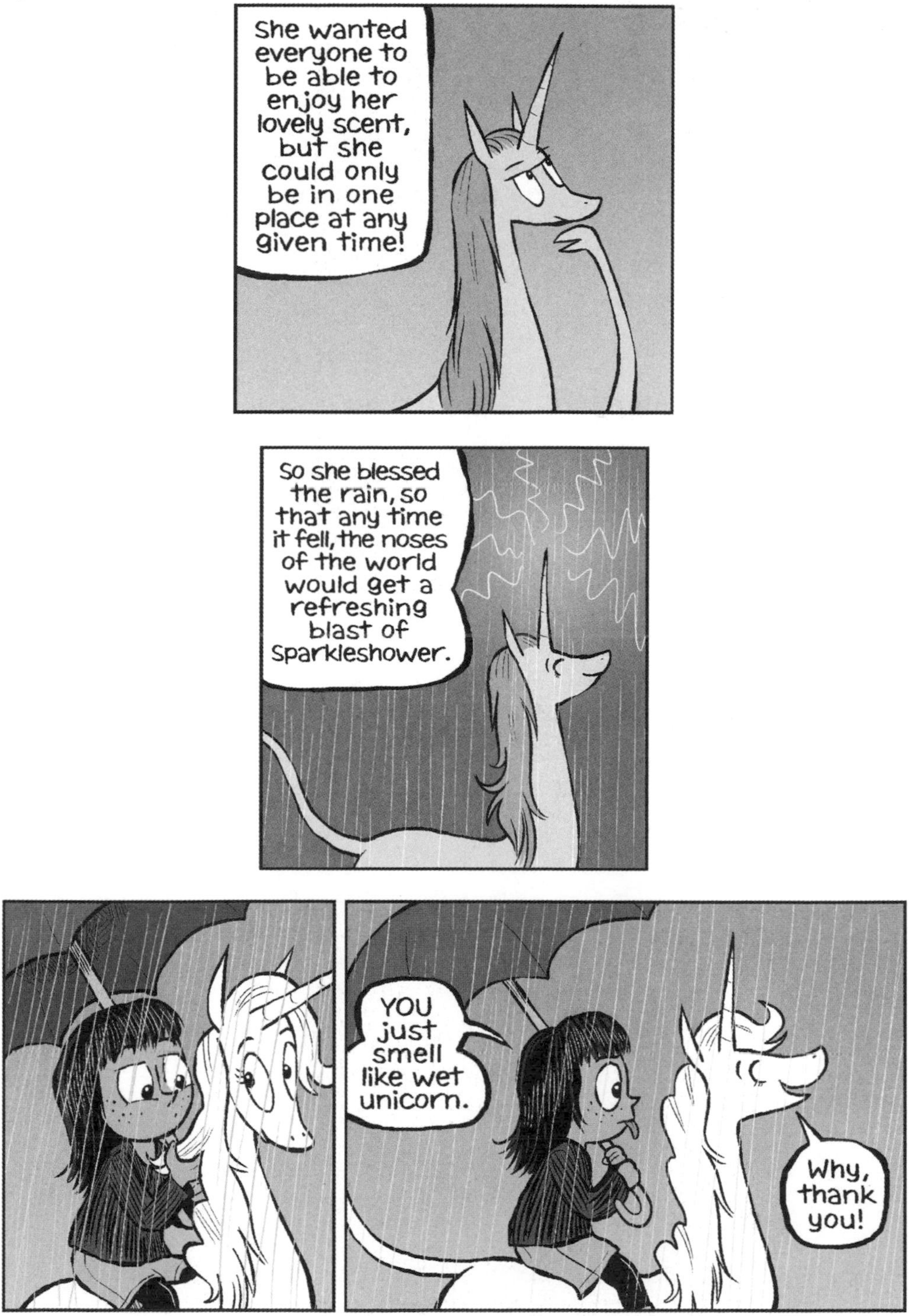
She wanted everyone to be able to enjoy her lovely scent, but she could only be in one place at any given time!
So she blessed the rain, so that any time it fell, the noses of the world would get a refreshing blast of sparkleshower.
YOU just smell like wet unicorn.
Why, thank you!

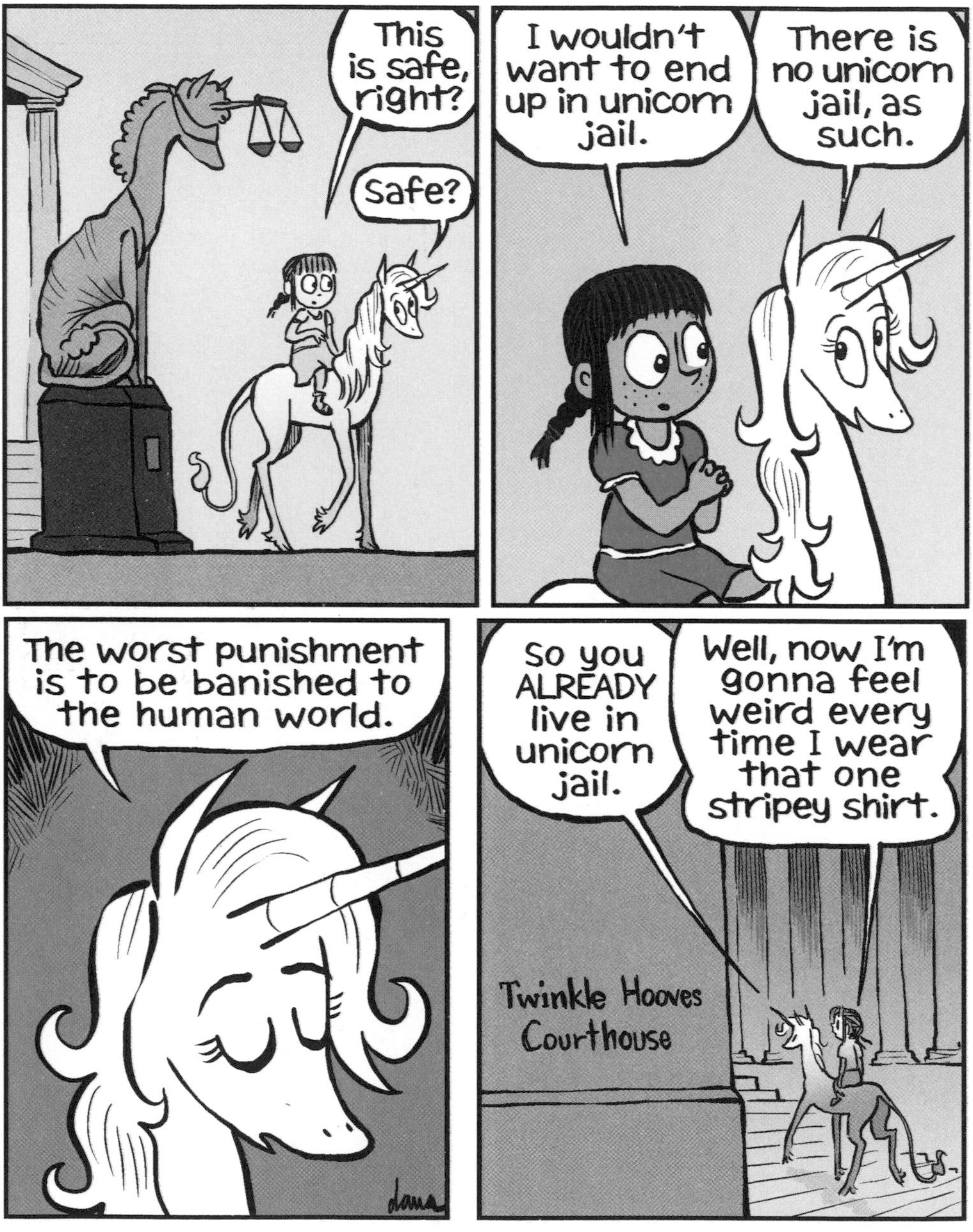
This is safe, right?
Safe?
I wouldn't want to end up in unicorn jail.
There is no unicorn jail, as such.
The worst punishment is to be banished to the human world.
So you ALREADY live in unicorn jail.
Well, now I'm gonna feel weird every time I wear that one stripey shirt.
Twinkle Hooves Courthouse
dana

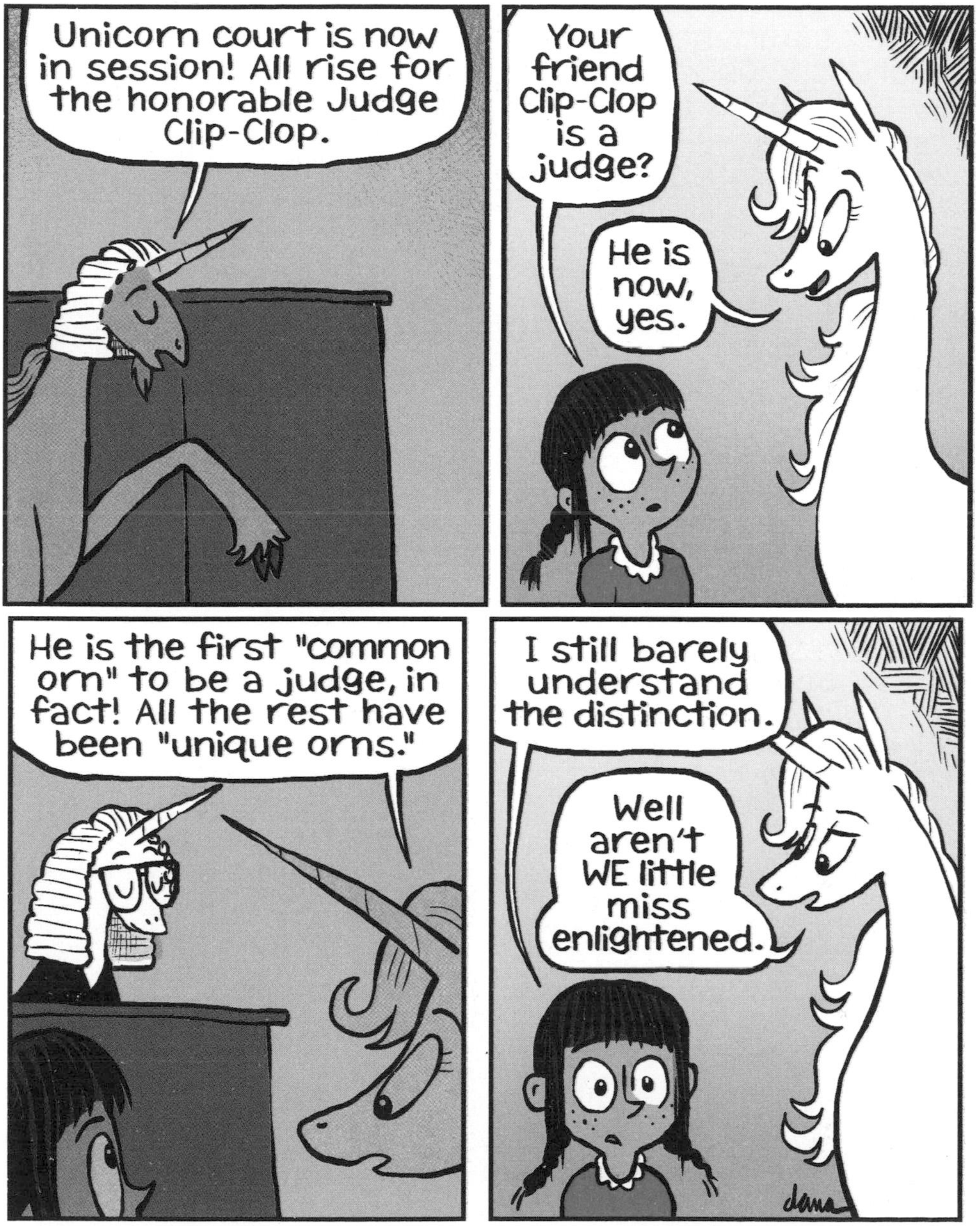
Unicorn court is now in session! All rise for the honorable Judge Clip-Clop.
Your friend Clip-Clop is a judge?
He is now, yes.
He is the first "common orn" to be a judge, in fact! All the rest have been "unique orns."
I still barely understand the distinction.
Well aren't WE little miss enlightened.

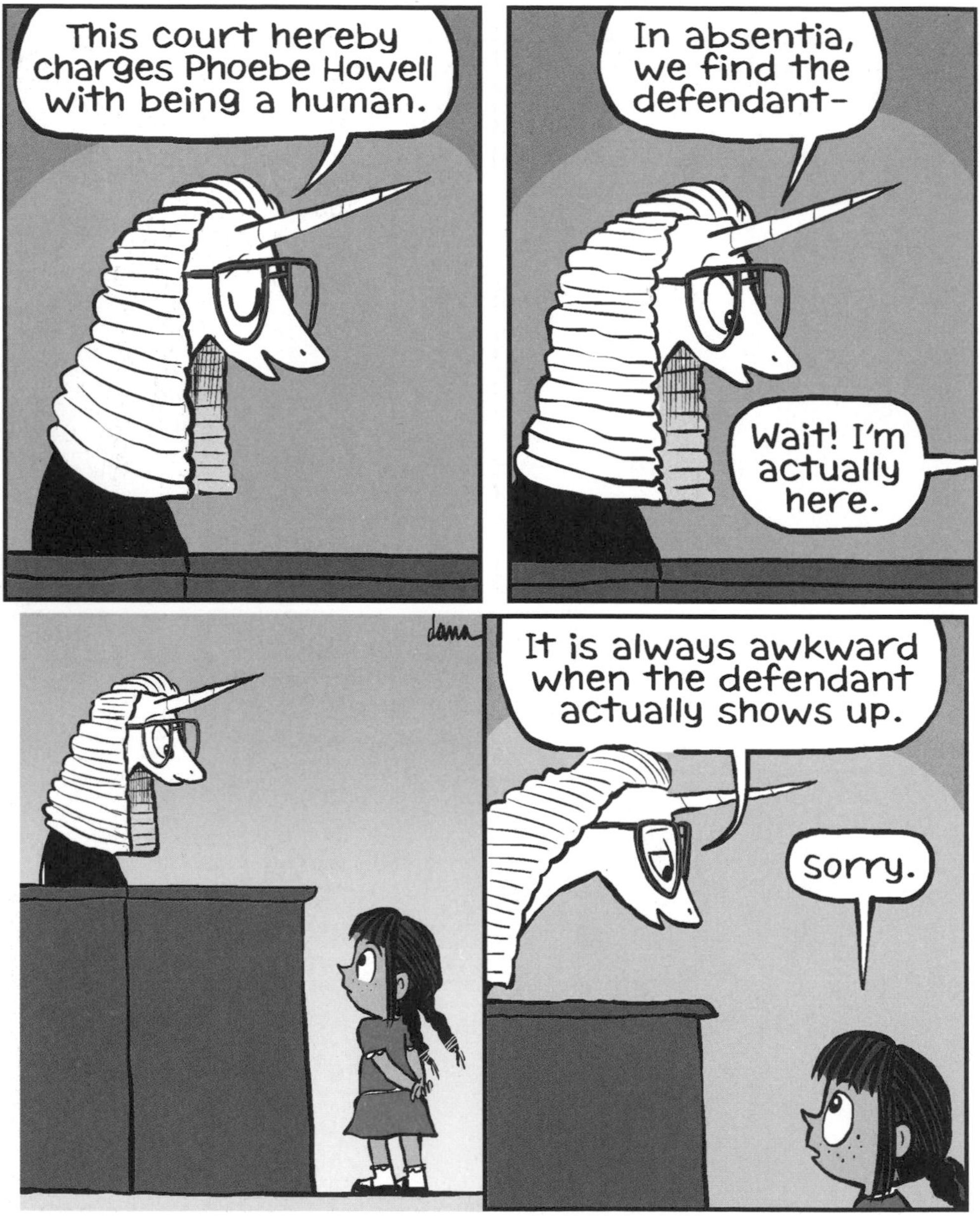
This court hereby charges Phoebe Howell with being a human.
In absentia, we find the defendant-
Wait! I'm actually here.
dana
It is always awkward when the defendant actually shows up.
Sorry.

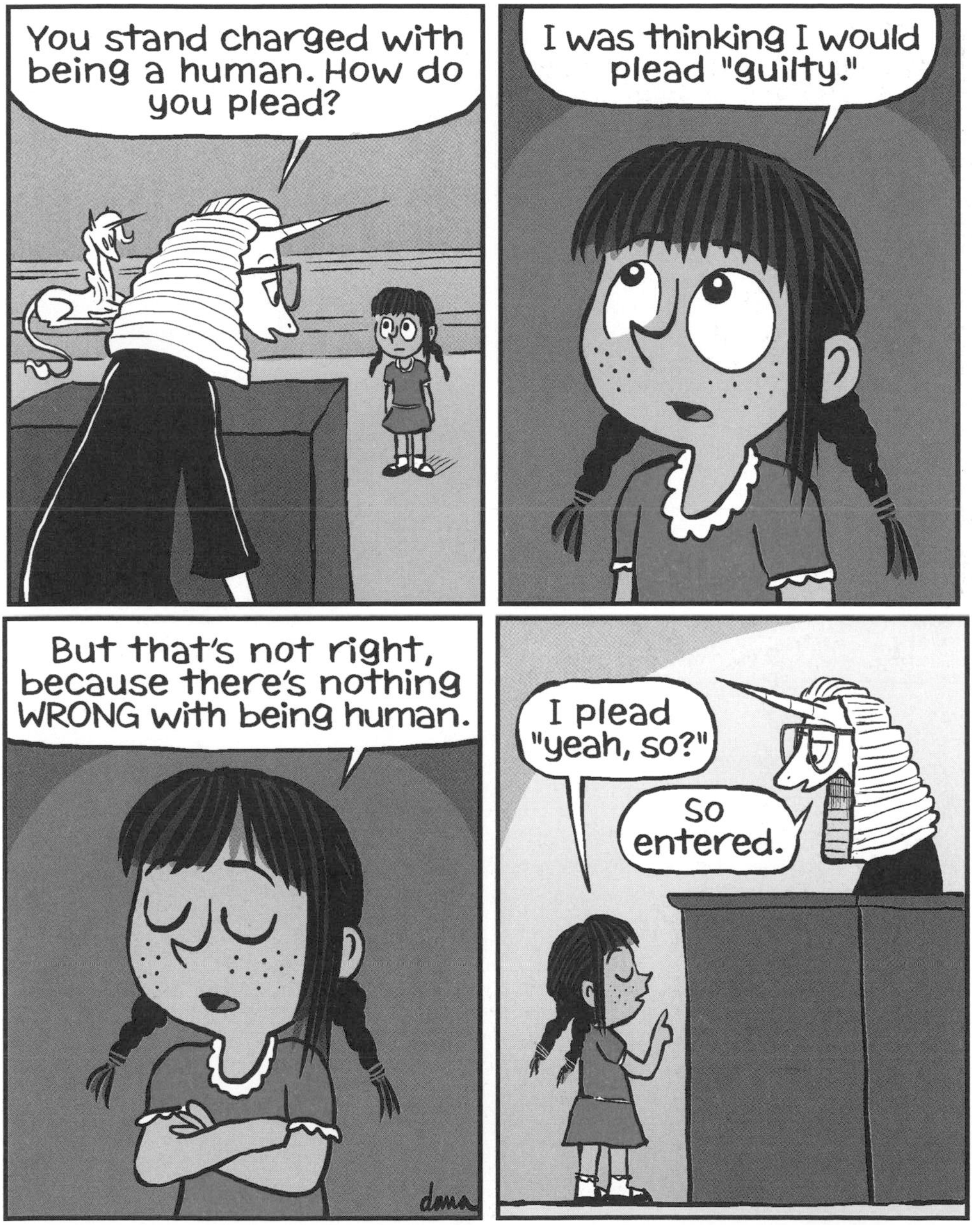
You stand charged with being a human. How do you plead?
I was thinking I would plead "guilty."
But that's not right, because there's nothing WRONG with being human.
I plead "yeah, so?"
So entered.
dana

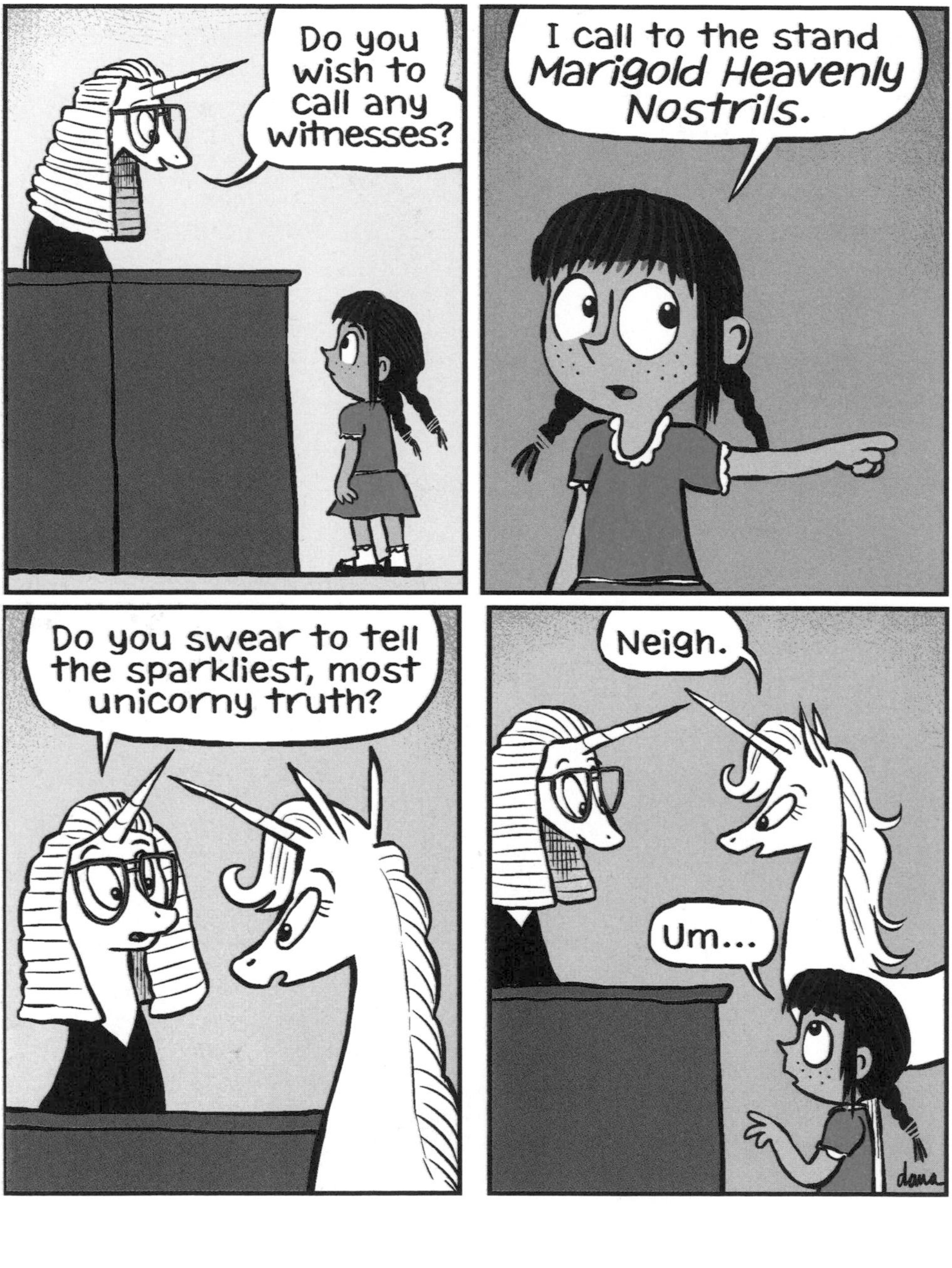
Do you wish to call any witnesses?
I call to the stand Marigold Heavenly Nostrils.
Do you swear to tell the sparkliest, most unicorny truth?
Neigh.
Um...
dana

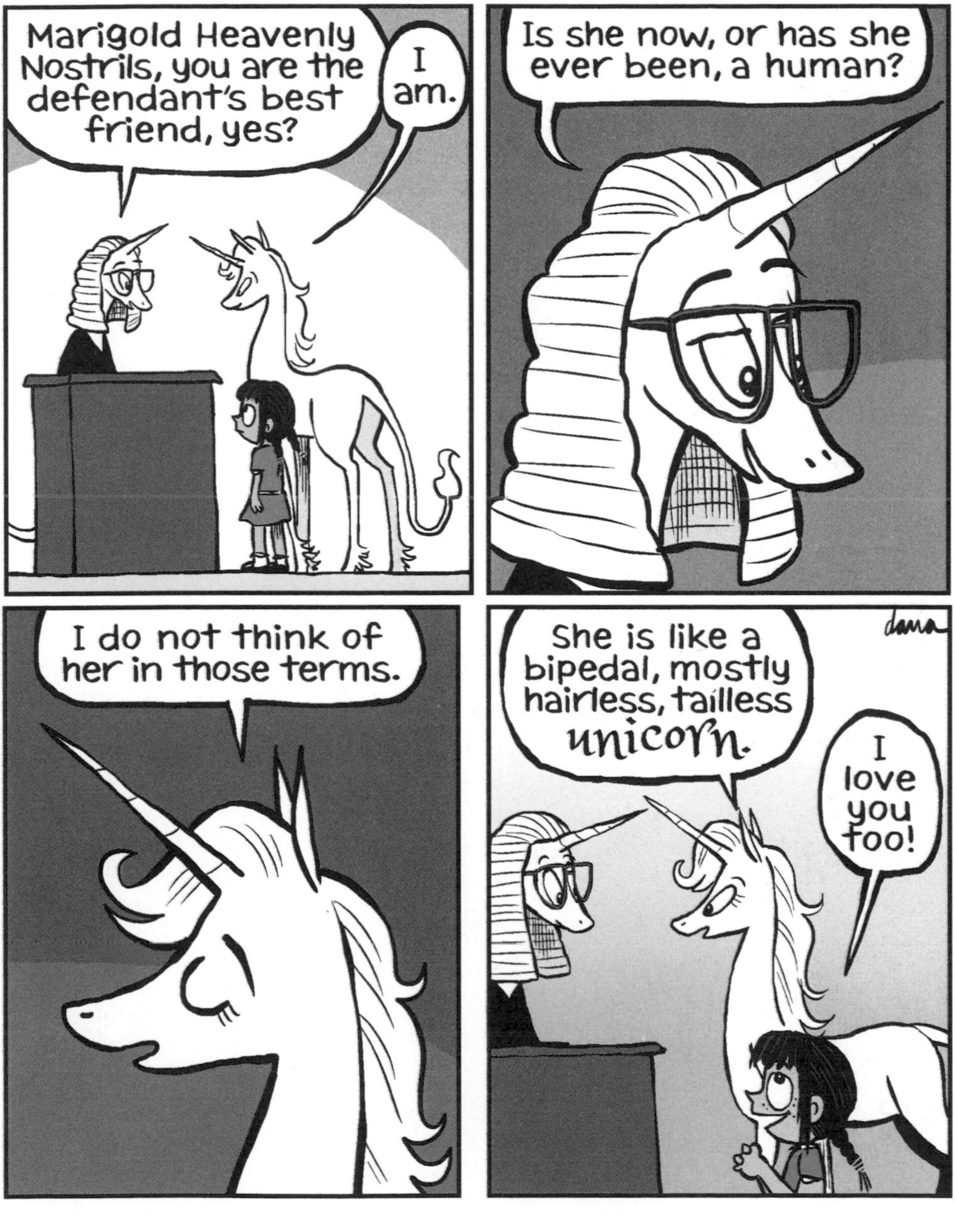
Marigold Heavenly Nostrils, you are the defendant's best friend, yes?
I am.
Is she now, or has she ever been, a human?
I do not think of her in those terms.
She is like a bipedal, mostly hairless, tailless unicorn.
I love you too!
dana

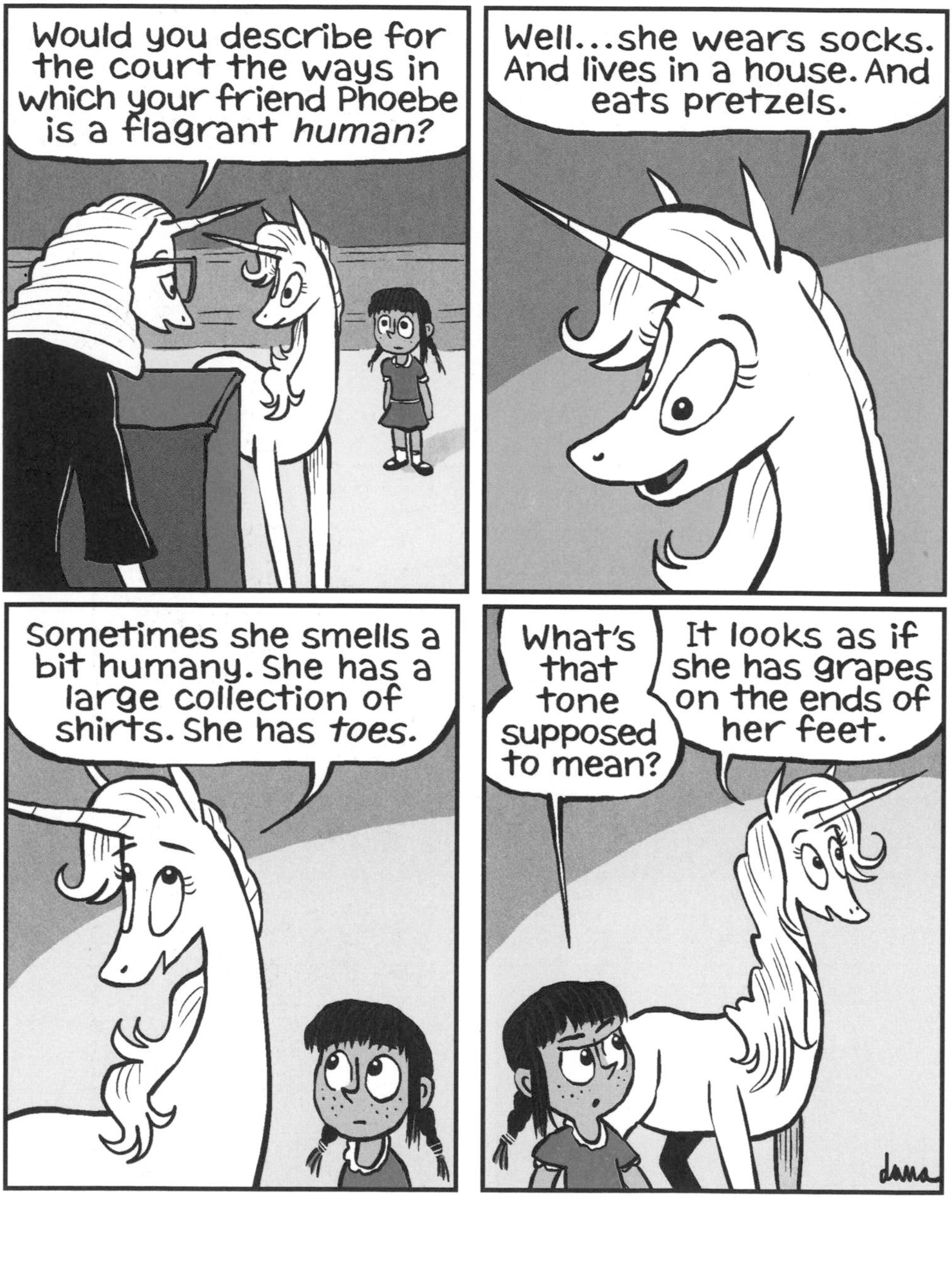
Would you describe for the court the ways in which your friend Phoebe is a flagrant *human?*
Well...she wears socks. And lives in a house. And eats pretzels.
Sometimes she smells a bit humany. She has a large collection of shirts. She has *toes.*
It looks as if she has grapes on the ends of her feet.
What's that tone supposed to mean?
dana

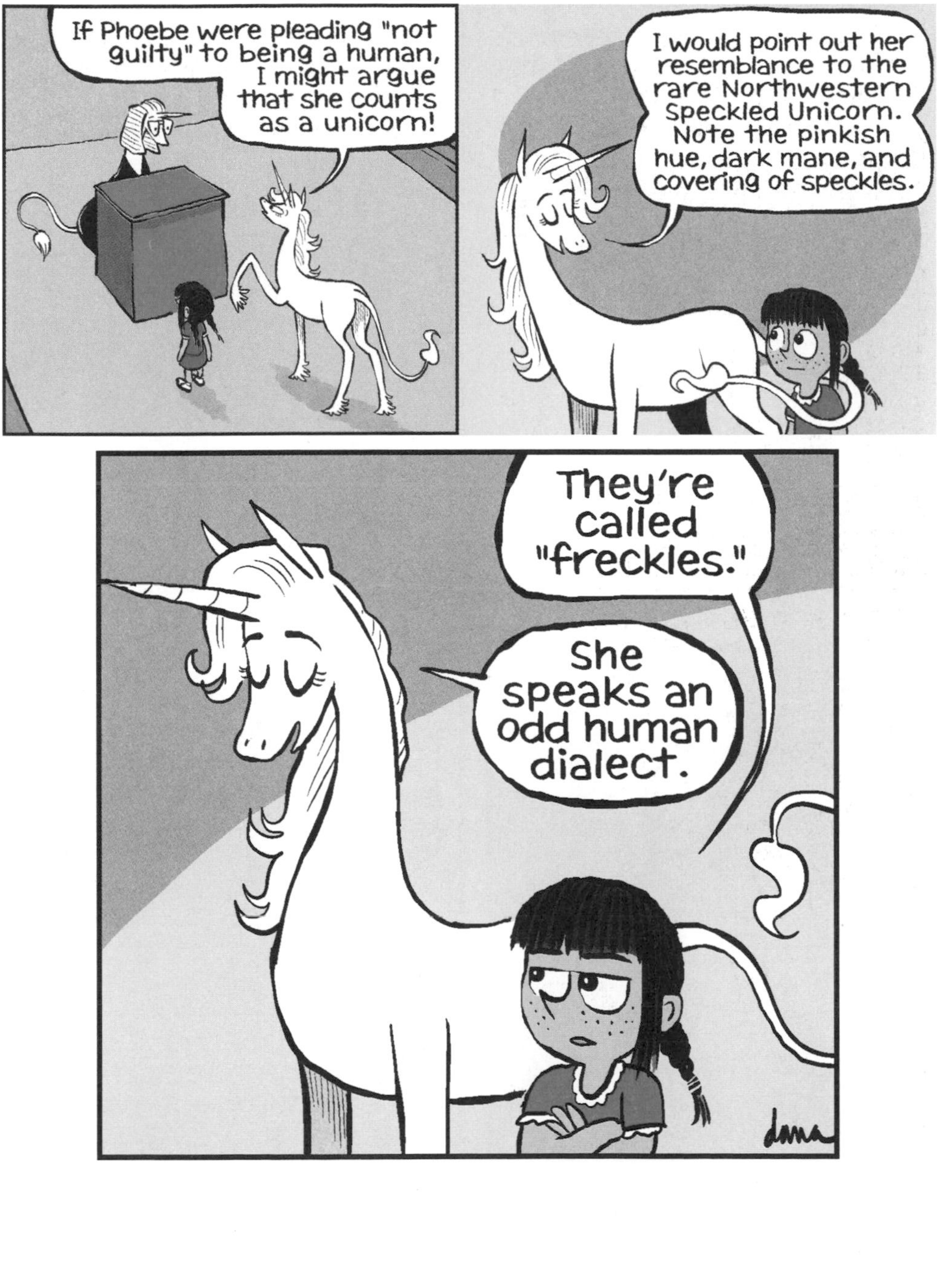
If Phoebe were pleading "not guilty" to being a human, I might argue that she counts as a unicorn!
I would point out her resemblance to the rare Northwestern Speckled Unicorn. Note the pinkish hue, dark mane, and covering of speckles.
They're called "freckles."
She speaks an odd human dialect.
dana

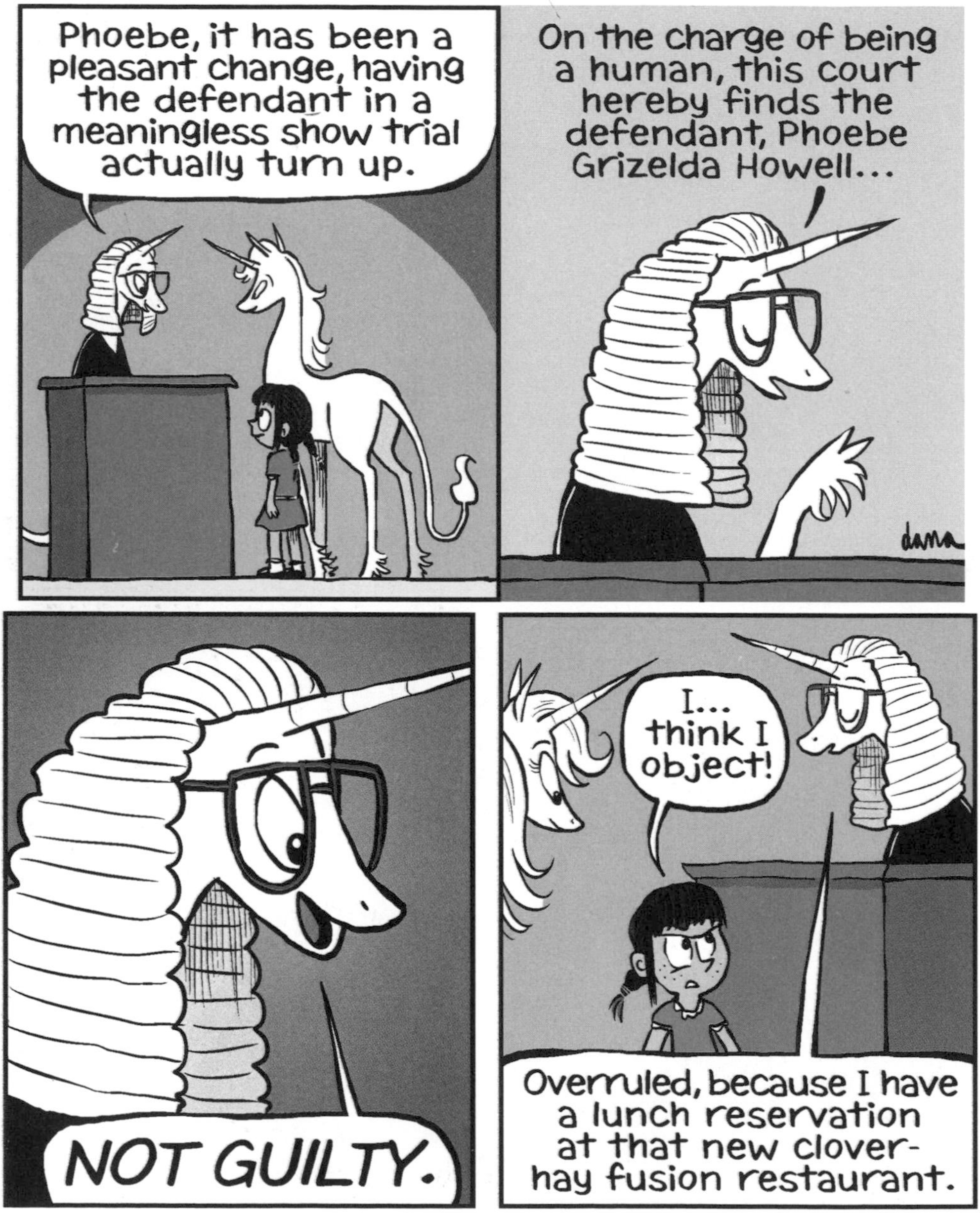
Phoebe, it has been a pleasant change, having the defendant in a meaningless show trial actually turn up.
On the charge of being a human, this court hereby finds the defendant, Phoebe Grizelda Howell...
dana
NOT GUILTY.
I... think I object!
Overruled, because I have a lunch reservation at that new clover-hay fusion restaurant.

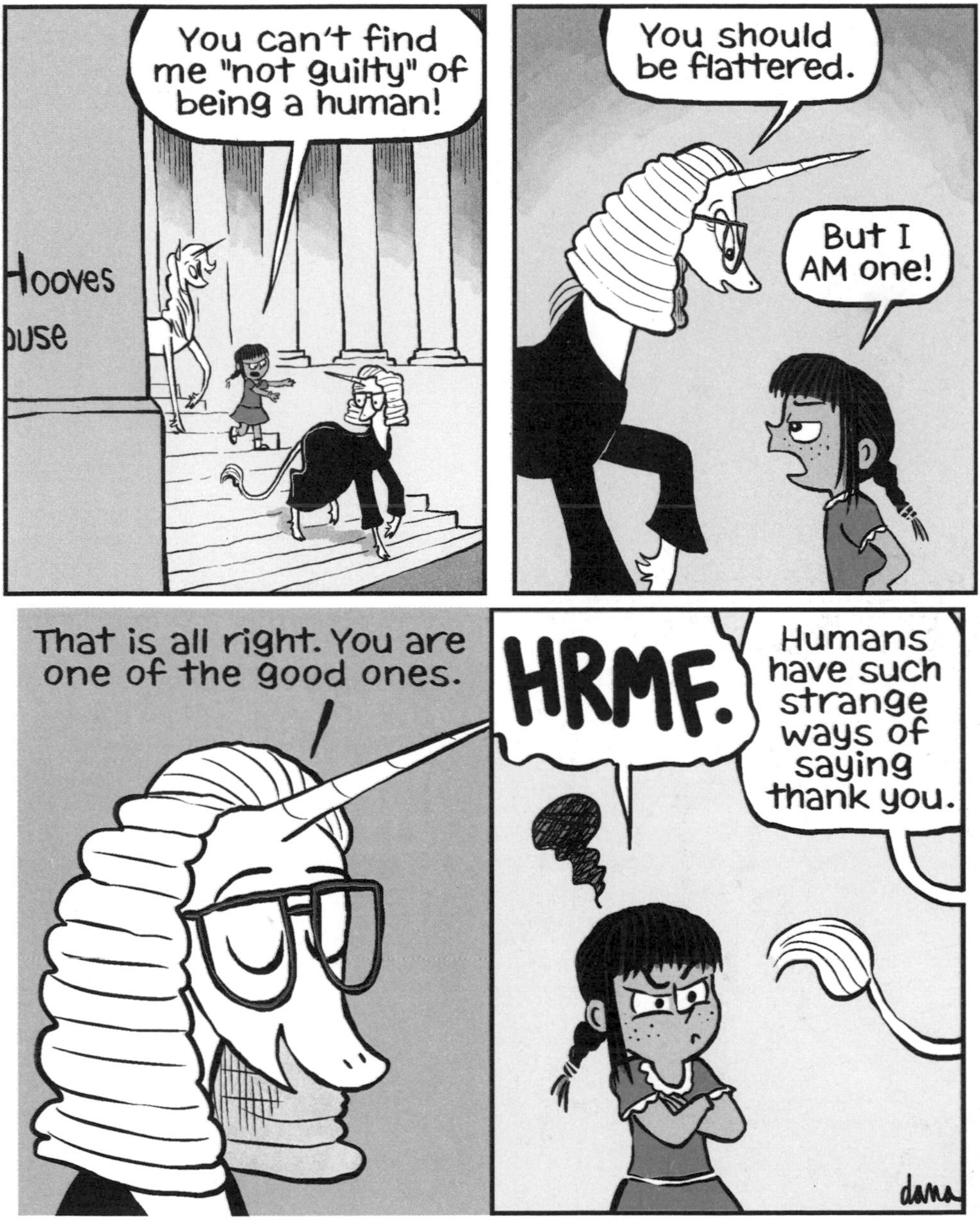
You can't find me "not guilty" of being a human!
Hooves
ouse
You should be flattered.
But I AM one!
That is all right. You are one of the good ones.
HRMF.
Humans have such strange ways of saying thank you.
dana

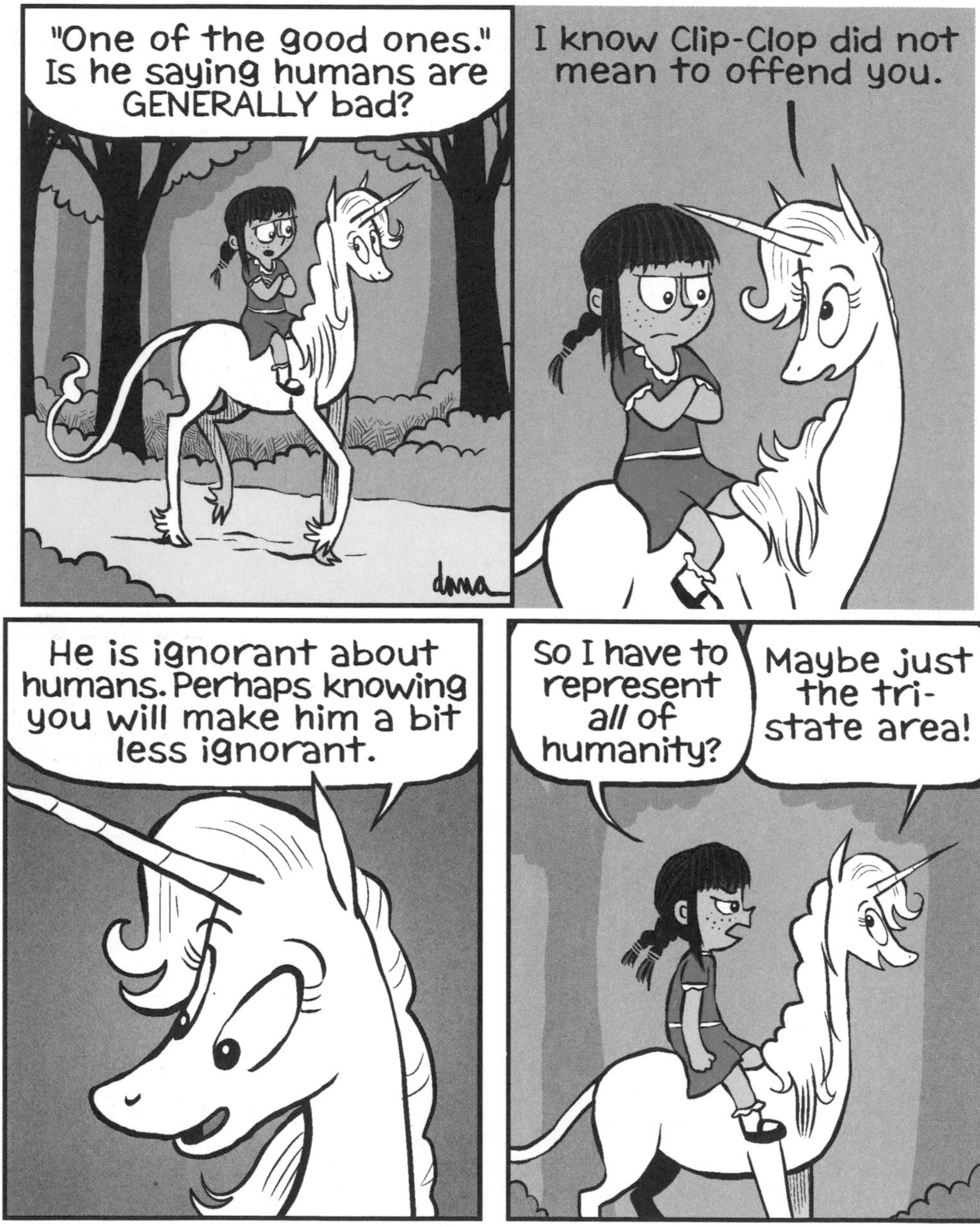
"One of the good ones." Is he saying humans are GENERALLY bad?
dana
I know Clip-Clop did not mean to offend you.
He is ignorant about humans. Perhaps knowing you will make him a bit less ignorant.
So I have to represent *all* of humanity?
Maybe just the tri-state area!

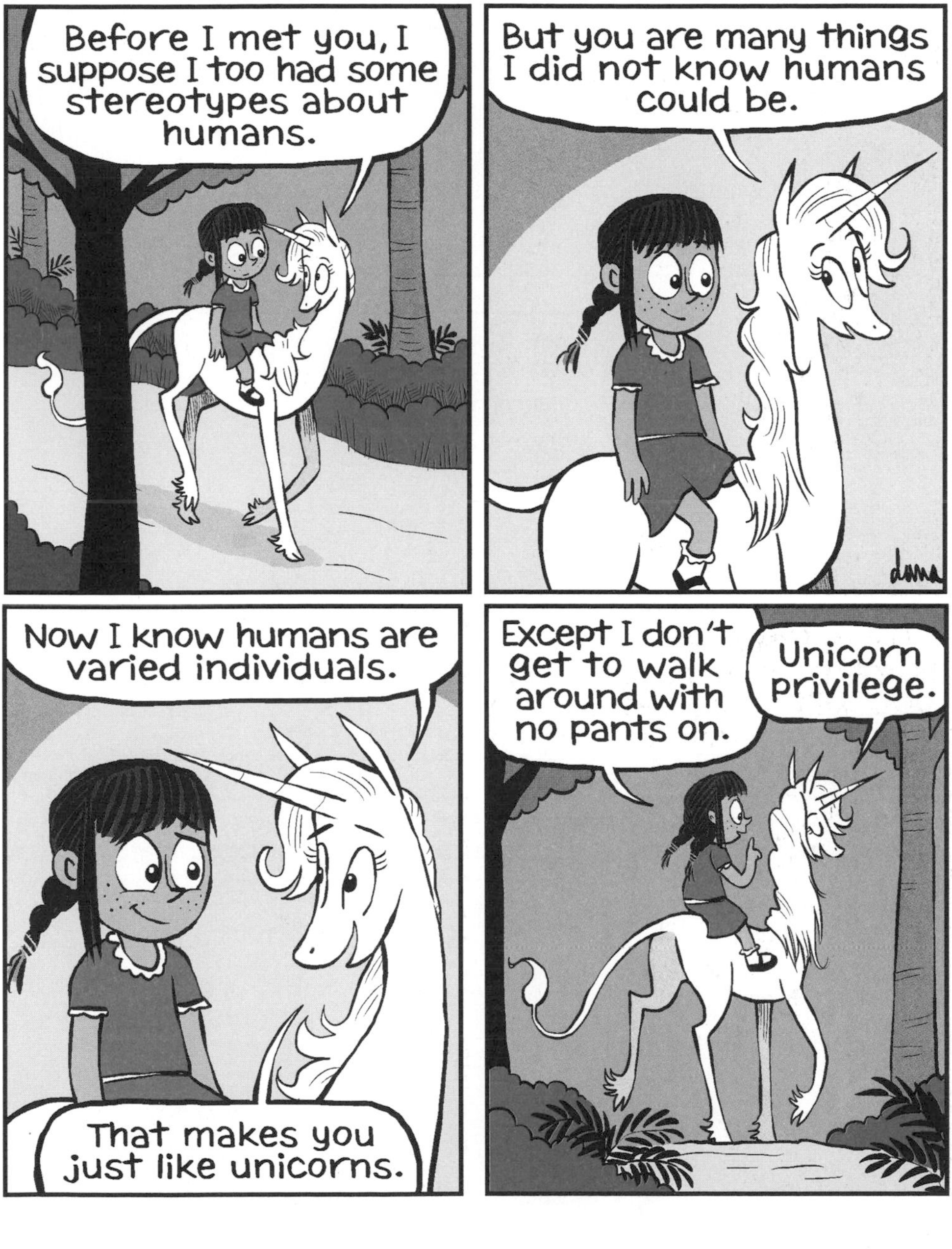

Before I met you, I suppose I too had some stereotypes about humans.
But you are many things I did not know humans could be.
Now I know humans are varied individuals.
That makes you just like unicorns.
Except I don't get to walk around with no pants on.
Unicorn privilege.

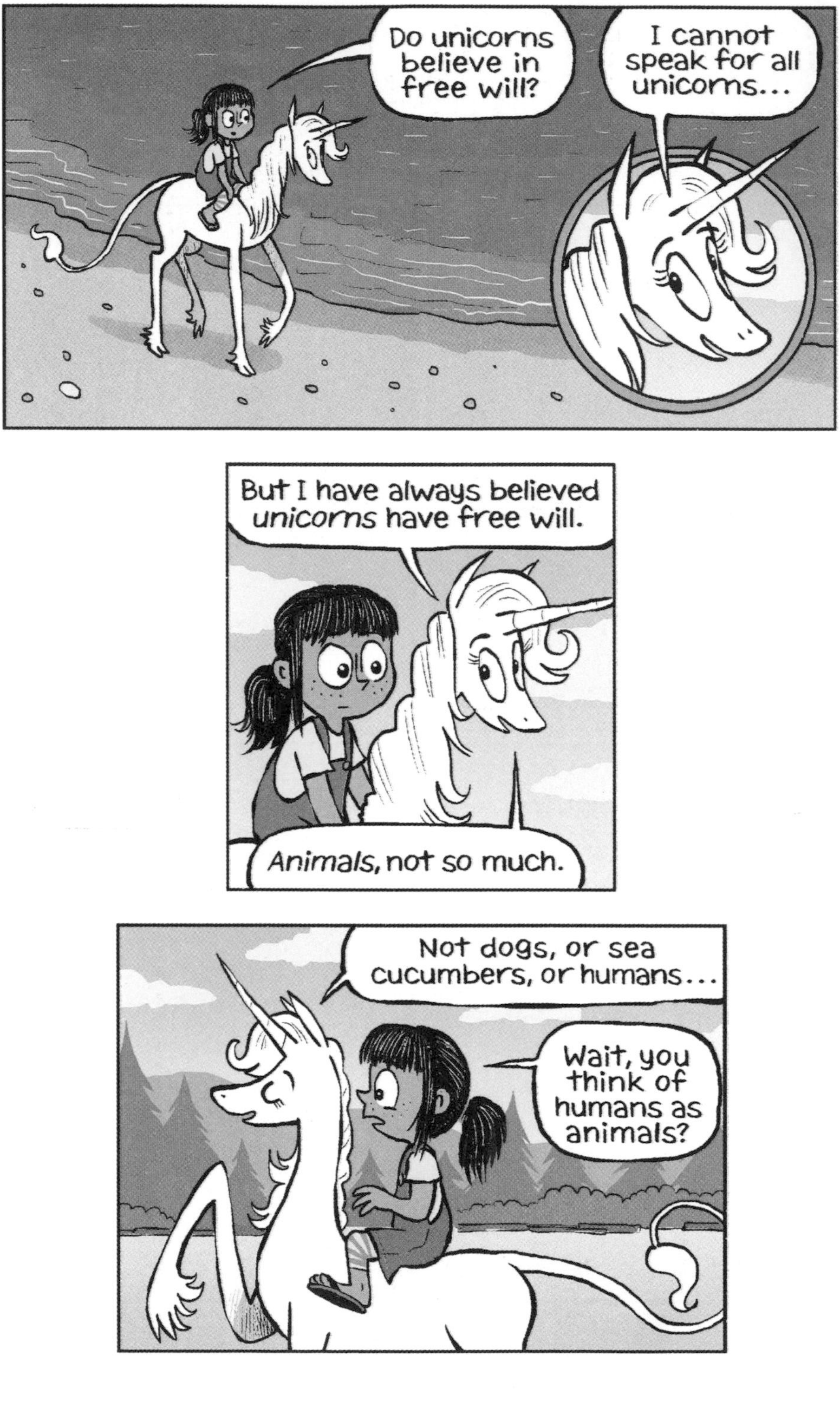
Do unicorns believe in free will?
I cannot speak for all unicorns...
But I have always believed *unicorns* have free will.
Animals, not so much.
Not dogs, or sea cucumbers, or humans...
Wait, you think of humans as animals?

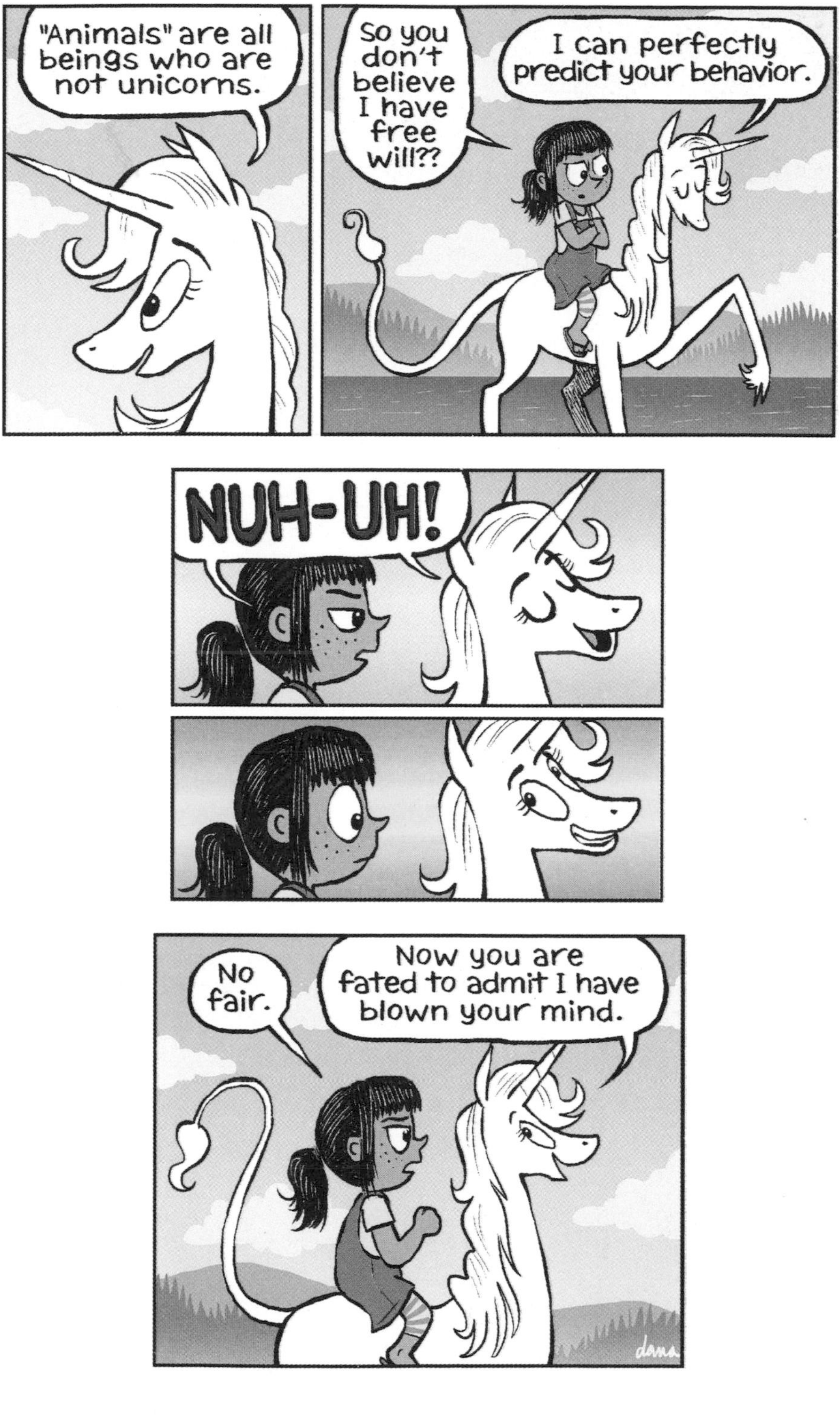
"Animals" are all beings who are not unicorns.
So you don't believe I have free will??
I can perfectly predict your behavior.
NUH-UH!
No fair.
Now you are fated to admit I have blown your mind.
dana

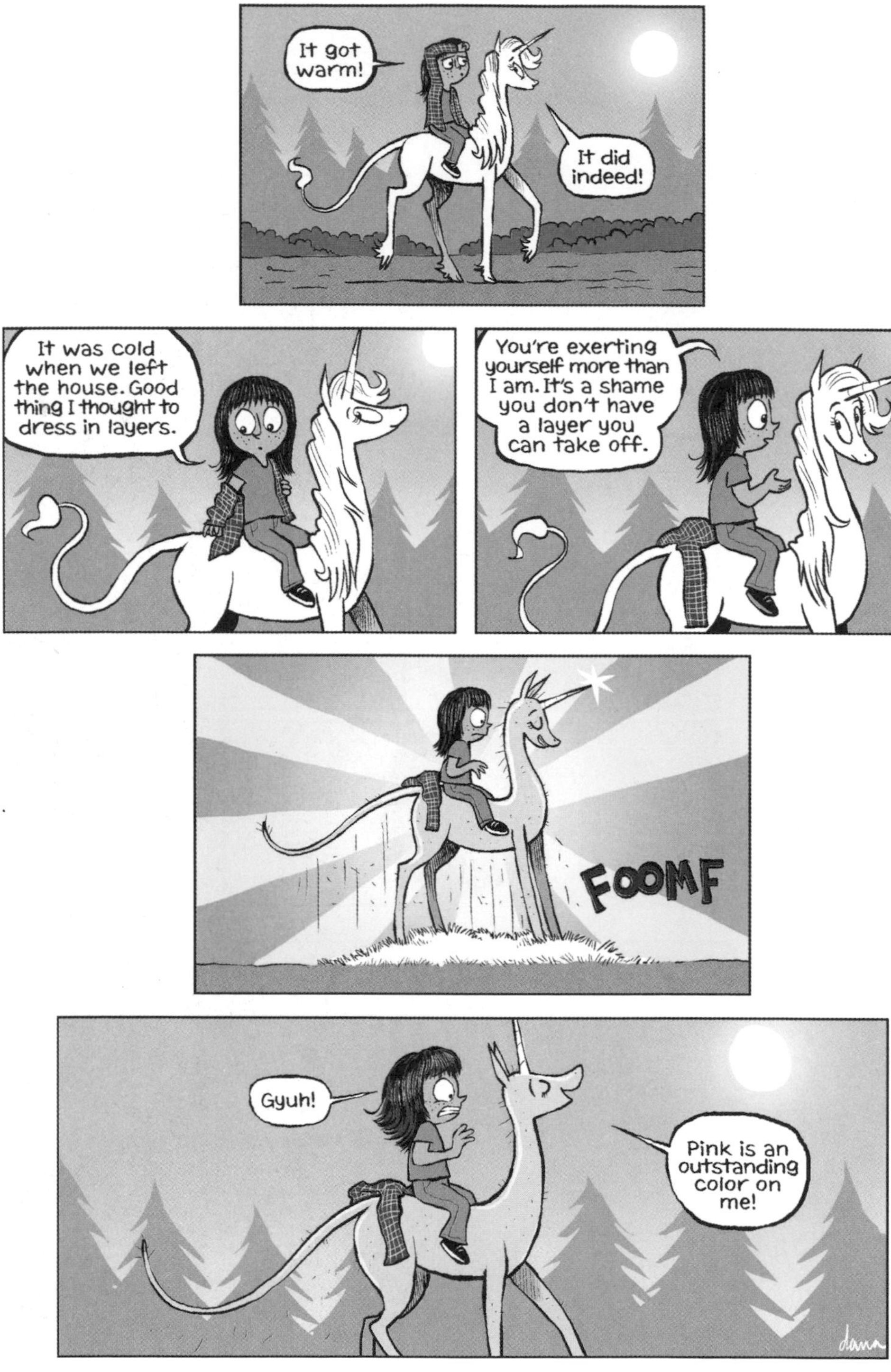
It got warm!
It did indeed!
It was cold when we left the house. Good thing I thought to dress in layers.
You're exerting yourself more than I am. It's a shame you don't have a layer you can take off.
FOOMF
Gyuh!
Pink is an outstanding color on me!
dana

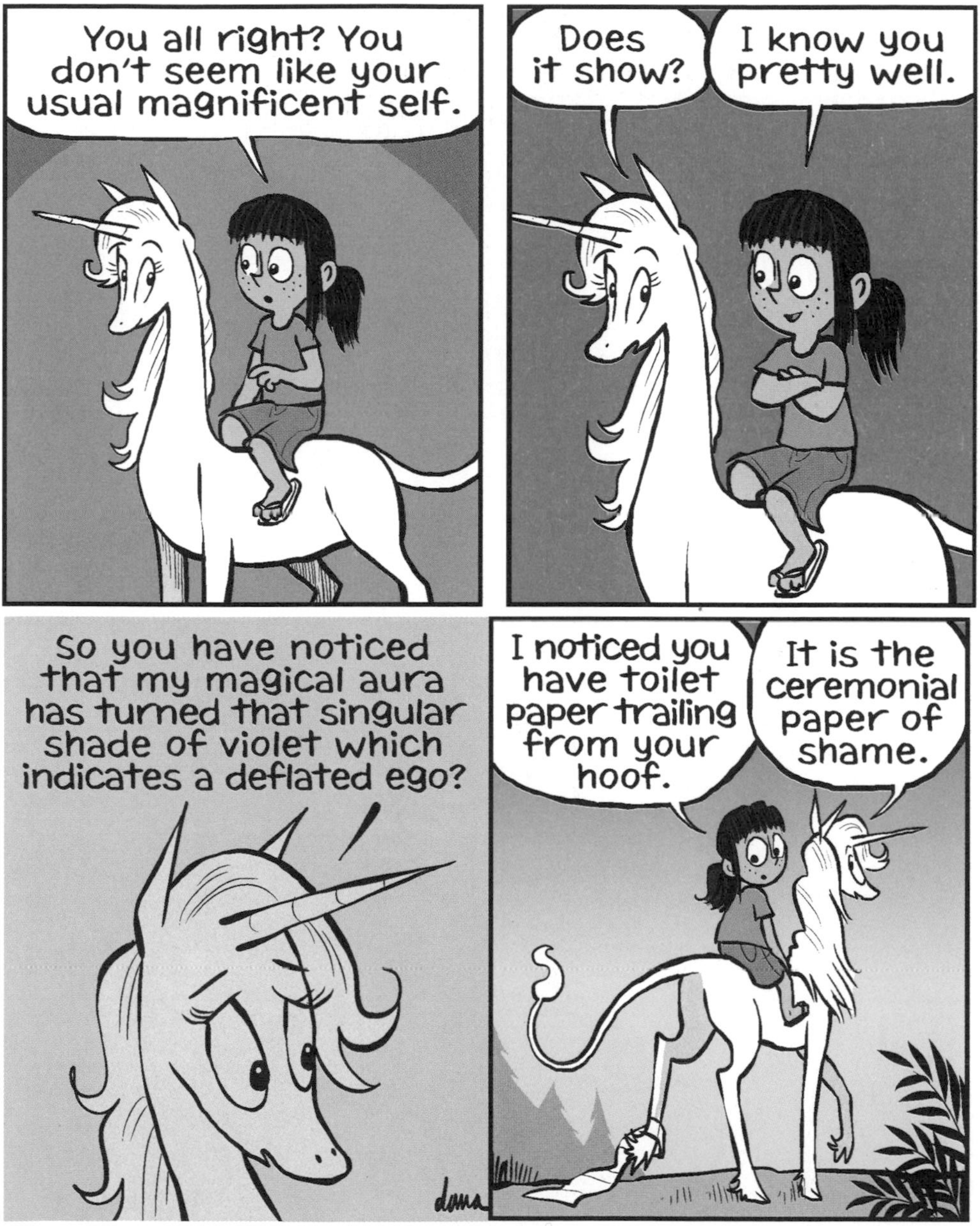
You all right? You don't seem like your usual magnificent self.
Does it show?
I know you pretty well.
So you have noticed that my magical aura has turned that singular shade of violet which indicates a deflated ego?
I noticed you have toilet paper trailing from your hoof.
It is the ceremonial paper of shame.
dana

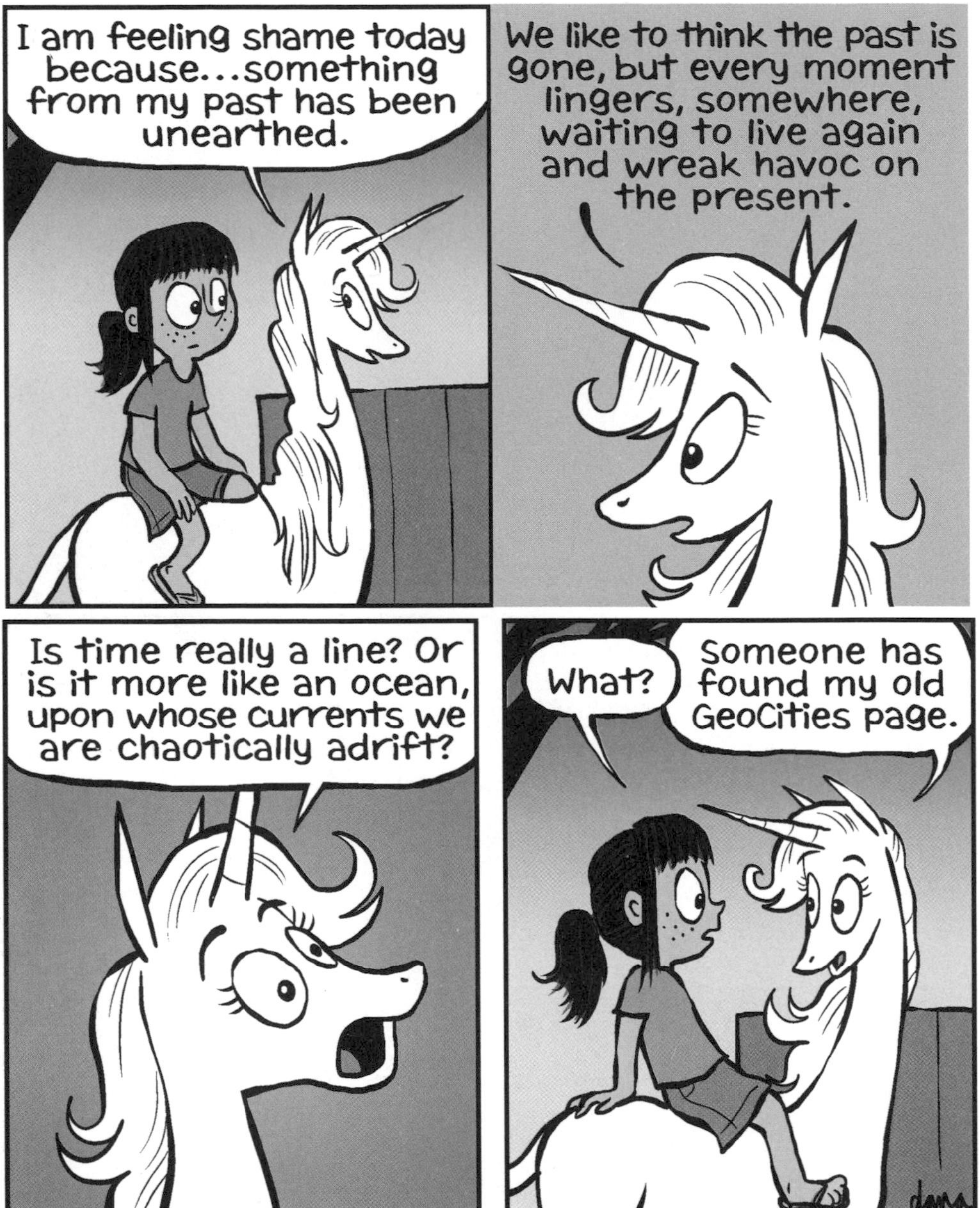
I am feeling shame today because...something from my past has been unearthed.
We like to think the past is gone, but every moment lingers, somewhere, waiting to live again and wreak havoc on the present.
Is time really a line? Or is it more like an ocean, upon whose currents we are chaotically adrift?
What?
Someone has found my old GeoCities page.
dana

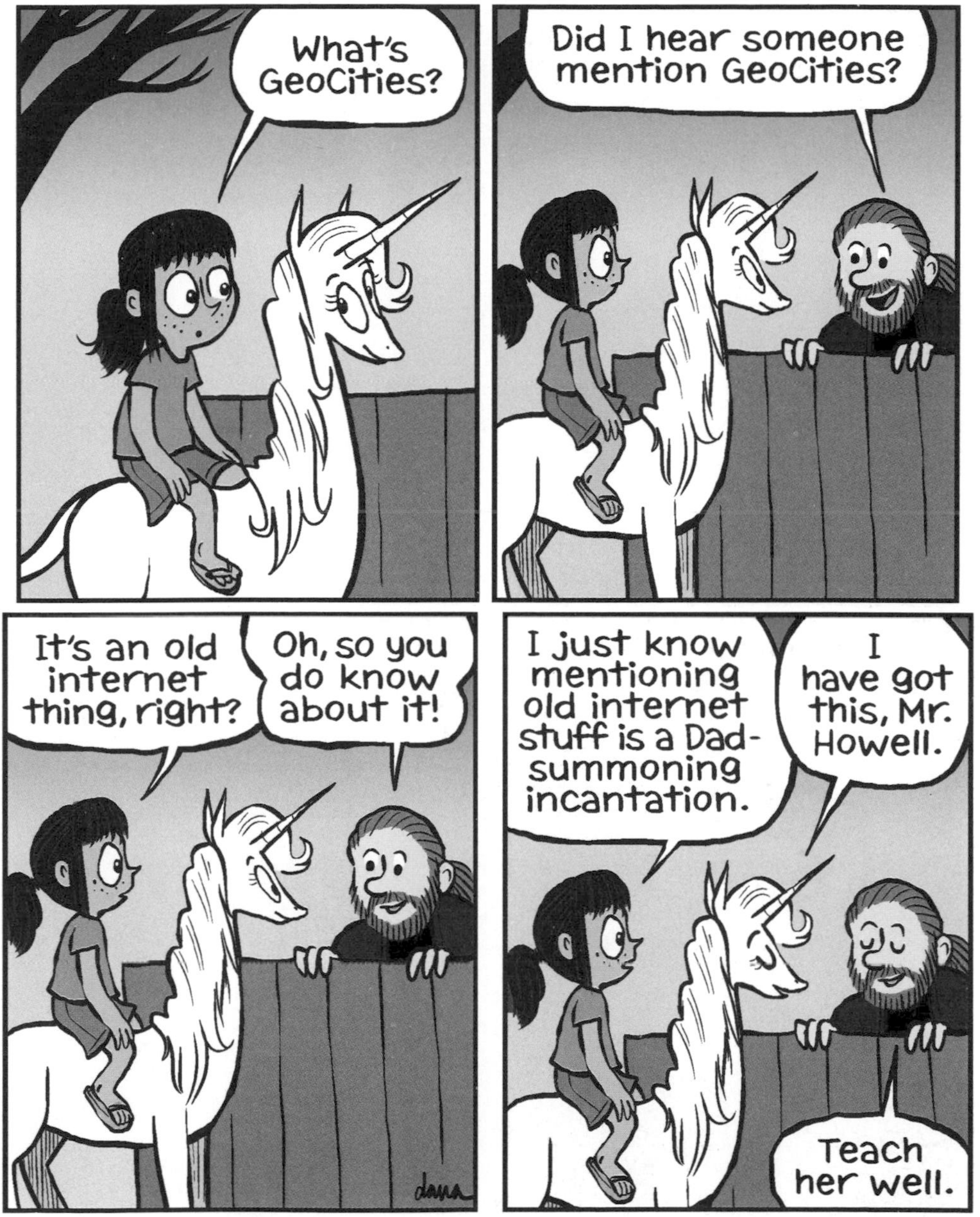
What's GeoCities?
Did I hear someone mention GeoCities?
It's an old internet thing, right?
Oh, so you do know about it!
dana
I just know mentioning old internet stuff is a Dad-summoning incantation.
I have got this, Mr. Howell.
Teach her well.

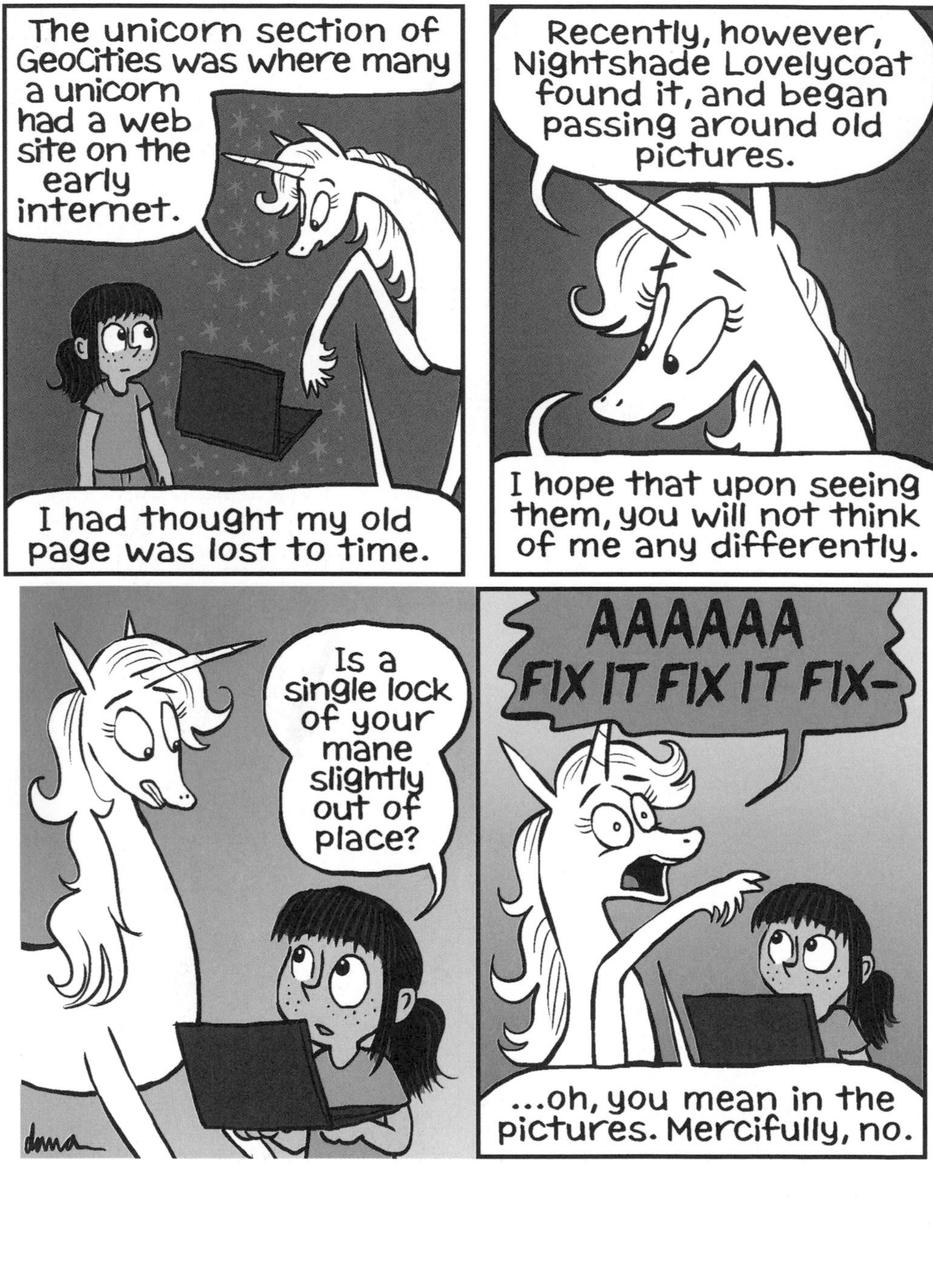
The unicorn section of GeoCities was where many a unicorn had a web site on the early internet.
I had thought my old page was lost to time.
Recently, however, Nightshade Lovelycoat found it, and began passing around old pictures.
I hope that upon seeing them, you will not think of me any differently.
Is a single lock of your mane slightly out of place?
AAAAAA
FIX IT FIX IT FIX-
...oh, you mean in the pictures. Mercifully, no.

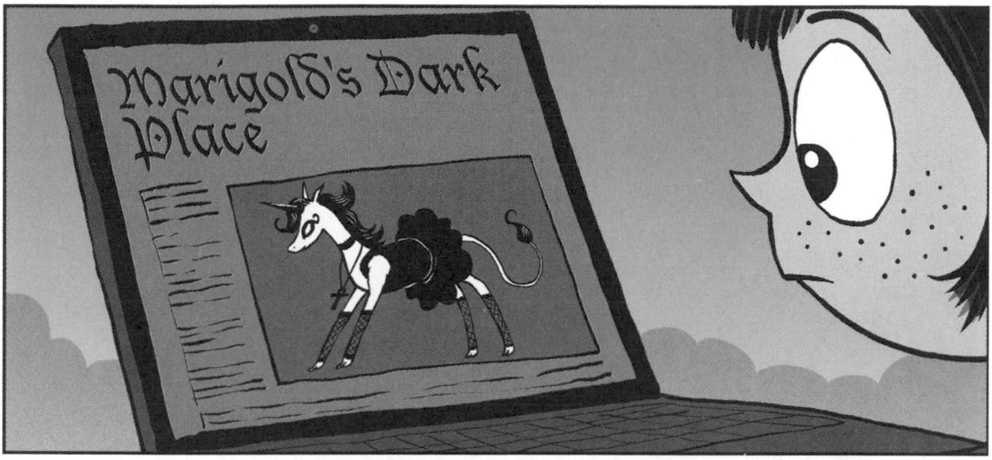
Marigold's Dark Place

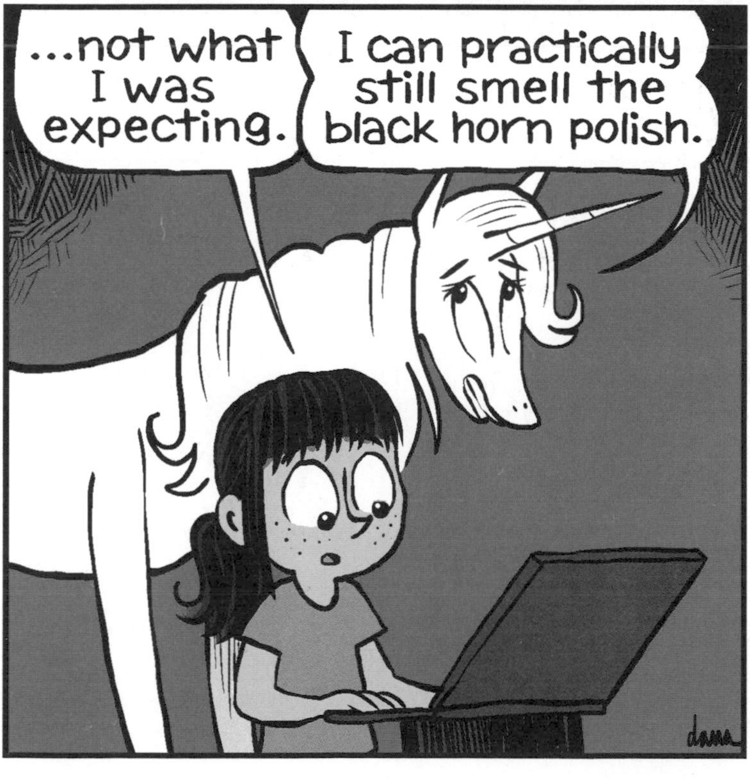
...not what I was expecting.
I can practically still smell the black horn polish.
dana

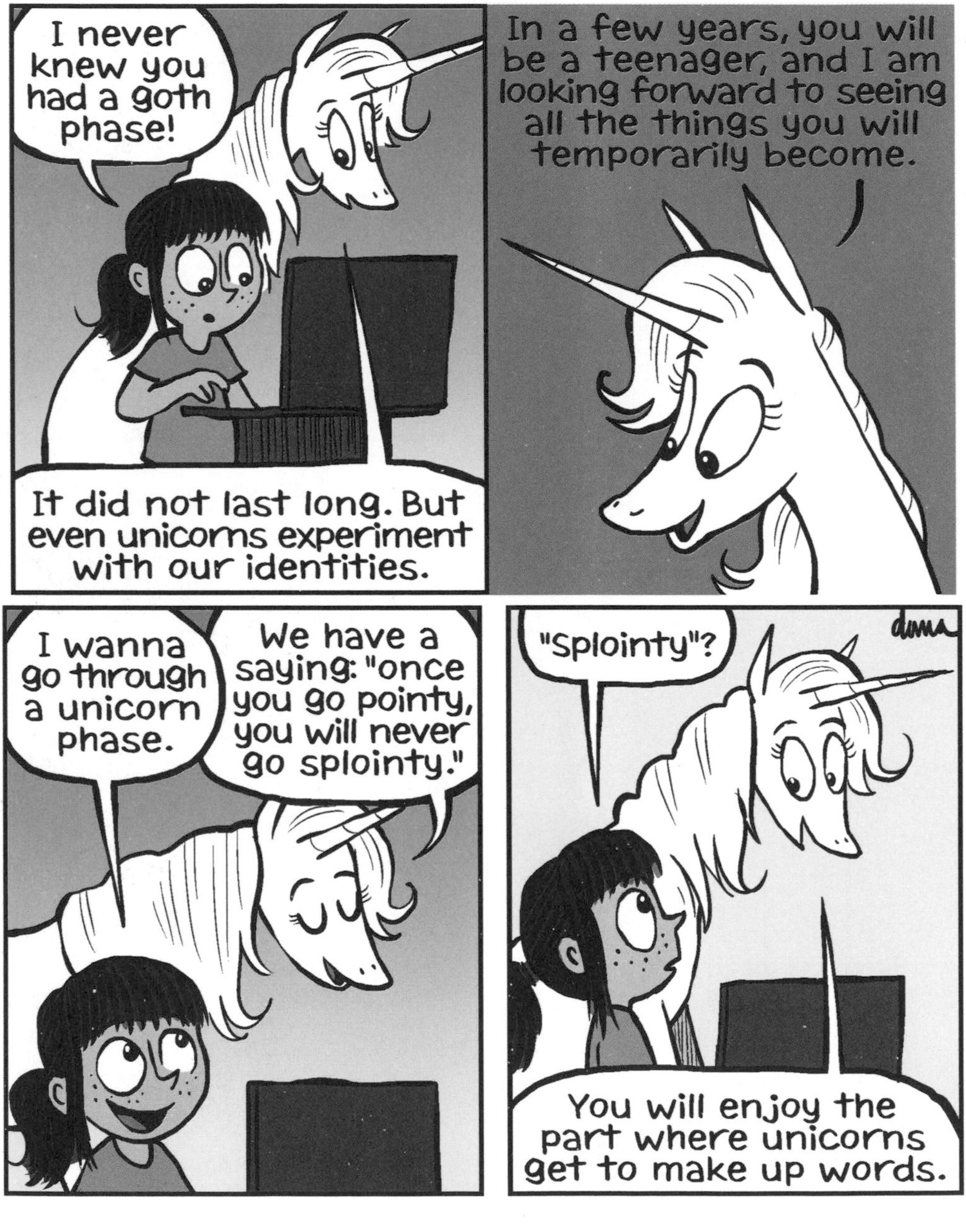
I never knew you had a goth phase!
It did not last long. But even unicorns experiment with our identities.
In a few years, you will be a teenager, and I am looking forward to seeing all the things you will temporarily become.
I wanna go through a unicorn phase.
We have a saying: "once you go pointy, you will never go splointy."
"Splointy"?
You will enjoy the part where unicorns get to make up words.
dana

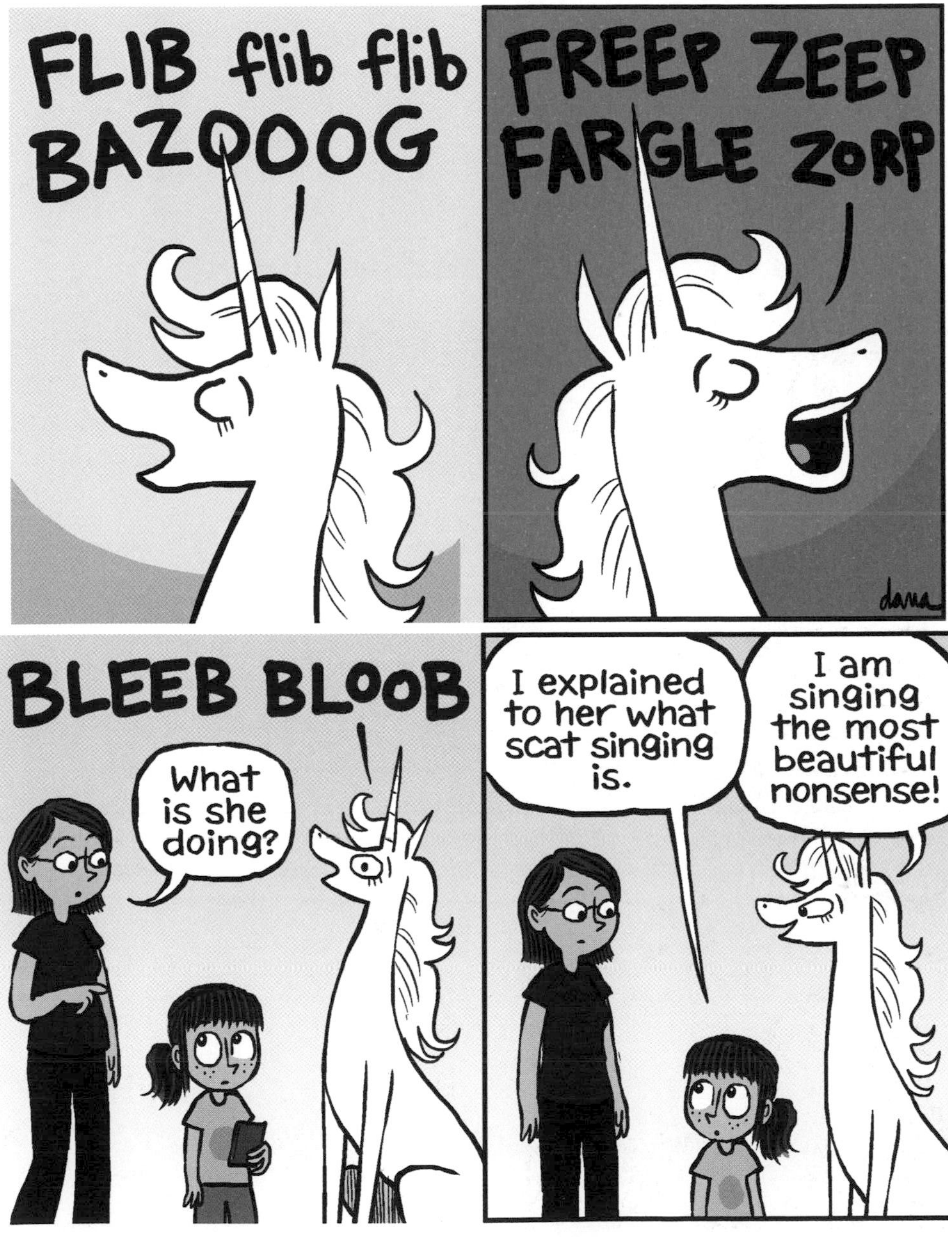
FLIB flib flib
BAZOOOG
FREEP ZEEP
FARGLE ZORP
dana
BLEEB BLOOB
What is she doing?
I explained to her what scat singing is.
I am singing the most beautiful nonsense!

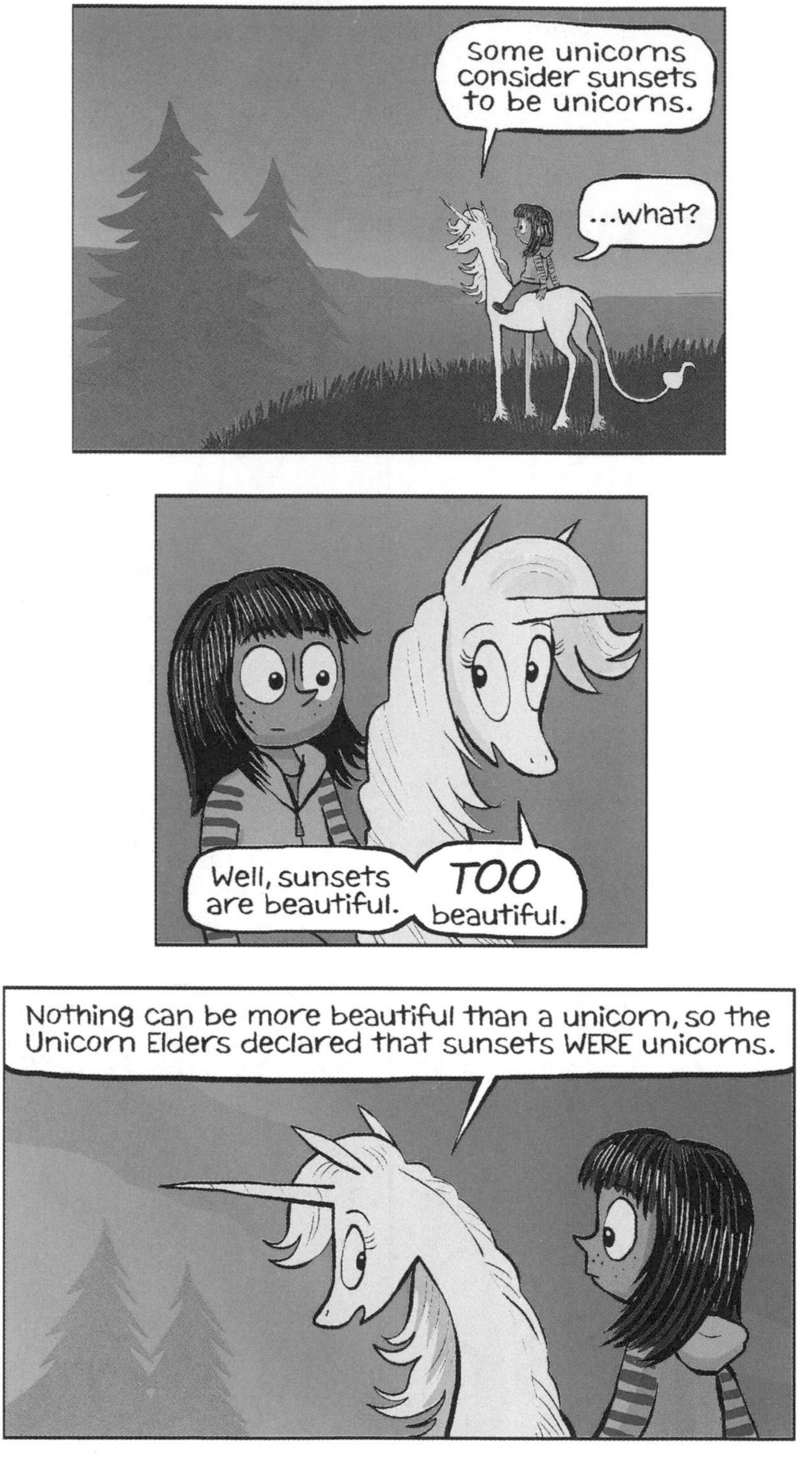

Some unicorns consider sunsets to be unicorns.
...what?
Well, sunsets are beautiful.
TOO beautiful.
Nothing can be more beautiful than a unicorn, so the Unicorn Elders declared that sunsets WERE unicorns.

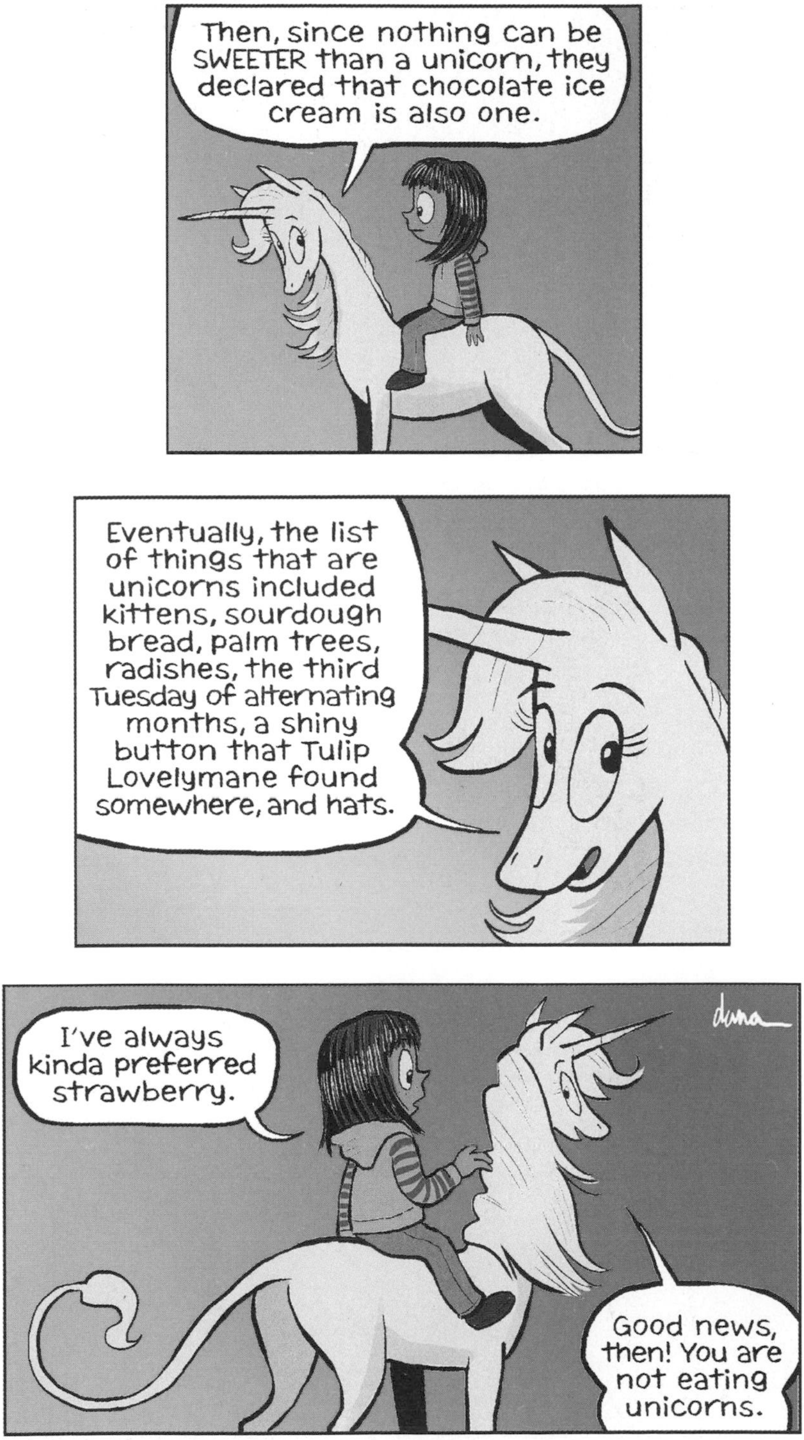
Then, since nothing can be SWEETER than a unicorn, they declared that chocolate ice cream is also one.
Eventually, the list of things that are unicorns included kittens, sourdough bread, palm trees, radishes, the third Tuesday of alternating months, a shiny button that Tulip Lovelymane found somewhere, and hats.
I've always kinda preferred strawberry.
Good news, then! You are not eating unicorns.

MORE TO EXPLORE! A special section featuring fun activities and words to learn!

How to Draw Marigold

Marigold's head has a circle at the center of it.

Before I draw her unicorny features, she kind of looks like a dinosaur.

Horn has four spiral lines
Eyes are ovals, spaced about one eye apart

Her horn is just above her eyes.

(In the very first strips, I wasn't super consistent about this, and she kind of had Wandering Horn Syndrome.)

The front part of her mane is basically a swoop, and is on the far side of her head and horn no matter which way she's facing.

(It's magic.)

A few lines to show her hair's not a solid object
eyes have little highlight dots
little heavenly nostrils

Marigold is kind of swan-shaped, with a long slender neck.

Her body is based on two circles
"shoulder"
"elbow"
"wrist"
"knee"
"ankle"

Her legs have the same joints as your arms and legs, just arranged a little differently.

Her hooves are cloven (two-pointed), like a deer's. Also she has fluffy fetlocks.

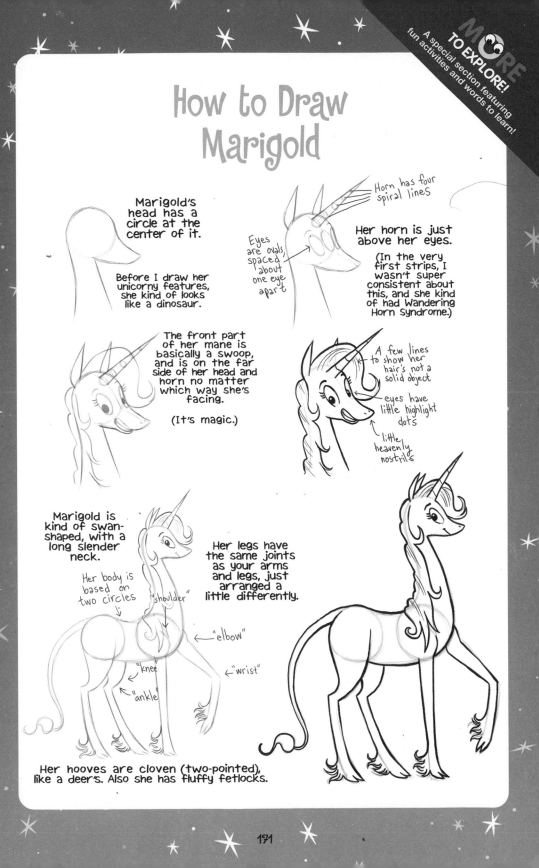

How to Draw Phoebe

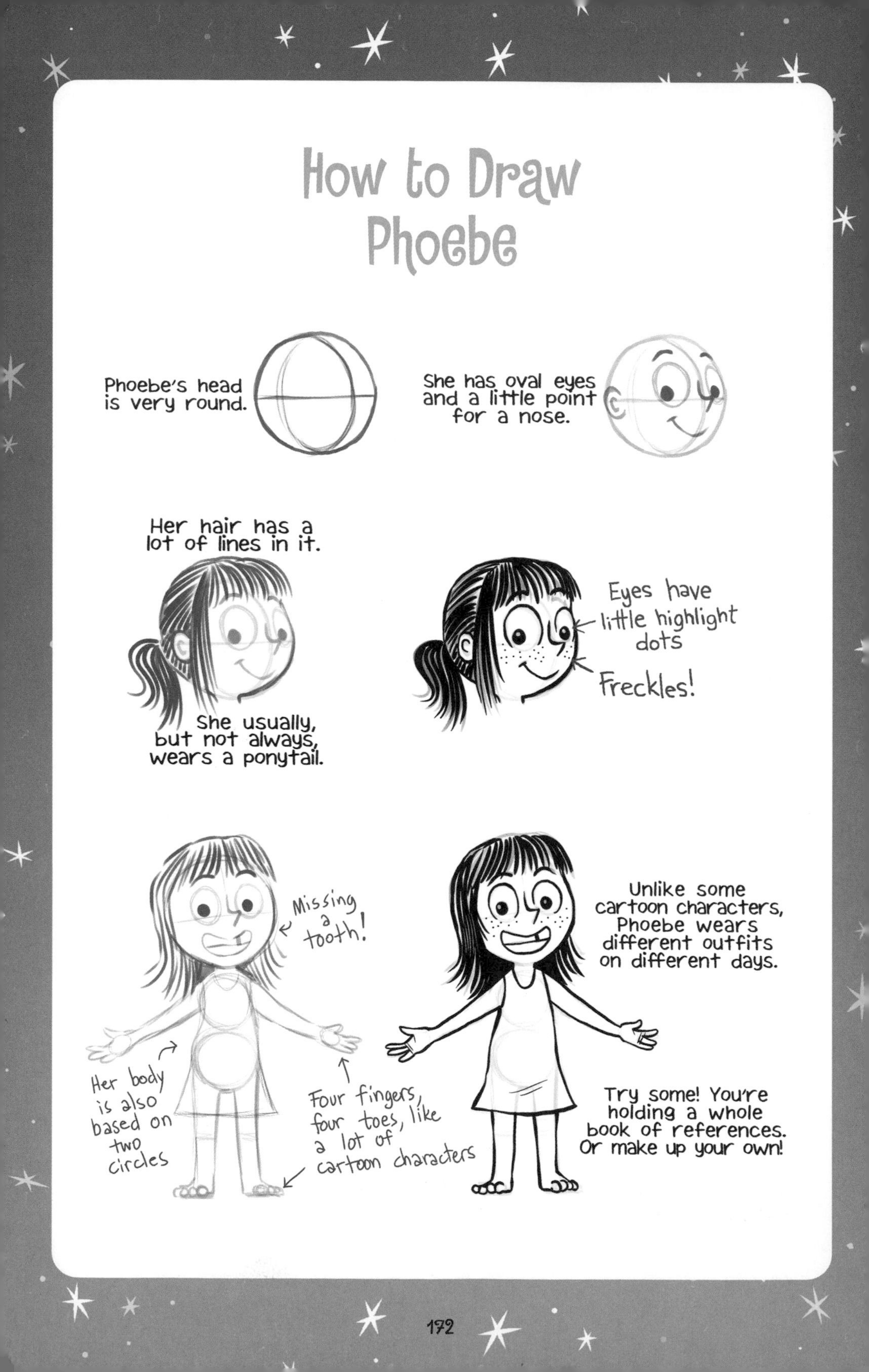
Phoebe's head is very round.
She has oval eyes and a little point for a nose.
Her hair has a lot of lines in it.
She usually, but not always, wears a ponytail.
Eyes have little highlight dots
Freckles!
Missing a tooth!
Her body is also based on two circles
Four fingers, four toes, like a lot of cartoon characters
Unlike some cartoon characters, Phoebe wears different outfits on different days.
Try some! You're holding a whole book of references. Or make up your own!

GLOSSARY

acquiesced (a-kwee-esd): pg. 125 – verb / accepted or agreed to something without argument

binge (binj): pg. 114 – verb / to use or watch something in unhealthy amounts

cinephile (si-neh-file): pg. 59 – noun / someone with a passionate interest in movies

confront (kon-front): pg. 93 – verb / to face a challenge or obstacle

cynical (si-ni-kuhl): pg. 102 – adjective / a negative or distrustful attitude

desist (di-sist): pg. 136 – verb / to stop doing something

dignity (dig-ni-tee): pg. 111 – noun / having self-esteem; acting with seriousness and pride

explicable (ek-spli-ki-buhl): pg. 23 – adjective / easily explained; understandable

impale (im-payl): pg. 78 – verb / to pierce something with a sharp object

impeding (im-peed-ing): pg. 30 – verb / to slow the progress of or stop from happening

incantation (in-kan-tay-shun): pg. 97 – noun / spells or charms that are spoken or sung

insufficiently (in-suh-fi-shent-lee): pg. 50 – adverb / not enough; not good enough; lacking

linguistic (ling-gwi-stik): pg. 125 – adjective / of or relating to language and words

luscious (luh-shus): pg. 47 – adjective / satisfying to the senses, thick and expansive

opalescent (oh-puh-le-sent): pg. 40 – adjective / reflecting a rainbow of colors

percentile (per-sen-tile): pg. 101 – noun / a measure on a scale of 100: for example, if you are in the 90th percentile on a test, it means you scored better than 90 percent of other people

perplexing (per-plek-sing): pg. 34 – adjective / difficult to solve; causing confusion

project (pruh-jekt): pg. 111 – verb / to signal or display to an audience

punchier (pun-chee-er): pg. 40 – adjective / more vibrant or spirited

relish (rel-ish): pg. 77 – verb / to enjoy; have a strong liking

retroactive (re-tro-ak-tiv): pg. 58 – adjective / something happening now that affects the past

savor (say-ver): pg. 109 – verb / to enjoy something to the fullest

standardized (stan-der-dized): pg. 98 – adjective / the same for everyone; consistent

therapeutic (ther-uh-pew-tick): pg. 48 – adjective / helpful to the body or mind

typecast (type-cast): pg. 61 – verb / to cast an actor or actress in only one type of role

undertone (un-der-tone): pg. 43 – noun / flavors, sounds, or characteristics other than the main ones; a hidden trait

Andrews McMeel Publishing
a division of Andrews McMeel Universal
1130 Walnut Street, Kansas City, Missouri 64106

www.andrewsmcmeel.com

20 21 22 23 24 SDB 10 9 8 7 6 5 4 3 2 1

ISBN: 978-1-5248-6070-7

Library of Congress Control Number: 2020933091

Made by:
King Yip (Dongguan) Printing & Packaging Factory Ltd.
Address and location of manufacturer:
Daning Administrative District, Humen Town
Dongguan Guangdong, China 523930
1st Printing—5/25/20

ATTENTION: SCHOOLS AND BUSINESSES

Andrews McMeel books are available at quantity discounts with bulk purchase for educational, business, or sales promotional use. For information, please e-mail the Andrews McMeel Publishing Special Sales Department: specialsales@amuniversal.com.

Look for these books!

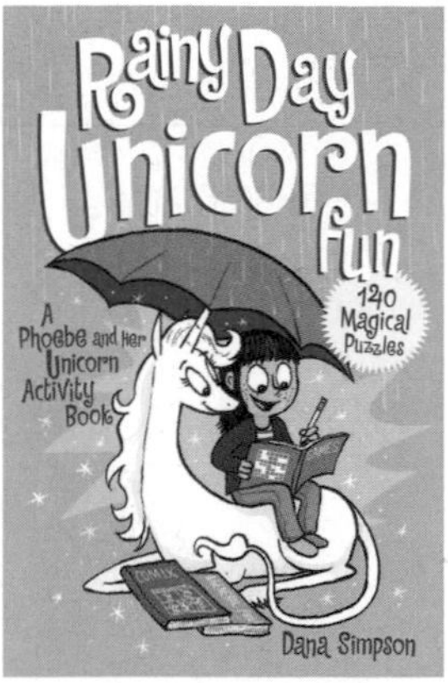
Rainy Day Unicorn Fun
A Phoebe and Her Unicorn Activity Book
140 Magical Puzzles
Dana Simpson

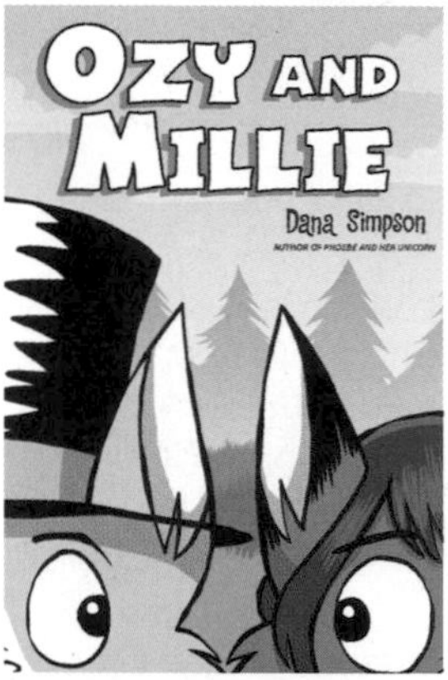
OZY AND MILLIE
Dana Simpson

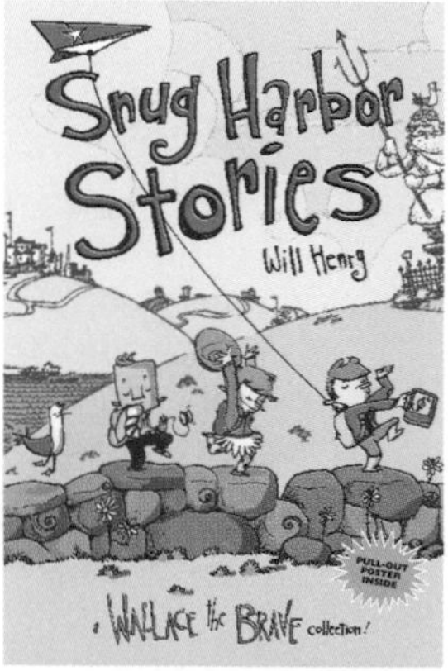
Snug Harbor Stories
Will Henry
PULL-OUT POSTER INSIDE
a WALLACE the BRAVE collection!

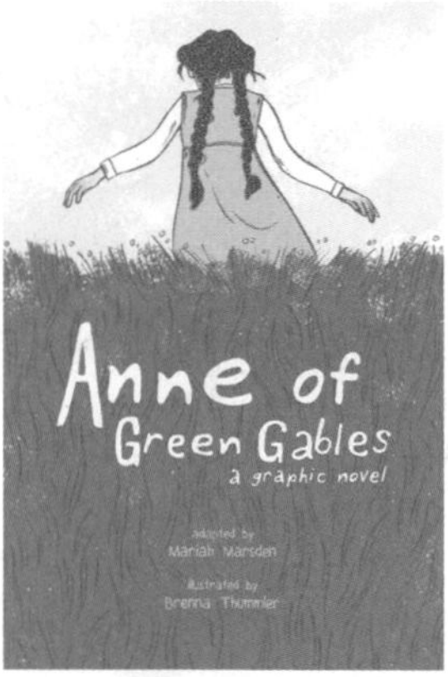
Anne of Green Gables
a graphic novel
adapted by
Mariah Marsden
illustrated by
Brenna Thummler

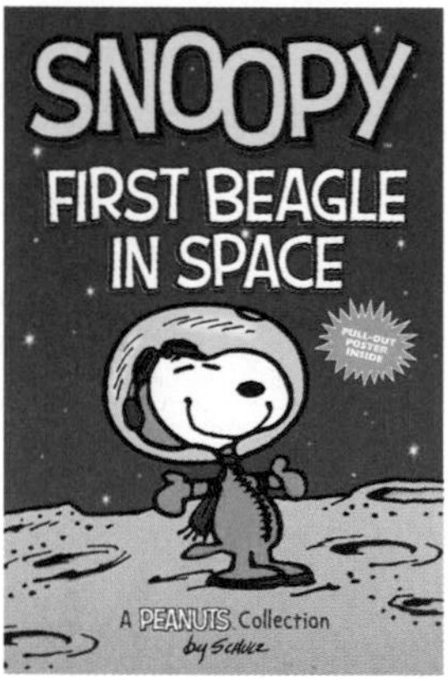
SNOOPY
FIRST BEAGLE IN SPACE
PULL-OUT POSTER INSIDE
A PEANUTS Collection
by Schulz

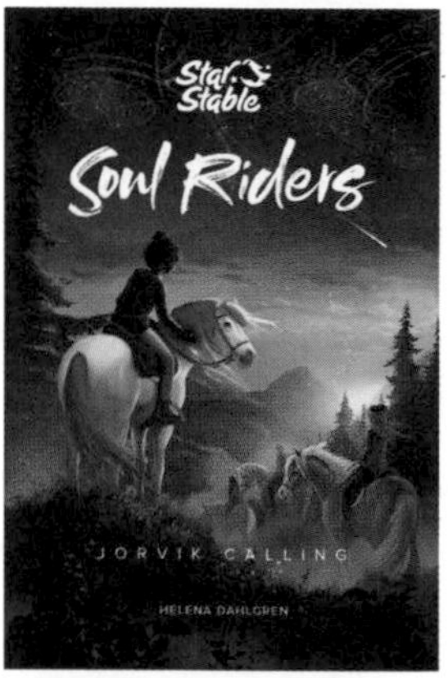
Star Stable
Soul Riders
JORVIK CALLING
HELENA DAHLGREN

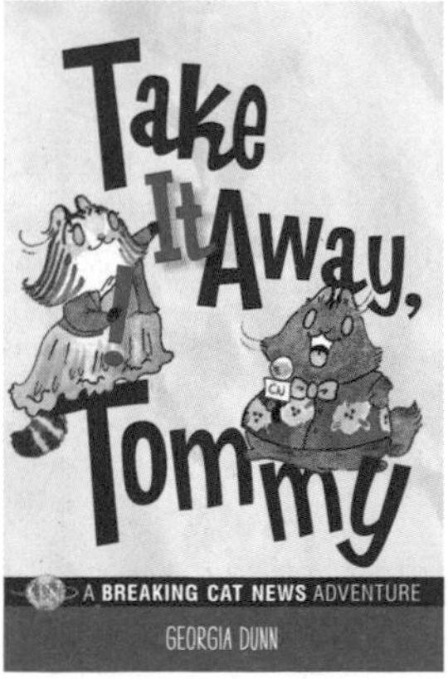
Take It Away, Tommy
A BREAKING CAT NEWS ADVENTURE
GEORGIA DUNN

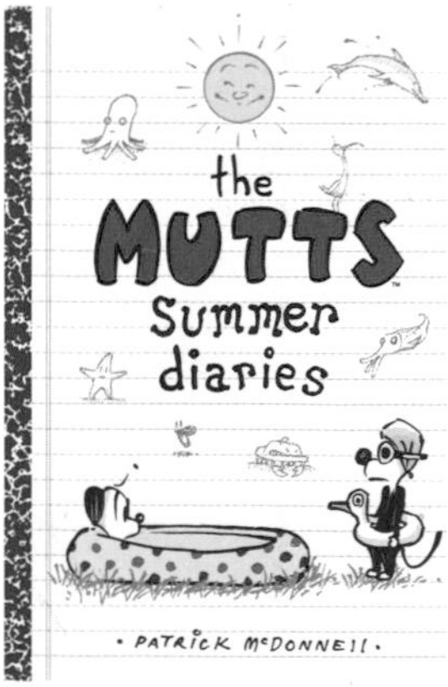
the MUTTS Summer diaries
PATRICK McDONNELL

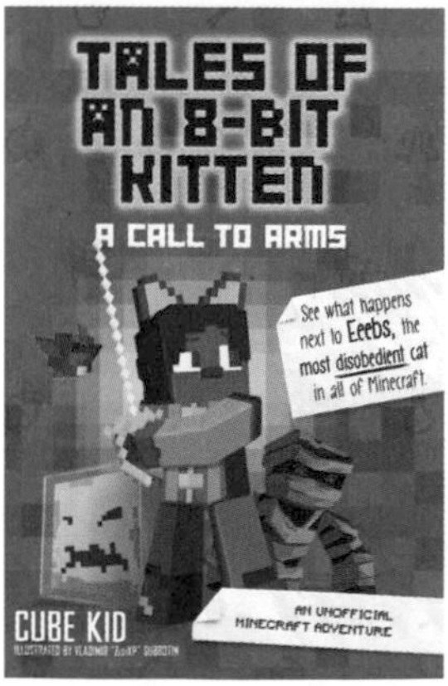
TALES OF AN 8-BIT KITTEN
A CALL TO ARMS
See what happens next to Eeebs, the most disobedient cat in all of Minecraft
CUBE KID
AN UNOFFICIAL MINECRAFT ADVENTURE